SHADOW MAN

L.L. BARTLETT

Cover by Wicked Smart Designs

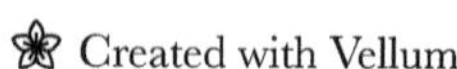
Created with Vellum

Description

Grief is love's shadow.
The presence of absence.
An unbearable weight of emptiness.
—John Mark Green

Jeff Resnick and his brother, Dr. Richard Alpert, are on the front lines of that emotion when it comes to their current investigations for their new consulting firm, R&A Insights. As Jeff tries to help a comatose man, whose brewery is in trouble, transition to the great beyond, Richard's cold-case arson is heating up in the here and now.

While Jeff grapples with the death of a relationship and the end his client's life, Richard faces his own demons and jealousies until their worlds collide to fight against the evil that confronts them.

Acknowledgments

As always, my thanks go to members of The Lorraine Train, who continue to support the work that I do: Amy Connolley, Pam Priest, Rita Pierrottie, Linda Kuzminczuk, and Debbie Lyon.

Cast Of Characters

Jeff Resnick, a former insurance investigator and bartender; reluctant psychic

Richard Alpert, MD, Jeff's older half-brother

Brenda Stanley, RN, Richard's wife

Maggie Brennan, Jeff's lady friend

Emily Farrell, associate at R&A Insights

Louie Susskind, owner and founder of Horse Hockey Brewing

Abe Bachmann, brewmaster at Horse Hockey Brewing

Bethany Susskind, younger daughter of Louie Susskind

Teresa Susskind Barton, older daughter of Louie Susskind

Nick Susskind, an attorney and Louie Susskind's son

Omega Dustin, end-of-life doula hired to attend to Louie

Nancy Clark, daughter of murder victim

Sam Neilson: Jeff's friend, who works at *The Buffalo News*

John Destross, Detective, Buffalo Police Department

Chapter 1

I arrived at the offices of R&A Insights only fifteen minutes late on that cold, cloudy March Monday morning, but our associate (fancy name for a receptionist), Emily Farrell, had already beat me to it. We'd met a little over two years before during a dark period in both our lives and reconnected in time for me to solve the case of a missing child—who just happened to be Emily. As a young, single mom, she was eager for a steady job that paid well—and boy were we paying her well.

It wasn't Emily's fault we had little in the way of work for her to do. I just wish we were actually pulling in money on a regular basis and making a difference.

It was my older, half-brother's idea to open R&A Insights—a brilliant name based on the initials of our last names. I'm Resnick, he's Alpert.

Dr. Richard Alpert was filthy rich and had never really practiced medicine, at least in the traditional sense. He'd done some volunteering but had spent the bulk of his professional career working as a researcher for a think tank in Pasadena, while after a way-too-long four-year stint in the army, I'd gone into the insurance business as an investigator. Crimes scenes had been my specialty until I could no longer stand looking at blood spatter patterns and moved into management—a big mistake on my part—and I hadn't lasted all that long in a position of authority. I'd been unemployed longer than I'd had benefits and had just found another job as a low-end investigator with yet another insurance company when I'd been brutally mugged.

I'd emerged from a coma to be blessed (cursed, more like) with an incredibly annoying new skill: sensing what other people felt and, on occasion, flashes of clairvoyance. Take my word, if it hadn't happened to me, I'd be just as skeptical as you must be. Some people call me a psychic. I hate that "P" word and don't like to use it, but it's a shortcut if I need to convey what I'd come to accept as my new-found abilities. With a cracked skull and a broken arm, and about to be evicted, I needed somewhere to go. Richard rescued me.

For the first two years after the mugging, I'd suffered crippling headaches. Lately, they hadn't been so bad. After three years, I'm pretty much recovered—except that my so-called gift hasn't gone away. In fact, it seems to get stronger as the months go by. I'm not a mind reader, but as I mentioned, I *can* sense things and sometimes I know about things before they happen. Oh, and I can sometimes talk to the dead, too.

I worked as a bartender for two years before I got hit by a car and lost that job, too, which is how Richard convinced me to become a consultant.

Which brings me back to R&A Insights. Richard has a volunteer job with one of the local hospital boards, but he was also bored. He thought we should tackle cold cases, but so far he hasn't put much sweat equity into the endeavor. I wasn't convinced we were going to be able to solve cases the cops had given up on. Okay, we had a website and business cards, but we were essentially depending on word of mouth to bring in clients. So far that strategy wasn't exactly panning out.

On that raw day in March, Emily wore a black turtleneck, slacks, and matching flats—what we called a Steve Jobs day. Once, we'd both turned up in all black and had a laugh. There wasn't nearly enough laughter in our office suite on Main Street in Synder—a suburb of Buffalo, New York.

Emily welcomed the cup of Tim Horton's best brew and a bear claw I'd bought her. I got a fruit explosion muffin for myself, pretending it was a healthier option—not that I really cared.

"How do you always know the days I don't have time for breakfast?" Emily asked as she took the plastic lid off of the paper coffee cup.

I shrugged and perched on the edge of her tidy desk. "It's a gift."

Gift? More like a curse. And, I wasn't in a hurry to share this aspect of my life with Emily, although I was pretty sure it was bound to come up sooner rather than later.

Emily took a sip of her coffee and shivered. "I can't seem to get warm. I checked the heat and it's seventy, but…." She let the sentence trail off. The temperature seemed fine to me. But then I'd read a story in *The Buffalo News* that said office temps were set at men's comfort levels and that women felt the cold more deeply. We should probably set the thermostat higher. Either that or give her a heater for under her desk. I'd mention it to Richard.

"Will Dr. Alpert be in today?" Emily asked.

I shrugged. "That's anyone's guess. He was dropping off his car to get an oil change and then had to go to the hospital to consult with someone on a case."

"Our kind of case?" she asked eagerly.

I shook my head. "A medical matter."

Emily reached for her bear claw and bit her lip, looking pensive. "I know I've only been employed here for two months, but I feel like I'm stealing from you guys."

Not me. I didn't have a nickel invested in the business. Richard had paid for the whole shebang. The office subscribed to a number of magazines that Emily and I read during the off hours, but so far no one else had and they sat neatly on a glass-topped table waiting for the next month's issues to take their places.

The phone rang, startling us both. Emily grabbed it before it could ring again. "R&A Insights; this is Emily. How can I help you?" She listened. "Oh, sure, Dr. Alpert, he's right here." She handed me the phone.

"Yo, bro—what's up?"

Richard sighed. "The service department is backed up. They say it's going to be at least three hours before they can get to the Mercedes. Can you pick me up and take me to the hospital?"

I had nothing better to do and figured I may as well play Uber driver. "Sure. Can I finish my coffee first?"

It took a few moments before he gave a resigned, "Yeah."

"Be there in about twenty minutes."

"Okay. See ya."

I handed the receiver back to Emily and wondered how badly I'd burn my esophagus if I chugged my cup of Joe.

"He needs a lift?" Emily guessed.

I nodded.

"How long do you think you'll be gone?"

Again, I shrugged. "Maybe we'll be back before lunch—maybe not. I'll give you a call or text." I knew breakfast wasn't going to happen so I closed the paper sack that held my muffin and stowed it in the little fridge behind Emily's desk, which already held an opened quart of 2 percent milk, several bottles of water, and Emily's brown-bagged lunch. "If you want to take that muffin home for Hannah—" Emily's six-year-old, "—you're welcome to it."

Her smile was sweet. "Thanks, Jeff. You guys are way too good to me."

Were we? I sure hoped so because sharp people need stimulating work. Emily was sharp, and we hadn't given her much to do. Even money can't hold an ambitious person. We all needed a case we could sink our teeth into and soon because the partners and only employee of R&A Insights were all bored silly.

I PULLED into the dealership's lot and saw that Richard stood behind the Service Department's plate-glass door, looking impatient. Upon recognizing my car, he burst outside and practically jumped into my passenger seat.

"About time you got here," he said, chagrined.

"I beat my estimate by five minutes."

He didn't comment.

"And we're going to?" I asked unnecessarily because he'd already told me.

"Sisters."

That meant Sisters of Charity Hospital on Main Street halfway to downtown, where Richard had done his residency more than two decades before.

"Why?" I asked.

My brother looked grim. "I don't suppose you remember Nick Susskind."

"Should I?"

"I think I introduced him to you at the Park Club that night—"

"Yeah-yeah," I cut him off.

I didn't want to be reminded of that terrible evening when I'd had to face the fact that my girlfriend, Maggie Brennan, had left me and strolled in, dressed to the nines, with her former fiancé on her arm. He'd dumped her years before, but after I'd found out that she cheated on me with him, I told her we were done. Long story short, we did get back together after the prick had betrayed her a second time, but things between us have never been the same since. And now, she was leaving Buffalo—and me—to take a new job. It was supposedly only a three-year assignment in San Diego, but in addition to leaving me, she apparently felt no qualms about leaving her five-year-old golden retriever, either.

Holly had gotten used to staying with Richard and his family when Maggie went on business trips to the West Coast. Richard, who'd never owned a pet, had at first rejected the idea of a dog and its upkeep—for all of three days—when he presented a demeanor of indifference. I don't get vibes from him like I do from most of the world at large, but I knew without a doubt that he had bonded with the dog after Maggie's third or fourth trip. Richard took Holly for walks, fed her, and brushed her. The only thing he didn't do was clean up the yard after her. That work was left to me. I love Holly, too, so I don't mind … too much.

But now Maggie was making a longer-term move, and Holly would be coming to stay in the Alpert household indefinitely. It was going to take some time to get used to the new arrangement—for all of us.

"Nick's father," Richard continued, "is in a coma. He asked me if I would evaluate his condition."

"Are you in a position to do so?" I asked.

"Nick's had a palliative care physician do so and wants a corroborating opinion from someone he trusts."

"And he trusts you, who is not his friend and only a casual acquaintance—plus not someone trained in end-of-life issues?"

Richard shrugged. "It seems one of Nick's sisters is resisting the diagnosis."

What that had to do with anything was anyone's guess. I pulled off of Main Street.

The Sisters Hospital parking garage is a pain to navigate. Or maybe I felt that way because I didn't want to be there. I remember back when I was a teen and had my appendix yanked how much I hated the joint. Curtis Johnson, Richard's family's elderly chauffeur, had been even more creeped out than me. His wife had died there and he'd never forgiven the institution, whereas I'd merely been grossed out.

Sisters had a smell—of death. But truth be told, I wasn't sure if that odor was real or a product of my vivid imagination. I followed Richard into the institution, wondering if I should have just stayed in the car. But then, the hospital was a lot warmer than the parking garage on that dank March morning.

I had no clue how Richard felt about evaluating his friend's father's chart. Was he antsy because he had to confirm a grim diagnosis, or worried for some other reason? To say my brother had been crabby of late was putting it mildly.

We made our way up to the hospital's cardiac unit. I thought we were going to meet Richard's friend … colleague … whatever, but he strode over to the nurse's station and struck up a conversation with the guy in charge and soon was glancing at someone's computerized chart. The patient names were listed outside the cubicles and I saw a dry-erase board with the name Susskind scribbled on it. I craned my neck to look inside and saw a balding, white-haired man sitting on the window sill. He was dressed in a shabby pair of brown pants, a faded plaid flannel shirt, and wearing scuffed suede slippers. He looked up at me and, feeling on the spot, I gave him a nervous wave. He did a kind of double-take, slid off the sill, and in seconds covered the expanse of tiled floor to intercept me.

"Hey, you can see me." The old guy sounded positively jubilant.

Uh-oh. I had a bad feeling I knew where this was going.

And, yeah, not only can I talk to the dead, I *can* see them, too.

Then again, I could hear the monitor beeping with every beat of the guy's heart in the room before me.

"And you are?" I asked tentatively.

"Louie Susskind."

"Relative of the patient?" I asked, already aware that I probably looked like I was talking to myself.

"Hell, I *am* the damn patient!" He gestured toward the bed and the guy lying in it.

Okay, this was weird, even for me.

"You're not dead?"

"Of course not. How could I talk to you if I was dead?"

"How are you talking to me now?" I challenged.

For a moment the guy looked thoughtful, then shrugged.

Richard approached the room and gave me a nod. "You better wait down the hall."

"With pleasure," I said as he walked right through Louie. He didn't seem to notice, but Louie kind of freaked out.

"I hate when that happens," he groused with a shudder.

"Come on," I muttered under my breath and led the way to the door at the end of the hall marked EXIT and away from prying eyes, wondering if the joint was full of ghosts and almost-specters. The next time I had to drop Richard off at the hospital, I would definitely stay in the car.

I took out my phone and held it to my ear. This way, I wouldn't look demented by talking to myself. Yeah. "So what's your story?" I asked Louie.

He shook his head. "Eh, bad ticker. I've had CHF for like the last ten years." Congestive Heart Failure. "It doesn't look like I'm going to bounce back this time."

"I'm sorry to hear that."

He nodded toward Richard. "Who's the guy you're with?"

"My brother's the doctor that just went into your room."

"He doesn't look like a regular doctor. Is he slumming?"

"It's his day off," I commented. "Apparently your son called him in. He's an acquaintance."

Louie's expression dissolved into a scowl. "That sonuvabitch wants to pull the plug on me." He nodded in the direction of his private room. "He wants that new quack—your brother—to agree with him. I've heard Nicholas talking on the phone. He wants me dead ASAP."

"What's his motivation?"

"To save his inheritance—what else?"

I eyed Louie's shabby attire. "What are you leaving him?"

"Unfortunately, my company. These last couple of years, the bastard has nagged us to sell to the highest bidder."

What kind of company? The old guy looked like he might repair shoes.

I asked the question.

"Horse Hockey Brewing."

I'd heard of it. I'd drunk a few bottles of the stuff. It wasn't bad. They had a quirky cartoon horse mascot with buck teeth. A costumed version often showed up at sports and charitable events. I'd heard rumors that beer giants like Anheuser-Busch and a couple of Canadian breweries were interested in acquiring the establishment.

"Have you got any other kids?" I asked.

"A daughter, Teresa. She's a saint. She took care of her mother and then me. My son? He's been a pain in the ass his whole life."

"I'm sorry to hear that." What else was I supposed to say?

"And then there's Bethany, my youngest. She's been helping me with the brewery since day one." Louie's gaze kept traveling toward the cubicle, his expression pensive. "So, are ya gonna help me?"

"What can I do?"

"Well, for one, stop Nick."

"How?"

"How should I know? Call the cops—talk to my lawyer."

"And say what? That some nearly dead guy told me his son is a jerk. Is there a will that gives him control of the company?"

"Not exactly. But unfortunately, just before this last CHF bout, he got me to sign a bunch of papers. I didn't exactly know what I was signing," he muttered.

"And how am I supposed to prove that?"

"I dunno. You look like a smart fella." He scrutinized my face. "By the way, what do you do?"

Shit.

"Well, as it happens … I'm a consultant with R&A Insights. I'm R. Jeff Resnick."

"Consultant? What the hell does that mean?"

"It means … I investigate crimes."

"Being forced to sign papers against your will is definitely a crime," the old man asserted.

"It's morally corrupt, but how can it be proved you *were* coerced?"

"That's up to you to figure out."

"And how are you going to pay me?"

"Talk to Abe Bachmann at the brewery. Tell him I sent you."

And how would that play?

"How long have you been in the hospital?"

"A week."

"And what do I tell him when he asks why I didn't show up sooner?"

"That's up to you."

I let out a breath and thought about Emily sitting there filing her nails or playing games on her phone all day, and me filling in page after page in a cheap pulp book of Sudoku puzzles with nothing better to do. "I guess I could look into it. But how am I going to report to you?"

"Show up here at the hospital."

And if his body was near organ failure, then what?

"Can you leave this floor?"

The old man looked thoughtful. "I can't say as I've tried."

"Well try now, because it's family only that gets to visit patients, and, sure as shit, your family isn't likely to let a stranger visit."

"Talk to Abe at the brewery. Convince him to get Bethany to give you permission."

This was stupid. This was impossible. This was friggin' weird.

I let out a long breath. "Okay, I'll give it a shot."

Chapter 2

Richard Alpert had stopped practicing medicine for the first time more than two decades before. Well, not entirely. He'd been on staff at a big think tank in Pasadena for eighteen years and during that time he'd dispensed the odd Band-Aid, ordered tests for strep throat and high cholesterol, and gave flu shots, but mostly he'd sat in front of a computer evaluating proposed drugs and medical equipment and procedures. More recently, he'd done almost a year of volunteer work at a low-income clinic when he'd called it quits a second time. He just didn't like dealing with people whose lives were coming to an end.

And then the evening before, Nick Susskind, from the hospital charitable foundation where Richard volunteered, had called him with his tale of woe. They weren't friends. Richard barely knew the man except that Nick was also on the foundation's board as a layman from the community. There were a couple of those seats and it was said they were bought by donations for the cause. Richard wasn't about to judge, since the same might be said of him after he'd given the foundation a check with a whole lot of zeros after the number the year before.

After evaluating the patient, he found his brother sitting in the family waiting room, scanning through his iPhone. Richard nodded in the direction of the exit and Jeff got up and followed. Neither of them spoke until they got to the car.

"So?" Jeff asked and shoved the key into his car's ignition.

"I don't feel like talking about it."

"The son wants to pull the plug, right?"

Richard scrutinized his brother's face. "Yeah." How'd he know that? But then Jeff had ways of knowing stuff he had no logical way of identifying.

Jeff nodded and turned the key. "What are you going to advise him?"

Richard shrugged. "I agree with the staff palliative care physician. The old man is sinking fast."

Jeff nodded, looking thoughtful. He threw a look over his shoulder before backing out of the parking space. He was quiet for the time it took to get to the bottom of the ramp and pay the parking fee. He pulled out onto Main Street and turned east. "Well, as it happens, while you were otherwise occupied, I accepted a job for R&A Insights."

"Really?" Richard asked, elated. "Did Emily call?"

Jeff shook his head. "I met a guy up on the cardiac floor and he hired us to straighten out a mess for his company."

"So who is this guy?"

"Louis Susskind."

Richard blinked. "That's impossible. Louis Susskind is the patient I just evaluated."

"He's also a disembodied spirit who says his son is trying to hurry him into the grave."

"You spoke to him?" Richard asked skeptically.

Jeff nodded. "He seems to be an okay guy. He said his son is itching to sell his company—Horse Hockey Brewing."

"My God, what a stupid name."

"Yeah, but the beer isn't half bad. More than one conglomerate has been putting out feelers to buy them out. Louie wants to hold out until the company is more profitable."

"That makes sense."

"Yeah, but your buddy, Junior, wants a quick profit. Makes you wonder why, huh? How well do you know that guy?"

Richard shrugged. "Enough to make small talk."

"And on that basis he asked for your medical opinion?"

"Complete strangers have asked me for medical opinions on countless occasions. How is this a case?"

"When we talked about starting this business, you agreed we would help restless spirits gratis."

So he had. "Wouldn't this be a kind of conflict of interest?"

"How so?"

"Because his son asked me for a medical opinion and I agreed to give him one."

"Were you going to charge him for it?"

"Of course not."

"Then where's the conflict?"

"I guess that depends on where our inquiries take us and what we do with whatever information we uncover."

"We might not find out anything other than what Louie already told me."

"And what if the old man dies before you have a chance to report back to him?"

It was Jeff's turn to look skeptical. Then again, Jeff saw and spoke to the dead on a semi-regular basis.

"Where do we start?" Richard asked.

"Before you came out, I had a chance to look at the Horse Hockey website. I didn't learn much except a brief history of the place, the beers they make, their tasting room menu, and their street address. So let's go check out the place."

"And talk to whom?"

"Louie's second-in-command, a guy named Abe Bachmann."

Richard shrugged. "I guess we can try. Or at least you can try. I may want to hold back until we know if there's anything untoward going on."

"That makes sense. Do you want me to drop you off at the office?"

"No. I'll go home and have lunch with Brenda and Betsy." His wife and toddler daughter. "Maybe Brenda will drive me to the dealership to pick up my car this afternoon. I'll call and let you know."

"Fine with me."

Richard gazed out the passenger-side window, unease creeping into his gut. They'd been waiting for a case to fall into their hands. Was this it?

I DROPPED Richard off at home and headed toward Transit Road. It's as straight as an arrow—a testament to the surveying skills of Joseph Ellicott. After getting bonked on the head with a baseball bat during the mugging, I'd forgotten a lot of what I'd learned in the past, so it was with a bit of pride that I remembered this particular piece of history. The fact the guy did the survey back in the seventeen hundreds with the most basic of equipment was a testament to his ability. As I traveled down that straight tract, I wondered if Ellicott drank a lot of beer. I like beer, but I like bourbon better. I wasn't going to get that at a brewery.

Horse Hockey brewing was located at the northern end of Transit Road on the Amherst side. It sat in a somewhat forlorn-looking strip mall that had once housed a now-defunct big-box store. The building had been divided with the brewery taking up at least three-quarters of the formerly empty space.

At the side of the structure was an outdoor area that boasted chairs and tables—covered in ice and unused at this time of year—with an entrance to the brewery's indoor tasting room. According to their website, they served stuff like chicken wings, nachos, wraps, and other light fare.

I parked the car in front and got out. At that time of day, the tasting room wasn't open for business, but I figured there might be someone I could speak to on the premises who could introduce me to Abe Bachmann.

The door to the tasting room was locked, so I walked around to the back of the building, trying to avoid black ice and hunks of snow still littering the pot-hole pocked drive that circled around the north side of the building. A white truck with the Horse Hockey logo imprinted on it was backed up to a raised concrete loading dock and was being stocked by a couple of guys bundled in parkas and ski hats. I watched as kegs of the latest brew were moved into the truck and waited a few moments to see if they'd acknowledge my presence. They didn't.

I tried the door to the left of the dock and found it locked. I rang the bell beside it. For a while, nothing happened, then the door opened. A woman who looked like she might be closing in on forty, her mousy brown hair streaked with blonde highlights opened the door. She wore a purple sweatshirt under a black jacket with the Horse Hockey logo on the upper right. "Can I help you?"

"I'm looking for Abe Bachmann."

"Why?" she asked, not at all welcoming.

"Louie Susskind sent me."

Her eyes widened. "I doubt that. Mr. Susskind is in the hospital, in a coma."

"We spoke before he ended up there," I fibbed.

"Who are you?" she demanded.

I reached into my back pocket, pulled out my wallet,

extracted one of my cards, and handed it to her. I hadn't performed that feat all that often. It felt pretty good.

She read it and glowered at me. "Are you some kind of investigator?"

I shook my head. To be an investigator, you had to have apprenticed with a private detective for three years and be licensed with the state. Who had time for that? "I'm a consultant."

"And how did Mr. Susskind contact you?"

"We ran into each other and he told me a little about his business. He asked me to speak with Mr. Bachmann."

She kept looking at me and I could practically read her thoughts: should she trust me?

"Hey, Bethany," one of the guys on the dock called, sounding concerned. "Need any help?"

She shook her head. "I'm okay." She looked back at me and scowled. "Come on in."

I followed her into the shipping area, which was lined with pallets filled with six-packs of beer bottles wrapped in shrink wrap and row after row of silver kegs. She kept a brisk pace, leading me through the building past a long and complicated bottling machine that was blessedly silent, toward what looked like office space that had been carved out of the cavernous room.

"Are you Louie's daughter?" I asked as I struggled to keep up.

The question brought her to an abrupt halt and she pivoted, looking wary. "Yes."

I wasn't sure what to say next. I was supposed to convince Bachmann to have Bethany give me permission to visit her father and now I'd met her face-to-face. Maybe I should have given this whole thing a bit more thought before barging onto the premises.

She turned around and we approached glass cubicles along

the far wall. A tall black guy dressed in a white lab coat over a flannel shirt stood behind a desk, talking on the phone. Bethany pursed her lips and stood there, waiting for the man to notice her. When he did, he gestured to the phone. We stood there, and half a minute later he hung up and waved us in.

Bethany opened the door. "Sorry to interrupt."

"That's okay." He nodded toward me, his expression not at all welcoming. "Who've you got there?"

I was hit with a wave of suspicion. It seemed Louie's concerns were well founded.

I pulled out another of my cards and handed it to him. "Louie sent me."

Bachmann studied the card, looking away. "What for?"

"He was concerned about the business. That it might be sold out from under him."

"Over my dead body," Bethany muttered.

"And mine," Bachmann added.

"It can't happen," Bethany stated.

"Then I assume you don't know about the paperwork Louie signed."

Bethany's and Bachmann's panicked gazes darted toward each other.

"Paperwork?" Bachmann said warily.

I nodded. "He wasn't sure exactly what he'd signed—but he said he didn't trust Nicholas." And it looked like neither did the two people in front of me.

"When was this?" Bachmann asked.

"Louie was kind of hazy on the details." Not a satisfactory answer, but the truth as far as I knew.

The tension emanating from those two people shifted into high gear.

"Did my father hire you?" Bethany asked.

"We never actually got around to signing a contract."

“Then that makes you a pretty poor businessman. Are you any better as a consultant?” Bachmann asked.

“My partner usually handles those kinds of details. And Louie wasn’t in the best of health when we spoke.” They seemed to accept that statement.

“What do you think you can do for us?” Bethany asked.

I shrugged. “Poke around. Ask some questions.” I laughed. “Try a glass of your beer.”

Their expressions remained stony.

“Then how about a brewery tour? I’d like to know more about the business your dad—” I nodded in Bethany’s direction, “expects me to save.”

“Save?” Bachmann asked. “You?”

“That’s what he asked of me.”

Bethany crossed her arms defiantly. When she spoke, an edge had crept into her voice. “And how do you propose to do that?”

“Right this minute, I have no idea. But a good place to start is right here at the brewery. Can you give me a bit of a tour—tell me more about the company?”

They looked at each other, unhappy with my suggestion, but acquiesced.

The tour was cursory at best; a brief rundown on the brewery’s history, the fermentation process, and the dead quiet bottling line. There seemed to be a lot of canned and bottled product stacked in pallets with shrink wrap up against the wall. The guys on the loading dock had been loading kegs.

Eventually, my guides led me back to the brewery’s back door.

“Thanks,” I told them sincerely.

“Is there anything else you’d like to know?” Bethany asked.

“Not so much know as do.”

“And that is?” Bachmann asked.

“I’d like to visit Louie.”

"What for? He can't speak. He's hardly been awake for a week," Bethany groused.

"You'd be surprised what people in a coma can hear."

Bachmann snorted. "Are you speaking as the voice of experience?"

"As a matter of fact—yes."

Both looked startled, but I wasn't about to give them the lowdown on my medical history.

"I guess I could put your name down on the list of visitors … not that it will do any good."

"You never know," I told her.

Bachmann didn't look pleased. Was he on the list of visitors? Or maybe he didn't relish the idea of visiting his friend who was on the downslide into death.

"Okay," Bethany said. "I'm going to visit him later this afternoon."

"Great. Give me a call at the number on my card. In the meantime, can you tell me why your brother Nicholas wants to sell the brewery?"

"Besides the fact he's an asshole?" Bethany asked.

I nodded.

Bethany's expression darkened. "Nick's trying to salvage a nineteenth-century sailing ship from the bottom of Lake Ontario."

"Sounds expensive," I offered.

Bethany shook her had. "You have no idea."

"What's the name of the vessel?"

"The Bonnie Rae. They say it's cursed."

That sounded like something in my wheelhouse.

"What's the attraction?"

"It's said one of our relatives was onboard," she said.

"And the significance of the vessel?"

"Nick probably thinks if he can salvage the cargo, he'd not

only be a gazillionaire, but some kind of hero." Bethany rolled her eyes in disdain.

And to finance such a venture took a lot of capital. It might be something my partner, the skilled researcher, might be able to suss.

I nodded. "Until we speak again."

I opened the door and let myself out. It banged shut behind me and I heard the deadbolt thrown.

I walked back to my car and thought about the encounter. Bethany and Abe were suspicious of me, and rightly so. But I wasn't sure I trusted them all that much, either. It wasn't the best way to start a new business arrangement.

I got in my car and started the engine, backing up to pull out of the lot. Something about the brewery felt very wrong.

How long would it take me to figure out what that something was?

Chapter 3

Emily's car was still parked in the small lot behind our office when I returned from my travels. I'll give her that—bored as she was, she never skipped out early. I probably could have gone straight home, but I figured I should write up notes on my meeting with Louie and then the brewery visit. Our shared file cabinet would be a lot less rocky when it was filled with something other than air.

Emily looked up as I entered the office. "I didn't expect you back today. And, hey, you actually look happier."

"I do?" I asked, shrugging out of my coat and placing it on a hanger on the built-in rack.

"Yeah, like a big weight has been lifted from your shoulders."

I managed a smile. "That's because we have a case."

Her eyes lit up. "We do? Tell me all about it."

My smile faded. How was I going to explain Louie and the task he'd given me? "Well, when I took my brother to the hospital, I met a man who's got some trouble he wants us to look into."

"Just like that you met a client?" she asked, her eyes going wide.

"Uh, he kind of sought me out," I fudged. "Anyway, the guy owns a craft brewery and wants me to nose around to see what's what."

"And what is what?"

"I don't know yet," I answered honestly. "I'll have to do some more digging."

Emily's expression went from interested to wary in almost a heartbeat. "What does Dr. Alpert think about the case?"

"He's not quite as enthused as me. It's complicated."

Emily frowned and shook her head. Maybe she was disappointed that I wasn't more forthcoming. She continued to study my face. "I gotta say, Jeff, you're the strangest boss I've ever worked for."

Had she doped out my secret or was she fishing?

"Strange how?" Did I creep her out? If so, I can't say I'd be surprised.

Emily shook her head. "You're not like regular guys."

That was true. I sometimes thought I was the unhappiest person on the planet who hadn't committed suicide, although I'd tried it not all that long before. Not of my own free will, mind you—but I'd attempted it all the same.

"It's your eyes," Emily offered. "They're usually kind of … dead." Then her eyes widened in horror and she raised a hand to cover her mouth. "I'm sorry. I shouldn't have said that."

I shook my head. "It's nothing I haven't noticed myself."

She bit her lip and I could almost sense her mind whirring.

"You know all about me and my past," Emily said, "but I really don't know much about you."

"There's not much to tell."

She looked skeptical. "Dr. Alpert said you were a crime-scene specialist before your accident."

"It wasn't an accident. It was a mugging that left me with a skull fracture and a broken arm."

"That job had to be a terrible toll on your soul."

"Sometimes," I admitted, thinking about the last grisly crime scene photos I'd examined—those of my dead wife. Yeah, quite a toll.

"And you got hurt last summer when you got hit by a car," she continued.

It was an SUV, but who cared about the details? "Did my brother tell you that, too?"

"No, you did. You had a cane when we met that time in the grocery store, remember?"

So I had.

Eventually, Emily was going to have to learn the unique aspect that I brought to our business, but now was not the time to detail my so-called psychic gift—which I considered an enormous hindrance in my life.

"Did you ever see the movie *Sixth Sense*?" I asked.

Emily shook her head. "Why?"

"You've got Netflix, right? Why don't you watch it … and then we'll talk."

She frowned. "Why?"

"Just watch it—and not with Hannah," I quickly added. "It's kind of a scary movie."

Her expression darkened. "I don't like scary movies."

"Neither do I."

Emily looked more than a little uncomfortable. It was time to change the subject.

"I need to type up my notes. You don't have to hang around until five."

"Are you sure?"

"Did we get any calls while I was gone?"

She shook her head.

"Then I'm sure I can handle things here."

"Well, okay," she said, opened her desk drawer and pulled out her purse, and then retrieved my abandoned muffin from the fridge before walking over to the coat rack. She donned hers and pulled out her car keys. "I guess I'll see you in the morning."

"Bright and early," I said, trying to sound cheerful but I had a feeling things were going to sour in the next hour or so. I just wasn't sure why and wasn't eager to find out, either.

I watched as Emily headed for the door, looking back to give me a rather uncertain wave. I forced a smile and waved back. She closed the door.

I stood there, my gaze dropping to the Berber carpet. Had I just made a big mistake asking her to watch that film? Would she do it that night or put it off for a few days—maybe not watch it at all? If so, we'd soon have to have a much different conversation. One I wouldn't look forward to. Of course, I could just have Richard talk to her about my gift. But that was the coward's way out.

Right then, I felt like taking the easy way out. Sometimes life was just too friggin' awkward. But awkward didn't kill you, even if embarrassment just might.

I turned and entered Richard's and my office, a space I spent way more time in than him. Setting up this consulting business had been rash—and, in my estimation, a huge mistake. I should have just looked at the want ads and found myself another bartending job. But Richard had pushed to establish R&A Insights. Why hadn't he put more effort into getting the firm started?

It was a conversation we needed to have.

And why was I so reluctant to do so?

A STRANGE CAR sat in Richard's driveway. A visitor? I parked my wreck in the garage's farthest bay and headed over to the big brick house. I lived across the drive above the garage, or carriage house as his late grandmother had called it, on Richard's property, along with my cat, Herschel.

The big house's back door that led to the butler's pantry was unlocked and I stepped through it and into the kitchen where I found Brenda and Richard sitting at the table with my lady friend Maggie in what had been her usual spot during the many dinners the four of us had shared in that house, with toddler Betsy strapped into her highchair, eating Cheerios. Richard had megabucks, but they pretty much lived a middle-class life because that's the way Brenda wanted to bring up Betsy—otherwise known as my little Cherry Pie.

Maggie's dog, Holly, sat in the corner next to Richard, looking distinctly unhappy, that is unless a Cheerio bounced off her nose. She knew.

I bent down and gave Maggie a quick kiss on the cheek. "Hey, I thought I was going to pick up you and Holly tomorrow," I said, taking off my jacket and hanging it on the back of my usual chair before sitting down.

"I had a change of plans," Maggie said, sounding just a little too cheerful.

I'd seen the crate and other doggy paraphernalia stacked in the pantry when I'd entered.

"My Mom and Dad decided they'd like to take me to the airport tomorrow."

It must have been their car that sat in the drive. I hadn't looked in it, but I knew they weren't fond of Holly. Maggie had no doubt covered the seat with towels and had probably been made to promise to vacuum it out before returning it. Holly had never been allowed to visit the elder Brennan's home. They weren't pet people. Another strike against them. When we'd first discussed her travel arrangements, Maggie had said no one in her family was available to take her to the airport and would I mind. Of course not. That they'd changed their minds on the eve of her departure didn't come as much of a surprise, either. It looked like we'd be saying our goodbyes in the middle of Richard's driveway.

"Maggie was just telling us her plans for the evening," Richard said, his tone neutral.

"I've got to make one more sweep of the house, and the people renting are coming within the hour to collect the keys. They intend to move in tomorrow."

I nodded. I thought it was a mistake of her to rent and not sell—the place gave me the creeps—but she insisted she was coming back … eventually. I wasn't sure I believed that, either. We were at the point where I just wished she'd go and that didn't feel good, either. For a while, she'd meant the world to me. That I could sense I was no longer that important to her was demoralizing.

I was tired of feeling that way.

An awkward silence fell over the table. It seemed like none of us wanted to look each other in the eye. Finally, Maggie pushed back her chair.

"I have loads to do—including laundry. I'd better get to it." She stood. "Come and say goodbye to your mommy, Holly."

The dog lay at Richard's feet and didn't move. Her tail didn't even wag.

"Holly," Maggie tried again, and this time her voice cracked. Still, the dog didn't move. It was only when Richard stood that she got to her feet and finally padded over to Maggie but it seemed more as a gesture of duty than desire. Had Holly already resigned herself to accept a new master?

Maggie crouched down and gave the dog a hug and a quick kiss on the top of her head. Then she straightened, cleared her throat, and quickly donned her jacket, grabbing her purse. She held her arms wide for Brenda. "Until we meet again."

Brenda stepped over and gave Maggie a big hug, patting her back. "You'll always be welcome in this house. And I expect a phone call—if not tomorrow, then on the weekend."

"You'll get it," Maggie promised. "I'll have loads to tell you about the job and how I'm fixing up my apartment. I already have plans to go to the big flea market not far from work on Saturday."

Brenda stepped aside so Richard could have his turn at a hug. "Safe travels, Maggie. And don't worry about Holly. We'll take good care of her."

Maggie's gaze drifted to me.

I shrugged.

Again she cleared her throat. "I'd better get going. Walk me to the car, Jeff?"

"Of course."

I shrugged back into my jacket and gestured for her to go before me.

"Bye," Richard and Brenda chorused.

"Bye-bye!" Betsy called and opened and closed her hand in a wave that Maggie didn't see.

She walked out the door and I pulled it shut behind us.

When she arrived at the car, Maggie turned, and I could see there were tears in her eyes. I could feel the pull of conflicting emotions within her. Disappointment that her dog hadn't made more of a fuss of her, but also a thin thread of regret. Very thin.

"This isn't forever," she promised.

"I know," I said and stepped forward, putting my arms around her and pulling her close for a kiss, although neither of us felt any kind of passion.

"I feel sad," she admitted. "But … excited. I've never had this kind of opportunity given to me."

"You worked hard for it," I said, parroting what she'd told me countless times.

She managed a smile. "I did. We all make sacrifices when it comes to our careers."

"Yeah." What more was there to say?

She hurled herself at me, holding on for dear life. "It'll be okay."

"We'll get through it," I said into her hair and managed to hold onto her just a little bit tighter.

Maggie pulled back, gave me a more impassioned kiss, and then quickly turned, wrenched open the car door and got in.

It was cold. I shoved my hands into my jacket pockets and watched as she backed the car out of the driveway, knowing Richard and Brenda were watching from the kitchen window.

At the end of the drive, Maggie's gaze was focused on the road. I waved, but she didn't.

So, I was alone.

Again.

BY THE TIME Jeff reentered the house, a glass of scotch on the rocks sat before Richard. "Beer or bourbon?" Brenda asked.

Richard was surprised she even bothered to ask.

"Bourbon."

"Coming right up," she said, playing bartender.

Richard watched as his brother took off his jacket and sat down once again. Moments later, a glass appeared before him. Brenda took her seat and set down a glass of white wine for herself. "We should have a toast." She picked up the glass. "To Maggie, may she find what she's looking for."

"Or what she's abandoning," Richard muttered under his breath.

Holly, who'd repositioned herself between Richard and the

highchair, gave a little woof as though in agreement. The three of them clinked glasses.

"So," Richard said after taking a sip. "How did it go at Horse Hockey Brewing?" What was the point of discussing what had transpired minutes before in that kitchen?

"I spoke to the owner's daughter—your friend's sister—and the brewmaster."

"And?"

"They were reluctant to level with me about what's going on at the brewery. But I got a strong vibe that they're both scared."

"Of what?" Brenda asked.

Jeff nodded in Richard's direction. "Maybe of your friend —Nick."

"He's not my friend," Richard said defensively. "And how do you know he doesn't have his father's and the brewery's best interests at heart?"

"All I know is what Louie told me and gauging from the reactions of the people I met today, the situation warrants more investigation."

"And what will that entail?" Brenda asked.

He let out a rather chagrined sigh. "I'm not sure." Jeff looked in Richard's direction. "Of course, you could shut this whole thing down right now."

"What do you mean?"

"It all depends on how loyal you are to your hospital friend."

"He's not my—"

"Okay—your colleague," Jeff corrected himself. He sipped his bourbon on the rocks. "I need to talk to Louie. I thought I might go this evening. Do you want to tag along?"

Richard shook his head. "I'd only be listening to one side of the conversation." He had a point, but he could see the disappointment in Jeff's expression.

"Do you want to stay for supper?" Brenda asked.

Jeff looked around the kitchen, where obviously there'd been no food prep. "Pizza?" he asked.

"You got it."

He shrugged. "Okay."

During their makeshift supper, they didn't discuss Maggie or the situation at the Horse Hockey Brewery. They didn't talk about anything of note, and somehow that just felt wrong.

A pall of depression seemed to hover over them. Only baby Betsy maintained a sense of *joie de vivre*. And later, when everyone else was tucked in for the night, Holly planted herself on the floor next to Richard's side of the bed. He let a hand hang over the side and was rewarded with the nuzzle of a damp nose.

How sad was it that it was the highlight of his day?

Chapter 4

I waited until well after official visiting hours were over before heading out to the hospital to see Louie, figuring I'd find a better parking space. Richard no longer had admitting privileges, so I couldn't borrow his pass and had to pay to park. I made a mental note to add it to a list of expenses … not that I was sure we'd make a nickel on this little endeavor.

Other sad-eyed visitors wandered between a waiting area and the corridor of hospital rooms, hoping and praying for miracles. I checked in at the nurse's station and found that Bethany had added my name to the list of authorized visitors.

Once again, Louie's spirit sat on the window sill and, upon seeing me, leapt into the air like a gymnast, something his physical self probably hadn't been able to do for decades.

"Resnick! You came back. How's my brewery?" he asked without waiting for me to even say hello.

"As you can see, your daughter authorized me to visit; now will you move to the other side of the bed so that it looks like I'm talking to your body."

"Sure, sure," Louie agreed and scooted around me to stand at the head of the other side of the bed.

I pulled out the uncomfortable plastic chair—no doubt to cut such visits short—and sat down.

"So, what have you got to tell me?" Louie badgered.

I waved my hand at him as though flicking at an annoying fly. "Give me a chance, will ya?"

Louie's spirit scowled at me.

"How are things going here?"

He glanced down at his physical body, looking depressed. "Not good. I'm dying."

"Eh, we're all dying," I said and shrugged, hoping to make him feel a little better.

"Some faster than others," he grunted. He looked up at me. "What have you got to report?"

"Not much. I spoke to Abe at the brewery. He grilled me—wanting to know where I had met you. He's not one to trust easily."

"And why should he?"

"It makes it harder for me to help you. Needless to say, they weren't thrilled to hear about the papers you'd signed."

"Yeah, well, I'm not, either."

"I don't know what their legal recourse is. You signed them. They probably can't prove you did it under duress."

"There must be something we can do."

"How good is your lawyer?"

Louie shrugged. "He's no supreme court contender."

"Has the brewery got the bucks to hire someone better?"

"You got someone in mind?"

"I know of a pretty prestigious firm that's got a good track record. But they're pricey. My partner has an in with them. If nothing else, they could stall things until Abe and Bethany can figure out something else."

"And bill us by the hour."

"You get what you pay for."

Louie frowned. "It sounds to me like you're giving up."

"I don't yet see a way out of this."

"What would it take?"

"You'd need to recover."

Louie scowled. "I don't think that's going to happen."

"What would happen to Bethany and Teresa if Nick sold the company out from under them?"

"They'd get a share, but it wouldn't be enough for Bethany to start over again."

"I guess that depends on how much she wants it."

"Bethany's poured her heart and soul into the brewery. To have it sold off from under her…."

"Have you got a board of trustees—anything like that?"

Louie shook his head. "I never wanted the business to leave the family."

And it sounded like he hadn't erected any safeguards to prevent it, either.

"So, what's your next move?" Louie demanded.

I thought about it. "I've got a friend who works for *The Buffalo News*."

"What can he do?"

"Possibly get me in to talk to Nick…without him knowing my connection to you or that my brother and I are in partnership."

"What good will that do?"

I shrugged. "Maybe nothing. But it's a start."

Louie looked more than just a little depressed. He gazed down at the immobile figure of himself lying on the bed attached to monitors and an IV drip.

"You know, after you die you don't *have* to go," I told him gently.

Louie started. "I don't?"

"I've met a few restless spirits." Okay, maybe just four … that I knew of … five if I counted Louie.

"I'm not dead," the old man protested.

Yet. But from the look of it, he wasn't far from it, either.

"What would keep me here?"

"Unfinished business."

"I've got a lot of that," Louie groused. "What would I be able to do?"

"That's the thing…not much if anything."

"Then there ain't much point in hanging around, is there?"

I shrugged. Louie was probably thinking about passing through the pearly gates and being reunited with his wife and others he'd loved. Good luck with that.

"Can you talk to this reporter guy tonight?"

I glanced at my watch. "I'll text him."

"You do that."

I stood. "Do you need anything?"

"Yeah, a new heart."

"Something else is bothering you," I observed.

The old man shrugged, looking back at the inert form that lay on the bed. "Today Teresa brought in a deathmonger."

"A what?"

"A death doula."

I'd only heard of doulas assisting women who were about to give birth, not guiding those to the afterlife. "And that bums you out?"

"Yeah. I'm *not* dead."

"How old are you?"

"Seventy-five. I shoulda had another twenty years. My dad did—and my mother lasted almost as long."

But had they smoked, drank, or engaged in other unhealthy pursuits?

"So, what's next on your agenda to save my brewery?" Louie asked, his penetrating gaze fixed on mine.

"Like I said, I'll contact my friend and see where that goes. I'd like to meet Teresa and this death doula, too. Any idea on when they're likely to show up?"

"Teresa told the deathmonger she'd meet her here in the afternoon. Come around four to see the show."

"You make it sound like a circus."

"It's something like that," Louie groused. "Just wait."

I'd have to do a little Internet sleuthing between now and the next afternoon. "Is there anything else—or anyone—I should look into?"

Louie considered my question for long seconds before he snapped, "No."

I eyed him critically. He wasn't being totally honest with me and I had no idea why. I decided to push him.

"Is there anyone else at the brewery I should talk to?"

Again Louie snapped, "No!"

A knock on the doorjamb distracted me. I looked over my shoulder as a nurse entered the room.

"I need to turn the patient," she said. "We don't want him to get bedsores."

The man was dying, unconscious, and as far as I knew, wasn't feeling a damn thing, but it was the humane thing to do.

"I was just about to leave," I said and rose from the uncomfortable chair. "I'll see you tomorrow, Louie."

The nurse shook her head. "It's not likely he heard you."

"Maybe…maybe not."

"She's an idiot," Louie groused.

I reached to squeeze Louie's body's hand. "I'll come back tomorrow to see you."

"You better," his disembodied self growled.

Chapter 5

It was already after nine on Tuesday morning when Richard entered his study to check his email, with Holly hot on his heels. By the tracks in the dusting of snow on the driveway, he knew Jeff had already left for their R&A office, yet he felt in no hurry to follow him—or even if he needed to.

Richard turned on his computer and logged into his primary email account while Holly made herself comfortable near the heat return on the floor nearby. Scrolling through the emails, he was surprised to see a note from a familiar name. He clicked to open the message and sat back to read it.

FROM: Det. John Destross, Buffalo PD
Subject: Possible Cold Case

DR. ALPERT. If you're still available, I may have a case you might be interested in looking into. If so, call me at the number listed below.

Thank you.

RICHARD PICKED up the receiver on his desk phone, punched in the number given, and was pleased when the call was picked up on the second ring.

"Detective Destross."

"Hello, detective. This is Richard Alpert. I received your note. How may my firm help you?"

"Thanks for sending me the brochure about your service. If you're willing to look at another *pro bono* cold case, I've got one that I think you might be interested in."

"Tell me about it," Richard said.

"First off, I didn't work on the original investigation, but I know one of the detectives who was in charge of the case. The department doesn't have the resources to spend investigating old cases. But this one bothered my former colleague."

"I'm listening. What's his concern?"

"Arson—and murder. The victim died in the fire."

"When did this happen?"

"Twenty-two years ago. The woman was well-known in the neighborhood, but if anyone knew about the crime, they weren't willing to turn snitch."

That didn't bode well.

"If you're interested, I can send you an email with the case notes attached."

"That sounds good. Can you give me the gist of the case now?"

"The surviving family has been reluctant to talk about one of their own who was the prime suspect and disappeared within days of the crime."

"That's what R&A Insights is all about, detective," Richard said rather glibly.

"Yeah, well, you might not sound so assured once you meet

the family. None of our officers were successful in getting them to talk freely. There's definitely something to tell, and they haven't been willing to share that story."

"R&A Insights has a number of resources we're able to utilize."

"Perfect," Destross said. "I'll get that information to you this morning."

"Thanks. We'll talk again soon," Richard said. He hung up the phone, glad the detective had contacted him. Jeff had his own case and it would be a blatant conflict of interest for Richard to collaborate with him. Destross's arson case was an opportunity for him to prove his mettle as a consultant. It rather irked him that this was to be a pro bono job, whereas Jeff's case might actually land them income, although being hired by a comatose man unable to write his signature on a check was no guarantee of future payment, either.

Richard would tell Jeff about this case … but not until after he'd spoken to the family. And even then, it might not be something they'd even want to take on. He'd just have to see.

Even so, the fact the detective had consulted them was a cause for celebration.

Although the sun was nowhere near the yard arm, Richard crossed the expanse of his study to stand before his dry bar. He poured himself a neat Scotch and returned to his desk. Sitting back in his big leather chair, he lifted his glass and took a sip of that fine eighteen-year-old whisky. Finally, he had a case he might be able to sink his teeth into.

He savored the Scotch and the victory, even if both were premature.

EVEN BEFORE I left for work—God, I liked the sound of that—I texted my friend Sam and said I'd be calling him later that morning about a possible story idea. He replied: *Great.*

I arrived half an hour before R&A Insights' listed hours of operation, flicked the light switches, and started a pot of coffee. While it brewed, I picked up my phone and tapped one of the names on my contacts list. It rang.

"Sam Nielson, *Buffalo News*."

"Hey, Sam, it's me."

"Jeff? Where the hell have you been?"

"I'm proud to say I'm now gainfully employed."

"Doing what?"

"Well, that's kind of why I'm calling. Are you doing anything for lunch?"

"Have you got an expense account?" he asked, his tone sly.

"Yup."

"Then I'm as free as a bird."

"Great. How does the Falcon's Nest up on Main Street here in Snyder sound at noon?"

"Make it twelve-thirty."

"Fine."

"See you then."

I set the receiver down. It had been a while since I'd seen Sam. Since I'd even spoken to anyone other than Richard, Brenda, Maggie, Emily—and now Louie. To interact with another living human being was a major event in my ever-shrinking social circle.

Emily arrived five minutes before opening, called out her presence, but didn't bother to address me further.

I'd finished reading the paper and had done all the puzzles I wanted to complete before I left my office to get a second cup of coffee. Emily sat behind her computer, playing Candy Crush on Facebook. I wouldn't have thought someone her age had an account on that platform, but maybe she used it to keep up with relatives or long-distance friends.

She looked up. "Need anything?"

I proffered my mug. "Just another cup of Joe." I refilled it and doctored it.

"Will you be leaving on your airport errand soon?"

I shook my head. "Canceled."

"Oh. But, I thought she was…." Emily didn't finish the sentence.

Yeah, I thought so, too.

"And Holly?"

Emily had already met Holly on several occasions, thanks to her staying with the Alperts, and Richard bringing her to the office.

"She's with Richard. Maggie brought her over last evening."

Emily looked like she wanted to say more.

"Yeah, it was a surprise to me, too."

Emily nodded. "Um…Dr. Alpert said your girlfriend was going to leave her dog with him to take a job in California."

"That's true."

"Does that bother you? I mean her going away. Everyone knows long-distance relationships are hard to maintain."

She was right and it was a conversation Maggie and I had avoided but needed to have. Then again, I pretty much knew that if an opportunity for sexual fulfillment came her way, Maggie was likely to embrace it. As soon as she'd told me she'd taken the job, I knew our exclusive relationship was over. She was a sexual being and from past experience—and despite her protests—I knew she wouldn't feel fettered to a hard-and-fast commitment. I loved her. I'd always love her, but I no longer thought of her as a soulmate. I'd been in denial about that aspect of our relationship. Richard had never believed it. My psychic mentor, Sophie Levin, hadn't, either. Brenda had never voiced an opinion. I'm not sure she'd have ventured one even if I asked, although I'm sure she had one.

"Yeah, they are," I admitted.

"So, what will you do without her?"

Emily was a nosy little thing.

"You're alone. I could ask you the same question."

Emily shrugged. "I do laundry, clean the apartment, and help Hannah with her homework. Just normal mom stuff."

"I do laundry, clean my apartment, and my cat and I watch basketball on TV." I probably drank too much, too. She didn't have to know that.

Emily's expression darkened. "I watched that movie you told me about," she said coldly. "I didn't like it."

"It made a lot of money," I observed.

"It was creepy. It scared me." She glared at me. "You're not dead like the guy in the movie … so, do you see yourself as the character of the little boy?"

"Kinda … sorta…" My heart sank. "Yeah."

Emily's expression soured. "Well, I don't believe it's possible. My faith won't *let* me believe it," she said with more than a touch of arrogance. She probably thought I was crazy.

Hmm. Maybe I was.

I shrugged, but I thought I should warn her that I could tune into at least a portion of her emotional life. I just wasn't sure how to do it without sounding like some kind of voyeur. No matter, I needed to offer her a choice.

"I'll understand if you decide you'd rather seek employment elsewhere."

Her eyes widened in sudden panic. "I didn't say that."

"No, but if you don't feel comfortable being around me, as one of the firm's partners, I encourage you to reconsider working with us. I am the way I am. Much as I'd like to go back to the way I used to be, it's not my decision. So, you're free to leave—or stay. It's up to you."

Emily's head dipped so that I could no longer see her eyes. "I'm going to have to think about it."

"Well, don't take too long," I said coolly. "Once things ramp up, we're going to need an associate who can work with us on any project that comes our way. If you're not up to the challenge, you need to let us know—and soon." God, I felt like the worst corporate prick I'd ever had to deal with when I'd worked for those big insurance companies back in Manhattan.

Emily said nothing. What could she say?

"Tell me more about what you *think* you can do," she said, her tone more than a little dismissive.

I knew things about her that she probably wouldn't be comfortable about me knowing. I'd connected with her the first time I'd touched her two years before. At one point, she'd even felt an attraction—albeit slight—toward me. I'd have to tread carefully.

"Sometimes I pick up vibes left behind after people touch inanimate objects."

"Such as?" she demanded.

The mail sat on her desk. Had her touching it tainted it? No way to find out unless I picked it up. I sorted through the junk mail and picked up something…probably from the mailman who'd dropped it off. His boots leaked and he was sick of dealing with cold, wet feet. That wasn't something Emily was going to accept. I told her anyway.

"You can't prove it," she remarked.

Okay, it was time to pull out the big guns. I grabbed the coffee cup that sat on her desk, holding on tight. Slowly, vague, murky images began to seep into my mind. But as I thought more about it, my understanding bloomed.

"Hannah wants a puppy…but there's no way you can have a dog because of your job. You can't see how it would work with training it and would feel guilty leaving it in a crate all day."

Emily's eyes widened.

"You've thought about getting an older dog, one already house-broken, but then—"

"Shut up!" she commanded, her cheeks darkening. "That's a flagrant violation of my privacy!"

"Hey, you asked for proof."

"No, I—" But then she didn't continue. Her brow wrinkled and she looked confused. "How…how do you know about the whole puppy deal?"

I shrugged. "I told you. I get vibes. But not always. I have no idea how it all works, and it doesn't all the time. It's kind of like tuning into frequencies on a radio. Sometimes the signal comes in strong, and sometimes not at all."

"Such as?"

I shrugged. "I can tune into my sister-in-law, my niece, and my girlfriend, Maggie, but my brother is a complete blank to me. Believe me, it's not a gift. This whole thing is a gigantic burden."

"Well, I don't want you tuning into me," she blurted

I frowned. "It's not something I can control, which is why you need to consider if working for R&A Insights is best for you. It's your choice."

For a moment, I thought Emily might burst into tears, but then I could feel a resolve build within her. She needed this job, and had based certain expenditures on her increased pay base.

"I need to think this over," she said coolly.

"You do that."

Meanwhile, my coffee had gone cold. I could nuke it in the microwave that lived in the conference/break room or pour it down the sink. I chose the latter, and went back to my office, forcing myself not to close the door.

It was now up to Emily. Would she stay or would she quit her job?

I hoped she'd stay. I liked her—had since the day I'd met

her two years before—but if she decided to get a job elsewhere, I could live with that, too. We'd had a slight connection, but I'd had that with countless other people who'd moved into and out of my life.

I could live without her, too.

And yet . . . I wasn't sure I wanted to.

Chapter 6

Richard had taken the time to read through and study the case notes Detective Destross had forwarded to him. Leaning forward, he picked up the phone's receiver, and punched in the number the cop had given him earlier that day. It rang four times before someone picked up.

"Hello."

"Is this Mrs. Nancy Clark?"

"Yes," the voice said warily.

"I'm Dr. Richard Alpert. I wonder if I might speak to you about the arson that took place in your home over twenty years ago."

"What for?"

"I'm a partner at R&A Insights in Amherst. I'm working with the police to—"

"No, thanks."

The connection was broken.

Startled by the brevity of the conversation, Richard placed the phone's receiver back on the switch hook. The woman's reaction shouldn't have been a surprise. After all, if the cops hadn't been able to work with the family, what luck was he going to have?

Yet someone had died in that fire and the prime suspect was a family member, but still....

Okay, if Mrs. Clark wasn't going to speak to him, he wondered if someone else associated with R&A Insights might have better luck.

But first, Richard headed upstairs to brush his teeth before he sought out his wife. She didn't have to know about his celebratory drink—premature though it possibly was.

He found Brenda in the kitchen, folding the baby's laundry. They had a set-up in the basement—the washer, a dryer, and a large workbench, that she and Jeff still referred to as the dungeon—but she preferred to use the kitchen table as a workspace. Their daughter was seated in her highchair playing with toy beads that were attached to the tray by a suction cup, keeping her occupied.

Brenda looked up. "Hey."

"Hey, yourself."

Richard stooped to kiss the top of Betsy's head before he took a seat at the table and grabbed one of the little pink shirts to fold. "I may have just received a new case for R&A Insights."

"Oh?"

He explained about Destross's email and subsequent phone conversation.

"I read through the case notes—such as they are—and I'd like to give it a shot. I was hoping maybe you could give me a hand."

"What do you want me to do?"

"Talk to the victim's daughter."

Brenda squinted at him. "And why's that?"

"Because Mrs. Clark won't talk to me."

Brenda frowned. "And why's *that*?" she insisted.

Richard blew out a snort of breath. "Because I'm a white guy. The family has no reason to trust me."

"Uh-huh," Brenda said. "And what makes you think she'd talk to me?"

"Well, isn't it obvious?"

"Because I'm black?"

"Well, yeah," Richard reluctantly admitted.

Brenda shook her head. "If they don't want to trust you, why should they trust me?"

"Because you're a compassionate person?"

"Mama mama mama," Betsy said and banged her fists on the highchair's tray.

Brenda's penetrating gaze was not at all sympathetic.

"The thing is, I understand one of the lead detectives on the case is no longer on the force and is quite ill, but he really wants to solve the old lady's death before he passes. Could you live with yourself if you didn't at least *try* to help me figure out who killed the old lady and bring that person to justice?"

Brenda's lips pursed. "Well, if you put it that way."

"You're a valued member of our team. We won't ask all that much of you—but if you could help bring closure on a cold case, would you be willing to help?"

For a moment, Brenda looked like she might explode, but then she shook her head with what seemed like resignation. "Okay. What do I need to do?"

"Call the victim's daughter and ask if they'd like resolution."

"And if they don't"

"Well, then, we're pretty much done," Richard admitted.

"What if I said no?"

"Well, you *are* a part of R&A Insights," he said, knowing he was playing the guilt card.

"Is my name on the door?" she pressed.

"No, but you agreed to be our moral compass."

"And what does that have to do with speaking to Mrs. Clark?"

"Because she isn't likely to open up to me."

"And we both know why."

Yeah, they did.

"Pretty please?" he asked.

Brenda glared at him.

"With sugar on top?"

Brenda pursed her lips, let out an exasperated breath through her nose, and shook her head. She scrutinized his face. "Why is this so important to you?"

"We need to establish the business. We're not exactly inundated with work."

Brenda continued folding the little shirts and pants, balling the tiny pink socks, and setting them into the white plastic laundry basket. It seemed like a long time before she spoke again.

"I . . I guess I could help. *This* time." Did that mean she might not be open to the prospect in the future?

"I'd like this business to succeed. We—I—need your help, at least in the beginning."

Brenda's expression soured. "I'll help. For now."

What did that mean for the long term?

Richard wasn't sure he wanted to know.

I HADN'T BEEN to the Falcon's Nest all that often. I'd taken Maggie there at least once, but I remember it being a big deal when I'd been a kid living with Richard. His grandparents had liked the place—it had been around that long. Not that Richard had ever taken me there. We went to a few franchise burger joints—definitely nothing special—when he could spare the time. I'd chosen not to be bitter about those years. Well, *most* of the time.

The Falcon's Nest had been in business under a number of owners for more than a hundred years and sported a colonial vibe, and was still patronized by a distinctly older crowd. Nothing wrong with that, either, especially since their prices were reasonable and the drinks good.

As I didn't have far to go to get there, I arrived first, was seated, and had thoroughly perused the menu by the time Sam arrived only five minutes late. He took the seat opposite me.

"So, what's the deal?" he asked.

"Hello to you, too."

"You didn't invite me here because you missed me," he said and picked up his linen napkin, shaking it open over his lap.

"I kind of thought we'd at least catch up before I got down to business. We can do that after the entree."

"Whatever," he said.

I shrugged and signaled for the waitress, who arrived promptly.

"What can I get you gentlemen to drink?"

"Labatt Blue for me."

"I'll second that," Sam said.

"Would you like to order now?"

I shot Sam a look, but he shook his head.

"We'll order when our drinks arrive," I told her.

"I'll be right back," she said and turned.

"What kind of trouble are you in now?" Sam deadpanned.

"Trouble? I'll have you know I'm gainfully employed."

"So you said—with that consulting business your brother wanted to start," Sam remembered.

I nodded.

"And how's that going?"

"Uh, not particularly well. We've got an office and a secretary, and that's about it."

"But it's about to change?" he suggested.

"I was hired by a client just the other day."

"And you want me to go nosing around on their behalf?"

"Only if you think the story might be worthwhile. Are you doing features these days?"

"What's the subject?"

"Possibly salvaging a nineteenth-century schooner at the bottom of Lake Ontario."

Sam actually looked mildly interested. "And your client wants some publicity to raise funds to do it?"

"No. It's his son who's the history buff." I explained how Nick had apparently duped Louie into signing over his power of attorney and how Horse Hockey Brewing might end up in the hands of a conglomerate that was likely to trash it.

He shrugged. "Happens all the time."

Our Canadian beers arrived and we were forced to order. We made it easy on the kitchen staff: Two beef on weck sandwiches.

"Can't your client get a lawyer to help him out?" Sam asked, taking a sip from his pilsner glass.

I shook my head. "He's…indisposed."

"In what way?"

"He's kind of in a coma."

Sam's brows shot to the top of his tall forehead. "Oh, yeah?"

I nodded.

"I can see where that would be a problem," he remarked.

I explained how I'd met Louie and Sam merely nodded. My "gift" and how it impacted me, no longer surprised him.

"If I contact Nick Susskind, what's my story? How am I supposed to have heard about him?" Sam asked.

"You're a creative writer. You figure it out."

"And I suppose you'll want to tag along."

"That's a given."

"As my trusty photographer?"

"I've replaced my broken Nikon." In fact, Richard had done so after a foray with Sam that had gone terribly wrong and it had been smashed. I hoped he still felt a little guilty for pushing me to help him look for the missing assets of a crook who'd scammed thousands in a Ponzi scheme. He hadn't won a Pulitzer for that piece of journalism, but he'd admitted he'd garnered a hefty raise after he'd written about it.

"So, what do you think?" I asked.

He shrugged. "Give me some contact info and I'll make some calls."

Realistically, that was all I could expect.

"Got anything else going on?" Sam asked.

"Our business isn't exactly thriving." Before I could elaborate, the waitress arrived with our sandwiches.

"What's going on with you personally?" Sam asked, picking up a potato chip and popping it into his mouth.

"Nothing much."

"I got that feeling."

"What do you mean?"

"It's your eyes. They remind me of a shark's. Kind of dead."

I glared at him. Emily had said the same thing.

"What's eating you?" he persisted.

"Nothing."

"Bullshit. If you've got a problem, I'm willing to listen."

"I don't have a problem."

"Yeah, you do. Something's eating at your soul."

I let out a breath and moved the chips around on my plate. Yeah, something *was* eating at me like acid. I let out a breath. "My girlfriend took a temporary assignment with her company in San Diego."

"How temporary?" Sam asked and took another swig of his beer.

"Three years."

Sam frowned. "That's not temporary. That's a sentence—at least for you."

Yeah, it was.

"What are you going to do?" he asked.

I shrugged. "Nothing."

"I hope you didn't take a vow of celibacy in her absence."

"She'll be coming back to Buffalo every so often."

"So does the solstice, and the intervening months are pure hell, especially during the winter."

"Not in San Diego," I corrected him.

"You ain't there, buddy."

"Eh, winter's back is nearly broken."

"Blizzards can still happen." Not that we'd had a truly miserable winter.

I didn't want to talk about it—to Sam or anyone else. Yeah, I was in denial.

The person I needed to talk to was Maggie, and it wasn't going to be a pleasant conversation.

That said, Sam was right. I'd felt hollow for quite some time and it had only recently dawned on me why. It was Maggie. She loved me … but she wanted more, which was why she'd been so eager to take the job in California. It seemed avoiding the long, cold Buffalo winters was more important to her than her time spent with me. Yeah, winter weather in Western New York is the pits, but she'd endured it her whole life. She wasn't at the snowbird stage and yet she was willing to give up her new home, her dog, *and* me to bask in the California sunshine.

Did that make her shallow or just environmentally practical? And what about the devastating climactic changes occurring in the Golden State? Was she willing to ignore all that just to avoid wintry weather? Sure, if she wanted to ski she could visit any number of resorts in what was to be her new, albeit (supposedly) temporary home, but she'd never voiced that desire to me in the three years we'd known each other.

You're thinking about this too hard, some voice within me preached.

Maybe, but another little voice in the back of my brain whispered that it was time for me to move on.

The question was…was I willing to listen?

Chapter 7

Brenda had things to do, like put the baby's laundry away, prepare lunch, and then put Betsy down for her nap before she was ready to make the call to Mrs. Clark. She even insisted on reading the case notes before she felt comfortable enough to make the call. But finally, Brenda sat behind Richard's desk and tapped the number on her cell phone's keypad. She hit the speaker feature so Richard could listen in. It rang three times before being answered.

"Hello?" The woman who answered still sounded wary.

"Is this Mrs. Clark?"

"Yes,"

"My name is Brenda Stanley. I believe you spoke to my husband earlier today about the arson that took place in your former home."

"Somebody called," the woman said, suspicion lacing her tone.

"We're partners in R&A Insights and we look into cold cases."

"For the police?"

"Sort of," Brenda admitted. "I suspect I know why you

want nothing to do with *them*. We *all* know." An edge had crept into what Richard had come to know as Brenda's "urban" voice.

"That man who called said you were working with the police."

"It's true they did bring your case to our attention, but we're independent."

"Uh-huh," the woman said, still skeptical.

"Would you be willing to speak to me in person about your experience and your fears? It would be totally off the record," Brenda said.

"Why should I?"

"The chief suspect in the arson was your son. The victim was your mother. Much as you love him, if your son was responsible for your mama's death...." She let the sentence trail off.

"He did *not* set the fire. He did *not* kill his nana, but the police didn't want to hear that," Mrs. Clark said angrily.

"I understand. Do you think you know who set the fire?"

"No, ma'am," came the reluctant reply.

"Wouldn't you like the opportunity to see justice for your mother *and* to exonerate your son?"

The woman let out a sigh. "I sure would. But I just can't trust...."

She didn't have to say more.

"I—we—would like to help you resolve this situation. But I assure you, if after speaking with me, you decide not to move forward, our company will not proceed any further."

Richard glared at Brenda, but she simply looked away.

"Well...I guess it wouldn't hurt to talk to *you*."

"Thank you. When would it be convenient for me to visit?"

"Tomorrow."

"I can be available anytime during the day."

"How about two o'clock?"

"That would be fine." Mrs. Clark supplied her address, which agreed with the information Detective Destross had provided. "I'll see you then."

"All right. Good-bye."

Brenda hung up the phone, but her expression was anything but friendly. "Happy?" she taunted.

"Yes, thank you." He frowned. "Why are you so angry?"

"Because I was supposed to be a *silent* partner in this little adventure you've undertaken."

Adventure?

"Are you saying I don't take the company seriously?"

"How often do you actually show up at your supposed place of business?"

Richard glowered. "As often as I need to."

"You spend considerably more time with Maggie's dog than at the office you pushed to open."

Heat rose up Richard's neck to color his face. He *had* left the day-to-day operation up to Jeff. But then, they really hadn't had much to do until now. But she was right. He wanted to solve old cases, but he hadn't done as much as he should have to find them. He'd spent his time taking delight in his baby girl and forging a bond with the golden retriever he was beginning to think of as *his* dog.

"Okay, you've made your point. What do you want me to do?"

"I have no idea. But you need to do *something*. Either that or decide you're retired, concentrate on philanthropy and—should summer ever arrive—golf. Isn't that what millionaires do?" she asked acidly. "And by the way, you haven't done all that much to give away the money you say you want to be rid of."

How long had Brenda been holding back these opinions? They hurt more because of the source, but she wasn't wrong, either. That said, he wasn't ready to admit his failings aloud.

"Do you intend to go to Mrs. Clark's house alone?"

"Hell no. You can take me."

"What about Betsy?"

"I'm sure we can snag Jeffy to watch her for an hour or so, either at home or the office."

Richard nodded. Jeff never said no to an opportunity to babysit his niece. "Okay, I'll ask him."

"You do that," Brenda said. She rose from the chair and left the room.

While his wife had agreed to his request to help with his first case, Richard felt nothing near happiness. Once again, he questioned his grand scheme to establish R&A Insights. Was it just a fool's errand? The thought left him feeling vaguely depressed and his gaze wandered to the dry bar across the room.

It took all his self-control not to cross the distance to pour himself a drink.

You don't have a problem, a little voice inside him said.

The rational part of his brain begged to differ.

HAVING Sam's potential help with part of my investigation would be an enormous help, but I needed to get to the hospital to meet with the death doula Louie had mentioned the evening before. Upon arriving at the hospital, I learned that Louie had been downgraded to palliative care. Were plans being made to move him to a potentially cheaper place to die? Would he be shoved out the door to die at a nursing facility or a hospice home—which would be cheaper still?

I nudged past the partially open door to Louie's room and saw a hefty woman with salt-and-pepper roots marring the part in her bleached blonde hair, seated by his bedside, holding his hand, her pale face drawn, her eyes brimming with tears.

Louie's disembodied spirit sat on the window sill, scowling. "So you're back."

I nodded as the woman, who had to be Louie's other daughter, Teresa, looked up. "Excuse me. Who are you?"

"Jeff Resnick. I'm a business associate of your father."

Teresa scowled. "Why are you here?"

"Your sister Bethany gave me permission."

Teresa's scowl deepened, her lips merging into a thin line. She was an overweight, middle-aged woman whose face was creased with an excessive amount of worry lines. Louie had said she was a saint for looking after her now-deceased mother, but I sensed another load of grief weighed her down.

I stepped deeper inside the room.

"About time you got here, Resnick," Louie's spirit groused.

Teresa's sad expression brightened. "How nice of you to come to visit daddy. Even members of his own family are too busy to come," she said bitterly. "I'm Teresa Barton, Louie's daughter." Barton had to be her married name.

"Glad to meet you," I said and nodded.

"You say you're a business associate? Where did you meet Daddy?"

"Tell her at the poker club," Louie directed.

"Uh, at the poker club."

She nodded, the tension in her facial muscles relaxing.

"I understand you've employed a doula."

"Yes."

"I'd very much like to meet her."

"Why?" Teresa asked suspiciously.

I bowed my head and told a bald-faced lie. "Because I might need the same kind of service soon."

Teresa's mouth trembled. "Ideally, I should have consulted her before dad's health deteriorated. Then he could have told us his end-of-life plans."

"Not to friggin' die," Louie groused unhelpfully.

"Is it something you think your father would have approved of?" I asked.

"Yes," Teresa answered without hesitation.

"Not a chance," Louie shouted for only me to hear. "Goddamn waste of money. If she thinks my estate will pay for this, she's got another thing coming to her."

And just who was the executor of Louie's estate? It was a question I needed to ask—but not just then.

From behind me came the sound of someone clearing her throat. I turned to face a petite African-American woman.

"It's the deathmonger," Louie said contemptuously.

The woman stepped inside the room but didn't offer me her hand. "Hello, I'm Omega Dustin." She was dressed in what my mother had called a muumuu that seemed to be made of red and yellow silk—or some reasonable facsimile. Several necklaces of silver adorned with pendants, including a pentagram, hung from her neck, and all her fingers were decorated with silver rings. Several bangles clanked around her wrists. She set down her near-to-bursting tote on the floor.

I introduced myself.

"I'm happy to meet you," Omega said. Her voice bore a slight accent that may have been Haitian—if it was real. I had no reason to trust anything about her.

She moved to stand beside the bedside. Since oxygen was being used to assist Louie's breathing, no candles burned. But a small device on the bedside table was plugged into the wall housed a pool of melted wax, giving off the same scent of hops I'd inhaled when walking through Horse Hockey Brewery.

"Daddy loved the smell of beer," Teresa explained unnecessarily.

Had she brought it, or was it Omega's contribution?

Omega turned her attention to Teresa. "Is it all right if I touch him?"

"Yes, of course," Teresa encouraged.

"No!" Louie's spirit cried emphatically.

Omega rested her fingers on Louie's forearm, tracing an infinity symbol against the dry skin. She then raised her hand to touch his head, smoothing his bald pate as one would pet a beloved dog.

"Ugh," Louie's disembodied self-proclaimed and grimaced. "I don't like strangers touching me. The truth is, I was never a touchy-feely kind of guy."

I refrained from asking him why.

"Are you in tune with the people you minister to?" I asked the doula.

"You mean spiritually?"

I nodded.

"Sometimes."

"And your connection with Louie…?"

Omega looked thoughtful.

"I ain't feelin' nothin' but creeped out," Louie said with vigor.

"Not as deep as I would have hoped," Omega admitted.

Was she a sensitive? I'd have to touch her to see if I could get a vibe from her. If I couldn't, it didn't mean she wasn't authentic since I can't connect with everyone I meet, either. But it might be telling.

"How soon do you think daddy will pass?" Teresa asked.

Omega looked thoughtful. "While his condition is dire, he still has a few days."

"Is he suffering?" Teresa asked, her voice cracking.

Omega shook her head. "No."

"Listening to this crazy broad is fucking painful," Louie groused.

"Have you read the pamphlet the palliative care physician gave you?" Omega asked her benefactor.

Teresa's head dipped. "No."

"Because you're in denial?" Omega asked.

Teresa's mouth trembled. "Maybe."

"And yet you hired me," Omega remarked, her voice the epitome of calm.

"It was so hard losing my mother. It nearly broke me. I thought if I had help to get through it, this time it might be easier."

"We are all going to die," Omega said reasonably. "But I'm here for you as well as your father." She reached out to rest a reassuring hand on Teresa's arm.

"Oh please," Louie complained to the ceiling.

Omega turned her attention to me. "And why are you here, Mr. Resnick?" Her stare was penetrating.

"Mr. Susskind is—was—concerned about the fate of his brewery."

Omega nodded sagely. "Yes. I've felt that vibe."

"Vibe—schmibe," Louie groused.

"He does not want it to be sold to the highest bidder," Omega said.

"That's the first sensible thing the woman has said," Louie grunted.

"How do you feel about that?" I asked Teresa.

Again, her mouth trembled. "I'm torn. I love both my siblings, but . . . they both have good arguments pro and con."

"Go for the con, Tessa," Louie implored, rising from the window sill.

"Where do your loyalties lie?" I asked. "With Bethany or Nick?"

"I'm not sure," she replied, her eyes filling with tears. "I know I could have the deciding vote when it comes to the future of the brewery, but I'm just not sure what to do."

"Cut your brother out!" Louie's spirit practically shouted.

"I have my family to consider. My husband has early-onset dementia. And my daughter is on dialysis. I could use an infusion of cash," she continued.

Not a good place to be. Even so, she wasn't likely to see a nickel until after probate. And who was Louie's executor? One of his kids? A lawyer? A family friend? Would Louie even be willing to tell me or would he think the question impertinent?

"I'm so sorry," I said.

"Sorry hell!" Louie growled. "If she doesn't side with Bethany, she's dead to me."

I wished I could have called him out on that statement. Poor Teresa was between the proverbial rock and a hard place.

"Are you good to stay with Daddy through the night?" Teresa asked Omega. "I can be back here at eight tomorrow morning to spell you."

"Yes, thank you. I'm sorry I can't be here for him twenty-four/seven, but I'm only one person."

"I'm good with that. I've lined up help from my friends and cousins to help take care of my husband and get my daughter to her appointments."

"Losers—all of them," Louie chimed in.

Losers? For helping a woman who was obviously overwhelmed? I'd say they were more like saviors, or at least saints. When Louie died, his oldest daughter would at least have a compassionate support system to help her through her grief. I wondered about the other two siblings.

"Dear lady," Omega said and patted Teresa's arm. "When you get here, you get here. In the meantime, I will hold vigil for your dear father."

Teresa's eyes filled with tears and she practically leapt forward to hug the death doula. "Thank you," she whispered harshly, her words filled with a terrible, raw emotion that threatened to draw me in like a riptide.

I stepped away.

Omega pulled back. "Go home. Take care of your family. I'll be here through the night."

Teresa wiped the tears from her eyes with the second

knuckle of her right hand before gathering up her tote bag and purse and practically fled from the room.

Once she was gone, Omega and I exchanged rather relieved looks. I'd experienced Teresa's cascade of emotions, although thankfully not at an intense velocity. I wasn't at all sure what—or if—Omega had perceived them.

Omega looked toward Louie's body for a long moment, but then her gaze raised in the direction of the window for a few seconds before turning back to me. "And why are you here, Mr. Resnick?" she asked.

"As I said, Louie asked me to help save his brewery."

"Yeah, and what the hell have you done so far?" Louie demanded.

"I've spoken to his daughter Bethany, his brewmaster, and hope to speak to his son."

"And they said?" Omega inquired.

"I'm still trying to process it all," I admitted.

Omega took off her coat and draped it over the back of the chair before nodding, letting her gaze wander from the opposite wall to the ceiling and back to the window sill before settling on the floor where the hem of her dress obscured her feet.

"If you want to take a break, I can stay here with Louie for a few minutes," I offered the doula.

She seemed to weigh the offer for a long few moments before answering. "Yes, I do believe I'll get a cup of coffee. I should be back in five minutes or so," she said, and grabbed her purse before she gave me a nod and left the room.

"Thank God," Louie groused once the doula was gone.

"Hey, give the lady a break," I admonished him.

"Why? I don't want her here."

"Yeah, well, your daughter does."

"And where is she getting the money to pay for the deathmonger?"

"Don't call her that, it's rude."

"I could call her a helluva lot worse," Louie threatened.

I was sure he could—and possibly would.

"I came here to update you on my investigation. Something's funky going on at the brewery."

Louie's eyes narrowed. "What do you mean?"

"I mean the bottling line is silent. Nothing's happening. There's a skeleton crew working. Is that normal?"

Louie didn't answer. Instead, his spirit self looked wary.

"Well?" I demanded.

"We take a break from production now and then," Louie said, rather reluctantly.

"And why's that?"

"When we've got too much inventory."

"I'd think after eighteen years you'd have the hang of that."

"Yeah, well…." But he didn't elaborate.

"Is it usual to lay off the entire production staff?" I pushed.

"Sometimes."

I scowled at him. "Why can't you be honest with me?"

"What do you think I'm lying about?"

"Not necessarily lying, but you aren't telling the truth, either. Why the hell should I work for someone who isn't going to be upfront with me?"

"Who says I'm not telling you the truth?"

"Me!"

"Well, what do you want to know?"

"Everyone I met at your brewery looks scared. Of whom or what?"

Louie scowled. "That's bullshit."

I threw my hands up in the air in exasperation. "I'm outta here."

I moved toward the door.

"Wait!" Louie called.

I turned at the open doorway.

"Okay," he admitted. "Lately, we've had a tough time at the brewery. Someone working on the inside is trying to ruin us."

"Why didn't you tell me that in the first place?" I asked, venturing back into the room.

"Maybe because I'm ashamed."

"What have you got to be ashamed of?" I asked and expected yet another avoidance tactic.

"I thought I'd built the best team. I thought I was a great boss. I pay better than most craft breweries. But for some reason, not all my people have been grateful for the perks I give them. They always want more."

"Is there anyone, in particular, you don't trust?"

"I've had a few blow-ups with our accountant."

"But he isn't likely to try to ruin your business," I countered.

"And some of the distribution crew have been causing trouble."

"In what way?"

"Saying we send out product too near its use-by date."

"I'd think your customers would be happy about their dedication."

"I can't afford to throw out batches of beer when sales are slow."

"And you can't afford to sell skunky beer and lose your customer base, either," I argued.

Louie merely shrugged.

"Is there anyone you want me to check out?"

"I can tell you who *not* to bother to check out and that's Bethany and Abe. I'd trust them with my life."

My gaze wandered to the old man's body lying on the bed. Perhaps I should ask Richard if there were ways to kick off a bout of congestive heart failure—then again, I could just Google the subject. I made a mental note to do just that.

And since he'd specifically asked me not to look into Bethany and Abe, I put them at the top of my list of people *to* check out.

"Can you give me *some* direction on what I need to learn to save your brewery?"

"Getting Nick to back off is the key. You said you might have a way to get to him."

"I'm working on it."

Louie looked at his inert body. "You'd better make it quick. I'm running out of time."

I quite agreed. But then, I felt like I was running out of time, too. With Maggie, with Emily, and with R&A Insights. Maybe running out of time was the wrong descriptor. I was running out of patience—with the whole damn lot of them.

Chapter 8

It was after four-thirty when I returned to the office. Maybe I should've just gone home and let Emily close down for the night as the reception I got from her earlier in the day was chilly to say the least. She had what some might call a "puss" on—her eyes narrowed and her responses to my questions about what had gone on in my absence were answered in a clipped tone.

I tried to ignore that less-than-warm reception and settled behind my computer to see what I could find out about Bethany Susskind. She had a LinkedIn profile that told me that she worked for Horse Hockey Brewing since its inception and was now its manager. Not helpful. Digging a little deeper, I found that despite the fact she'd gone to Nardin Academy—an all-girls college-prep high school—she'd done as Louie had said and gone to Vermont to intern at the now-defunct Catspaw Brewery. She listed no hobbies. Her Facebook profile, which hadn't been updated in several years, listed her as divorced, all the photos were of Horse Hockey events. Talk about a yawn.

Abe Bachmann didn't have a LinkedIn profile. I couldn't find him on Facebook, Instagram, Twitter, or even Pinterest.

The guy didn't strike me as being especially shy. I searched every database I had access to—six—and could find no trace of Abe Bachmann. Was he pulling some kind of Social Security scam? There was no mention of him on the Horse Hockey Brewing's website as being their master brewer. None of the newspaper articles written about the business mentioned him. There weren't many black brewmasters in the country, let alone Buffalo. One might think it would be good PR for the company to tout that fact.

So, what was the story? Was Horse Hockey paying him under the table? Where did he live? A generation ago, it was possible to live without a paper trail, but it was highly unusual in these days of phones that tracked your every move and cookies on your computer spying on your online usage.

I needed to dig a little farther. But it was getting on toward dinner time, although I probably wouldn't have noticed if Emily hadn't shouted goodnight before leaving.

I shut down my computer, turned off the lights, and thought about everything I'd been through that day. As I drove home, I considered what Sam had said about my relationship with Maggie and I wondered if I should talk about it with Brenda. But then, her loyalties were divided. Maggie was the first person she'd become friendly with when she'd first moved to Buffalo. She still communicated with her friends in California, but that was a lot different than having a buddy in the same city to actually visit with and talk to, and even that was ending for her. Did she feel Maggie's departure as deeply as me? I wouldn't know unless I asked, and I wasn't sure I wanted to.

Since I ate most of my dinners with the Alpert clan instead of heading for my apartment over the garage, I parked my car, closed the garage door, and trudged across the driveway to the big house. Whoever coined the phrase "a heavy heart" could have been talking about me.

I hung up my jacket in the butler's pantry and entered the kitchen where Brenda was stationed behind the stove and Betsy was in her highchair singing to herself and sounding oh so pleased, despite the fact it was all gibberish.

"Hey, there," Brenda said as she stirred the pot before her. Whatever it was she had on tap for supper, it smelled good.

"Is it okay if I'm here?" I asked. After the day I'd had, I wasn't sure anybody would be glad of my company.

"You know you're *always* welcome in this house," Brenda said. Her smile was so warm and inviting that I almost wanted to cry, but that would have been a stark admission of my way-too-vulnerable state.

I took my usual place at the table and gazed fondly at my little Cherry Pie. "Hey, kiddo."

"Jha-Jha," Betsy squealed and banged her palms against the tray on her highchair. "I love you, too, baby girl," I told her.

"Beer or bourbon?" Brenda asked me.

I knew she'd judge me by my answer, but I gave her my preference.

"Bourbon."

She nodded, and there was just a hint of disapproval in her expression. Still, she brought out a bottle of Maker's Mark and poured a shot and a half over ice, topped it with more soda than I preferred, and handed me the glass.

"Thanks."

Brenda nodded and turned away.

Richard appeared at the doorway with Holly trotting behind him.

"Hey," he called, and headed for the cabinet where the liquor resided. He took down a bottle of Lagavulin. He grabbed a glass from another cabinet, plopped in a couple of ice cubes from the fridge freezer and poured himself a generous amount of the breath of the Heather—with no soda

—before taking his usual seat at the table. Holly settled herself at his feet. "How'd your day go?" he asked.

"Louie's still hanging in there, but his oldest daughter brought in a doula."

"Who's having a baby?" Richard asked and sipped his whiskey.

"She's a *death* doula. She's supposed to ease Louie into the next world—as well as support his family."

Richard shrugged. "Whatever."

Considering he'd been consulted on Louie's proximity to death, I thought he might have been more interested. "How'd your day go?"

Again my brother shrugged.

A frowning Brenda turned to look at him but said nothing.

"Looks like something's bothering you," Richard said, and took another sip of his drink. I hadn't started mine.

I let out a breath. "We may have an employee problem at R&A Insights World Headquarters," I said.

"Problem?" Richard asked blandly.

Brenda took some plates out of the cupboard, but I got an anxious vibe from her.

"Since I've been working with Louie, the subject of the unusual cases we might take was bound to come up."

"Oh, dear," Brenda said and began to set the table.

"What did you say to her?" Richard asked.

"I suggested she watch the movie *Sixth Sense*."

Brenda looked horrified. "Was that a good idea?"

"If restless spirits are gonna be a part of our business, we need to employ someone with an open mind. Emily let me know that her religious beliefs precluded the idea of earth-bound spirits."

"Hmm, that *could* be a problem," Brenda said. As far as I knew, she'd never encountered a disembodied spirit, but she wholeheartedly believed that I had.

"And what was her reaction?" Richard asked guardedly.

"She thought I was shitting her. So I gave her a little taste."

"Such as?" Brenda asked. She seemed a lot more interested than Richard.

"Just some innocuous stuff that she hadn't confided to anyone."

"Jeffy!" Brenda chided me.

"Her daughter wants a puppy."

Brenda frowned. "Oh."

"But I also gave her an ultimatum."

"And she quit?" Brenda asked, aghast.

"Not yet. She likes the money too much."

"If she decides to leave, we might want to advertise for a receptionist who's watched at least one of the Ghostbuster movies and hope he or she is open to the paranormal," Richard offered.

It was a poor joke. "It may be that we end up doing our own scheduling and rely on an answering service. It sure would be a lot cheaper in the long run—especially since we're currently working with a negative cash flow."

"I guess you're right," Richard said, sounding depressed. I knew he liked Emily. I did, too, and maybe a little too much. But the fact she had such an ingrained negative mindset meant that she wasn't likely to accept me and how I was able to approach any given investigation.

The more I thought about it, the better the idea of employing an impersonal answering service became. Of course, it sure would be lonely sitting by myself in that little office day after day. I was lonely enough after losing my bartending job since the demise of The Whole Nine Yards. With Emily—and even Maggie—gone, all I'd have was Richard, his wife, and daughter.

My life seemed to be getting smaller and smaller by the day.

"What's for supper?" Richard asked.

"Meatloaf," Brenda replied.

Richard frowned. He wasn't a fan of ground beef unless it was a grilled patty on a decent hard roll with the works. Brenda was determined that Betsy would have what she called a normal—meaning a middle-class—childhood. That meant a diet of regular food with no pâté de foie gras or caviar served.

"It's just about ready. I just have to mash the potatoes and corral the peas," Brenda said.

"Da-Da!" Betsy cried, diverting all our attention.

A lot of silent sipping of different varieties of distilled spirits ensued as Brenda made gravy, mashed the potatoes, put everything into serving bowls, and placed them on the table

We served ourselves, and Brenda made a plate for Betsy to mash into her face and hair. Conversation from the adults was at a minimum with, with only requests to pass the potatoes, peas, or gravy.

It didn't take long for us to finish.

"I'm heading back to my study," Richard said, pushed himself away from the table, and got up.

"I'll be there with Betsy in a few minutes," Brenda said.

Richard waved over his shoulder and left the kitchen, with Holly following in his wake.

We watched him go, and then Brenda and I looked at the table filled with dishes and serving bowls. We were on our own when it came to cleaning up.

Brenda got up first and attempted to mop up Betsy's mess while I stacked plates. "You've been awfully quiet," she said as she stepped over to the sink.

"I've got a lot on my mind."

"Besides Emily?"

"Well, the women in my life *are* giving me a lot of grief."

"Maggie?" she asked.

I considered what I might say and then figured *what the hell.* "I think she's about to cheat on me."

Brenda's mouth drooped, and for a moment I thought she might cry. "Oh, Jeffy."

I shrugged. "It doesn't come as a surprise." From her expression, the thought wasn't new to Brenda, either.

I carried dirty plates to the sink.

"What aren't you allowing yourself to do?" Brenda blurted, running warm water over a dishcloth.

I decided to answer honestly. "Walk away from Maggie."

Brenda said nothing, but I could tell she wanted to.

"Talk to me," I implored.

She wrung out the dishcloth. "It's not my place to voice an opinion on the subject."

"But what if I asked you to?"

"You know I have conflicting concerns—and loyalties," she admitted—which I already knew. "I love you both." She grabbed a clean dishcloth, stepped over to Betsy's highchair, wiped her face, and tried to get some of the potatoes out of her hair.

"But?" I asked as I started to rinse the plates.

Brenda seemed to shrink. "But I love you more, and … I'm sorry to say that I don't see a future for you with Maggie."

Neither did I, but I decided to lie. "In the near term, no. In the future…."

"Oh, come on Jeffy. She left her dog with us," Brenda practically wailed.

I gaped at her. "Are you saying that Holly should have been more important to her than me?"

"Real dog people *never* abandon their pups," she remarked.

"You've never been a pet person," I accused.

"No, but I know plenty of them. I've known women who've kicked their boyfriends to the curb if their dog or cat gave a paws-down assessment. And if Maggie *does* come back to

Buffalo, there's no way Richard will give Holly back. As far as he's concerned, she now belongs to him—and it could get messy in the end."

Somehow I managed a smile. "I had the same impression. How do you feel about her?"

Brenda's smile was rather conspiratorial. "She's already making one hell of a good family dog."

I couldn't agree more.

"What's your gut telling you?" Brenda asked. "*Will* Maggie come back?"

"Yeah. Eventually."

"And will it be messy?"

My heart sank. "Yeah." Real messy.

Brenda let out a breath. "Well, the end of her assignment is three years in the future. We won't have to worry about it until then."

If Maggie stuck it out that long. But I also got the feeling she wouldn't be ready to come home any time soon, either. She had a great job, the possibility—perhaps *already*—a new love and a wonderful place to live. Who could want more?

I brought the last of the dishes over to the sink and passed them to Brenda, who rinsed them before putting them in the dishwasher. She cleared her throat. I got the feeling she wanted to tell me something important.

"How'd your day go?"

She shrugged. "The usual. Laundry was the highlight."

Something in her tone told me it wasn't.

"Oh, and Richard asked me to help him with his new case."

That statement stopped me in my tracks. "Oh?" Richard hadn't said a word about it to me during dinner. *Me*, his business partner.

"He spoke with some detective—the one you guys met with last year."

Bonnie Wilder or John Destross? I felt like I'd been doused with a bucket of cold water. "And?"

"Apparently it's an unsolved arson where an elderly woman died."

"And *you* and Richard are handling it?"

"I guess he didn't tell you about it," she said, her voice rising.

She *knew* he hadn't.

"Nothing's written in stone," she continued. "He was given the name of the family and a phone number. We're going to meet with someone tomorrow."

I nodded and waited for her to say more.

She didn't.

We finished returning the kitchen to its usual immaculate state before I headed to the butler's pantry to grab my coat.

"Thanks for supper. You make a great meatloaf."

"Thanks. It's just like my mama used to make."

"You've done her proud," I said neutrally.

"See you tomorrow?" Brenda asked, sounding hopeful.

"Probably." But maybe not. More and more, I felt like I was intruding on their lives. And lately, I found the connection with my brother growing weaker. It wasn't me who was responsible for it. That he hadn't told me about his own investigation said a lot.

An awful lot.

And I wasn't sure what I could do about where I stood in his world.

I needed a Plan B.

Only I wasn't sure what that should be.

Chapter 9

Richard was comfortably ensconced in his office with a glass of single malt Scotch—neat—clasped in his hand and feeling just a little smug when his wife entered the room. Brenda said nothing as she deposited their daughter into her little playpen and then sat on the worn leather couch with what could only be described as a flourish.

Richard lowered his glass to sit on his thigh, out of Brenda's sight.

"Anything wrong?" he asked innocently.

"You bet your ass," she said, sounding rather menacing. "Why on earth didn't you tell Jeffy about your investigation?"

Richard held out his left hand in supplication. "Because I don't know if there will even *be* an investigation. It all depends on *if* and *what* the family will tell you tomorrow."

Brenda didn't seem mollified by that explanation. "He's been totally transparent about his investigation, and you're not willing to tell him what you might be doing—in a business you profess is half his."

"Why are you making me out to be some kind of villain?" he asked, feeling put upon.

"Because if you aren't honest with your own brother, what would *you* call it?" she challenged.

"Cautious."

"Bullshit!" she countered vehemently. It wasn't like Brenda to swear.

"Look, if we get anywhere with the victim's family, I'll have plenty of time to level with Jeff."

"And include him in your investigation?" she demanded.

Richard hesitated before answering.

"What do you have to prove? That you're better than he is when it comes to investigating? Because if that's true, you shouldn't need *me* to help you get the information you want."

Richard's hand tightened around the glass. He did need Brenda to get what he had to know to solve who was responsible for the arson and the old lady's death. "You're right. I don't know what I was thinking." He was thinking exactly what she'd accused him of and felt ashamed.

"*You're* the one who wanted to start this business. You coerced Jeffy into helping you pull it off. But *he's* the one who goes into the office every day. *He's* the one who has to deal with an employee who thinks he's some kind of freak. *He's* the one writing the checks and doing all the grunt work while you sit behind your desk here at home every day, sneaking drinks behind my back or walking the dog and ignoring the business you wanted to start. When was the last time you actually went into the office?"

Richard wasn't sure. Maybe two weeks? But then they'd had no cases—and now they did—potentially two of them. And how had she known about his stolen moments of pleasure with 20-year-old Scotch? He washed his glasses in the powder room sink near his office. Was she measuring the liquor level of the bottles on the cocktail cart across the way?

Yeah, she probably was.

"You're right. I guess I just assumed. . . ." But he hadn't

assumed anything. Back at the think tank in Pasadena, he'd been responsible for everything that went on in his unit, from supervising his colleagues to overseeing a yearly multi-million dollar budget. He *had* dumped all that kind of work on Jeff, wrongly figuring that his financial contribution was of equal value if not greater than the time Jeff put into the project. It wasn't exactly a secret that Jeff was unhappy with their lack of meaningful work.

"Let's see how tomorrow goes, and then, either way, we'll tell Jeff about it."

"Too late, *boss.*" Brenda had called Richard by that descriptor when she'd worked for him at the think tank—*before* they'd become intimate. Now she used the term as a slur.

"You mentioned it to him?"

"You bet your ass I did. If you're not willing to be honest with your own brother, I, at least, am!"

Richard took a moment to contemplate that statement. "And how did he react?"

"He didn't. That's how he is. But he was hurt. I *felt* it."

Was that another dig proving that his wife and brother shared a connection he could never experience?

Finally, Richard spoke, dreading the answer to his question. "Are we still on for tomorrow?"

Brenda glared at him. "Only if you're going to be upfront with Jeffy."

"Of course," he agreed amiably. He had to. And yet he felt resentment at her command.

He also felt like a shit.

Richard's hand tightened around the glass of Scotch. What the hell was wrong with him? He knew the answer to that question, but wasn't willing to acknowledge it. Not yet. Maybe not ever.

Richard pursed his lips and fought the urge to succumb to tears.

Brenda pushed herself up from the couch. "I need to give Betsy a bath. Goodness knows those potatoes in her hair have practically petrified. Don't be surprised if you hear a banshee wail when I try to comb it all out."

Richard nodded, swallowing. "Do you want a hand?"

"No, I want you to talk to your brother," she said pointedly.

"Okay, I will."

She didn't ask him not to pour himself another drink because she must have known he might be unable to make that promise honestly.

Brenda scooped up Betsy and carried her out of Richard's study without another word or even a backward glance.

Once she was gone, Richard stared at the phone. He could call his brother. Yeah, that would be easier than having to face him in person. Richard picked up the receiver, not sure how he could begin such an awkward conversation. He punched in the number, and the phone rang four times before it went to voice mail. He hung up. Had Jeff left his house and gone out? Well, Richard decided, he'd tried his best.

His gaze strayed to the dry bar across the room.

No. He would not have another drink. At least, not that night.

Ha! He actually felt like he'd successfully thwarted his wife.

He frowned. It was a hollow victory.

"Rich?"

Richard closed his eyes and cursed inward. Then he opened them to see his brother standing in the open doorway.

Richard swallowed. "Hey, I just tried to call you—your landline, that is."

"I left a load of laundry downstairs. It's wrinkled as hell. I've got it tumbling with a couple of wet socks to try and fix it."

Whatever.

"Why'd you call?" Jeff asked.

"I wanted to mention that Detective Destross called me the other day," Richard said.

"So I heard," Jeff said neutrally.

"Uh, he's got a cold arson case he wants us to look into."

"I'm working on the Susskind project," Jeff reminded him.

"Yeah, I know. That's why I thought I could handle this one by myself. So far, I'll just be interviewing the suspect's mother."

"Whatever," Jeff said quietly.

"The thing is, the woman is black and won't speak to me."

"And?"

"She's agreed to talk to Brenda."

"And?" he said again, unsurprised. How much had Brenda told him?

"Brenda doesn't want to take Betsy with. Would you be willing to look after her for an hour or so?"

"Of course."

"The appointment's at two tomorrow. We need to leave at least half an hour before."

"CP's nap time."

"Yeah."

Jeff frowned. "I have an appointment with your buddy Nick Susskind at noon. I've enlisted Sam Nielson as a cover to meet him, but I can cancel."

"No, don't. We can drop Betsy off at the office. Do you think Emily would have a problem looking after her until you get there?"

"Probably not."

Why did he sound anything but sure?

"I'll make sure I'm back by one-thirty, or at least pretty damn close to it. Will that work for you?"

"Yeah."

"So tell me more about this arson," Jeff said.

"There's not much to go on. An elderly woman died, and the cops think her grandson was to blame."

"Did he do it?"

Richard shrugged. "He disappeared afterward and hasn't been seen or heard from since."

"Which doesn't paint him in a good light."

"No," Richard agreed. "How's your case going?"

Jeff frowned. "It's complicated."

"What does that mean?"

"Not only am I having problems with my spectral client, but like I mentioned, I'm having some with Emily, too."

"I thought the two of you got along well."

"That was before I leveled with her about my…gift."

Richard grimaced but shrugged. "It is a lot to ask of someone."

Jeff glowered at him. "Yeah, well, if she's going to continue to be snarky toward me, I won't want to spend up to eight hours a day with her."

"Are you ready to fire her?" Richard asked, concerned.

"Not yet. I'm willing to cut her some slack, but not indefinitely."

"I'm surprised you're making the situation so personal."

Jeff's brow furrowed, and his voice rose. "*I'm* the one who has to spend an entire workday with her. As an employee, she shouldn't get to control the atmosphere we both have to operate in," he said firmly.

Another dig that Richard didn't spend enough time in the office? He could easily rectify the situation by coming in every day for at least an hour or two. Perhaps he should try to do so in the future. He liked Emily, and he'd hate to lose her….

As though sensing something was bothering him, Holly got up from the plush bed near the heat run and trotted over to Richard's chair, sitting and resting her golden head on his knee, looking up at him with adoring eyes. He wished Brenda had looked at him with such admiration mere minutes ago. He stroked the dog's silky head.

"Don't fall in love with Holly," Jeff warned. "When Maggie returns, she'll expect to get her dog back."

Richard frowned. "It might already be too late for that. I'm sorry I didn't get your affection for your cat. I never had a pet before. Now…I get it."

"His name is Herschel," Jeff said for perhaps the thousandth time.

"Yeah." Richard waited for a long moment before he spoke again. "So we're good to go tomorrow?"

"Yeah."

"Great. I might drop by the office in the morning."

"Good," Jeff said. "I'm sure that would brighten Emily's day."

"Okay. See you there."

Jeff's gaze traveled down to the parquet oak floor. Richard hadn't meant his words to sound so dismissive, but Jeff turned and left the room without a word.

Once again, Richard glanced at the bar cart across the room, feeling like a total shit.

WHEN I RETURNED to my apartment, my cat Herschel was ecstatic to see me and wound around my ankles, purring like a well-maintained motorboat. I felt guilty leaving him alone for far too many hours in the day, but taking him to the office wasn't practical, either. I reached down to scratch the top of his head.

"I'm glad to see you, too, buddy."

I opened a can of his favorite fishy cat food, doled a sprinkle of dry food into the bowl, and he immediately abandoned me to chow down.

I looked at the clock. It was five o'clock back in San Diego—Maggie was three hours behind me, time-wise. I couldn't call her and actually find her in for another couple of hours. If she *was* in.

I thought back to my conversation with Richard. I could have been more enthusiastic during our chat, but I was pissed at him, something that had been building for weeks. I wasn't sure how—or even if—I wanted to resolve the situation.

To work off my frustration, I killed time by scaring the shit out of my cat by vacuuming my apartment, changing the litter in the cat box, and emptying the dishwasher before settling in front of the tube to channel surf and not finding much of anything to interest me.

I was still wide awake when the eleven o'clock news came on and it was with dread that I punched in Maggie's cell phone number. Would she answer? I wasn't sure. I wasn't even sure I *wanted* her to answer.

Okay, I did and didn't because this was going to be a difficult conversation. It probably wasn't a good idea to try and figure out our new normal, but I had to know where we stood. Or at least where *she* stood. Because if she....

Did I honestly want to know where we stood?

I was about to abort the call when Maggie picked up.

"Hey, Jeff, " she answered cheerfully. Caller ID had immediately identified me.

"Hey, Maggs, how are you?"

"Just fine," she said cheerfully. "I've spent the afternoon getting the apartment fully set up before I go back to work full-time next Monday. What's up with you in miserable old Buffalo?"

Did she hate the city of her birth so much?

"Oh, not a whole lot. Just missing you," I said, not quite a true statement.

"I miss you, too," she said, but her tone was just a little too jovial. She launched into a one-sided dialog on how she was settling into her new condo. How she loved the area she'd chosen and how it was so close to work and came with amazing amenities. I heard what she was saying, but I didn't take in much of it. I had to wait until she ran out of steam before I could voice what I'd been thinking, and I had to ease into it slowly.

"I'm glad you're starting to feel at home there—but I hope you don't get *too* comfortable."

She laughed. "Are you saying you don't think I'll eventually come home?"

"Well, it is a possibility…isn't it?"

She laughed again, but it sounded rather mocking to my jaded ears. "Not a chance."

I wasn't sure I had the patience to dance around waiting for the answers I needed to hear. Things I hadn't been able to ask her face-to-face before she left. Being on the phone, where I couldn't see her eyes or expression, made the whole conversation so much less personal.

"Uh, have you thought about how we can sustain our relationship long distance?" I asked.

"Unlike most couples, we're connected on a different level," Maggie said confidently.

Yeah, we were. But she didn't seem to realize that I connected with her in a more visceral manner. I already knew she was open to connecting with another…and there was already someone else she'd identified with as a potential lover. Would she indulge in that powerful urge?

Hell, yes. She'd cheated on me before. It seemed inevitable that she'd stray again.

I'd thought—and mistakenly so—that she was my soulmate. What else had I gotten so wrong?

Instead of pushing the issue, I backed off. It was cowardly, but I was pretty sure I wasn't at a point where I could face hearing the truth.

"I can't tell you how good it feels to hear your voice. When do you think you'll come home next? Mother's Day? Memorial Day?"

"Maybe."

What the hell did that mean?

"Maybe?" I queried.

"It all depends on my job. I'm the new girl in the office—low man on the totem pole. It stands to reason I'll be the one who has to work while others with more seniority get time off."

Yeah, but she was working in a supervisory capacity. Surely she'd have first dibs on holiday hours. What she wasn't saying was that she could possibly have that time off but wasn't willing to spend it or the money to come back to Buffalo. Not when she had a much more upscale place to spend her time ... and with who knew whom.

"Hey, Maggie, can you help me with this?" said a male voice in the background.

"In a minute," she said, her voice sounding muffled. She'd obviously put her hand over the phone's microphone.

"Maggs?" I asked.

"My workmate, Tony, is helping me set up my computer and printer."

It wasn't exactly rocket science.

"Nice of him."

"He's part of the team that moved out west from Buffalo. It's nice to have a built-in friend," she said brightly.

Sure it was.

I shook myself. Was Tony more than just a work friend, or was he her potential new lover?

I felt too uncomfortable to ask.

"There's the doorbell. Pizza has just arrived," Maggie said. "I'll let you go. Call me soon, okay?"

"Of course. Love you," Maggie sang.

"Love you, too," I echoed, not feeling at all assured that either of us had spoken the truth.

The connection was broken, and I set down my phone. Our conversation only exacerbated my fears.

Maggie felt upbeat and positive.

I felt doomed.

Chapter 10

Though it was well past my bedtime, I backed my car out of the three-car garage and down the driveway. Wet, fat snowflakes fell as I drove to the bakery on Main Street. I'd lost count of how often I'd visited the little shop with the chipped and faded blue paint covering its shingled facade. On those trips, I didn't even bother to get out of my car. If the lights were off, then Sophie wasn't there. She hadn't been there for nearly nine months.

Had she finally left this early plane? She'd told me she was only here for me...and if so, she damn sure hadn't been available for what seemed like forever.

To my astonishment, on that night the lights in the back of the shop *were* on. My heart pounded as I whipped around the corner and parked, then jogged to the bakery. I stood on the concrete slab in front of the shop and pressed the doorbell. Nothing happened for long moments, and then the silhouette of a stooped figure appeared.

She just stood there.

I braved a smile and waved.

She didn't move.

I gestured for her to enter the shop and unlock the door. She moved as though to take a step away and my heart sank, fearing she might disappear. But then her shoulders slumped even lower, and she slunk forward, as though every step was an effort.

She unlocked the door and stepped back, crossing her arms and hugging them as though her moth-eaten maroon sweater was suddenly not giving any warmth.

"Come in, come in," she practically barked, pivoted, and turned toward the back of the shop.

I dutifully closed the door and followed her.

The battered card table and metal folding chairs stood in their usual places, but there were no cups or a plate filled with fresh-baked cookies. The hotplate above the sink was turned off, too. No tea or cocoa for me. Sophie stood stiffly and as far away from me as she possibly could. She may have let me in, but she obviously intended to continue punishing me.

I unzipped my jacket and took my usual seat at the table. "Long time no see."

Sophie shrugged.

"So, what have you been up to?" I asked, knowing the answer was not a damn thing.

Sophie shook her head.

"Do you want to hear what I've been doing?"

She shook her head in disgust.

I had a decision to make. Bluff and I might never see her again. But if she was going treat me so shabbily…maybe I wouldn't want to come back.

Bluff it was.

I stood and zipped my coat.

"It was nice to see you again. Maybe we can do this again sometime."

I turned and headed for the door…but not too fast.

I stepped into the shop with its refrigerated glass display cases and kept walking.

I paused at the door and reached for the handle, my hand lingering for long seconds. Then I turned it.

"Wait!"

I closed my eyes and let out a breath before I turned back to face her.

She sighed and shrugged. "You may as well come into the back."

"Not if you're going to be mean to me."

The color rose in her cheeks. "When have I ever been mean to you?"

"Every day you kept me from seeing you—being with you."

Her mouth drooped.

"You either love me, warts and all, or you don't," I told her bitterly.

A tear cascaded down her cheek, and when she spoke, there was shame in her voice. "I do love you with all my heart. And…I'm sorry."

"I love you, too. And I've missed you. I count on your wisdom. I don't have anyone who understands or cares for me like you do."

Her features seemed to crumple, and she raised her hands to cover her face in embarrassment. I rushed toward her and gathered her into a gentle embrace. "I love you, Sophie Levin," I whispered.

"And I love you," she managed between sobs.

I held her for a long moment, and then she pulled back and straightened, her expression grim but resolute. "Would you like cocoa or tea?"

"Cocoa, please."

She nodded and bustled toward the back room, suddenly all business.

I followed.

While she prepared the cocoa, carefully measuring it into the cracked-and-stained mugs, I unzipped my jacket and took my usual seat again.

Once the hot chocolate was ready, she placed a mug before me and took her seat, looking at me expectantly.

"We haven't charged any of our clients," I told her. She'd been appalled at the idea of Richard and me setting up a business where I'd use my psychic gift and charge people to solve the cold cases we received.

"That's because you could hardly call your business successful."

"There's that," I admitted. "Richard pays me a living wage. That's all I ask." Or at least had accepted.

"But I sense you are not happy in this work."

She had that right.

"I thought we might be more successful than we've been," I admitted. "We've got two cases right now. One I'm working on, and Richard's exploring something else."

"And you sense something's amiss?" she asked.

I reluctantly nodded. "Yeah. I hoped you might help me figure out why."

"What do I know?" she replied flippantly.

"A lot more than me when it comes to interpreting our… gifts." God, I hated calling this psychic crap anything other than a friggin' curse. And it was *her* side of the family that was responsible for inflicting it upon me.

Sophie picked up her mug and thoughtfully sipped its contents. "You should not believe everything you hear."

"I try not to. Can you tell me who to listen to?"

She shook her head. "I'm not privy to that kind of information. I just know that not all you are learning is true."

Great. And how was I to figure out the truth from lies?

"But your work is not all that's on your mind," she said.

"No," I admitted.

"It's Maggie," Sophie said, and her tone was the epitome of sadness.

"Yeah," I admitted. "I don't know what to think about that situation."

"Yes, you do," Sophie countered.

Yeah, I did.

I let out a breath. "She's going to cheat on me again while she's in California. She won't tell me about it, but I'll know when it happens because—"

"Because you have a connection."

"Yeah."

We sipped our cocoa.

"You thought you were soulmates," she stated, her tone neutral.

"I did."

"She was a balm for your battered soul when you needed it most."

Yeah, but not without a lot of drama.

"Your Maggie has had a lot to contend with, as well."

"Are you saying you approve of her cheating on me?"

Sophie shook her head vehemently. "I'm just saying that the woman has her own demons."

Yeah, her husband cheated on her but not with a woman. She accepted it. Learned to live with the fact and even embraced her ex-husband's husband. And did she feel his infidelity gave her license to do likewise?

What did it matter in the long run? Maggie was a sexual being, and she wasn't going to deprive herself of that aspect of life just because she was thousands of miles away from me for an extended period.

I still had strong feelings for her, but she was on a new adventure in California, and I knew she was determined to squeeze every ounce of the experience to the max.

"She is *not* your soulmate," Sophie commented.

She was right. I'd gotten that wrong. Oh, boy, had I gotten that *wrong*. And now Sophie was warning me that I'd gotten something I was investigating wrong, as well. Only I didn't know what that was, either.

"Will I ever find anyone in that regard?"

Sophie's deep brown eyes met mine. "You already have."

For some reason, my gut roiled at the notion. The only women I had any actual contact with were Brenda and Emily. Brenda was off the table—at least in this lifetime—and . . .

"Emily?"

Sophie shrugged.

"But she thinks I'm some kind of freak."

"And yet she still comes to work every day."

"Because she needs the money."

Sophie shook herself. "I wish I had some cookies for you. Or some Makowiec."

I hadn't had poppy seed roll in half of forever. Still, her suggestion hadn't kept me from noticing how she'd deliberately changed the subject. I wouldn't get anything else from her—at least that night—when it came to Emily.

I was fifteen years older than our R&A receptionist. That was an even bigger age gap than between Richard and Brenda. She was just a kid. A kid *with* a kid.

I didn't want to think about it—or her.

Was I in denial or just so angry that Maggie had forsaken me that some part of me wanted to retaliate?

"You have to get up early to go to work. You have a lot to do," Sophie said in what was obviously dismissal.

I looked down at my cup. It was empty. I hadn't even sipped the cocoa she'd made me. Was everything that transpired between us just a wish—or a dream?

I stood. "Can I come back and see you soon?"

Sophie shrugged. "You know I'm here for you for as long as you need me."

"Then I guess you'll be here forever."

Her expression darkened. "Nothing lasts forever."

Her words cut me cold.

"I can dream."

Sophie shook her head.

"Then can I hope?" I asked.

"There's always room for hope," she said enigmatically.

I knew that was the best I could expect.

I rose from my chair and zipped my jacket. "I'll be back soon."

"And I'll be here," Sophie promised.

Some of the weight that held my soul hostage lifted. I kissed Sophie on the cheek and headed for the bakery's front entrance.

"Stay safe," Sophie told me.

"I always try," I told her flippantly.

"I mean it," she said more forcefully. "Take care in all you do."

My stomach did a little flip-flop, and I knew grilling her for more information wouldn't give me any more answers.

"Good night," I told Sophie.

"Don't let the bed bugs bite," she countered.

If her warning was to be believed, they were the least of my worries.

Chapter 11

I didn't stop at Tim Hortons for coffee and pastries the following morning, but I was pleased to see that Emily had a fresh pot of java already brewing when I arrived only two minutes after eight. After hanging up my coat, I availed myself of a cup and faced my surly employee. After my conversations with Richard and Sophie the evening before, I decided it was time for an ultimatum after all.

"So, what have you decided?" I asked.

Emily looked at me through hooded eyes. "About what?"

"Are you going to quit your job with us?"

Emily pursed her lips, her cheeks turning pink. "I can't afford to," she practically growled.

"Well, if you aren't willing to work with me, you can't work here."

"I'm perfectly willing to coordinate with Dr. Alpert."

"And you've seen how much time he spends in the office."

She looked away.

"I don't have cooties. And if you can't expand your mind enough to accept—"

"Who says I can't?" Emily challenged.

"Well, you haven't done much to disprove it."

Her scowl deepened. "I never said you had cooties."

"But you sure intimated it."

Emily looked even angrier.

"Look, have I ever mistreated you?"

"Well, no," she reluctantly admitted.

Yeah, I'd brought her coffee, pastries, and sometimes lunch with leftovers enough to give her and her kid supper. How did that make me an ogre?

"What will it take for you to get past this?" I asked in my most conciliatory tone.

Emily actually looked humbled. "Time."

How much time?

I asked the question.

"I've had a lot of crap to accept since we first met," she remarked.

Yeah. Her faith had been tested. She'd learned her parents weren't the people who'd brought her up, and now I was asking her to believe in something the faith she'd been indoctrinated into told her was bogus.

"I don't know," she said honestly.

I guess I could accept that. But we still had to work together—even if there wasn't much actual work to do.

"Okay," I said. "Let's move on."

Could she?

Emily shrugged. "Okay."

She'd agreed because, as she'd said, she needed her paycheck.

"What's on tap for today?" Emily asked, a scowl warping her pretty face.

"I've got an appointment to interview someone at noon. Richard has something else going on later this afternoon and is going to drop off his daughter—"

"I wasn't hired to be a *babysitter*," Emily interjected, her tone sharp.

"Who asked you to be one? And who says I'd even trust you with our girl?"

Emily blinked, her mouth gaping, her attitude vaulting from umbrage to insult. "Well, I've managed to nurture my own daughter to age six without fatal consequences."

"And I've taken care of CP since she came home from the hospital. I don't *need* any help. I'll try my damnedest to be back here in time, but if I'm a minute late, I hope you'll at least be willing to accommodate us."

The door to the office opened before Emily could reply. We both straightened, hopefully anticipating a potential client, but it was only Richard, accompanied by Holly on a leash. The dog shook the snowflakes off her head and pulled toward the table that held the coffeemaker, cups, and accouterments. She knew where the doggy treats resided.

Richard unclipped the leash, letting the dog loose, took off his topcoat, and hung it up. "That coffee sure smells good."

"Let me get you a cup," Emily volunteered with a smile, her demeanor doing an abrupt one-eighty. She'd never offered to fetch me coffee.

She bustled about doctoring Richard's brew just as he liked it. She'd obviously taken note of it. Would she complain to him if she had to care for his daughter for a mere five minutes?

I was pretty sure I knew the answer to that.

Emily handed Richard his cup. "What brings you in today? We don't see you often enough."

And, apparently, she saw me far too much.

"Thanks. Just checking in. I'm working on an arson case. I thought I should come in to type up my notes."

Which, according to what he'd told me, was next to nothing.

"Would you like help with that?" Emily asked sweetly.

Richard shook his head. "I'm good."

Holly gave a yip, reminding us that she hadn't been given a treat. Emily and Richard rushed forward, bumped into each other, and laughed. Richard reached for the glass jar that held the bone-shaped treats and tossed one to the dog, who caught it with Olympian skill. They both laughed.

Why did I feel like the odd man out?

"Did Jeff mention that my wife and I have an appointment to talk to a witness today?"

"Why, yes, he did," Emily answered blithely.

"I hope it won't be too much of an imposition if you have to look after our little girl for a few minutes if Jeff is late from his appointment."

"Not at all," Emily said agreeably.

I ground my molars together.

We all looked at each other for long seconds, and I got the feeling I should make a hasty exit. "Well," I began. "I've got things to do."

"So do I," Richard said and started after me to our shared office. Holly dutifully trotted behind him.

"Let me know if you need anything," Emily called after us.

Richard didn't pull the door closed after him, which meant that it would be up to me to do so if we were to have a frank conversation. It wasn't likely to happen as I'd already told him about my reservations when it came to Emily, so I didn't bother.

We both took our seats at our desks and fired up our computers while Holly hunkered down under Richard's desk.

"Do you have much to write about your investigation so far?" I asked my brother.

"Enough," he answered cagily.

When he'd pitched the idea of going into business together, he'd made it sound like we'd be working together, but that wasn't the vibe I was getting. He'd told me damned little about the case Detective Destross had asked him to look into. He hadn't asked me all that much about my case, either. Yeah, it could be seen as a conflict of interest, but all the same….

Richard didn't bother hitting the Internet but opened a Word document and began to type.

My gaze didn't stray to his thirty-four-inch screen, but I wondered by the staccato sound of the clacking keys if he was typing and retyping THE QUICK BROWN FOX JUMPED OVER THE LAZY DOG. Meanwhile, upon booting up, I stared at the picture of Machu Picchu that my computer had offered. I wasn't sure Sam would ask the right questions of Nick Susskind. Would I, as his pseudo-photographer, be taken seriously if I made my own inquiries?

I sipped my coffee slowly, and my thoughts drifted to Holly, whose tail stuck out from beneath Richard's desk, which thumped the floor every so often. She seemed perfectly content with the way things were. Before Maggie's ex-mother-in-law had a stroke and went to live with her son, Holly had spent most of her days with the old lady. She'd been exiled to doggy daycare before Maggie had prevailed on Richard and Brenda to look after her during her frequent one-to-two-week trips to the west coast before transferring there for her three-year assignment.

She'd easily abandoned her dog and me to grasp the brass ring of what she thought would be a better life. I already knew that she'd one day feel bitter about that choice, but it was something she wasn't yet able to hear. Saying so would not endear me to her, either.

I shook myself. Thinking about such things wasn't going to brighten my life, which felt pretty shitty just then.

I glanced at the clock. It was hours before Sam and I would get to talk to Nick Susskind. With every hour that passed, his father's vital signs waned. Louie didn't have much more time.

It seemed like everything in my life was going sour. I hadn't felt this low since shrink Krista Marsh had entered my life. The thought of that nightmare of a bitch had me swallowing down bile. And suddenly, I felt almost as bad as I had nearly two years before. It was a wicked darkness that seemed to close around my soul. I had to remind myself that at least a few souls loved me. Brenda, CP, Herschel, and—apparently now-forgiven for a stupid transgression—Sophie. It was always touch-and-go with Richard, and now Maggie was giving me iffy vibes, too.

I shook myself. Was my ego so fragile that I needed to beg for acceptance?

Sorta…kinda…maybe….

I took a fortifying sip of coffee, sure that I was being ridiculous. Countless other people had no one on their side. The sick, the elderly, the homeless—and here I was, feeling like I'd been abandoned.

Grow up! the voice inside me commanded.

Yeah, I had a job to do. To save Horse Hockey Brewing, and I would try to do so despite the conflicting messages from the family members who owned it. And as the minutes ticked by, I grew less and less sure I was going to be able to help my sort-of client.

Chapter 12

Richard didn't hang around the office for long, didn't show me the notes he'd written, and shut down his computer so I couldn't access them, either. Why all the secrecy? And should I have called him on it? Instead, I turned my attention to my own case.

It didn't take long for me to hunt down information on Omega Dustin, whose legal first name was Zelda. I don't blame her for choosing the last letter of the Greek alphabet as a substitute—it sounded way cooler.

I pored through my various sources and found that Omega had never been arrested. Her LinkedIn page listed her previous occupations as a child-care provider, secretary, and mortician beautician—presumably, the latter inspired her current occupation. She had a website that listed the duties she was available to perform, including at-home respite care for the families of the dying, help with paperwork associated with a death, and washing and dressing bodies for burial in cases where embalming was not part of the funeral process. It was all rather creepy to me. But then I stumbled on a Youtube channel called 'Ask A Mortician' and fell down a rabbit hole and spent a couple of hours learning how funeral mores had changed during the last century so that Americans had pretty much removed themselves from the process of taking care of their dead—gladly foisting the unpleasant job onto those willing and able to take on the task and often for a hefty price.

During my YouTube investigations, I'd heard the sound of Emily's cell phone go off and the soft murmur of her voice but hadn't paid much attention to it. But at the end of one of the videos, I'd looked up to see her standing in my doorway.

"What's up?"

Emily sighed, her expression darkening. "My biological parents have decided to sue my—" She stopped. "The people who brought me up."

I sat back in my comfortable office chair. "What do they hope to gain from it?"

She shrugged. "Nothing monetarily. They want…justice."

That wasn't likely to happen.

"And how do you feel about that?"

Emily shook her head. "When I was little, I loved the Ohio people—unconditionally. Something they didn't return when they found out I was pregnant with Hannah. They abandoned me. Left me to shift for myself. So, in some ways, I'm all for it. And yet…."

And yet her heart ached that the people she'd loved most of her life had treated her so shabbily.

I could identify with that kind of hurt. I'd experienced it with my own mother. She'd been devastated by the death of her first husband and then her in-laws stealing their child—Richard. She'd never really recovered from those losses, and I'd been collateral damage.

"What if you're called to testify against them?" I asked.

"I'll answer truthfully. If nothing else, that's what they taught me to do."

"Do you still love them?"

For a moment, I thought Emily might cry, but then she sort of shook herself before answering. "Yes. They were the only mom and dad I knew. But I can never forgive them for not only stealing me away from my biological family, but abandoning me when I was most vulnerable."

"Do you want to see them punished?"

"I don't know. For my new family's sake—yes. What Joanna Farrell did was despicable. And yet…."

She didn't have to say more.

"What will you do?"

"I guess just try to stay neutral."

"And what if criminal charges are brought against your Ohio mom? What will you do?"

"I don't know. Probably feel guilty."

"Why? You had no choice in the matter."

"Is that how you feel about the so-called power you think you have?"

A wave of anger flared within me, but it was pointless to argue with her. I know what I know, and if she couldn't accept me, too bad. But her words did nothing to endear her to me, either.

"Let's stick to your problem," I said, although I'd lost a significant portion of empathy I might have had for her situation.

Emily shook her head. "It's not something you need to worry—or even think—about."

Then I wouldn't. At least not too much.

Oh, shit. Of course, I would because I'm not a friggin' prick. But as her employer, I couldn't afford to get emotionally involved in her problems, despite my part in reuniting her with her biological parents.

"You've been busy," she said, her tone indicating she thought I'd been wasting my time on the Internet.

"Yeah. I got stuck in a loop learning the ins and outs of a death doula."

"A what?" she asked, appalled.

I explained how I'd met Omega Dustin the previous day.

Emily's expression conveyed her revulsion.

"Louie wasn't impressed, either."

"Who's that?"

"The guy who hired me. He's in a coma. He's dying."

Emily's eyes widened, and she took a step back. "And I suppose you can talk to him?"

"So far."

Emily shook her head and scowled.

I was then reminded of Richard's joke days before about the movie *Ghostbusters* being required viewing for our new hires. As a kid, I'd watched the movie on network TV every time it came on. The Annie Potts character, Janine, the secretary, had blithely accepted the outrageous idea of collecting riotous spirits as only a jaded denizen of Manhattan could. Emily was no Janine. If she continued to work for us, she would have to embrace that persona, and I wondered if I should suggest she watch that movie, too.

Maybe I needed to take Emily on a field trip so that she could see I wasn't just some asshole charlatan. She needed to be reassured that my investigative prowess was not dependent on whatever psychic vibes I experienced and was grounded in actual observational fact.

I glanced at my watch. "I've got to go," I said and shut down my computer. Emily retreated to the reception area and was sitting behind her desk when I grabbed my coat. "See you later," I said and dashed out the door.

I left the office half an hour before my appointment and met Sam, who'd parked on the street near our interviewee's place of work.

Nick Susskind was a partner in the law firm Stanley,

Sweeney, Kennedy, and Susskind. His office seemed more like a maritime museum than that of an attorney. Instead of certificates and diplomas, various lake-faring souvenirs hung on the walls and filled oak bookshelves. A painting of the ill-fated Edmond Fitzgerald in a gilded frame graced one wall, while small-scale replicas of other doomed vessels that once cruised the Great Lakes sat on shelves and atop cabinets. Maps and charts decorated the walls, and a vintage life jacket was preserved in a chunky shadow box.

"Thank you for speaking with us today, Mr. Susskind," Sam said, offering his hand.

Susskind shook it. "Call me Nick." He looked in my direction. "And you are?"

Before I could speak, Sam answered. "Ernie—"

"Preston," I interrupted before Sam could inject his tired old joke of calling me Ernie Pyle, the Pulitzer-prize-winning World War II journalist who'd died in action. Sam wasn't a dad, but he told bad dad jokes, which were received with the enthusiasm you'd expect.

"Thanks for contacting me," Nick said. "I'm ecstatic at the prospect of drawing attention to my organization and our quest for recognition of the history of sailing and shipping on Lakes Erie and Ontario." Nick ushered us into the seats before his desk. "How'd you hear about me and the foundation I've established?"

Sam shot a look in my direction before fibbing. "A friend of a friend. I've got a boat moored on Grand Island—nothing much," he demurred, "and I'm fascinated with stories of what happened in the past and think my readers would be entertained by them as well."

Nick's eyes practically sparkled.

"I understand you want to find and survey wrecks," Sam began. "Any in particular?"

"There's the Anna Dupré, a French Canadian freighter

that sank in Lake Ontario a mile offshore from Wilson. Our team believes we may have found her and her cargo of coal."

"Do you hope to salvage it?"

Nick shook his head. "Not when most coal plants have already been shut down. And I agree with the surviving families—and the Canadian government, as opposed to our own—that these wrecks are grave sites and warrant our respect."

I frowned. From what Louie had told me, Nick couldn't wait to put the old man in the ground to see his salvage ambitions fulfilled. It seemed at odds with the regard he seemed to feel for those lost on the lakes.

"What does your organization hope to achieve?" Sam asked.

"Generally to chart and identify the vessels and honor their crews."

"Sounds expensive."

Nick frowned and nodded. "But if you were a survivor of one of the men lost, wouldn't you want some kind of closure?"

"How many decades out?" I asked.

Nick's gaze flickered to me, and his expression hardened. "Does it really matter? The loss of these sailors is passed down through the generations. Many of the families grieve for the loss of a grandfather or uncle they never knew just because of the stories they've been told."

"Are you such a survivor?" Sam asked.

"Yes. My great, great, great uncle Melvin Susskind was the captain of a freighter—the Bonnie Rae—that sank in Lake Ontario in nineteen oh three during a freak October storm. It's my hope that we'll find that ship."

"How will you do that?" Sam asked.

"With the purchase of a submersible vehicle."

"Sounds expensive," I said.

"You better believe it," Nick agreed. "Maintenance is the most costly aspect. Obviously, we wouldn't be able to use it during winter months, but paying to hire a compatible sub would be just as—if not more—expensive. And there's the opportunity to lease it out to other organizations when it's not possible to use it locally, which would help to pay back the cost."

"I understand you intend to finance this sub by forcing the sale of your family's brewery," Sam said.

Nick's eyes narrowed. "Where did you hear that?"

"A source," Sam said obliquely.

Nick's expression darkened. "My sister, no doubt." He sat back in his chair, his spine stiff. "It isn't true. We're a limited liability company and have a fundraising wing. But when it comes to the brewery," he began, "without my father in charge, it hasn't got a chance to survive."

"Why not?" I asked. "You've got a brewmaster who knows his stuff."

"Yes, but…." Nick paused as though trying to come up with the proper words. "I'd hate to see all dad's hard work go down the drain."

"I understand your father's currently hospitalized," Sam said.

"Yes. And not likely to recover. My sisters and I need to consider what's best for the brewery and its employees and how to protect our father's legacy."

"And selling out is your best option?" I asked.

Nick glared at me as though a photographer shouldn't be allowed an opinion. He answered succinctly. "Yes."

"I understand your sister, Bethany, is currently in charge of the brewery," Sam said.

"Yes. We've had an offer to sell to a national brand. It's my opinion that we should accept it. That can't happen while my father is in a coma."

"How close to death is he?" Sam asked.

"Days away."

Not if Louie had anything to say about it.

"How severe is the struggle to control the brewery's future?" Sam asked.

"When—or if—my father dies, Bethany has control of the brewery, but I have power of attorney. Bethany's had the most input and knows the ins and outs of running it. If we sold the business, she'd not only be well compensated but could easily find another position with any of the many craft breweries in the area. If not, she'd be in a position to open her own establishment. If I were in her shoes, selling the brewery would be my top priority."

"Why is she so hesitant to sell?" I asked.

Nick shrugged. "Loyalty to our father. But he worked his whole life and has so little to show for it. I'm sure he could have been persuaded to sell if Bethany hadn't been so negative about it."

That wasn't the vibe Louie gave me. He'd intimated Nick was greedy and that he'd signed papers he wasn't sure about—probably the power of attorney as Nick had mentioned. But that would be canceled upon Louie's death—unless Louie had signed a codicil to his will, making Nick his executor. Or had signing off on pages of legalese been the figment of a mind slowly sinking toward death? The Louie I had spoken to was as sharp as a tack. The man in the hospital bed was just an inert body to me. That Teresa could be persuaded to see things Nick's way was something I needed to consider. Louie trusted Bethay with his life and business.

"Tell me more about your foundation's plans," Sam said, and I tuned out most of that conversation. I was too busy trying to weigh what Louie had told me and how I'd perceived the players in the brewery saga.

The weak link in the chain seemed to be Bethany. My impression of her was of a woman with something big and possibly destructive to hide. And there might be a lot of guilt associated with whatever shadowed her soul.

Bethany had permitted me access her father, which was a point in her favor. Was whatever she'd hidden from the rest of the world a burden on her soul, and did she hope an interloper like me might expose that darkness to the world at large—or was I giving myself way too much credit on that account?

I wanted nothing more than to head to the hospital to grill Louie about his son, but instead, I glanced at my watch and remembered that I had an obligation to Richard and CP, which was more important. But I still had a few minutes to spare and tuned back into Sam's and Nick's conversation.

"Thanks for letting us speak with you today," Sam said.

"When do you think the story will run?" Nick asked.

"Unfortunately, I'm pretty sure my editor will want to hold it until the weather warms—but that's not unusual. Would you mind if Ernie here took a few pictures of you and your memorabilia?"

Nick rose from behind his desk, his smile broad. "Not at all."

So I slid into photographer mode and hoped the story would run, giving me at least photo credit if not pay for the results.

Nick beamed for the camera, and as I clicked through the shots, I knew I'd done a good job of capturing him and the story he wanted to push.

Now I had to ask Louie why his assessment of his son differed so greatly from mine.

Chapter 13

I probably should have been arrested for speeding after hightailing it out of Nick Susskind's office, but it was only one thirty-five when I drove into the parking lot R&A Insights shared with the building's other tenants, and saw no sign of Brenda's van. Had they already dropped off CP, or were Richard and Brenda late?

I hurried into the office to find that CP was already there, sans snowsuit sitting in her stroller in the middle of the front of the office with Holly sitting by her side, acting as her guardian.

"Damn. I'm sorry I didn't get here before they dropped Betsy off," I apologized to Emily.

"They've been gone less than five minutes. We're okay, aren't we, Betsy?"

CP shook her favorite kitty stuffed animal and giggled. That girl was just a bucket full of giggles.

I hung up my coat and grabbed the stroller's handles.

"Where are you going?" Emily asked.

"Into my office. I told you. I don't expect *you* to take care of her."

"I appreciate that. But what are *you* going to do with her?"

"Watch her." What did she expect? "Right about now, she should be taking her afternoon nap."

"Well, you can't put her down to sleep here."

"She'll fall asleep once I get her out of her stroller and toss her over my shoulder."

"Bet you five dollars she won't."

"You're on."

Once again, I grabbed the stroller's handles, pushing it into my office, with Holly following right behind. CP raised her arms to me, and I lifted her out of it. "Come on, baby girl. It's nappy nap time." I settled the baby against my left hip and headed for my desk. Emily stationed herself at the office door.

CP waved her stuffed black kitty, calling "Sho-Sho." That's what she called my cat, Hershel.

"That's right. You, me, and Sho-Sho are going to take a nice nap, aren't we, baby girl?"

CP giggled.

"And I've got a bridge in Brooklyn to sell you," Emily muttered.

Of course, getting CP to sleep wasn't quite as easy as I'd implied. First, we had to investigate all the stuff on my desk, including the stapler, tape dispenser, and a cup filled with pens. And then we had to sing a couple of songs for Sho-Sho before CP nestled her head against my shoulder and obediently fell asleep.

Emily glowered. "How did you do that?" she quietly demanded.

I raised a finger to my lips, leaned back in my chair, and was prepared to drift off to sleep as well…but it wasn't likely to happen. My mind was filled with turmoil. After listening to—and speaking with—Nick, I had many more questions than answers. The whole situation between the brewery's owner and beneficiaries felt wrong. Well, maybe not wrong, but I was operating under conflicting stories and loyalties. And the undercurrent of conflict among the players was palpable. One thing was for sure; I needed to have a follow-up conversation with Bethany Susskind. She'd been the most guarded of the siblings, and I wasn't sure why.

But then I felt my body relax as a tiny fist snagged my shirt collar and the warm little body nestled closer against me, comforted knowing CP felt safe in my embrace.

I leaned my head back farther, and in no time at all, I drifted off to dreamland, too.

RICHARD SHRUGGED DEEPER into the confines of his heavy winter coat and contemplated starting the van's engine once again. He wasn't exactly fuming but was decidedly unhappy. He should have brought something to read. And the fact that he had to start the car every ten minutes or so to warm it enough to stay mildly comfortable on that bitter March day was annoying. But he admitted that Mrs. Clark was unlikely to speak to a white man about the fire that had destroyed her former home as well as her family. Brenda could probably communicate with whales under the sea, so Richard wasn't surprised that the few minutes he might have spoken with the woman had turned into half an hour with Brenda. Then three quarters and it was a full hour and five minutes before his wife left the shabby wood-frame home, with Mrs. Clark watching her get into the car from her living room window.

"What did she say?" Richard prompted.

"Not here," Brenda said.

Richard started the van and pulled away from the curb. "What took so long?"

"Mrs. Clark invited me to have a cup of tea with her."

"How nice," Richard groused.

"Yes, it was," Brenda snapped, which was unlike her.

"I'm sorry. My feet are cold. It makes me snarky."

"Which is nothing compared to what that poor woman has gone through."

A wave of guilt coursed through him, and Richard's fingers tightened around the steering wheel. "I'm sorry," he apologized once more. "Did she tell you anything of significance?"

"Only that she continues to believe in her son's innocence."

"And where is he? Does she still keep in contact with him?"

"She didn't say, and I didn't ask."

Richard glowered. "Why not?"

"You wanted me to build her trust, didn't you?"

"Of course."

"Then be a little patient," she admonished.

"Does that mean you're open to speaking with her again?"

"Of course. But only if you can dig up something to bolster her belief in her son's innocence."

"And how am I supposed to do that?"

"Isn't that why you opened R&A Insights in the first place? Find a way!" Brenda commanded.

She was right. And Richard *had* been sitting on his laurels, waiting for cases to fall into their laps and magically resolve themselves. But that wasn't the way life worked.

"Did she give you any clue as to who might have started the fire?"

"The landlord, for one."

"Why?"

"Abbots Boulevard was in the midst of gentrification at the time."

Since the fire, the once decrepit neighborhood had undergone a magnificent transformation. Gentrification was a double-edged sword. It brought derelict properties back from the brink of demolition, but it also made rents—and property ownership—out of reach for the people whose families had lived there for decades.

"Did she give you the name of the landlord?"

"Yes. William Margolin."

"Did she give you any other information on the man?"

Brenda shook her head. "Just that he was hard-assed and *white*."

"That's not a lot to go on," Richard said.

"You've got a name and the year. That should be a pretty good start for a consulting firm that wants to take on cold cases," Brenda bluntly pointed out.

Why did she have to sound so damned condescending? Still, she was right. And now Richard had a starting place. If nothing else, his particular skill *was* sifting through the minutia, be it on the Internet or through more primitive means—microfilm, fiche, or printed matter—to catalog a trove of information.

He steered through unfamiliar streets until he came back to more well-traveled thoroughfares. Although no sensitive like his brother and to some extent his wife, Richard knew he had to address the tension between them.

"We can't do this," he said as he turned left.

"Can't do what?"

"I'm sorry I asked you to get involved. I don't want what Jeff and I might do to come between us."

"What are you saying?" Brenda asked, sounding confused.

"I can't help that I'm a white guy. I can't—and won't—defend the crap that has gone on in the past and continues today. All I know is that I love you and I want to make things better for everybody. Black, white, purple, and green."

Brenda scowled. "I don't know anyone who's purple *or* green."

"Ah, but what if we're visited by purple aliens tomorrow?"

Brenda's scowl deepened. His feeble attempt at levity did not amuse her. "Then I hope they won't be exposed to the same prejudice my people have experienced."

Richard let out a breath. "I'm not a horrible person."

"Yeah, but too many white men are," Brenda countered.

Richard couldn't refute that.

"I'm sorry. I'm really sorry."

Brenda's expression softened, and she reached across the space between them to rest a hand on his shoulder. "I know. I don't mean to take it out on you, but we have to find a way to help Mrs. Clark find closure."

"But what if—*what if*—her son was responsible for the fire?"

"And what if he wasn't? Would you work as hard to prove him innocent?"

"You better believe I will."

Brenda squeezed his shoulder. "That's all I can ask."

Richard braked for a red light. "For what it's worth, I wouldn't be at all surprised if the cops *were* just lazy and were looking for a scapegoat. But I have to give them—and Mrs. Clark's son—the benefit of the doubt. As a researcher, my aim is always to be impartial."

Brenda gave a sad nod. "I know."

The light turned green, and Richard pressed the van's accelerator.

"Mrs. Clark also said that her son had some trouble at school," Brenda remarked.

"What kind of trouble?"

"There was a fight. Marcel tried to break it up. There was bad blood between him and several other boys."

"What else did she tell you about her son?"

"That he had earned a chemistry scholarship to UB."

"That's impressive. What else?"

"He'd been president of the school's chess club and was a member of the basketball team."

"Chemistry and chess don't sound in the same league as a jock."

"That's what she said. Is that enough information to get you started?" Brenda asked.

That was a good question.

"It's pretty obvious why Marcel Clark disappeared. Did Mrs. Clark give you any indication if she knew his whereabouts—or even if he's still alive?"

"Of course not. But I did let her know I was sympathetic. I may only have seventeen months of experience as a mom, but no way would I let anyone threaten my daughter and get away with it."

Richard felt that same sense of devotion.

"What happens next?" Brenda asked.

"Research. That's my job."

"If you want my opinion—and I'm not sure you do," Brenda said pointedly. "You need to try to prove Marcel's innocence. I don't know of any grandsons who'd want to see their grandma dead—no matter how horrible she might be."

Was that a dig at Richard's paternal grandmother, who had driven his mother to a psychiatric facility? Scarred her so badly that she'd so horribly mistreated her second son—Jeff—so that he was nearly as damaged as their mother?

They drove in silence for long minutes before Richard spoke again.

"Do you want to go anywhere else?"

Brenda shook her head. "We'd better pick up Betsy and Holly and go home. We've already inconvenienced Emily and Jeffy. I can run errands another day."

"R&A Insights isn't a corporate entity. We can afford to be flexible when it comes to unusual circumstances."

"Babysitting wasn't on the job description when Emily signed on."

"No, but we pay her an awful lot. Surely she can accommodate us now and then."

"I doubt she'd agree if you asked her to clean the washroom," Brenda muttered. "I know I certainly wouldn't."

Richard didn't want to get into the subject further, and they didn't say much to each other. He didn't like feeling at odds with his wife. And what if Marcel Clark had started the fire that killed his grandmother? Casting doubt on that assumption might be all he could hope for.

Would that be enough for Brenda?

Chapter 14

Richard and Brenda arrived back at R&A HQ just after three. By then, CP and I had both awakened from our naps and were deep into reading *Green Eggs and Ham*. She didn't understand much of it, but she giggled at the funny rhymes just the same.

Brenda entered my office, with Richard leaning against the door jamb. "Has my baby girl been good?" Brenda asked, holding out her arms.

"Mama," CP cried and eagerly let her mom take her up.

"The best girl in the whole wide world. How did your meeting go?" I asked.

Brenda's expression turned pensive. "We'll just have to wait and see," she said, grabbing CP's jacket.

I didn't bother to press either of them. I got up from my desk. "I need to get going. Got to check in with my client and his death doula."

"We need to get going, too. I want to get supper going. You'll join us, won't you, Jeffy?"

"Be there with bells on," I said, giving her a heartfelt smile.

"Wonderful."

"See you then," Richard said as I headed out of our office

without Richard asking me one question about what I was up to or sharing a word about his own case. That wasn't a way to operate a business. I didn't have time to contemplate the implications just then.

I grabbed my coat, telling Emily I'd call or text to let her know if I'd return to the office that day, and headed for my car.

When I arrived at the hospital, I found Louie's spirit again sitting on the window sill looking depressed—so much so that he barely acknowledged my presence. Omega sat alone at Louie's bedside. A small speaker attached to an MP3 player sat on a stand on the bedside table, issuing the soothing sound of tinkling metal wind chimes and ocean waves. Once again, the room was filled with the heady scent of hops from her candle warmer, and she held onto Louie's hand, stroking his thumb with her own while she perused her cell phone's screen with her other. She looked up as I entered. "Oh, it's you, Mr. Resnick."

"Call me Jeff. How is Louie today?"

She shook her head. "Sadly, inching closer and closer to death."

"*She'll* be the death of me," Louie griped from his non-corporeal state.

"Do you think I could have some private time with Louie?" I asked.

Omega squeezed Louie's hand just a little harder. "Well, I could use a bathroom break and get myself something to eat. Will you wait for me to return before leaving? Mrs. Barton doesn't want him to be alone."

"I'd be glad to."

Omega nodded, gave Louie's pale countenance a sad nod, and disengaged her hand. "I may be gone half an hour."

"That's okay. I don't have any other plans for the day." With no other clients and Maggie three thousand miles away, boy, was that the truth.

Omega stood and grabbed her purse from the over-bed table that had been pushed to the side. She smiled at me and seemed to float out of the room, her colorful muumuu swishing as she walked. I pushed the room's door closed behind her.

"Can you get this bitch to leave me alone in peace?" Louie implored. "She gives me the heebie-jeebies."

"Sorry. That's up to your daughters, and Teresa seems enamored with Ms. Omega."

"Crazy as a loon," Louie groused, and shook himself. "What have you been doing on my behalf?"

"This morning, I went with that friend of mine from *The Buffalo News* to interview Nick."

Louie's eyes widened in anticipation. "And?"

"He told us about his non-profit and about your great great uncle who died on the freighter Bonnie Rae. He's pretty passionate on the subject."

Louie scowled. "He's an idiot. Uncle Melvin was a drunk and an adulterer. The family was relieved when the damn ship sank, and they could be rid of the old bastard."

"That wasn't the impression Nick gave me."

"Eh, he's a dreamer," Louie said with disdain.

Okay, so Louie didn't give a shit about his forebears. I have to admit, I pretty much felt the same about mine, save for Sophie.

"What do you want me to do next?" I asked.

"I don't want all that I've worked for to sink to the bottom of Lake Erie or Ontario. You've got to stop all that crap."

I glared at him. "Did I mention that as an individual in a coma, you aren't in a position to pay me for my services?"

"Appeal to Bethany."

"And say what?"

"That I've given you the authority to do so."

I shook my head. "We've got nothing in writing. So why would she agree to pay me?"

Louie's gaze hardened. "Does that mean you're going to bail on me?"

"I didn't say that. But I've found that if people don't pay for a service, they don't appreciate the work that's done."

Louie looked at the pale form of his body on the bed. "I guess. If you don't turn a profit, after a while the Feds will decide it's a hobby. It took us operating in the red for far too long before we made a profit. And now Nick wants the fruits of *my* labor to pay for his damned expensive hobby—to the detriment of the rest of the family—the selfish bastard."

"That's not the impression he gave me," I reiterated.

Louie's eyes narrowed. "I told you, he wants to sell the brewery."

"Couldn't your daughters buy him out?"

"Teresa's in his court."

Which I'd already suspected.

"She'll probably want to invest in some cockamamie scheme. Maybe bankroll that charlatan, Omega."

"What about her husband and daughter?"

"Jim's lost his marbles, and Chrissy always was a hypochondriac."

"Not if she's on dialysis," I muttered. "You said Teresa was a saint when it came to caring for your wife."

"She *was*," he said as though emphasizing that it was all in the past.

"She seems pretty devoted to you, too."

"Probably feeling guilty. She was always her mother's child."

That wasn't helpful. The whole family seemed to be a major problem, but I needed to get down to what was really going on at the brewery.

"Let's change tacks," I said.

Louie scowled.

"What's going on at the brewery that needs the most attention?"

"I'm not sure what you mean."

"Well, when I visited, the place seemed dead. The production line was down. There were only a couple of people there besides Bethany and Abe." It suddenly occurred to me then that Abe Bachmann was an odd name for a black brewmaster. The surname was just as Jewish as mine, and he certainly didn't fit that descriptor—or was I just being persnickety?

Louie's eyes narrowed. "It takes time for beer to ferment."

"But surely you time it so that the batches mature at different rates so that you always have product going out the door."

"Yeah, most of the time." Something in the timber of his voice caused my hackles to rise.

"And what does that mean?"

Louie's brow furrowed, and he glared at me. "What does it matter? Nick is trying to force the sale of the brewery from under us—and just because I've got this damn heart failure." His expression darkened and he looked at his physical body with disdain. "Fucking useless doctors," he groused. "They always pulled me out of CHF before. If they *really* cared, I'd have been back on my feet in a week—just like before."

But it had probably taken him longer and longer to recover after each bout, something he wasn't taking into account. Yeah, congestive heart failure could be managed—and for several years—but it wasn't something anyone who suffered from it would fully recover from—not without a transplant.

I got the feeling that Louie wasn't being completely honest with me—but for what reason?

As a former insurance investigator, the word *fraud* floated into my mind. But what kind of fraud had Louie, Bethany, and Abe been perpetrating? Did Nick know about it and want to be rid of the brewery before it was discovered?

One thing was for sure: Louie wanted to steer me away from looking into that angle. Should I abandon him and give up the quest or keep digging until I exposed the truth? I didn't have anything to lose either way. R&A Insights wouldn't see a nickel out of whatever I uncovered, and I didn't have anything else to occupy my time, either.

"I need you to be clear about your goal," I told Louie.

"I told you. Stop Nick from forcing the sale of the brewery."

"And how do you think I should go about that?"

Louie's expression hardened. "Nail him!"

"How?"

"He's cheated on his wife in the past."

"And you want *me* to expose that?"

"That's what I hired you to do."

"And again, I have to remind you that I have no contract with Horse Hockey Brewing, you, or your heirs."

"You have a moral obligation to help me," Louie asserted.

I didn't see how or why. I could just walk away that second, but what if Louie died and *could* haunt me—make every day of the rest of my life on earth a living hell?

"What if I keep digging and you don't like what I find?"

Louie seemed to mull over my question. "I guess it's a risk I'll have to take."

As far as I could see, he bore no risk. While I, on the other hand....

"I'll see what my newspaper friend says and get back to you."

Louie looked at the prone figure of himself on the bed, his mouth drooping. "You'd better be quick about it. I don't know as I'll be here much longer."

It was a possibility that could solve my problem of dealing with the whole situation—or not.

"All right. I'll visit the brewery again and talk to Bethany. It seems she's got the most at stake to keep the brewery open."

"Damn right," Louie said.

She wouldn't want to meet with me at the end of the workday, but I didn't want to go back to the office or home, despite the guilt I felt at leaving Herschel alone for so many hours. I'd already promised I'd see Brenda for supper, but I wasn't sure I wanted to talk to my brother.

"Hey, Resnick!" Louie asked. "You going to cry or somethin'?"

"I'm fine," I lied.

"Well, don't shed any tears for Nick or Teresa."

I hadn't planned on it.

The heavy wide door to the room swung open. Omega had returned.

"Did you have a nice visit?" she asked, setting her purse down on the bed table once again.

"Peachy," Louie muttered.

"Oh, yeah." I cleared my throat. "I'd better get going," I said to the room at large.

"Have a good evening, Mr. Resnick. I shall say a prayer for you."

"She's been praying at me for two days now. Hasn't done a damn bit of good," Louie commented.

"Thank you," I told Omega. "I'll probably be back tomorrow afternoon."

"I'll be here," they both said in unison.

Somehow, I didn't doubt it.

Chapter 15

After yet another night of crappy sleep, I got up, set up the coffeemaker, and took a shower while it brewed, then shaved and dressed. I fed Herschel and myself before leaving for the office. I left the radio on for Herschel, so he'd hear voices and music during the day, hoping he might not feel so alone.

For once, I got to the office before Emily. I started the coffee, perused the mail, and emailed Bethany Susskind before Emily arrived one minute before eight.

"You're here early," she said as she hung up her coat and scarf.

"I couldn't sleep and had nothing else to do," I explained. It was more or less the truth. "I need to talk to our client's daughter today. I sent her an email. If I hear back from her, would you like to go with me?"

Emily's eyes widened. "Really?"

"Yeah. I think it might help to have you get more involved in the business."

Her eyes narrowed. "Because you think she might open up to *me* and not you?"

"Exactly."

Emily frowned. "Isn't that just a little dishonest?"

"In what way?"

"Well, because…." But then she didn't seem to have an answer for that. She let out a sigh. "What am I supposed to do?" Emily asked, sounding deadly serious.

"Listen—and ask questions, but only after taking my lead."

"About what?"

"How Bethany Susskind feels about her father's impending death and the brewery she's about to inherit—along with her siblings," I hastened to add.

"I think you'd better fill me in on the whole situation," Emily said.

"I can do that on the way to the brewery. Are you game?"

Emily's eyes practically sparkled. "Yes."

"Fine. I'll catch up on things in my office and hope I hear from her." Just then the phone rang. Emily answered.

"R&A Insights. This is Emily. How can I help you?" She listened. "One moment, please." She handed the phone to me.

"Mr. Resnick? It's Bethany Susskind. You wanted to meet with me to talk about my father?"

"Yes. Would you have time this morning?"

She let out a long breath before answering. "How about eleven o'clock?"

"That's perfect. I'll see you then."

She ended the call.

"Looks like we've got the green light to go. We should leave around ten thirty—just to be safe."

"I'll be ready," Emily said, excitement coloring her tone.

"Great." I gave her a nod and headed back to my office… to goof off for two and a half hours. God only knew I didn't have anything else to do.

That wasn't true. I decided I should do more research on

wrecks on Lakes Erie and Ontario. The nitty-gritty of locating wrecks, the pros, cons, and legalities of salvage, and the lore of traversing the Great Lakes. The subject was fascinating, and the hours passed in what seemed like a heartbeat.

"Jeff—it's ten twenty-five," Emily called at last.

"Thanks," I called and put my computer to sleep. I got up and entered the reception area.

"Grab your stuff and let's go."

We donned our coats, hats, and scarves and locked up the office to trudge to my car in the back lot. I unlocked the passenger-side door for Emily to enter.

She frowned. "Wow. Your ride is quite a comedown compared to Dr. Alpert's Mercedes. Why's that?"

"Because this is what I can afford."

"Yeah, but…isn't Dr. Alpert—?"

"Incredibly wealthy?" I asked.

Emily scowled and ducked into the passenger seat without commenting.

I walked around the front of the car and got in, buckling my seat belt before starting the engine.

Emily faced me, looking puzzled. "I'm not sure I see where you and your brother are coming from. I mean, I figured you're half-siblings, right?"

"Yep."

"And you were brought up differently than him."

"Very astute."

"So, what's the story?" she asked.

I didn't feel kinship enough with Emily to spill Richard's and my history—at least not then.

"That's not something I want to talk about today. Instead, I'll tell you what I know about the brewery's players so far."

Emily shrugged. "Whatever."

I shoved the gearshift into reverse and backed out of the

parking space, heading for the tiny lot's exit. During the twenty-plus-minute drive to Horse Hockey Brewing, I told Emily everything I thought I knew about the Susskind family and employees and what I'd been told, but not my suspicions. I wanted her to come to her own conclusions and report back to me.

This time, I parked in the brewery's back lot. The temperatures had risen, and the lot no longer resembled a skating rink so we didn't risk life and limb as we advanced toward the employee entrance. I rang the bell a couple of times before a woman employee in a blue jumpsuit opened the door.

"We're here to see Bethany. We've got an appointment."

"R&A Insights?"

"You got it."

"Come on in," the woman said. Her jacket was embroidered with her name: Portia. "Bethany's in the office."

She ushered us in and past the brewery's still-silent production line to the inner office.

"Bethany, your guests are here."

Bethany didn't rise from behind her desk as Emily and I entered. Her lieutenant, Abe Bachmann, stood in one corner, acknowledging us with the barest of nods.

"Thanks for seeing us," I began. "Let me introduce you to my associate, Emily Farrell."

Bethany nodded in Emily's direction. "Nice to meet you," she said before returning her attention to me. "What can I do for you today, Mr. Resnick?"

"Jeff," I encouraged.

She said nothing.

"I've been to see your father a couple of times."

"And I'm still not sure why you wanted to do that. Poor Dad is little more than a vegetable."

"It's given me time to think about what he said to me before he lapsed into a coma."

Bethany's eyes narrowed. "Such as?"

"Well, he was dead set against selling the brewery to a national concern."

"You've got that right." She pursed her lips and for a moment I thought she might burst into tears, but then her features seemed to relax into resignation.

"What if, after he passes, your brother forces a sale?" I asked.

"Then he'll have to fight it in court, which could take years. In the meantime, the brewery will only increase in value," Bethany said confidently.

"That sounds like a prudent strategy," I agreed. "But from what I understand, your sister Teresa might also back a quick sale."

Bethany scowled. "That's because she's got financial problems of her own. "She's got a husband with early-onset dementia and a daughter with health problems. Yeah, she needs the money."

Which corroborated what both Teresa and Louie had told me. "What do you think about her employing an end-of-life doula to ease your father into the afterlife?"

Bethany's gaze hardened. "That she can damn well cough up for the cost of that crap on her own nickel. I may not see eye-to-eye with my brother on most things, but I think we'd both agree that a death doula is something Dad wouldn't have tolerated or expected to have to pay for."

She had that right.

I nodded. "I'm curious as to why the brewery's production line is at a standstill."

Bethany bit her lip and shot Abe a glance before answering. "We're between batches. Once our fermentation tanks are ready, the bottling line will be brought back to life."

That sounded reasonable…if they had all the time in the world and no employees to pay.

"Where's your workforce? Surely it takes more than four people to bottle a couple-thousand-gallon tanks of beer."

"They're on hiatus. We're reformulating our most popular brew—making a bigger batch. We'll be back online in a week or so," she said, but something in her tone said otherwise.

And what were her presumably unpaid employees doing during the interim? Sitting around twiddling their thumbs or sending resumes to every craft brewery in the state and beyond?

"You say my father hired you to work for us. I'd like to see the contract," Bethany said.

I let out a breath. "Unfortunately, your father and I never signed an agreement before he fell ill."

"And exactly what did he hire you to do?" Abe asked, standing taller, and looking just a little menacing.

"I'm supposed to stop Nick and Teresa from forcing the sale of the brewery."

Bethany shot Abe a look that was a cross between hope and triumph. Abe's expression remained skeptical.

"And how do you propose to do that?" Bethany asked.

"I haven't had much time to come up with a strategy," I admitted.

"Why are you bothering?" Abe asked, his tone bordering on hostility. "It's got to be obvious to you that we're under no obligation to compensate you—no matter how the situation is resolved."

I glared at the man. "I would hope," I said calmly, "that your firm would honor the verbal contract between Louie and me."

"I guess that would depend on the outcome," Abe said.

I turned my attention to Bethany. "So, if my efforts on your behalf fail, you'd be unwilling to pay my fee?"

Bethany's expression soured. "I don't know you. I have no

clue who you are or if you're bullshitting me. I have no reason to trust you."

"Nor I you," I countered. "Your father hired me to try to save this brewery from being yanked out of your control and sold to the highest bidder. If that's not what you want to happen, let me know now, and I'll walk away because I've got no stake in what happens to you or the brewery. I'm only trying to honor my promise to a dying man."

My words seemed to have struck a nerve with Bethany, whose mouth trembled, her eyes growing damp.

"Okay," she said finally. "What's our next move?"

"Have you any idea what's in your father's will?"

Bethany didn't answer.

"Surely he spelled out what he wanted to happen to his assets and how they'll be distributed."

Bethany shot Abe a rather panicked look. He shrugged. Bethany turned her attention back to me. "I wasn't made privy to daddy's will. I have no idea what's in it."

Since Bethany had been her father's staunchest supporter when it came to the brewery, she would likely have the most to gain. That is, if there *was* a will. The survivors of people who died intestate could really be fucked if the state determined the distribution of a deceased person's assets. If Louie had no will, Bethany might well be forced to sell the brewery so that the estate could be equally split between the heirs. Despite what Nick said, it wasn't likely she'd have enough to start over again. That said, she had the skills to establish another business *if* she could find financial backing. I'd ask Louie about it, but I needed to know whether Bethany would work with us. I studied her face. She looked distinctly unhappy.

Emily stepped forward. "It's in your best interest to help us save your stake in the brewery."

"And how am I supposed to do that?" Bethany asked.

"By being honest with us. As Mr. Resnick said, your father

hired us to help save the brewery and keep it independent. We're doing our best, but can't fulfill that verbal contract without your help."

Bethany's gaze drifted to the floor, where it stayed for long seconds. "I don't know if it'll help, but our attorney is George Weston. We've been working with him since dad set up the operation. His office is in Amherst. I don't have his number off hand. You can Google him."

I made a mental note of the name—not that the guy would talk to me without Bethany giving him the green light. "Thanks."

"Are we done?" Abe asked. He seemed to want to get rid of Emily and me.

"For now," I answered. "With your permission, I'll keep digging."

"If it were up to me, I'd send you packing," Abe said.

I turned to Bethany.

"I want to keep the brewery—at least for now. The time isn't right to sell. Dad knew that."

I nodded in agreement. "We'll talk soon," I said, and turned for the room's exit.

Once again, Portia, the jump-suited woman, guided Emily and me to the brewery's back entrance. We walked back to my car in silence. I unlocked the car doors with my key fob but didn't open the passenger side for Emily. She was more than capable of getting inside by herself.

We didn't speak as I pulled out of the lot and headed south. I decided to break the quiet.

"Thanks for speaking up back there. I wasn't making much headway, but you got Bethany to think."

"All part of my job, right?" Emily said diffidently and looked at the clock on the dashboard.

"Yeah." I braked for a red light. "It's almost lunchtime. I

thought I might like to go for Chinese. Want to come along?" I asked.

"Only if I pay for myself," Emily said bluntly.

"I'm not asking you out on a date," I replied flatly. "I'm asking if you want to accompany me to a restaurant and get something to eat."

"I'm open to that," Emily said. "I can save the salad I brought for lunch and split it with Hannah for dinner."

Good for her.

The light turned green, and I pressed the accelerator pedal.

Her tone annoyed me. I was beginning to wonder why I ever thought I liked this woman. But now we were committed to breaking bread—or at least crispy fried noodles dipped in apricot sauce—together.

I thought my less-than-friendly tone had done the trick because the drive to the Golden Pond restaurant couldn't be called chatty, and I was grateful for the radio that I seldom turned on when I drove. I'd punched in the local soft rock station, but Emily didn't seem at all pleased by that selection. Not that she voiced her objection. It was just the vibe I received. Yeah, it wasn't my favorite, either.

Once at the restaurant, we entered and were greeted by a large—more-than-life-sized version—of a gold Buddha in the doorway.

"Let me show you to your table," said a pretty young Asian woman in a peach silk brocade jacket.

We settled into a banquette that overlooked the parking lot out back with its mounds of dirty snow almost six-feet high. The hostess left us with thick binders of the restaurant's offerings.

Emily shimmied out of her coat, and I did likewise.

"So, what did you think about our visit to Horse Hockey Brewing?" I asked.

"First, thanks for introducing me as your associate. It sounded so much more important than a mere receptionist."

"We didn't hire you with the thought you'd stay in that position."

Her eyes widened and, when she spoke, she sounded genuinely surprised. "Really?"

"It'll take a couple of years—maybe more—to build up the business. We realize there isn't much for you to do right now, but hope you'll take the opportunity to learn and grow as the work comes in."

She leaned in closer. "What can I do to make that happen?"

It was a good question—and one I hadn't discussed with Richard but I had my own ideas.

"For one thing, when and if we ever have them, read our case notes and any background information we collect."

"We don't currently have any sharing capability with our computer system."

As Richard was such a computer nerd, I wondered why he hadn't built that into our system. Why did he want to hide what he was investigating from Emily and me? We were supposed to be partners. Before that day, it hadn't occurred to me that we might be working on different cases at the same time, although I suppose it was inevitable. But it wasn't as though our current projects were taking up all that much of our time, either.

"I'll see about fixing that glitch."

"What else can I do?" Emily asked. "Right now, I feel pretty useless."

I could feel her sense of frustration.

I thought about it for a moment. "You could contact all the police agencies within a twenty-mile radius and ask if they need help with unsolved cases."

"With what criteria?"

"We should work on the wording," I suggested. "Why don't we take a stab at it this afternoon, and then we can discuss it?"

Emily nodded, and the waiter arrived with a stainless steel pot that contained tea and bowls of fried noodles, duck sauce, and hot mustard.

"Ready to order?" he asked.

We hadn't even perused the menu. "Can you give us five minutes?" I asked.

"Sure thing," he said and headed back up the aisle to his station, where he could survey the entire—mostly empty—restaurant.

Emily picked up her menu and scanned the offerings. "I'm not all that versed in Chinese cuisine. I pretty much always get the same thing."

"I like dishes heavy with veggies," I said.

"Such as?"

"The Hunan Pork usually comes with a lot of broccoli. Moo goo gai pan is good, too."

Emily wrinkled her nose. "I like the meaty ones. I usually get sweet-and-sour something or other."

I wasn't a big eater and could easily make a Chinese lunch extend to at least three meals.

"What kind of soup do you want?" I asked.

"Egg drop. And you?"

"Hot and sour."

I'd already made up my mind, but Emily was still staring at the menu when the waiter arrived for our orders. I gave him mine, but we had to wait a few moments for Emily to decide on hers.

"I'll have the sweet-and-sour pork with the egg drop soup," she said.

The waiter nodded, retrieved our menus, and left us alone.

I poured the tea. I wasn't a big tea fan, but Maggie was and had gifted me a pot and a couple of fancy bone china cups that were seldom used—especially now since she rarely visited my humble abode over Richard's three-car garage. Several times she'd prepared for us an afternoon tea with three different types of sandwiches—egg salad, cucumber, and salmon—with scones, strawberries dipped in chocolate, and cocoa-dusted truffles. I could never eat even a quarter of that bounty, but she enjoyed the preparation and was happy to partake of the leftovers.

Maggie always set a fine table.

I'd seen Emily's apartment when we'd first met. Her dishes were pretty much Corelle ware and thrift shop decor—not that there was anything wrong with that. Maggie's home had been filled with yard sale and thrift store finds, but she'd refinished and repurposed everything and often used starched and ironed linen napkins at mealtimes.

Was I being a snob?

Why was I giving Maggie a lot of credit and Emily such short shrift? Emily wasn't my friend, but she wasn't cheating on me, either.

Emily rapped her knuckles on the table. "Hello!"

I shook my head. "Sorry. I got lost in thought. What did you think about our meeting at the brewery?"

"That there's no way we'll to see a dime from them."

I nodded. "It's a distinct possibility."

"Then what's the point?"

I wasn't sure how to answer. Luckily, the waiter arrived with our soup. Once he'd left, Emily picked up her spoon, dipping it into her bowl. She blew on the steaming liquid before sampling it. "Why didn't you and Mr. Susskind sign a contract?"

"I told you. The man's in a coma."

Emily looked at me as though I'd sprouted a second head. "I thought you were joking."

"Nope."

"But you spoke to him?"

I nodded.

She shook her head. "That's not possible."

"Tell Louie that," I muttered, and wished I'd ordered a bourbon on the rocks.

Emily turned her attention to her soup. She took a couple of spoonsful before she spoke again. "Okay, if I suspend my disbelief like they say about fiction, why should I believe in any of this crap you keep telling me about Mr. Susskind?"

"Because...." But then, I didn't have a logical explanation. "Well, I guess you don't have to. But why would I make it up? How else could I know about the trouble the brewery is going through?"

"It's got me stumped," Emily admitted, and dipped a fried noodle into duck sauce and chewed it. "But what you've told me seems to be upheld by what Bethany Susskind told us."

Yeah, it did.

"What happens next?" Emily asked, echoing Bethany's question.

"I'll try to talk to their lawyer."

"What will that accomplish?" she asked, and returned her spoon to her soup.

"To find out the brewery's legal standing."

"If he'll speak to you."

"Exactly. If I'm lucky, Bethany will phone him to let him know I'll be calling."

"And if she doesn't?"

"I'll have wasted only a few minutes."

I tried my soup. Not bad.

Emily poured tea for herself. Apparently, it didn't occur to her to offer me any.

Was I becoming invisible?

I poured some tea for myself, if only to wet my whistle.

"When we get back to the office, why don't you write up

your impressions of our visit so we can add it to the official file."

Emily looked up, pleased. "I will." She stabbed a piece of pork, letting some of the rice stick to the sauce. "Thanks for taking me with you to the brewery. For the first time, I actually feel like part of the R&A Insights Team."

Lucky her. I was still waiting for that feeling.

Chapter 16

Richard spent the morning reading through his case notes before reviewing the minutes from the last hospital board meeting he'd attended, the latter of which took up most of the morning. Concentrating on *real* work made him feel useful, more so than what he was doing for R&A Insights. He lifted his cup to sip his coffee and noticed it had gone cold. He wondered if Brenda had tossed the morning's brew. He could make another pot.

Getting up from his desk, he grabbed his cup and, when he passed his dry bar, felt a surge of pride that he hadn't made himself an Irish coffee.

Brenda was sitting at the kitchen table, staring at her phone.

"What's up?"

"I got a text from Maggie a little while ago," Brenda said, and, for some reason, Richard's gut tightened. "Oh?"

"She's deliriously happy with her job and the warm weather in San Diego."

"Our weather will be almost as nice in a few weeks."

Brenda scowled. "Not a chance."

Yeah, the weather was likely to suck for at least another two months, albeit with hints of summer to come. Still, Richard had never doubted his decision to leave the Golden State to return east, and neither had Brenda.

"Do you think she's as happy as she claims?" Richard asked.

Brenda's frown deepened. "I'm a terrible friend because I think she took that job because she's infatuated with one of her co-workers and wanted to pursue it, much to Jeffy's detriment."

"I wish you hadn't told me that, and whatever you do, please don't tell Jeff. "

"You know I wouldn't."

Yeah, he did. And yet he wasn't surprised that Maggie had cheating on her mind. She'd done it to Jeff before, and while he'd been willing to forgive her, Richard hadn't been able to do so. He'd put on a brave face for the sake of harmony, but he doubted he'd fooled Brenda or Jeff.

"Do you think Jeff knows?" Richard asked, already knowing the answer.

"Of course he does. Those two are connected, mores the pity," Brenda groused.

Goddammit.

They didn't say anything for far too long a time while Richard rinsed out the pot and made a fresh brew. "What do you think we should do about it?" Richard finally asked.

"Not a damn thing."

"But we've got to support Jeff," Richard said, even if he'd kept other things to himself.

"I agree."

"And how do we do that?"

"You could talk to him," Brenda suggested.

"I don't know about that," Richard said, refusing to meet his wife's gaze.

Brenda scowled once again. "It seems to me you haven't been talking to him nearly enough lately."

"What do you mean?"

"Are you going to update him on what we found out yesterday?"

"Of course," Richard said. "I just wish I'd made more headway."

"And why haven't you?" Brenda asked tartly. She'd obviously bonded with Mrs. Clark and empathized with the woman over her son's absence in her life and how it must have gnawed at the poor woman's soul.

"Marcel Clark dropped out of sight right after the fire and there's been no trace of him since. I suspect his family knows full well where he is and has been clandestinely communicating with him."

"And on what do you base that?" Brenda asked.

"Gut feeling."

Brenda rolled her eyes. She who claimed to have the gift of second sight—if only to a minor degree. "Then he's probably left the area and is living—discretely—in some large urban area thousands of miles from Buffalo."

Richard looked thoughtful. "I don't think so."

"And on what do you base that assumption?"

Richard's lips quirked into a smile. "Gut feeling."

Brenda's expression darkened. "You *could* be right."

"I sure hope so. And let's assume Marcel was innocent of his grandmother's death. Why hide out for nearly twenty years?"

"It's obvious. The cops made him the prime suspect. They decided to pin it on him with no real evidence just to clear the case. It's not as though that was unusual for the time—or even now," she added pointedly.

No. It wasn't.

The silence lengthened between them. The coffeemaker

had finished its cycle, and Richard poured himself a fresh cup. "You want some?"

Brenda shook her head.

Richard studied his wife's so-loved and familiar features. "Did Mrs. Clark give you any other background on her son? His likes, loves, hobbies?"

Brenda looked thoughtful. "Not really. I mean, we didn't get into any of that. And if you're right that she's still in contact with him, she's not likely to speak to either of us again." Brenda frowned. "How do you propose to find out what made him a person of interest?"

"Maybe check out his high school buddies."

"How can you figure that out?"

"There are yearbooks online. I could start there."

Brenda looked skeptical. "Sounds like a shot in the dark."

Richard shrugged. "Lots of cold cases are solved by so-called shots in the dark."

"And gut feeling?" Brenda asked.

Richard nodded.

"Then please don't sit around waiting for stuff to happen. Mrs. Clark is a woman with a terrible weight on her soul. If we can do anything to relieve her pain, we have to do it."

"Agreed."

They looked at each other for long seconds before Richard picked up his coffee cup. "I'd better get to it, then."

Brenda said nothing. His gaze dipped to look at her phone once again, looking so sad.

Richard knew he should say something, *do something*, to lift the weight from *her* soul. But instead, he left the kitchen and returned to his study. He had work to do.

AFTER RETURNING TO THE OFFICE, I called Weston's office, but it was a no-go. I left a message asking Bethany to talk to the guy and get the okay for me to speak to the attorney.

As the afternoon went on, I felt like the walls were closing in on me. I'd never felt claustrophobic before, but my thoughts had taken a dark turn—like I was about to have a panic attack…if that's the right term. I'd never had one before. I even drove back to Richard's property with the car windows open, gulping air. A short and chilly ride. I felt a little better when I arrived at my apartment. Herschel seemed to sense something was up, for he followed me around like a puppy. I hung up my suit coat and realized the hamper in my closet was again about to spill over. It was past time I did some laundry. I figured I could do it later.

After such a big lunch, I texted Brenda and told her I wouldn't show up for dinner. Instead, I decided to assemble the paperwork for filing my taxes, thinking it would be a diversion from thinking about Louie and Maggie. Both situations were starting to feel impossible.

After a couple of hours, my tax forms were filled out. Next year, it would be a whole lot more complicated … if R&A Insights was still in business.

After that, I boxed up everything that reminded me of Maggie, stuffing it into my dark room. I hadn't realized how much influence she'd had when it came to my living quarters.

It was after seven, and the place looked sparse. I needed to put my own stamp on the apartment, that is if I stayed there. I looked around and the pile of laundry was the only blight in that immaculate apartment. There was only one way to fix that. I'd have to go across the driveway and wash the stuff. I could hide in the basement and choose not to interact with my family—mostly avoiding my brother. Unfortunately, when I entered the house, I could see Brenda standing over the kitchen table folding laundry while CP sat in her highchair chewing on Sho-Sho, her favorite stuffed kitty.

I lifted the stuffed pillowcase I held. "Great minds think alike, huh?"

"When you have a toddler, it's never-ending."

I nodded and looked down at the bulging sack in my hand.

"We missed you at supper," Brenda said. She did. I doubted Richard did.

"You know how big those portions are at Chinese restaurants."

She scrutinized my face. "Are you okay?" Brenda asked, sounding worried.

I swallowed before answering. "Not really."

She looked at me with sympathy. "I'm not a physician, but I've been around the block more than once."

"What does that mean?" I asked, dropping the pillowcase and joining her at the table, picking up a couple of little pink socks and balling them.

"I think you might be clinically depressed."

That wasn't exactly a startling revelation. "Go on," I said.

"Depression runs in families. I'm afraid you and Richard are on the same sad path, but for different reasons."

"Have you spoken to him about it?"

"No, but I probably should. And I'm pretty sure neither of you will seek professional help."

Not a chance in my case. It seemed to me that these so-called professionals were more interested in categorizing people coming through their doors so they could get reimbursement from insurance companies. I'd been screwed before by a therapist. I'd never again spill my guts to a shrink or a psychologist ever. I might to a trusted friend—but I really didn't have that option, and I wasn't going to subject Brenda to that kind of emotional assault, either. But I'd always been able to talk to her. Maybe I should say something now. I mulled the idea over as we folded the last of Betsy's little pants and T-shirts.

"I never had a problem being alone...until lately." I made eye contact to gauge her reaction. I saw only sadness and compassion. I did my best to explain. "When Shelley," my dead wife, "left me, I was a mess...but I could handle it. Now, after the last couple of years, I'm not so sure."

"Why's that?" Brenda asked, her tone soft.

I wasn't sure I could articulate all the crap that seemed to be showering over me.

"Is it Maggie?" Brenda asked.

"Partly."

Brenda's mouth tightened before she spoke. "I think we might be getting the same vibes."

A flush of relief coursed through me. I *wasn't* crazy. Maybe I *could* trust my feelings after all.

"The thing is, except for Emily—and she and I aren't exactly chums right now—I've got practically zero when it comes to social contacts. God, I can't tell you how much I miss the bar and its regulars. They weren't my friends, but I got to actually *talk* to people. Nine months without that kind of contact has been harder than I thought it would be."

"Oh, hon, we've got two guest rooms. If you want to come stay with us, you know the welcome mat is always there."

I frowned. "Yeah, well, that's you talking."

"Jeffy, you know Richard would never turn you away. He's the one who brought you back to us."

"I haven't exactly gotten that welcoming kind of vibe from him lately. He's been pretty guarded when it comes to his investigation.

Brenda's brows furrowed. "Yeah, I know."

"And Holly and Hershel aren't exactly friends," I said, offering another barrier.

"It could be that they haven't spent enough time together," Brenda said reasonably.

Yeah.

And now it was time for truth. I swallowed hard before speaking. "I'm not sure I can trust myself to be alone much longer."

Brenda's eyes grew damp. I'd tried to kill myself after Maggie cheated on me almost two years before. It wasn't exactly my idea at the time…but I'd done it just the same. And still, I couldn't talk about it—even to Brenda.

She cleared her throat. "Hon, I *want* you to come stay with us. Will you do that for me?"

I looked away and swallowed.

"Please, please stay. For just a couple of days. Until this thing with Maggie gets resolved."

"She's kind of already resolved it by moving away."

Brenda shook her head, drew me into a hug, and we clung to each other for long seconds. When she pulled back, her eyes were full with tears. She wiped them away and straightened. "Now, you go right across the driveway, pack a bag, and come stay with us for as long as you need." She gazed into my eyes. "Jeffy, you will *always* be welcome in our home. You *and* Herschel," she amended.

"Thank you," I said sincerely. "But not until we square it with Rich. And I promise it won't be for long," I said as a wave of shame rolled over me. "I just need a little time to figure out how to disconnect from Maggie."

"I get that," Brenda said. "I'm finding it harder and harder to be her friend for the same reason."

"I don't want you two to part as friends because of me," I protested.

"Yeah…but it's inevitable," Brenda admitted.

I didn't dare react to that statement, but I was pleased that Brenda had reaffirmed her support for me.

"What do we tell Richard?" I asked.

"You let me take care of that," she said decisively.

"I don't want to put you in that position."

"I'm volunteering," she said adamantly.

Chicken shit that I am, I was relieved to hear her say so.

"Okay," I said, letting out a breath. "It will probably take me a few trips across the driveway to bring my stuff—and Herschel's, too—over here."

"Want my help?"

CP let out a shriek of joy and threw Sho-Sho on the floor.

"No, I'm good. Toss some sheets on the bed in the room that connects with CP, and I can make it up."

"Are you sure?"

"Yeah. I need the activity to kind of make the space more my own—you know?"

"I know," Brenda said with a nod.

It pained me to think that my brother might not know just how lucky he was to have such a beautiful, kind woman in his corner. It also pained me to think I might never find a kindred spirit.

I tried to put that thought away because I had practical matters to contend with, like grabbing clothes, my laptop, Herschel's litter box, food, and treats.

I wasn't sure coming to stay with them was a good idea… but I couldn't think of anything better. If nothing else, it would distract me from the darker thoughts that were taking up way too much real estate in my brain.

Chapter 17

Richard stared at the blank computer screen before him. He'd been trying to come up with a list of people to talk to about the Clark arson, but it had been so long, and how many would gave a flying fig about an incident that happened years before?

He heard a noise at the door and looked up to see his wife standing there. "What's up?"

She strode into the room with Betsy on her hip and deposited the toddler in the playpen. "Jeffy's coming over."

"What do you mean 'over'? He's here all the time."

"I mean, he's coming over to stay for a while."

Richard sat up straighter in his padded leather chair, suddenly annoyed. "Why?"

Brenda sighed. "In case you hadn't noticed, the poor guy is clinically depressed.

Richard frowned. "When did you earn your degree in psychology?"

Brenda glowered at him. "And when did you become a heartless prick?"

"Brenda!"

"Should I tell him he isn't welcome?" she asked, testily.

Richard ignored the question. "Is this because of Maggie?"

"Partly."

Richard nodded.

"I thought it would be good for him," Brenda continued. "I don't like the thought of him being on his own most of the day and all night."

"He has Emily during office hours."

"A woman who can barely tolerate him."

"That's an exaggeration."

"Is it?"

Richard shrugged.

"Look, if you don't want him here, just say so," she said irritably.

"I *didn't* say that," he countered.

"Then could you at least show him a little empathy? You know, that emotion you used to be capable of."

Anger flared within him, but he didn't reply.

Brenda turned.

"Wait," he called. "Where are you going?"

"To get the guest room ready. Or would you prefer he sleeps in the basement?"

"Brenda!" he scolded her, and Betsy began to whimper in her playpen.

"No, you listen to me. When you brought your brother back to Buffalo to live it was hard for us but even harder for him. You knew he had physical and emotional problems and my God, he has faced them with courage. I don't think I could have survived what's been thrown at him. I don't think you could, either. But if you can no longer muster that same compassion—"

Her words stopped.

"Then what?"

"Then you are no longer the man I came to love. To respect. To cherish."

"Brenda," he said, swallowing an almost overwhelming surge of confusion and pain.

"What in God's name has gotten into you?" she demanded.

Richard's gaze traveled to the dry bar across the room. "I … I don't know," he stammered.

"Then you'd better think long and hard about it."

Was she giving him an ultimatum? It didn't matter. He knew he was far better off with her than without her.

"I'm sorry I've disappointed you *and* Jeff. I promise I'll do better." He gazed into her eyes. "Can you believe that?"

It seemed to take a long time before she replied.

"You've never, to my knowledge, lied to me. So, yeah, if you say you'll try, I believe you."

Richard rose from his chair and rushed to meet his wife, capturing her in what he hoped she'd perceive as a loving embrace. "I promise."

Her arms wrapped around him, and she pressed her cheek against his chest. "We're a family. Maybe a ragtag team, but we *are* family. And don't you ever *dare* forget it," she said.

"No, ma'am,"

"And don't call me ma'am," she said firmly.

"No, Ms. Stanley."

She pulled back. "You *can* call me by my name."

A smile quirked his lips. "Brenda."

It was a beautiful name. And she was a beautiful woman who possessed a beautiful soul.

She patted his chest with her right hand. "I need to get things ready. Be nice to him," she said, regaining that firm tone.

He nodded. What else could he do?

She sighed and finally seemed to notice their daughter's fretful noises. She started for the playpen, but Richard held out a hand to stop her. "I'll take care of Betsy-Bets. You take care of Jeff."

She nodded and left the room, while Richard attended to Betsy, lifting her out of detention and giving her a quick kiss. "You're okay," he assured her as she wrapped her little arms around his neck. If only a kiss and a hug could solve all life's problems.

AS I STARTED PACKING a bag to take across the driveway, doubt began creeping into my thoughts. Was I nuts to want to spend time in a house where I'd been profoundly unhappy as a teenager? Where I'd felt like an inconvenience for nearly two months the summer before while my broken leg had healed? And during a time when my brother seemed perfectly content to cut me out of the loop when it came to our newly formed business partnership?

Yeah, I must be completely out of my mind.

But it wasn't Richard who would be there for me. It was Brenda and CP who offered me unconditional love. Hell, I could just avoid Richard most of the time. And I didn't plan to make his home my permanent residence. In fact, I hoped I could come to terms with my relationship with Maggie in days —not weeks or months—before I went back to my … I wasn't sure I ever wanted to call the apartment over the garage home ever again. I didn't feel good about being there. And how many times had that happened during the previous three years? I seemed to slip in and out of favor with my brother, aware that I'd always been a burden to him. I didn't like that feeling. Not one damn bit.

I was determined to find a part-time job and start saving. It might take me a year to have enough to strike out on my own, and I'd sure have to downsize my living accommodations, but I could do it. I'd lived rough before.

With that in mind, once I'd moved my duffle bag, laptop,

and chargers across the drive, I returned to my apartment and cleaned the litter box, glad it had clasps to hold the top to the bottom. Then I loaded an unhappy Herschel into his carrier and took him and his box next door. Once I showed him where to find his box and water and food dishes, I let him loose in the house he was already familiar with. He seemed to settle in much easier than me, seeking out familiar places.

I returned to the living room where Brenda watched TV with CP on the rug before her stacking and knocking over blocks.

"Everything okay in your room?" Brenda asked.

"Perfect. Thanks."

CP ground her little fists into her eye sockets.

"Looks like you've got a sleepy little girl on your hands."

"I don't think I've seen an entire TV show uninterrupted since the day she was born," Brenda lamented.

"I'll put her to bed."

"You wouldn't mind?"

"I'd be honored. I'll even sing her to sleep—albeit off-key."

"Well, if you want," Brenda said.

I bent down and scooped up my niece. "Bedtime, little girl."

CP giggled, that sound a balm to my soul.

"Kiss your girl goodnight," I told Brenda and bent low so she could plant a kiss on the top of her daughter's head. "Say night-night CP." But that silly little girl only giggled once again.

As I changed CP's diaper and zipped her into her pink thermal jammies, I thought about what I ought to do once she fell asleep—and that was to pay Louie another visit. That is, if he hadn't already checked out of this world. If he had, I wouldn't be bound to keep looking into the problems at the brewery.

Abe didn't want to pay R&A Insights for our services. Would he have been less belligerent if I'd told him my fee would be only one dollar? Maybe—maybe not. But then, he wasn't likely to value efforts that came so cheap, either.

I settled CP in her crib and sat in the rocker beside it. She offered no resistance to sleep. I liked to think that she felt safe with me beside her. I watched her little chest rise and fall as she slept and marveled at how special she was—and what lay ahead of her.

Finally, I turned off the light and crept out of her room, silently closing the door.

Once outside in the hall, I straightened. I still had work to do.

THOUGH I only planned to charge Horse Hockey Brewing a buck for my services, I wondered if they would at least pony up for my parking fees at the hospital. Of course, they'd have no idea I made these visits to consult with the brewery's founder, so it looked like R&A Insights would be eating that expense. Well, Richard could well afford it. Meanwhile, I needed to cut my expenses to the bone. Richard had given me a credit card with a twenty-grand max, but I only used it for gas for my car and groceries and used my ATM card to withdraw fifty bucks a week for miscellaneous expenses. Despite his millions, I wasn't living high on the hog at my brother's expense, something he had to know—and if he didn't, I'd be very surprised.

Because it was after visiting hours, I found a good spot in the parking garage, hunkered into my jacket, and crossed the concrete to enter the hospital. A couple of minutes later, I arrived at Louie's room. Once again, Omega was at his side.

"Welcome back, Mr. Resnick," she said, raising her gaze from the book on her lap.

"Where the hell have you been?" Louie's disembodied

spirit hollered from his perpetual perch on the room's window sill.

Omega's gaze traveled to the floor, and a chill ran through me, making me shudder. I hoped she was being paid by the hour. There's nothing more boring than sitting around and doing nothing—especially at a hospital bedside. Not that I dismissed her devotion to her vocation. If nothing else, I was pretty sure she believed that her services did help ease a dying person off to their next plane of existence while comforting those left behind.

"I'd be glad to spell you for a while."

Omega smiled. "I could stand to stretch my legs and get something to eat." At that time of night, the offerings were limited to vending machines with crappy choices for snacks and wretched coffee.

"Go already!" Louie's spirit self practically shouted.

Omega rose from her chair, clasped her back, and winced. "I'll be back in half an hour or so. That should give you more than enough time."

Enough time for what? But before I could ask the question, Omega grabbed her purse and exited the room.

I watched her walk slowly toward the elevator before returning to the cramped room.

"You might want to be a little less negative around Omega," I advised Louie.

"What the hell are you talking about?"

"She's a sensitive. She's aware of you. That you aren't just a vegetable." Our gazes turned to the body lying on the bed.

"Oh, crap," he muttered. "I've been a real prick saying a whole lot of nasty shit every time she held my hand."

"Then you might think about apologizing to her. She might be a big help to us—to help you convey to your heirs what you want to happen to the brewery."

The idea seemed to trouble Louie. "Yeah, but she's—"

Black? Was Louie just a prejudiced jerk? Maybe. And yet, he'd hired a black brewmaster. Abe Bachmann had been an integral part of Horse Hockey's success. Bethany seemed to trust her second in command, but did Louie?

I asked the question.

"Abe's a good guy," he said without conviction.

"But?"

Louie shrugged. "He's just another employee. Nothing special."

Oh, yeah? Then why wouldn't he look me in the eye when he said that? The brewmaster was *the* single most important employee when it came to making beer. Why was Louie downplaying Abe's role at the brewery? Was that an angle I needed to explore? I doubted I'd get very far pushing Louie for answers. Perhaps I should try to speak to Bethany one-on-one to get that information. Or was I grasping at straws? Louie's relationship with his brewmaster had little to do with his son Nick's push to sell the brewery.

"Hey, you should be talking to me," Louie growled.

"Okay. Your daughter doesn't think I need to be paid for my efforts to try to save your brewery from being sold out from under her—despite not even asking what my fee would be."

"Yeah, well, the brewery's at the mercy of the market. Cash flow can be a problem." He squinted at me. "How much were you planning to gouge us?"

I glared at the non-corporeal image of the man. I was really beginning to dislike Louie Susskind. "A buck."

Louie blinked, his mouth gaping. Then his brow furrowed. "Why so cheap? Are you working on so many other cases that you're giving us short shrift?"

It was evident Louie had never taken a Dale Carnegie course because he definitely had no idea how to win friends and influence people.

"At this time, you're my only case."

He frowned. "So, your business is a failure." It wasn't a question.

"To be honest, you're only my *second* case. We've only officially been in business for about a month."

Louie looked even more skeptical. "Why only a buck?"

I heaved a sigh. I didn't want to explain the predicament Sophie put me in, and I didn't think Louie would accept an explanation that had to do with me employing my unique gifts. And the way things were going, this might be my only case with R&A Insights. When Richard finally convinced me to go into business with him, I thought that would bring us closer together. Instead, he seemed to be using the case he'd acquired to drive us apart. That move didn't endear me to him. And, in fact, I now felt as pinned as I had as a teenager. Stuck with no authority and dependent on his goodwill. Decades later, I resented it just as much.

"Well?" Louie demanded when I hadn't answered his question.

I took a few long moments before answering.

"I have this…." God, it pained me to say the words. "—gift of being able to see—talk—to people in your predicament. Some are actually … dead."

"I'm *not* dead," Louie declared.

Not technically, but in a coma with his life signs ebbing as the hours ticked by, he was as good as gone.

"Souls in your situation can't pay, even if their survivors can. My contract is with you, and I'll try to abide by it as best as I can."

Louie shook his head. "Then you're an asshole."

Yeah, I was.

"What else do you want me to do?" I asked him.

Louie's eyes widened until they practically blazed, but he kept silent. If there was a transgression he was ashamed of, I had a feeling he wasn't about to reveal it to me. Had he once unburdened himself in a church confessional? If so, then he probably felt he was in the clear. Then why had his reaction to my question been so explosive?

Finally, Louie's head drooped, and he looked across the room to the sad, pale form on the bed. "Find some way to keep Nick and Teresa from selling the brewery. Please," he added as an afterthought.

He would never tell me the truth about what was wrong at the brewery and neither would Bethany or Abe. I was going to have to figure that out for myself.

"I'll try my best," I told Louie.

What else could I say?

Chapter 18

Richard resisted the urge to pour another drink and stared at his computer screen. His idea to contact Marcel's high school classmates, which had seemed like such a good idea hours before, now seemed daunting. He'd paid for a year's subscription to a website that featured PDF files of yearbooks and downloaded the edition for Marcel Clark's senior year. With more than three hundred graduates that year, the males had outnumbered the females by only ten. That meant a potential hundred and seventy guys he would have to vet. Forty percent were white, so he subtracted them from the mix, which was a calculated risk. Marcel had been a member of the school's basketball team, but there was no mention of his prowess on the court. There were five white dudes on the team. Marcel could have been best friends with any of them, but he concentrated on the names of the black teammates.

Marcel was only one of three black students pictured in the chess club's group photo. These extra-curricular activities were the perfect additions to include on a college application.

Marcel, the prime suspect in Mrs. Johnson's death hadn't been some kind of scholastic slacker. And it was only the redacted testimony of the unnamed source that had caused the cops to decide the young man should be considered their prime suspect.

Richard pulled up the reports that Detective Destross had provided for him. Two officers: Charles Taylor and Peter Jones, investigated the case. After a Google search, he learned that Taylor had been fired from the Buffalo PD for falsifying reports in a push for convictions. Six cases had so far been overturned because of his intimidation of witnesses. His partner had resigned as a consequence. If Richard could track either of them down, it might explain why they'd settled on Marcel as a suspect and give law enforcement a reason to consider the young man as their top suspect.

But the more he dug, the more downhearted Richard felt. Taylor had died by suicide more than a decade before. Was that because so many of the prosecutions he'd testified on had been overturned and that gave attorneys for the other people he'd fingered and still resided as guests of the state?

Richard found an old address and phone number for Peter Jones but when he called, the number had been reassigned. He wondered if Destross would give up the information as he would like to speak with Jones. The question was…would the man talk to him. And even if he did, would Richard believe anything he had to say?

ALL WAS quiet when I returned to the Alpert family home after I visited with Louie. I saw a crack of light under the door of the master bedroom. Brenda was probably reading, or more likely was asleep and had left the light on for when Richard came up from his study. I peeked into CP's room, where she was still asleep, and quietly closed the door.

I'd finished my nightly rituals and climbed into bed, leaving the door open a crack for Herschel to join me, and was about to turn out the light when my phone's ringtone sounded. I stabbed the call icon to quiet it and saw that it was Maggie calling. My heart actually skipped a beat as I answered it.

"Hey, Maggs, what's up?" I asked as a ridiculous thread of pleasure coursed through me. She'd called. *I* hadn't had to be the one to initiate the contact. A win—or was I just kidding myself?

"I just called to see if you want to talk dirty," she said slyly.

"Dirty?" It wasn't something we'd ever done as a prelude to sex.

"Yeah, you know—have a little phone sex."

Who was this woman on the other end of the conversation?

"Not particularly."

"Oh." She sounded disappointed. Had she been having phone sex with someone else?

"I hear you've moved back into the Alpert home," Maggie said with what sounded like a touch of scorn. She'd either spoken with or texted Brenda.

"Yeah," I said, my heart sinking. "But it's just for a few days."

"How come?"

I took a chance and spoke the truth. "Because I'm lonely." There, I'd said it out loud.

"Is that crack aimed at me?" she asked with an edge to her tone.

"No, it's a fact. My job isn't exactly going all that well and since the bar closed, I don't get to see a lot of people on a regular basis."

"What about little *Emily*?" she asked, her tone a tad snarky.

"She's an employee."

"And?"

"She makes a good cup of coffee, and that's about the extent of her job responsibilities right now."

"Then why don't you let her go?"

So I could be alone for another eight hours of the day?

"Richard hired her. It's Richard's business. He can do as he pleases."

"Then why are you the only one who goes to the office on a regular basis?" she challenged.

That was a good question. Had Brenda shared that tidbit, too?

"Richard does what Richard does. How goes *your* job?" I asked, not that I wanted to hear the answer.

"It was the best career move I've ever made," Maggie gushed, her demeanor doing a fast one-eighty and launched into a recitation of everything she'd accomplished that day, rhapsodizing about her wonderful workmates, and the incredible weather, and the great view from her apartment. I only caught a few words here and there as Herschel suddenly appeared, jumping on the bed and demanding my attention, which I was glad to give him. Maggie yammered on, and I petted my boy until a noise in the passage caught the cat's attention and he jumped down to investigate. I yawned.

"Am I boring you?" Maggie asked tartly.

"Maggs, it's after midnight, and I have to be at the office by eight."

"Oh. Sorry. I forgot about the time difference."

Sure she did.

"I go to bed a lot earlier than I did when I worked at the bar," I reminded her.

"And you *still* miss it?"

Desperately.

I kept my tone neutral. "Yeah."

"Maybe you should give up playing consultant." She hadn't voiced that she thought bartending was beneath me, but maybe she'd felt that way all along. Did she think I couldn't hack being an investigator, as well?

I ignored her suggestion.

"I'm glad you called," I lied. "But I'm bushed. I've really got to hit the sack."

"Okay. Talk to you soon," she promised. "I love you."

"Back atcha," I said, without feeling.

"Nighty-night."

I stabbed the end call icon. "Good night." That said, I was pretty sure I wouldn't have one.

I turned off the light and rolled onto my side, but I knew sleep wouldn't come any time soon. I wondered if I should get dressed and go to the bakery to talk to Sophie, but what was I going to tell her? She knew what I was up against and hadn't had any advice to give.

I could watch TV or read—goodness knows there were plenty of books on the shelves across the room, from mystery novels to DIY, most of them Brenda's books. Richard's choice of reading tended to lean toward medical journals.

Herschel jumped up on the bed once again and nestled against my chest, purring loudly. I rubbed his ears and he relaxed even more.

Did I feel better in Richard's house, or was I fooling myself? I wasn't sure. I wasn't going to get a lot of quality time with my family during the workweek, but spending time with CP and Brenda over the weekend (or weekends, depending on how long I stayed), would be good for my soul. And yet it was Richard I really wanted to connect with. Why was he being such a secretive jerk?

I knew one thing for sure; if he became snarky or resentful, my time in his home would be over. I'd slink back to my apartment across the driveway and start planning my next move to give up R&A Insights and once and for all get the hell out from under Richard's financial umbrella.

For all I'd been through these past four years, I was back to square one. No money, no assets, and now I had a cat to support.

"I'm sorry, Herschel," I apologized. "Maybe I should have given you up when old Chester died. You might have found a happy home with a family who loved you and given you a much better life than I've been able to offer you."

Herschel's purr revved up as though to refute my words.

"I love you, too, buddy."

My cat rested a paw on my hand. He was a cat. He couldn't possibly know how comforting that small gesture of outreach meant to me, but I soon fell asleep because of it.

And I dreamed.

Maybe it was Maggie's suggestion of talking dirty that caused my mind to dwell on sex, but something about this dream was different.

Oh, it was good...it was *really* good, but it was weird because...because....

Oh, that lovely climax....

Except...except....

It wasn't me who'd experienced that exquisite high....

It was Maggie ... and she hadn't experienced it alone.

I woke up sweating, my heart pounding.

And I wondered who'd been on the receiving end of Maggie's affection.

Chapter 19

The following morning, I left the house before the rest of the family woke up. Coward that I am, I didn't want to have to talk to Richard. The fact that he hadn't acknowledged my return to his home didn't bode well. But staying at his house meant I could be away for long periods knowing Brenda and CP would give Herschel lots of attention *if* he sought them out. He was used to them and especially seemed to enjoy CP's company. Damn, I loved that little girl. I had some hard decisions to make about my future. If/when I went out on my own, I'd probably have to cut ties. That meant losing a close connection with CP and Brenda. That would be the hardest.

But wasn't I getting ahead of myself? Richard had been an asshole for only a couple of weeks. Should I discard the previous three years because of that?

I wasn't sure.

I was also feeling crappy about Maggie. Had she just been dreaming the previous night and just transmitted her feelings and sensations to me, or had she actually been with another guy and I'd just been an accidental voyeur of their tryst?

I didn't want to think about it.

I arrived at the office more than an hour before Emily was due to arrive. We hadn't hired a cleaning service, which was my decision to keep expenses to a minimum for a business I wasn't sure would succeed. So it was me who vacuumed the place and cleaned the bathroom. After being tasked with cleaning the cans at the Whole Nine Yards for nearly two years, swabbing out the R&A washroom was a cinch. No puke or piss on the floor or backed-up toilets to plunge. It was practically heaven.

By the time Emily arrived for work, the place was tidy, and a fresh pot of coffee awaited her.

"Someone's been busy," she commented as she took off her coat, hat, and scarf and hung them up.

I expected her to grab a mug from the shelf under the coffeemaker, but instead, she went straight to her desk where she donned the sweater that hung on the back of her chair. I could sense a change in her demeanor, but I wasn't exactly sure what it was. Sadder somehow. And I wasn't about to ask her about it.

"Anything special happening today?" she asked.

I frowned. "Just trying to find a way to keep the Horse Hockey Brewery from being sold. I thought I might try to talk to Bethany Susskind alone, but I'm not sure she'd be up for it. She seems very tense."

"Something seems really wrong at that brewery," Emily commented.

"Yeah, but what?"

She shrugged. "I typed up my notes. Have you read them?"

"Not yet, but I will before I try to talk to her. I thought it odd that the production line was down," I commented.

"They have a lot of unsold product. What's with that?" she asked.

"A bad batch of beer that they know they can't sell?" I suggested.

"Maybe. If it got out that they had all those pallets full of cans and kegs full of skunky beer, maybe no one would *want* to buy their brewery. Maybe Bethany knows that, and that's why she's insisting it isn't the right time to try to sell the business."

Holy crap! Emily had figured out what I hadn't seen with my own eyes. And why was that?

"That's a great assessment," I told her. "But I think there has to be more to it than just that."

"Isn't that enough?" she asked.

I grabbed a mug and poured myself some coffee, doctoring it up. "I don't think so."

"Well, if you ask me, Bethany is screwing her brewmaster."

"Emily!" I scolded her.

"Well, wasn't it obvious?"

No, it hadn't been. But it made sense now that she pointed it out. "What made you think so?"

"The way she looked at him before answering any of our questions. Technically, she might be in charge of the brewery, but I don't think it's her who's calling the shots."

That made a lot of sense. Bethany might be the one dealing with the paperwork that kept the brewery in compliance with health codes, paying the bills, and everything else that went into keeping a business alive. But it was Abe who brewed the beer.

And it seemed like something had gone terribly wrong with a whole lot of beer—and maybe not one batch judging by the inventory sitting in their warehouse.

The word *sabotage* settled in my thoughts. But why would Abe, who *might* be Bethany's lover, want to sink the Horse Hockey ship?

Ship.

The thought brought me back to Nick's desire to sell the brewery to possibly fund his maritime pursuits.

Oh, what a tangled web … and there was more than one person trying to deceive me. Louie was at the top of that list.

But why? He'd recruited me, after all. That said, he wasn't the first who'd tried to distract me with a line of crap. When I'd been an insurance investigator in Manhattan, I'd had plenty of clients lie to me when filing claims. It was the main reason I'd moved to the crime unit so that I didn't have to deal with such bullshit artists. I excelled, but the work had been soul-sucking. Still, being good at the job meant I was pretty much left alone … until they'd elevated me to manage the unit, a promotion I should have turned down. Not because I stunk in the position but because it kept me behind a desk supervising a team of backstabbers who used every petty excuse to try to get rid of me. It took two years, but they finally succeeded.

Emily pulled a sleeve of saltines from her desk drawer and opened it. "So what do you think?" she asked before munching on a cracker.

"That you're right. Something very fishy is going on at Horse Hockey Brewing."

"I wonder if this would help." Emily shuffled through several envelopes from her in-basket before handing me a plain white one. "This came in yesterday's mail. To tell you the truth, I almost threw it away. I mean, it looks like junk mail. But then I thought some friend of yours or the doc might want you guys to know about it."

I took the standard No. 10 envelope from her and held the ends between the fingers of both hands, hoping to get some kind of vibe. Yeah, and I got one—Emily's. The top of the envelope had been slit and held a single piece of standard copy paper. Printed on that paper was an obituary from a local funeral home. It looked like a screenshot off a computer. These days, not many people want to pay for an obit in *The Buffalo News*. One word of the obituary immediately jumped out at me

—and why not, because it was highlighted in yellow: Unexpectedly.

I read the brief account

Roberto Gonzalez. Unexpectedly called to Heaven on March 10th at age 46. Predeceased by his parents, Antonio & Selena Gonzalez; sister, Marisol Torres. He is survived by his wife, Elena Gonzalez; children; Delores (Dante) Ortiz, Elenora Torres, & Roberto Gonzalez Jr.

It went on to tell the time of the viewing and internment.

So who was this guy, and why would someone want to bring him to my attention?

I closed my eyes, waiting for one of my funny feelings to come over me, wishing Emily hadn't touched the paper, because the remnants of her aura were interfering with whatever psychic signature was attached to it.

I looked at the envelope more closely. It was addressed exactly the same as my business card. I hadn't handed out a slew of them. The most recent went to Bethany Susskind, Abe Bachmann, and Omega Dustin, who I immediately discounted. I had a feeling Roberto was linked to the brewery.

So, had Bethany wanted me to know about Gonzalez without letting Abe in on her indiscretion? Or was it the other way around?

I gave the envelope the same touch test. Unfortunately, it, too, was contaminated by Emily's touch. I frowned. I really didn't want to have to open all the mail. But then, were we likely to regularly get stuff I'd need to touch to suss out information?

"Did you know the guy who died?" Emily asked.

I shook my head and topped up my coffee, then waved the envelope in her direction. "Back to work."

It didn't take long for me to find the source of the obit. One of the Amigone Funeral Homes. You had to love that name. I checked social media sites and found Roberto on Facebook. His photo album was filled with pictures of family members and events, and pictures taken at Horse Hockey Brewing and some of their promotions.

Bethany and Abe were still my top suspects for mailing the obituary. The question was, why?

It didn't take me long to track down where Roberto lived, and when I called the house, a woman with a Hispanic accent answered.

"Mrs. Gonzalez?"

"Yes."

"My name is Jeffery Resnick, and I'm a consultant working with Horse Hockey Brewing. I understand your husband was employed there."

"Si," she said with hesitancy.

"Do you mind if I ask what he did there?"

"If you work for the brewery, shouldn't you know?"

Damn. I'd hoped she wasn't going to ask that. I took a wild guess. "He was involved in a work accident, was he not?"

"Si."

Unexpectedly.

"Have you heard from the insurance company about—"

"I don't think I should be talking to you," she said and hung up.

I replaced the phone's receiver and sat back in my chair. So, Roberto died as a result of a work accident. But what? Would Louie, Bethany, or Abe answer if I asked them about it? It occurred to me that every time I'd visited the brewery, I felt … unsettled seemed the best descriptor. Was it because of Roberto's accident?

I tried Googling recent workplace accidents but couldn't find anything. Surely *The Buffalo News* or the local TV stations would have covered something like that…unless he hadn't died on site. Maybe he'd suffered an accident and died at the hospital or even en route.

I'd just have to keep poking around and hope I hit pay dirt.

Feeling antsy, I picked up my empty coffee cup and headed for the coffee station. As always, Emily sat behind her desk. She looked up. "Was that announcement of any use?"

"Some. The man suffered an accident at the brewery that ultimately killed him."

"Whoa. No wonder everybody there seemed to be looking over their shoulders. Do you think they're going to get sued?"

"I wouldn't be surprised. But that's just one of the things going down at the brewery. Now to figure out why someone wanted me to know about it. My first thought was that Bethany or Abe sent it, but now I'm not sure."

"Who else knows we're working with the brewery?" Emily asked.

"The family, maybe the woman who let us in the door yesterday—Portia. Oh, and Omega."

"Why don't you ask her?"

"I'm not sure she's been told anything about the business."

"You won't know until you ask. Maybe you should make that a priority, if only to rule it out."

My, but Emily was becoming a pushy broad.

"I could," I promised. "I wasn't able to find out where Omega lives, which is kind of odd. I could go to the hospital, but she seems to show up later in the afternoon."

"Maybe someone at the hospital knows about her."

"She does interact with the nursing staff and techs?"

"You could talk to them."

I sure had nothing better to do.

"Great idea. And if Omega's there, I'll try to speak to her—and not within Louie's earshot."

"Offer to take her to lunch," Emily suggested.

"And what if she isn't willing to leave him alone?"

"Maybe you could text her," Emily said.

It was worth a shot—if only I had her number. The doula

seemed to be attached to her phone 24/7. I might have to slip her a note to get it.

I abandoned the idea of another cup of coffee and instead grabbed my coat. "I think I'll head over to the hospital now. I'll let you know my plans for the rest of the day as soon as I figure them out."

"I'll be here," Emily said, sounding just a little more cheerful than she'd been all morning.

"See ya," I said, and headed out the door.

I FELT good about our conversation as I got in my car and drove toward Sisters Hospital. Though Emily was still freaked about what I could do when it came to talking to the nearly departed, she hadn't voiced a desire to quit. Of course, we paid her far better than she was likely to get anywhere else. Then again, I wasn't *forcing* her to believe. All she had to do, at least at this point, was answer the phone and perform the duties of a secretary.

It was only eleven-thirty when I arrived at the hospital. I parked and walked toward the elevators, recognizing one of the techs from Louie's floor standing in the cold and smoking a cigarette. You'd think someone in the healthcare field would be well aware of the hazards of smoking, but there she was—a woman of about thirty, dressed in maroon scrubs and an unzipped parka, puffing away.

"Excuse me." She gave me a wary look. "But you work on the fourth floor, and Louis Susskind is one of the people you take care of, right?"

"I can't give you any information on a patient," she said rather gruffly. She had a smoker's voice to boot.

"I was wondering about the woman who sits with him in the evenings."

Her eyes widened. "You mean the voodoo lady?"

"That's the one."

"They say she chants incantations over the old man's body, but mostly she just sits there and reads or is on her phone. I guess the family's paying her for that."

"Do you know when she comes in for the day?"

The woman shrugged. "She stays the night, then the guy's daughter comes for a few hours to spell her, I guess so she can go home, have a shower, change clothes, and eat something decent."

"What time does she usually show up in the afternoon?" I asked again.

"Around four, when the shift changes."

I nodded. "Thanks."

With this knowledge in hand, I decided not to visit Louie until later, hoping to catch Omega before she got to his room that afternoon.

Instead, I returned to my car and called my friend, Sam.

"Hey, haven't heard from you since we talked to Nick Susskind. Anything new?" I asked.

"Not a damn thing—at least on him. I did some digging, and the guy seems to be legit in his quest to protect the wrecks on the Great Lakes."

I was afraid of that.

"Have you got any theories?" Sam asked.

"Only that I think there's a lot of unsaleable beer sitting in the brewery's warehouse. I haven't been able to ascertain if it was a mistake or sabotage. Also, one of their employees recently died on the job. A Roberto Gonazales."

"Interesting," Same said.

"Can you look into it?"

"If I have time," Sam said. "Have you found out more about your almost-dead guy?"

"Not really. I've got a couple of leads I'll try to chase down today. I need to do a deeper dive looking into the brewery's black brewmaster."

"A black guy? I guess I always think of brewmasters as being German. You know, fat white guys wearing lederhosen, funny hats with feathers, and a damn great stein in hand, with maybe a polka playing in the background."

"Do you think you can sell your interview with Nick Susskind to your editor?"

"Hell, yes. Send me your photos. As I alluded, they're thinking the Sunday Home and Style page in May or June would be perfect."

Okay, it would be a few months before that happened, and Louie would be long gone by then, but whether his spirit had left this earth was another subject.

"What else have you found out?" Sam asked.

"Damn near nothing. But I've got a lead I'll investigate later this afternoon."

"Anything I can add to my story?"

"Sorry, I'm just accumulating background information."

"Well, if it amounts to anything, call me." Yeah, I owed him. I owed him a lot. But if he could squeeze a feature out of Nick Susskind's hobby, my debt to him would be a trifle smaller.

I didn't bother going back to the office, and I didn't return to Richard's home or my apartment, either. Instead, I stopped at a tavern and ordered a beer and a beef on weck sandwich. I sat alone at a back table with a pad and pen, noodling ideas. Ideas about Louie, his business, his heirs, and whether when—not if—he died if he'd tether himself to this world instead of moving on to whatever oblivion awaited him.

I probably should have gone back to the office or back to Richard's house since I still had a shitload of laundry that needed to be folded or ironed. Instead, I went to the Boulevard Mall, which was on life support, but it gave me an opportunity to walk its heated tile floors to kill time and think until I could return to the hospital and intercept Omega.

It also gave me far too much time to think about where I was with Maggie, staying with Richard, and how I was afraid I might—just might—be attracted to Emily.

She wasn't beautiful—but then neither was Maggie—although she had some appealing qualities. Maggie was four years older than me. Emily was fourteen years younger. Quite the age difference. Then again, Richard and Brenda had a twelve-year disparity, and they made it work. I was getting too far ahead of myself. During the past month, Emily's disdain for me had grown almost daily.

I felt conflicted. Part of me was attracted to her, and the other half was repelled and damned annoyed. That wasn't a place to encourage a relationship.

And why would I even think of her in that context? I was technically still part of a couple with Maggie. Technically described the problem because I knew Maggie was already cheating on me. I'd known that would happen from the first time she'd mentioned taking the so-called temporary assignment in San Diego.

So, were Maggie and I to be free spirits on different coasts who fucked who we pleased and just pretended to be monogamous? I didn't like that scenario, either.

I felt caught in the middle. If I cut ties with Maggie, her dog was still living in Richard's home. He loved Holly. Though it had only been a short time since he'd taken the dog on, it was obvious that he would never willingly give her up. Richard had deep pockets and if it came to a lawsuit, it was likely—though not a given—that he might prevail.

I glanced at my watch. It was time to head back to the hospital.

Chapter 20

I intercepted Omega on Louie's floor at the end of the corridor. She looked dead tired, no doubt from the seemingly endless days and nights she'd spent at Louie's bedside.

"Ah, Mr. Resnick," she said in greeting.

"Call me Jeff. Excuse me, but would you have time to have a cup of coffee and a chat with me before going to see your patient?"

She flashed a toothy grin. "I was wondering when you'd get around to asking. But we must make it quick. Mrs. Barton is expecting me shortly."

It didn't take much persuasion to convince her to skip the vending machine coffee for the real stuff in the hospital cafeteria. We got our brews and settled at a table in a corner, away from the visitors and staff, where I hoped we could speak freely without being overheard.

I'd rehearsed several ways to bring up the subject of Louie's disembodied spirit, but Omega saved me the trouble.

"You have a gift," she began.

God, I hated that word. "Some might call it that."

"I, too, have such a gift, but not as pronounced as yours."

She shook her head and took a sip of her coffee. "I was born with it, but I sense that you attained yours in another way."

"My grandmother told me I always had it, but it wasn't until I suffered a skull fracture that it—" I paused to think of the best descriptor. "Blossomed."

"And you've been communicating with Mr. Susskind for how long?"

I told her the circumstances of Louie's and my first meeting, and some of what we'd spoken about—but not everything. I wasn't sure how much I could trust this so-called voodoo lady with the pentagram pendant. Time was short, so I figured I'd better start asking questions and getting answers.

"Louie told me he's said some nasty things about you."

"I would not know that," she began, but then seemed to change her mind. "Exactly. I cannot communicate with the near-dead in the way that you do, but I do absorb feelings and attitudes. Mr. Susskind is a very angry man. He feels his work on this earth is not complete."

She had that right.

"Can you hear him speak?"

"Not exactly. It's more like a voice from far away, but not being able to decipher the words."

I nodded. "Why do you think he's hung on for as long as he has?"

Omega's eyes widened. "Because of you. Since you arrived, he has hope that you may solve his earthly problems. This holding pattern he's in has confounded the doctors and nurses," she admitted.

"And his children?"

"I am only privy to Mrs. Barton's thoughts on that."

"And what does she think?"

"She worries he's suffering. I have assured her he isn't. Do you concur?"

"Maybe suffering emotionally—about the brewery."

She nodded.

"Has Teresa indicated she'd like him to move on?" I asked.

Omega shrugged. "She would not be the first. I've often noticed impatience from family members. They love their dying relative, but waiting for the inevitable—an outcome they cannot change through prayers or good thoughts—is an agony they don't know how to bear."

I knew what she meant. In a way, I was spared a lot of that angst when my mother was dying in a hospital across the city from our crappy apartment. I was just a kid. All alone and with no support system, I concentrated my efforts to keep my life from unraveling by going to school, focusing on my homework, doing the laundry, and washing the dishes. I did everything I could to keep my mind from thinking about the cloud of doom that seemed to hang over me.

And then Richard showed up one day as I was leaving classes, and I knew my mother was dead.

"I'm sorry if my efforts are keeping you in this holding pattern," I apologized.

Omega waved a hand in dismissal. "But this is my work. This is what I'm paid to do, and it will not last much longer."

Was her pronouncement Louie's death sentence?

"Will he pass on soon?"

Again she shrugged. "There are subtle indications." She didn't elaborate.

I studied her tired features, wondering if I should trust her. After several long moments, I figured *what the hell.* Louie wasn't being honest with me. It felt like Omega was.

"Louie has not been truthful with me. He's hiding a secret—a shameful one. I think he's afraid I'll figure it out, expose it, and that it would harm—maybe destroy—the brewery."

Saying what I felt aloud made it sound overly dramatic but nonetheless true.

Omega studied my face. "Is this something you think Mrs. Barton would know?"

I nodded. "I think all three of his children know the secret, and all are terrified it will become known. I think that's why Louie's son and Mrs. Barton are so eager to sell the brewery. It isn't their secret, but it could bring shame to their family, potentially ruining their lives—at least in the short term."

"And selling the brewery would hide the secret?" Omega asked.

"Not necessarily. But it might separate them from the shame of what their father had allowed to fester."

Omega sipped the last of her coffee and looked thoughtful. "What do you propose to do to solve this situation?"

"I have no idea," I answered honestly.

Omega looked down at one of the many silver rings that graced every finger and thumb of her hands. "You may be looking in the wrong direction," she stated at last.

"In what way?"

"It's just a feeling. I don't think the family will be of help when it comes to deciphering what's going on. It's not in their best interests."

"I don't have a lot to go on."

"I think you do. You just haven't figured out what that is."

"And can you help me in that regard?"

Omega offered a wisp of a smile. "No. Once again, it's just a feeling."

That wasn't at all helpful.

Omega turned her attention to the big analog clock on the wall. "I must get back to Mr. Susskind's room. His daughter will be eager to turn her vigil over to me."

"How does that make you feel?"

"It's my job. It's what I do. I lessen the burden on my clients when death is near."

Her client being Teresa Barton, not Teresa's father.

"You see, Mr. Susskind's death is only the beginning of my work with the Barton family. I am there to comfort Mr. Susskind, but my primary job is to walk his survivors through the mourning process."

I sure wished I'd had someone to do the same for me when my mother died—and even when I'd lost the father I'd only known for days before he left this earthly plane. In some ways, that parting had been even harder to manage.

I didn't like to think about it.

"What do you know about hospice care, Mr. Resnick?"

"That patients are usually so doped up they feel nothing and just die."

"Not precisely. In Mr. Susskind's case, he is not being given drugs such as morphine. There's no need for that. But he is no longer being given the medicines that kept him alive. They've turned off his pacemaker. Lying flat on his back, he will most likely die of pneumonia, as they usually do."

She said the words so matter of factly, but then how many similar deaths had she witnessed?

"If you'd like, I can give you a pamphlet that explains the dying process. Perhaps if you knew what to expect, you wouldn't feel so anxious," Omega said.

Just talking about death the way she did made me feel anxious. "That's very kind of you."

Omega smiled wanly. "It's my life's work. You see, we both have our destinies, Mr. Resnick." She reached into her canvas tote bag, shuffled through its contents for a few moments, and came up with the literature, handing the booklet to me.

"I'll make sure to read it today."

She nodded and rose. We discarded our cardboard coffee cups and headed for Louie's room.

Once there, I hung back as Omega spoke with Louie's daughter, who seemed eager to leave the room of impending death. Yeah, much as she loved her father, Teresa seemed impatient that his struggle to hang onto life in a vegetative state was delaying his death. I felt sorry for the poor woman, who spent a moment thanking me for my visits to cheer her father.

"Cheer hell," Louie shouted at me from his perpetual perch on the room's lone window sill.

I ignored him.

Teresa gathered up her things and left in a hurry. I couldn't blame her. She had a family in crisis that needed her leadership. It was a heavy burden to shoulder.

Louie grumbled to himself as Omega settled in the chair beside his bed. She grasped his body's hand and squeezed it. "I'm here for you, Mr. Susskind. Feel free to tell Mr. Resnick what I may do to help you on your journey."

"Journey?" Louie shouted. "I sure as hell ain't goin' nowhere." Then he seemed to take in what Omega had said. "Are you guys in cahoots?" he accused.

"You might say that," I told him.

Louie's anger flared. "I don't want her here. Have you told her that?"

"She knows," I said. "She's here because it's a comfort to Teresa, so she doesn't have to feel guilty taking care of her own family, who aren't doing all that well."

"The hell with Teresa. And you can tell that—that black bitch that, too."

I knew the word he'd really wanted to say.

I stood straighter, my anger boiling. "Don't you dare call her that again, or you can up and die and I won't lift a finger to help save your fucking brewery."

Omega turned her gaze toward me, her dark eyes wide. She might not have heard Louie's words, but she had obviously understood the negativity he'd expounded. I needed another answer. "What happened to Roberto Gonzales?"

"Who's he?"

Had Louie been incapacitated before Roberto's accident?

Maybe.

This seemed a good time to push him on the secret he was harboring. I took a few moments to figure out how to phrase my questions.

"You haven't been honest with me. You've done nothing but lie and misdirect me since the moment we met. Why the hell should I continue to help you?"

"Because you've got no choice," Louie said, his tone a taunt.

"Bullshit."

"No, really—you're a sucker, Resnick. I see things a lot clearer in my current state. I can read people like the back of my hand. You, Teresa, and even Nick."

"And?" I asked.

"You can't walk away from me and my problems. You're stuck. Like your shoes are encased in cement. And if you don't do as I say, even when my body fails, I can be a thorn in your side for the rest of your life because, as you said, even if I'm dead, I don't *have* to go. I can continue on for decades—maybe even centuries. I can be here forever and ever and, if nothing else, I'll make your life a living hell," he sneered

"Why?" I asked.

"Because I *can.*"

Was that true? At that moment, Louie's spirit seemed to be anchored to that hospital floor. But what would happen when his body died? Would he then have free reign to terrorize the world at large—and especially me?

I turned to Omega. "I think you should leave."

"But why?" she asked.

"Because Mr. Susskind is a shit as a person."

"But as I told you, I'm not really here for *him,*" Omega said.

"I understand that you want to help his daughter, but—"

"Yeah, tell her to get the hell out of here, too!" Louie's disembodied self bellowed.

"He's toxic, and I'm worried that he could hurt you," I pressed.

Omega's eyes widened, and then her mouth quirked into a smile. "He cannot hurt me—nor you, either."

I wasn't so sure.

"Omega—" I implored.

She shook her head. "Go. You have other things to attend to."

How—or what—did she know? What was she *not* saying?

"Will you be safe?"

Omega's smile was enigmatic. "Oh, yes."

I had no option but to believe her. I stepped closer and reached for her free hand, squeezing it. "I hope you're right," I whispered.

She mouthed one word: "Go."

Without another word, I turned and left the room, but I hadn't gotten far when Louie's spirit chased after me, yelling abuse. I headed for the stairs, yanked the door open, and hurried down them.

As I suspected, Louie wasn't able to follow.

Would that be true once his body died?

I sure as hell hoped so.

I'D ARRIVED at the Alpert domicile just in time for dinner. That night, Brenda had prepared baked chicken thighs dipped in bread crumbs, garlic powder, Parmesan cheese, and Italian seasoning. It smelled terrific. Richard acknowledged my presence without a word but at least nodded as I settled at the dinner table. Brenda presented me with a watery bourbon on the rocks.

"Did you have a good day?" she asked. I could tell she needed me to answer in the affirmative.

"Kind of. I had an interesting encounter with Louie's death doula."

I could feel Brenda's apprehension hitch up at that descriptor.

"So, tell all," Richard said and picked up the glass. It was dark amber. No soda had touched that Scotch.

I told all.

Richard scrutinized the ice in his glass. "The family's harboring a dire secret?" he asked skeptically.

I nodded.

"What do you make of that?" Brenda asked as she set a bowl of peas before Betsy, who was once again strapped in her highchair.

"Something about the whole situation feels off. Omega's aware something is about to go down, but she didn't seem inclined to talk about it."

"Do *you* think something dire is in the offing?" Brenda asked.

She wasn't going to like my answer.

"Yeah," I answered honestly. "The question is, dire for whom?"

"As long as it's not you," she said, decanting the night's veggies into bowls. Peas, broccoli, and grocery-store rolls piled on a plate.

When everything was on the table and we'd helped ourselves, the conversation turned to other things, none of which was particularly interesting. That was actually good. I craved the ordinary. It helped blunt the sharp edges of too many areas of my life that irritated my soul.

As usual, Richard disappeared as soon as our plates were emptied, and I hung back to help Brenda clean up the mess. If

I say so myself, I'm damn good at rinsing dishes. It wasn't rocket science, after all.

"Thanks for helping."

"It's the least I can do."

Brenda scrubbed the last of the pots. "Have you spoken to Maggie lately?"

I wasn't sure I wanted to answer that question. Brenda noticed my hesitation.

"For what it's worth, I—" But then she didn't elaborate.

"Know she's cheating on me?" I asked calmly.

Brenda wouldn't look at me and kept scrubbing the same spot on the stainless steel saucepan.

"It's okay," I told her. "I already know for sure. Boy, did I get the message."

"Message?" Brenda asked timidly.

"We may be three thousand miles apart, but we're still connected on more than one level."

"Oh, God," Brenda muttered, scrubbing even harder.

"Yes, I do believe she called out that deity more than once during the episode."

Brenda let out an exasperated breath. "I'm so sorry, hon."

"What have you got to be sorry about?"

"Sorry what she's done to you. That you had to experience it. That it feels like a betrayal to you every time I read a text from her telling me how friggin' happy she is in California and pretend I don't know what's going on."

"I don't want to come between you guys—to ruin your friendship."

"Oh, I think that's already a casualty. That and the fact that Richard isn't likely to give up her dog without a fight." She shook her head, examined the now soapless steel wool pad, rinsed the pot, and handed it to me. I dried it and put it away while Brenda assessed the kitchen. It was clean, with no peas on the floor and Betsy dozing in her highchair.

"What will you do now?" Brenda asked me as she extricated the sleeping toddler.

I shrugged. "Probably feed my cat, go upstairs, and veg out in front of the TV."

"No, I mean about Maggie."

My gaze traveled to the floor. "I don't know. Try to ignore her."

"Can you do that?"

"I can try." It occurred to me that I might want to discuss the situation with Omega—but not just yet. Sophie had been no help. Could the death doula help me in more than one situation? I wasn't sure. I'd have to think about it.

Chapter 21

I felt like a teenager sneaking out of the house when, holding onto my shoes, I tiptoed down the hall and the grand staircase. Once downstairs, I slid into my loafers and headed for the butler's pantry and my jacket. After locking up, I crossed the drive to the garage, retrieved my car, and headed north up LeBrun Road. It only took five minutes to arrive and park on the side street near Sophie's bakery. The place was dark as I approached the door to the establishment, but seconds later, the light in the backroom flared. Moments later, my psychic mentor unlocked the door and let me in. "Goodness, I wasn't expecting you tonight," she said as she ushered me toward the back room where she held court. Did she ever know when I planned on visiting—because I sure didn't.

"What'll it be tonight?" she asked. "Coffee, tea, or cocoa."

"Cocoa." I was more likely to sleep after drinking that brew. Not that I thought I'd get any sleep that night.

I took my usual seat and watched as she ran water from the tap into a small saucepan and set it on the electric burner that sat on a shelf over the sink. Before I knew she was dead—and by electrocution—I used to worry about this arrangement. I was never really sure I ate or drank the refreshments on offer, so it didn't seem all that important.

It wasn't until Sophie made the cocoa, poured it into cracked restaurantware cups, tossed a couple of cut-out cookies on a plate, and sat down that we spoke.

"And what brings you here tonight?" Sophie asked, her bright blue eyes gazing into mine.

"I have several things to tell you. First, you don't have to worry about me charging people when I use my—" God, I hated the word "—gift to help them with whatever it is they're going through."admitted

Sophie's eyes narrowed, but she said nothing.

"I thought a dollar might be a fair price. What do you think?"

The tense creases on her face seemed to ease. "I see that as a fair price," she admitted and tasted her cocoa. She nudged the cookie plate in my direction. They were iced bunnies, chicks, and Easter eggs—appropriate for the season. "But telling me that was not the reason you are here this evening."

"No," I admitted. "Something's happened that I didn't anticipate when I told Richard I wanted to help restless spirits."

"And that is?" Sophie asked.

"That not all of them are people of good character."

"True of a lot of people you meet during a lifetime. And who have you met that's a problem?"

I told her about Louie, how I'd met him, tried to help him, and the sinister turn that had occurred earlier that day.

Sophie listened, her expression somber.

"I tried to warn you," she said.

"But surely there must be restless spirits, like you, who need my help."

"I am *not* restless," she asserted. No, she had told me countless times that she was only tied to the living world for one reason: to support me. Would she be there for me the rest of my life, or she just fade away one day? I hoped not.

"So far, Louie can't follow me past the floor of his hospital room, but he threatened me. He said if I didn't do as he wished that after he died he'd make it his priority to ruin my life—for as long as I lived. He's not a nice person," I added lamely.

"So it would seem," Sophie agreed. "This is one reason why I think your business endeavor is not a good idea."

"Richard's trying to figure out who set a fire that killed an elderly lady. There's no money in that, either, because it's a cold case."

"And what has he come up with?" Sophie asked.

"Not much. Nothing really."

"Who would you charge in that case?" Sophie asked.

"Nobody. I guess you could say that Richard's and my business is a hobby—at least the IRS is going to see it that way."

"A rich man's folly?" she suggested.

"Pretty much."

She nodded, picked up her cup, and sipped her cocoa. She set the cup back down again. "I wish I could advise you on how to thwart this Louie character, but I've never dealt with such a person. Not since…."

Since she'd died? And what would she have done when she was alive?

"Just talking with you about Louie has been helpful," I lied.

"You haven't told your brother about these problems?"

"Not in great detail."

"And why not? He's your partner."

"Yes, but what can he do to help?"

Sophie looked thoughtful. "More than you know?"

"And what does that mean?" I demanded.

She shook her head impatiently. "I'm not sure, but as you know—as you've known ever since the day you came back to

Buffalo—you two need each other. Depend on each other. He might not know right now how to help, but he could be helpful in understanding."

Understanding what? I didn't bother to ask. I knew better than to push her. Sometimes she was like the Magic 8 Ball someone had given me as a child. You turned it over and it gave vague answers to your questions, like "ask again later" or "cannot predict now."

"Is there a way I can know when *not* to engage with those kinds of restless spirits?"

"I'm afraid not. You have to ask yourself *why* these spirits are restless. There may be a very good reason—and not a pleasant one—as to why they have not moved on."

Her statement caused me to ask a question I'd often thought about. "What about you? Are you in contact with other spirits? The people you've lost?"

Sophie shook her head, her expression one of infinite sadness. "No. They've all moved on."

I'd always suspected as much but had never wanted to know for sure. Maybe things worked out differently for different people, and if they didn't—I didn't need to know why.

"When I met Alice Newcomb, who needed my help to move on, I sort of thought that might be my destiny. But now, after interacting with Louie Susskind, I'm not so sure. I have the best intentions, but how am I supposed to vet the good and bad spirits?"

"I'm sorry, but I can't help you there."

"I don't want Louie to haunt me for the rest of my life. After what I experienced today, I not only *don't* want to help him, I want to banish him from this earthly plane."

"I can't guide you there," Sophie admitted. "I'm afraid this is something you'll have to figure out on your own."

Thanks. Thanks a lot. I didn't say the words aloud, but I'm sure Sophie caught my drift.

"But this case of yours is not the only thing on your mind," Sophie said.

"No, it's not," I admitted. Sophie was astute to notice the sadness in my voice.

"It's Maggie."

I nodded.

She shook her head. "But you suspected—actually, you knew what the outcome would be when she went to California."

"Yeah," I admitted, my heart sinking. "She promised me she'd be faithful, but it was only days—not even weeks—before she cheated on me."

Sophie lowered her head, her mouth drooping into a frown. "I'm so sorry."

"Did you know this would happen?" I asked, almost desperately.

Sophie shrugged.

She *had* known.

How had I been so blindsided? Because Maggie wasn't a druggie like my ex-wife? That she seemed so normal? I'd heard that women lost their sex drive the older they got. Maggie sure bucked that theory.

I picked up a cookie and stared at it before setting it back down on the napkin before me.

"I guess I misinterpreted what Maggie and I have."

"*Had*," Sophie corrected.

The finality in her voice seemed to cause the ache around my heart to grip just that much tighter. "I guess I should try to extricate myself from her."

Sophie shrugged. "That's up to you."

"Are you saying I should give her another chance?"

Sophie's brows narrowed. "Not at all. But what I would rule out and you might accept are two different things."

She made it around like I'd be an asshole to give Maggie a second—no, third—chance.

"There are just some people who cannot be faithful," she said sadly.

Something in her words sparked within me. Had she been disappointed in her husband for the same reason? If so, I wasn't about to ask. I didn't want to cause her to relive anything that might have hurt her. But come to think of it, Sophie never talked about her husband. When she'd reminisced, she'd talked about her son—my father—and her grandchildren.

I decided to redirect the conversation. It wasn't like I could say, "How about those Bills?" when they'd lost in the playoffs yet again weeks before, but I wasn't sure I was ready to leave.

And then I thought of Emily and the twinges of feelings I'd had for her. If I was upset at Maggie cheating on me, I couldn't very well ask for permission to cheat on her. Then again, Emily hadn't shown any interest in me.

"You're feeling lonely," Sophie guessed—or was she reading my mind?

"I am."

She nodded solemnly. "We all go through those times. Eventually, we get over it."

I'd been lonely most of my life. I hadn't gotten over it and was pretty sure I never would. What was that quote about being lucky in cards and unlucky in love? Hell, I wasn't lucky at anything.

"It's getting late. You have to get up early for your job."

Did that mean Sophie now approved of R&A Insights? I didn't ask in case she gave me a thumbs down on it.

"You've been very helpful," I lied as I stood up. If I was

honest with myself, our conversation had only made me feel worse about the situations with both Louie and Maggie.

Sophie scooped the uneaten cookies into a white bakery bag. "Take these to little Betsy. She will enjoy them," she said, her eyes shining. "And next time you come, bring more pictures of that darling girl."

"I will," I promised as I zippered my jacket.

She walked me to the door at the front of the bakery and let me kiss her cheek. "Good night, Sophie."

"Good night, Jeffrey. Come back soon."

"I will," I promised.

She closed and locked the door and waved before I turned to walk back to my car.

Nothing was settled. I was pretty sure I'd have a lousy night's sleep.

And I was right.

I should have recognized those queasy feelings as the beginning of one of my skull-pounding headaches. The thing was, they weren't coming as often, and they hadn't been as bad of late.

This one was a return to the worst.

I made it back to Richard's house and checked the medicine cabinet, realizing I hadn't brought my whole arsenal of migraine drugs, but I was bushed and too lazy to cross the driveway to get what I needed.

Big mistake.

I awoke hours later, puked a few times, went back to bed, and couldn't sleep.

Brenda checked up on me several times during the next day, brought me my meds, and made me homemade soup, which I ate at the desk in my temporary room, and then I went back to bed.

A totally unproductive day.

Again.

Chapter 22

It was snowing when I awoke early the next morning, feeling not quite a hundred percent but much better than I had during the preceding twenty-four hours. I got up, showered, and dressed, remembering a brief conversation I'd had with Emily some days before. I looked online and found the big DIY store on Sheridan Drive opened at eight. Brenda was already in the kitchen with Betsy strapped in her highchair and invited me to have breakfast with them. I had a cup of coffee and a slice of toast slathered with peanut butter. Richard was nowhere in sight.

"You must be feeling better," Brenda opined.

"Yeah. And despite my down day, I'm encouraged because it's the first bad day I've had in over two weeks. I'd say that's real progress."

"Good progress," Brenda assured me, and we held our cups aloft in a toast.

I fed Herschel before I crossed the driveway to retrieve my car and drove to the closest home-improvement store. The wind was sharp, but the snow had tapered off as I entered the big store, a blast of heat greeting me.

There weren't a lot of shoppers that early on a Sunday morning—most likely people who'd started a DIY project the day before and found themselves short of a tool or parts, but I was startled to see that, despite the early hour, I spied a possibly friendly face.

Emily pushed one of the store's shopping carts with her daughter Hannah attached to the front, riding shotgun as her mother pushed.

"Emily!" I called.

She looked around, caught sight of me, and pushed the cart in my direction. Inside it was a gallon can of the store's premium paint.

"Funny meeting you here," I said. "Hey, Hannah."

"Hi," the little girl said shyly, ducking her head.

Emily scrutinized my face, frowning. "Are you okay?"

I shrugged. "Yesterday wasn't a good day. I sometimes get migraines," I said, shrugging it off like that miserable twenty-four-plus hours was nothing.

She nodded.

"Doing a home improvement project?" I asked, nodding toward the can of paint in her cart.

Emily lowered her gaze. "We're redecorating Hannah's room. It's low VOC." Meaning it was labeled as having low or no volatile organic chemicals. Safer and far less stinky than traditional paints.

"What color did you choose?" I asked the little girl.

"Purple!" she cried excitedly.

"Lilac," Emily clarified. "I asked for the same color when I was a kid."

"Did you get it?"

Emily's expression soured. "No. Joanna," as she now referred to the woman who brought her up, "wouldn't let me choose. I had a stark white bedroom, and God help me if the walls ever got marked up."

I felt bad for her—felt bad for anyone who'd had just as miserable a childhood as me.

"Do you have a little girl?" Hannah asked me.

"Kind of. My brother has one named Betsy, and he lets me share her."

"Would you like a little girl of your own?" she asked, sounding hopeful. She'd never had a hands-on dad. Was that something she'd wished for?

"That would be very nice, but I'm not sure it will ever happen."

"Mama says that once upon a time you brought me a reindeer cookie."

"I did."

"I don't remember," Hannah said sadly.

"That's okay. You don't need to."

"Maybe one day you'll bring me another one so I *can* remember it," Hannah hinted.

I laughed. "Maybe one day."

Hannah nodded and smiled. "I'd like that."

Emily seemed embarrassed by her daughter's request and changed the subject. "What're you here for?" Emily asked me.

I didn't want to spoil my surprise for her. "Light bulbs."

She eyed my empty cart. "Must be one heck of a light."

"In a place like this, you never know what else might jump into your cart," I said with a shrug.

Emily nodded. "So true. Well, I guess I'll see you at the office tomorrow."

"Bright and early," I assured her.

"See you then," she said.

"Bye, Mr. Resnick," Hannah said cheerfully.

Emily gave me a half-hearted smile and pushed her cart down the aisle.

I watched them go. I got the impression Emily wasn't at all

happy. It had nothing to do with R&A Insights, me, or even Hannah.

As I pushed my cart toward the back of the store, I wondered what was the cause of her somber aura, but had a gut feeling that whatever it was, there was no way I could help her solve the problem.

Maybe my surprise for her the following day might help cheer her. But I had a feeling that whatever was bothering her might flare up and bite R&A Insights—and me personally—in the ass.

It wasn't a pleasant thought.

I wandered around the store and soon perused their line of space heaters. I'd forgotten to mention to Richard about getting one for Emily and decided—fuck it—and bought something that could sit under her desk and quietly radiate heat. She could run it year-round if she found the office too cold during air-conditioning season. That is if R&A Insights was still around come summer. Three months seemed a long way away just then.

I RETURNED to Richard's house within an hour of leaving, but when I entered the kitchen, there was no sign of my extended family or the morning's meal. That was okay, but I wasn't sure how I would spend the rest of the day. I could hide in the guest bedroom where I'd taken up residency, return to my digs across the driveway to chill out or go into the office. None of those options seemed palatable. It was too early to get started on the gardens, although a load of sticks and other debris had accumulated in the yard over the winter. I decided to tackle that job. It would give me a chance to breathe in some fresh air and get some exercise.

I'd filled two trash cans with detritus when Brenda

appeared in the backyard. "Jeffy, it's lunchtime. I've made tomato soup and grilled cheese sandwiches."

"I'll come inside in a few minutes," I told her but I had no intention of doing so. Another forty-five minutes later, when the cans had been returned to their home by the side of the three-car garage and the yard was in tip-top shape (and free of Holly's contributions), I entered the big house again. As I'd hoped, there was no sign of Richard. A note on the table told me my lunch was in the fridge. The microwave did a good job of rejuvenating the soup and the sandwich.

It was a little after one. I still had hours and hours to kill before I could hit the sack and hopefully have a night without dreams, and still, I hadn't seen or spoken to my brother in almost two days. We weren't even passing like the proverbial ships in the night. I knew it was a conscious decision on my part. Had he made it his business to avoid me, too?

I ate my lunch in the silent kitchen and wondered where Brenda and Betsy were hanging out. In Richard's study? In the living room? Did I want to intrude on them? Brenda wouldn't care and, after all, I'd accepted her invitation to be here so that I wouldn't be alone. But after just a couple of days back in the Alpert manse, I didn't feel like much of a welcome guest, either.

It had been three years and a couple of days since I'd returned to Buffalo after an eighteen-year absence, and I didn't feel any closer to my brother than I did way back when. Our relationship had had its ups and downs since my return, but it was currently at its lowest ebb, and I had no idea what had soured him on me. And truth be told, I was too chicken-shit scared to ask. He hadn't exactly ghosted me, but it felt nearly as bad.

The TV was on in the living room as I tiptoed to the stairs that led to the home's second floor. It sounded like some Disney musical. CP was probably playing with her toys with the video on as background noise while Brenda worked on her latest needlepoint project. Richard was no doubt ensconced in his study down the hall. I escaped to my room and booted up my computer to watch videos of the latest popular cocktails to learn how to make them in case I ended up back behind a bar in the not-too-distant future.

I wasn't sure I wanted to go back to that grind, but I hadn't found office work to be much better. That wasn't entirely true. I liked the investigation part of the job. I liked having somewhere to go—even if it meant leaving Herschel for extended periods of time. Maybe I should get him a buddy to keep him company. Not in my current circumstances, of course, but sometime in the future. And antagonistic as she usually was, I liked Emily—not in any romantic way—I was far too old for her, I told myself. I thought about the little heater I'd bought—on Richard's dime—for her and figured I'd surprise her with it the next morning.

I yawned. With all that yard work and the fact that despite my incapacity the day before, I hadn't had much real, decent sleep and got up from the desk and stretched out on the bed, figuring I'd just rest my eyes for a few moments. But when I opened them again, it was three hours later.

I got up, went into the bathroom, threw some cold water on my face, and decided to head downstairs. Brenda would be expecting me to show up for supper.

It was with dread that I descended the stairs.

As I approached the kitchen, I could hear Betsy squealing with joy. I doubt I'd ever been as happy as that little girl. I envied her and hoped she'd never experience the kinds of lows I'd had to endure during my shitty childhood.

I paused at the kitchen's doorway and took in the scene. Betsy in her highchair, Richard at the table with Holly at his feet, and Brenda at the countertop making a salad. Suddenly it seemed obnoxiously chauvinistic that neither Richard nor I ever pitched in to help her make the evening's meal. If I was going to continue to be a part of this family, that would have to change.

"Hey," I said.

Brenda turned in my direction, giving me a warm smile. "Hey, yourself. Feeling all right?"

I stifled a laugh as my memory flashed. That was the title of a song my mother had loved and used to sing just a little off-key.

"Not feelin' too good myself," I answered.

Brenda laughed. She'd gotten the joke. Richard looked at me blankly. Obviously, he hadn't.

"I see you've rejoined the land of the living," he said.

Did I detect a note of sarcasm in his tone?

"Yeah," I answered, trying to keep my voice neutral.

He eyed me over his crystal glass filled with neat Scotch. "Great."

I ignored him. "Can I give you a hand, Brenda? I can chop veggies like a top chef."

Again she laughed. "Not right now, but thanks for the offer. We're having stuffed pork chops. Do you mind sharing one with me?"

"Not at all."

"Let me get you a drink," Brenda said, abandoning the carrot she'd been julienning.

I waved away her offer. "I can get it."

Richard said nothing, but I caught him looking over the top of his glass as he watched me pour myself a bourbon with soda.

That's when I decided I might leave work early the next day and move back across the driveway and into the apartment over the garage. I didn't need to put up with Richard's shit any longer.

And as soon as I could manage it, I wouldn't have to put up

with him at all. For some reason, the thought left a big empty space in my chest.

I took my drink and sat at my usual place at the kitchen table. I sneaked a glance over at my brother. Was there a hint of a sneer on his lips?

No. I had to be imagining that.

I looked down at my glass, not sure I wanted to drink it, but then I took a sip and changed my mind.

"You did a great job in the yard," Brenda said. "Thanks."

"Just part of the service," I said.

"We pay people to do that," Richard said, implying that my efforts weren't appreciated.

"You'd have to pay extra to get the dog shit taken care of."

Holly seemed to know I was mentioning her, and I heard her tail thump against the floor. At least *she* seemed to appreciate my efforts.

I didn't feel like telling Richard about my encounter with Emily at the home-improvement store or why I'd been there. I didn't want to have a conversation with him at all.

The awkward silence continued. But then Brenda filled the quiet with a long and involved story about how cute Betsy's reaction had been to her first encounter with Ariel, The Little Mermaid, and how adorable she'd look with fins and iridescent scales come Halloween. Yeah, she would.

I nursed my drink while Brenda chattered on. Finally, she started setting the table and minutes later doled out our dinners, with Betsy getting food she could feed herself.

Brenda kept up nervous chatter as we ate. I had to force down my pork, stuffing, peas, and apple sauce.

"Any plans for the evening?" Richard asked me.

Since my so-called girlfriend had abandoned me, I had no friends I could count on and no money of my own, I fought the urge to tell him so. "Just to get a good night's sleep," I said, although packing up my stuff for the move the next day was at the top of my agenda.

"How about you?"

"Nothing special."

Since we'd all just about finished our meals, I turned my attention to Brenda. "Thanks for another great supper."

"You're welcome."

"I'd like to repay you for it by cleaning up the kitchen, that way you can relax."

"You don't have to do that."

"I want to," I said sincerely.

Her brown eyes seemed just a little damp as she scrutinized my face. We had a connection neither one of us was comfortable acknowledging, and I was pretty sure she knew where I was coming from—my need to say thanks in a tangible way.

Richard got up from the table. "Well, I have work to do."

The three of us watched him leave the kitchen, with Holly trotting along behind him.

Brenda glowered after him. "I've just about had it with him," she growled. "I have a mind to—"

"Don't," I said in a tone I'd never used when speaking to her.

"But, Jeffy—"

"Whatever happens, Rich and I have to work it out for ourselves."

Brenda's expression hardened. "Lately, I've seriously wondered who the hell I'm sharing a bed with because the man under the covers sure isn't the one I fell in love with."

"This is just a rough patch we're going through," I said with a bravado I didn't feel.

"Well, okay," she conceded.

"And I meant it about cleaning up the kitchen. I've got a podcast to listen to, and I prefer to be busy when I do it."

"Are you sure?"

"Positive."

She didn't look convinced, but she got up and released Betsy from the highchair. "Thanks. You're a good guy."

"You're not telling me anything I don't already know," I bluffed.

"Yes, I am." Brenda could read me like a book.

"Now, get outta here," I said, rising from my chair. "I've got a podcast to listen to."

"Kiss Uncle Jeffy nighty-night," Brenda told Betsy and handed the baby to me.

"Night-night, sweet girl," I told my niece and kissed the top of her head.

"Nigh-nigh," Betsy babbled.

I waved as they left the room.

I did clean up the kitchen, but didn't listen to the podcast. I had too much on my mind. And when I made it back to the guest room, I didn't feel like packing up my stuff. I hadn't brought that much. I could do it in a couple of minutes the next day. Getting Herschel and his stuff back across the driveway was what would take time.

With that decided, I turned on the boob tube and vegged.

I didn't have anything better to do except worry—about Louie, about Maggie—and I didn't want to do that either.

Chapter 23

I made it to the office about fifteen minutes before R&A's scheduled opening and set up the heater I'd bought for Emily the day before. I made the coffee and put a pot of water on for Emily, who seemed to be on a hot chocolate kick. After that, I booted up my computer to look at the online want ads. There seemed to be quite a few openings for bartenders, but they weren't close to my home base and seemed aimed at joints that catered to a younger crowd where the music would boom loud enough to cause hearing damage and set off migraines that might set me back a year or two in my recovery. Was I an old fart now that I was close to hitting that forty-year mark? Then again, it was only the first day of my job search. I'd keep looking.

Emily arrived at the stroke of eight and called hello.

"Hello, yourself," I hollered back and closed the tab on my computer, wondering if I should clear the history, too. But then Richard had never messed with my laptop and I'd never tried to access his files. Then again, if he ever *had* accessed my computer, he was more than competent at erasing his tracks.

"Jeff?"

I looked up to see Emily standing in my office doorway.

"There's a heater under my desk. It's toasty warm where I sit." She sounded pleased.

"You mentioned being cold. I'm sorry it took me so long to fix the problem."

"That was very sweet of you. Thanks."

"You're welcome."

"Did you get your light bulbs, too?" she asked and laughed.

"About a dozen of them."

Her smile was genuine when she asked, "Can I get you a cup of coffee?"

I got up from my desk. Getting coffee for the boss was demeaning in this day and age. "I can get my own."

She watched as I poured myself a cup. "Ready for hot chocolate?" I asked her.

"In a little while. I had a mug with breakfast. What's on tap for today?" she asked.

I laughed. "More of the same."

She scrutinized my face. "Are you okay?"

"Sure, why wouldn't I be?" And then I remembered that she'd previously described me as having dead, shark eyes.

"I dunno. You look like you might want to run away."

"Well, it was snowing when I left the house. Getting away from winter would probably do us all good."

"The first day of spring isn't that far off." She moved to sit at her desk. "Where would you run away to? California to be with your girlfriend?"

I laughed, but it was mirthless. "No. I don't have any desire to travel. I did a lot of it when I worked in insurance. Airports, hotels, and cold room-service food don't hold much allure for me."

"I love hotels, especially those with swimming pools. Hannah does, too. I've thought about hitting one of the locals for a weekend, chilling by the pool with my best girl, and leaving all my troubles behind. She'd love the free breakfast, too. They have everything I won't let her have at home."

"Being a kid is tough these days," I commented.

"Not as tough a life as I had. But that's all behind me now." She actually sounded rather chipper about it, which was an improvement from her comments the day before.

"But that's enough about me. Let's move on to something else. What do you want me to do with that list of police stations and sheriff's departments you had me assemble? We talked about sending them all a letter announcing our new business."

Should I feel encouraged that she should include herself as part of the management?

"I came up with a sample letter we might want to send out." Emily extracted it from one of the drawers in her desk and handed it to me. I glanced through it. It was rough but covered all the major points Richard had outlined when starting the business.

"Good work," I said sincerely, "but I think we should hold off sending it out."

Emily's brow furrowed. "Why? Shouldn't we announce our service to *every* potential client?"

"Yeah, in a perfect world."

She scrutinized my face and frowned. "What is it you aren't saying?"

I wasn't sure where I stood—and worse, what could become of her and her daughter if I just walked away from R&A Insights. If nothing else, I owed her honesty.

"This business was my brother's idea."

She gave me a pained expression. "I don't know as I want to hear anymore."

"Well, you need to know. I'm not happy with the way things are going."

"And you aren't good at hiding it, either," she muttered.

She crossed her arms across her chest. "So, what are you going to do about it?"

Cut and run, I thought, feeling like a wimp.

Emily seemed to read my thoughts. "So, confront the doc. It's really obvious he isn't pulling his weight as a partner unless that was the deal all along. But if it wasn't, then it doesn't seem fair that you do all the work, and he just sits back and writes the checks."

Should I feel grateful that she felt comfortable enough to give me her opinion or tell her to mind her own business? I decided not to comment.

"It wasn't supposed to be that way," I remarked.

Her expression soured. "So, is this business just a rich man's plaything?"

"It's beginning to look that way. And if it's so, it's not something I want to be a part of." Crap. I shouldn't have said that out loud. "That doesn't mean you have to walk away."

She shrugged. "I could stay for a while, but much as I need the money, I can't just sit here day after day scrolling through my phone and watching TikTok videos. I like to think I've got useful skills and could do something of real value with my life."

We were on the same wavelength, although was I thinking too small, aiming for another bartending job? Was Maggie right? Should I be setting my employment sights higher?

Emily's expression darkened. "Well," she seemed to hedge. "I guess I'd have to talk it over with the doc. You ought to do the same."

She was right. Staying silent and just walking away was the coward's way out.

"It's the top item on my agenda," I lied. I don't think she was fooled.

I started to feel like I was being smothered. I had to get out of there. I headed for the coat rack.

"I've got to interview a witness," I said as I wrapped a scarf around my neck and donned my topcoat. "If I don't get back, can you handle things for the rest of the day?"

"Don't I always?" she deadpanned.

Yeah, we'd—*I'd*—asked a lot of her, but she certainly couldn't complain that we hadn't fairly compensated her. Still, the bitterness in her voice was hard to ignore.

I buttoned my coat and headed for the exit. "I'll see you when I see you."

"I'll be here," she said to my back. "Have a good one."

I closed the door behind me. I would *not* have a good one. I was going to have to have an honest talk with Richard about my attitude toward the business, and I was sure it wouldn't go well.

At that point, all I could hope was that he felt the same way.

IT WAS NEARLY ten when Richard arrived at R&A Insights. Jeff's car wasn't in the lot. Maybe that was good. He wasn't sure he wanted to talk to him just yet. Maybe it would be better to converse about personal things back at the house—or maybe just ignore the fact Jeff had moved back into the big house. For one, Richard didn't like seeing the litter box in the butler's pantry. Since Betsy wasn't yet using the Jack and Jill bathroom between her own and the guest room, it might be better for the cat to do his business away from the rest of the household. He'd mention it to Brenda.

"Hey, Doc, glad to see you," Emily said in greeting as Richard entered the receptionist's area of R&A Insights, but somehow her tone wasn't as welcoming as he expected. "What brings you here today?"

"I thought I'd come in to update my notes," he said and hung up his coat, then headed for his shared office. Of course,

Jeff was nowhere in sight. The idea didn't bother him, and he settled behind his desk and powered up his computer.

Emily showed up in the open doorway.

"What's up?" he asked, but his gaze strayed to the computer that insisted he input a code before it would allow him to access his files or the Internet.

"I was wondering what our purpose is."

"Purpose?" he repeated, distracted, still looking at the monitor before him.

"Yeah. I assume you guys wrote up a business plan and a mission statement when you set up this company."

"Definitely," he muttered, still distracted.

"Can I read them?"

Richard hadn't really heard her. "What?"

"I'd like to know what the business plan is for R&A Insights. I think it would be helpful for me."

Jeff had mentioned they do something along those lines, but Richard hadn't thought it necessary at the time.

"Uh, we don't exactly have one."

"You just said you did," she reminded him.

"I'm sorry. I guess I wasn't listening as hard as I should have."

Her eyes widened at his admission. "So, why didn't you put those parameters on paper?" she persisted.

"It didn't seem necessary at the time."

"Why not?" she asked again.

A thread of annoyance flared within him. "I didn't think we needed one."

"And why was that?" she persisted.

What was with her? She'd always been so nice to him. Why was she pestering him now?

"Because Jeff and I are on the same page."

"Really?" she asked, her eyes still wide, her tone skeptical.

"Yes."

She gave a mirthless laugh. "Then maybe you should have a serious talk with your brother because if you ask me—and I realize you didn't—he's about to call it quits on this little endeavor you've concocted."

It was the first time Emily had spoken to him in what sounded like derision. She'd always been such a sweet little girl.

The thought made Richard cringe. She wasn't a girl. She was a woman, and she didn't sound at all pleased.

"What are you saying?" he asked, trying to keep his tone neutral.

"Your brother is about to bail on this little business you've set up."

The anger flared higher. "He hasn't said anything to me about it."

"Well, I'm giving you fair warning. The poor man's a wreck, and if you haven't noticed it—then shame on you."

"Emily!" Richard chided her.

"I'm sorry, Doc, but someone needs to say it out loud, and if you fire me for it, well, I'll be sad. Because I think what you set out to do could be a good thing. It sure changed my life for the better. But Jeff can't do it all on his own."

"He doesn't have to."

"Well, if you're partners, shouldn't you be pulling the same kind of weight around here?"

"I do my share."

"Do you really think paying the bills is enough? Or that keeping your partner—your *brother*," she reminded him, "—in the dark about what you're doing is fair?"

Now she was truly making him angry—especially since Jeff had said he thought she might need to go, and Richard had stuck up for her.

"Did Jeff put you up to this?" Richard asked.

"Hell, no. *He'll* probably fire me when he finds out I spoke to you. That is if he ever returns to the office."

Richard studied her face. She was serious. And, if possible, considerably angrier than he felt.

He said nothing, his fists clenching.

"I'm going home," Emily announced, although the work day was only two hours old. "If you want to dock my pay for the rest of the day, I'm okay with that." She turned on her heel.

Richard didn't get up from his seat and listened. He heard the rustle of her putting on her coat, her soft footsteps on the carpeted floor, and then the click of the door as it latched closed. He sank back in his chair.

Jeff was going to bail on Richard despite him rescuing the guy after the mugging that had nearly killed his younger *half*-brother. Richard had paid off Jeff's debts. He'd coughed up for extensive renovations on the apartment over the garage, given him a home, and now, after all he'd done for him, not just in setting him up with a well-paying job, but everything else he'd done since Jeff was a fourteen-year-old orphan.

The anger within him erupted with the force of an exploding volcano, and Richard slammed his fist so hard on the cherry wood desktop that not only made his laptop jump, but pain skyrocketed through his hand and up his arm. He ground his teeth to keep from crying out, angry at himself for losing his temper, but even angrier at his ungrateful brother.

He sat there for a long time, his hand throbbing, knowing he should see if there was any ice in the little refrigerator in case it started to swell, but at that moment not caring. His swollen hand would be proof positive that he had suffered. Yeah, everyone felt sorry for Jeff for all he'd endured, but wasn't he just a perpetual victim?

Richard sat there for a long time, fuming—feeling like he'd been duped for three long years. *He* was the victim. He'd had Jeff foisted on him by a woman he hadn't even known—their mother—at a time when he was at the crux of his education as a medical doctor. He'd paid off his mother's debts, and her funeral, and he'd paid for Jeff's expenses until the kid had absconded and joined the army just to get away from the Alpert Home. And then Jeff had stayed away for nearly two decades.

That ungrateful bastard!

Those words kept echoing through Richard's brain until it seemed like they were burned into his gray matter.

But then little by little reason started to seep into his thoughts. Jeff hadn't *wanted* to come live with him after the death of their mother. He'd had no choice. Jeff hadn't *wanted* to accept Richard's support and had begged to get his working papers so he could do as much as a teen could do to support himself. He hadn't asked for a car like most sixteen-year-olds. He worked and bought a bike to ride to and from work. He bought most of his clothes. He'd stopped eating and was anorexic after Richard's grandmother had tormented him. Taking Jeff in after their mother's death had been more like sentencing the kid to prison. And Jeff had escaped at his first opportunity to join the military because he felt he had no other alternative.

Jeff hadn't wanted to return to Buffalo after the mugging. But after losing his job and about to be evicted, again he had no options. And Jeff had only asked to live in the apartment over the garage. It was Richard who insisted on a total renovation of the space. Jeff had never asked for it. Hell, he would have probably been okay with running water and a space heater for the winter months.

More guilt showered down on him. Jeff had not wanted to start a cold case consulting business. He'd railed against it. And yet, at Richard's insistence, he'd acquiesced. As far as Richard knew, Jeff's psychic mentor had abandoned him. He didn't question that Sophie Levin existed. How could he—he'd met her that one time. That she'd abandoned Jeff because of R&A

Insights had to be a terrible blow for his brother. And … even if Jeff saw himself as a victim, which Richard was pretty sure he didn't, he'd never portrayed himself as such. In fact, he seemed to go out of his way to downplay whatever psychic gifts he'd gained after that terrible brain injury that had nearly crippled him.

Richard's hand continued to throb, the pain worsening as the minutes passed, swelling so that his hand felt like a blown-up surgical glove about to burst.

It took a couple of minutes for Richard to power down the computer, struggling to do so with his left hand, turn off the office lights, don his winter coat—sans buttons—and lock up for the day before heading to his car. Instead of steering for home, he headed to his old stomping grounds—Sisters Hospital—to have his hand looked at. And how was he going to explain it to Brenda? Most likely, it was only bruised. But, still….

And he still had to confront Jeff.

Confront seemed such an adversarial term. Discuss was a better descriptor. And yet he wasn't sure what he wanted to say. Maybe he should take a few days to figure it out. But what if Emily was right? What if Jeff was ready to bail? Though he hadn't wanted to accept it, deep inside Richard knew that whatever success R&A Insight might achieve would be up to Jeff.

As Richard steered west on Main Street toward the hospital, his throbbing right hand resting on his thigh, guilt enfolded him. Yes, over the years he'd tried to be generous toward his brother, but as often as not, Jeff had never felt comfortable accepting Richard's help.

And now, feeling like a complete asshole, Richard realized—and not for the first time—that he'd been acting with a savior complex. That he was determined to save his brother … but from what? Yes, after the mugging Jeff had had crippling headaches, but he was on the high side of healing. Those headaches were fewer and fewer in number. He was prepared to go back to work. But now, according to Emily, Jeff was ready to bolt. And if Richard was honest, and rethinking his earlier anger, he really couldn't blame his brother for feeling left out. It *had* been a calculated move on Richard's part. He *had* been feeling just a little bit cocky.

Little? Yeah, over-the-top cocky.

Shame washed over him. Where the hell did he get off feeling so superior…and only because he had a fat bank account?

He would have to talk to Brenda about this. She was his reality check. She was the center of his universe. She made his life make sense, and he hadn't been listening to her of late because he had an ego as large as the amount in his checkbook. But that meant nothing when it came to dealing with people—his family.

And suddenly, six foot-two Richard Alpert felt pretty damned small.

Chapter 24

I drove around for a while with no set destination until almost noon. Days before, Brenda had mentioned taking CP with her for a lunch date with a friend from her volunteer days at the women's clinic. With Maggie out of the picture, she was trying to establish bonds with other women to secure a network of kindred spirits. I'd never been close to my former boss or my now-deceased co-worker, Dave, both of whom were now out of my life. I'd really fucked up when it came to establishing friendships here in Buffalo. I'd been content to keep to myself and limit my time to being with Richard, Brenda, and Maggie.

Maggie had been the weakest link in that chain. She'd cheated on me two years before, and now she was fucking someone else three thousand miles away and lying to me about it.

I returned to the house intending to pack up my cat and gear and be out of there before one o'clock. After that, I'd hit the hospital and check in with Louie. But then I got a phone call from Maggie.

"What's up, Maggs," I said as I started taking my clothes out of the guest room's dresser, not at all feeling the love.

"Oh, Jeff—the tenants in my house called to tell me that there's a problem with the main bathroom toilet. It's all backed up and overflowed. They want it fixed PDQ."

My face folded into a scowl. "And what am I supposed to do about it?"

"Could you go over there and fix it for me, please?" she asked, her tone nothing short of begging.

"Maggs, didn't you contract with anyone to take care of these things before renting the place out?" I asked, dreading the answer.

"Well, everything always worked fine for me."

Yeah, but did she stuff the toilet with an excessive amount of TP, which was probably the cause of the home's current problem?

"Maggie, I've got a job now. I can't be—"

"Jeff, this is an emergency," she stressed. "Are you saying you aren't willing to help me out?"

"No, but—" But I didn't want her to depend on me to take care of the home she'd abandoned for her three-year stint away from Buffalo.

"Can't any of your sisters or brothers-in-law take care of this?"

"They've got *real* jobs," she said, dismissing my partnership in R&A Insights. Okay, I wasn't entirely committed to that job, either, but…still.

"What do you want me to do?" I asked, hoping I'd conveyed through my tone how unhappy I was.

"Rent a snake and clear the line. I'm sure that's all it would take."

And what was *that* going to cost me? Because I had a feeling that she would expect me to cough up the cost as part of being a good pal.

I let out a long, exasperated breath.

"Will there be anyone at the house when I get there?"

"No. They'll be at work. But you'll probably have to mop the floor and make it all pretty again. Please, Jeff. I really need your help," she said, sounding oh-so-pitiful.

I waited a long few moments before I answered. "I can't do this on a regular basis. You need to hire an agency to take care of the house in the future."

"I'm sorry—it never occurred to me that I would need to do that, but you're absolutely right. And I'll look into that during my lunch hour. But you *will* go over there and make things right, won't you?"

God, no! I wanted to yell. Deal with her tenants' shit-filled toilet? No. Just, no! But like Louie said, I was a sucker. A stupid, goddamned sucker. "Just this once," I told her curtly.

"And that's why I love you," Maggie simpered.

If she loved me, why was she fucking some younger guy in California? The thing was, I had no tangible proof. She could deny it forever and a day.

I still had a key to her house. Her brothers-in-law probably didn't. I was determined to surrender it to one of them—probably her sister Sandy's husband. They lived closest to the little bungalow Maggie had bought the year before.

"All right," I agreed. "I'll get everything sorted. This. One. Time."

"Thanks. Thanks so much. I really owe you for this."

Did she ever.

She begged off, and I left Richard's house before I'd even had time to finish emptying one drawer. I gave Herschel a quick kitty massage and a treat before I went to hit the same home improvement store where I'd bought Emily's heater to rent a snake and headed to Maggie's house.

How could she have gone to California thinking there'd be no problems renting out her house with no one to take care of it?

She did owe me. Big time.

The scene at the house was even worse than I'd imagined. And I spent most of the afternoon dealing with nasty water, a stranger's turds, and making everything nice once more—which didn't include dealing with the awful aura I had to confront every time I entered that house. I had no clue what had gone down there—some kind of tragedy or abuse—but the bad vibes always hit me like a punch to the gut.

And when it came to problems with the tenants, I was determined never to come to Maggie's rescue again. If she wasn't willing to employ a rental manager, it would *not* be my problem.

Angry? You bet I was. And now, if I left Richard's house with him and Brenda there, it was likely to cause a messy scene. I decided to put off my move for one more day. I'd have to figure out the timing. All of which made me feel like the coward I knew I was. Why was I tippy-toeing around the problem—which was Richard? I was too angry—mainly at Maggie—to think, let alone talk, about the situation.

One more day. I needed to give myself that time to cool off.

I didn't want to talk to Maggie. Instead, I left a terse text: *All cleaned up.* Then I turned off my phone and headed back to Richard's house. It was already after five, and it had started to snow once again. I didn't have the patience to visit Louie—who may or may not have died since my last visit. And who would hound me if I didn't hit the hospital?

I was surprised to see that Richard's car was missing from the garage when I arrived back at the old homestead. I let myself into his house and stamped the snow from my shoes. I never called it Richard's and Brenda's house, although it was her touches that made that old mausoleum feel more like a home.

"Hello!" I called from the butler's pantry as I hung up my coat.

"We're in the kitchen," Brenda replied.

Sure enough, and except for Richard, the rest of the whole fam-damily was there. Brenda was stationed at the counter making a salad for the evening's meal, CP was in her highchair tossing Cheerios to Holly, who caught them in mid-air, while Herschel chased one around the legs of the chairs.

"Good evening," I called, sounding much more cheerful than I felt. Was that because my brother wasn't in attendance? I plunked down in my usual chair. "Where's Rich?"

"He called and said he'd be a little late," Brenda said.

"Why's that?"

"He didn't say." She turned to scrutinize me. "Is something wrong?"

I considered telling her about the afternoon's events but decided to forget it. I'm sure she'd hear a sanitized edition from Maggie. "Nah. Did you have a good time at lunch with your lady friends?"

"Great. I really needed time talking to someone other than—"

"Richard, me, and Betsy?"

She nodded and looked chagrined. "Yeah. Can I get you a beer or a bourbon?" she asked.

"A beer. I can get it." I got up and crossed the kitchen for the fridge, grabbing a bottle from what was left of a twelve-pack. I didn't bother with a glass and sat back down at the table, twisting off the cap.

Brenda finished chopping lettuce and turned to look at me. "Are you sure nothing's wrong?"

I could never fool her. We were pretty much in sync, which probably drove Richard crazy.

I let out a breath and took a sip of my beer. "Uh, a few things."

"How about telling me about the biggie?" she suggested."

I took a swig of my beer for courage and began. "This R&A Insights thing just isn't working for me."

"You guys haven't been doing it for long. Maybe you need to do a shake-down to get things going the way you want it," Brenda said, but her optimistic tone seemed a little forced.

It was time for me to be honest, at least with her. I needed her in my court before I worked up the courage to talk to Richard about it.

"What I need for that to happen is to have a real partner."

Brenda nodded. "I had a feeling you'd say that. I've been telling Richard the same thing for weeks." She sighed. "I don't know what's gotten into him lately." But then her expression darkened. "Well, I do." She let the sentence hang.

"And that is?" I prompted.

"He's drinking too much. Sneaking it, in fact."

My eyes widened. "You mean he's carrying around little silver flasks and hiding bottles between the couch cushions?"

"No, but he goes into his office and pours himself a glass of Scotch—neat—even before lunchtime. He thought he was fooling me by brushing his teeth."

I would hate for my brother to follow in our mother's footsteps. She'd been a drunk most of her adult life and had barely been a mother to me.

"Does he need an intervention?" I asked, my anger toward him receding just a bit.

Brenda shook her head. "Not yet. But if he doesn't straighten up, he's going to get one."

"Have you confronted him?"

She nodded.

"And did it do any good?"

She shrugged. "It's too soon to tell."

It was then that we heard the outside door open and close. It could only be Richard. The dog kept an eye on Betsy, waiting for another morsel. Herschel still chased a Cheerio around the kitchen floor like it was the best toy ever, and

Brenda and I waited for my brother to enter the kitchen. To say there was tension in that room was putting it mildly.

When Richard finally appeared, we immediately noticed the white gauze—or was it fiberglass—that encased his right hand.

"What on earth happened to you?" Brenda cried, rushing forward, grasping his forearm, and raising it into the air.

"I had a little accident," Richard admitted, sheepishly.

"What happened?" Brenda cried, obviously upset.

"It's nothing," Richard muttered and took in the room. "Hey," he said in my direction.

"Hey, yourself."

"I think I could use a drink," Richard said rather wearily.

Brenda shot me a worried glance, but then she hurried across the kitchen and pulled an old fashion glass from the cupboard and a bottle of single malt from the cabinet that held the liquor. She poured him a shot, then topped it with club soda from the fridge, which I was pretty sure my brother wouldn't have wanted. He said nothing, though, as he took his usual place at the kitchen table.

"Is everything okay?" Brenda asked as she placed the glass before him, taking a seat.

"Well, maybe not," he admitted. He turned his attention to me. "I had a very interesting discussion with Emily this morning."

My gut tightened. I wasn't ready to have this conversation, but it seemed inevitable.

I waited for him to continue.

Richard's eyes narrowed, his left hand clasped around his glass. "Are you going to give up our business?"

Anger flared within me. "Emily had no business telling you what we'd talked about."

"Well, she did. Now I want to know where you stand?" he said gruffly.

I glanced at Brenda, who gave me a nod that seemed to say, 'go for it.'

I took a breath for courage. "I don't see a future for me in the business."

"Despite your case?" Richard asked bluntly.

"More likely *because* of it," I countered.

"And why's that?" he challenged.

"My client has done nothing but lie to me. His family members are either in denial or just as reluctant to talk about what's happening at the brewery. And like I told you, there's some kind of secret everyone is tippy-toeing around and don't want the public at large to know—whatever it is. I don't know how to handle it. Being as Louie is close to being a restless spirit and a pro bono case, I'm not sure I give a damn enough about any of them to keep going."

Just saying the words made me feel like a huge burden had been lifted from my soul.

Richard just stared at me. Brenda looked worried, and Betsy squealed with delight as she knocked the rest of her bowl of Cheerios off her highchair tray, causing Holly to scarf up the cereal booty.

Brenda reached for the empty pink plastic bowl and set it on her lap.

"Well?" I demanded of my brother.

"I'm not having much more luck on my case."

"Yeah, I figured as much because you sure as hell haven't shared a damn thing about it with me," I said, fighting to keep my frustration at bay. I glanced at his bandaged appendage. "Now, why don't you at least be straight with us about what happened to your hand."

Richard's gaze dipped to the table where his hand rested. He picked up his glass with the other one and sipped his watered-down Scotch before answering.

"I was pretty damn angry after my talk with Emily."

Brenda's eyes widened, and her mouth dropped open. "My God, you didn't hit her, did you?"

"Of course not," he said vehemently. "I punched the desk."

"And?" she demanded.

He let out a breath. "I fractured two bones in my hand."

Brenda's eyes blazed. "In front of her?"

"No, I held my temper until she left," he muttered.

"How often have you done something—" I stopped myself from saying *as stupid*, "—like that?"

His answer was adamant. "Never."

Brenda and I exchanged glances. I was puzzled. She was downright angry. Holly barked, letting us know the Cheerios were all gone, while Herschel batted his lone piece of cereal toward the butler's pantry. Betsy banged her palms against the highchair tray and squealed with delight at the pet antics, and Richard wouldn't meet our gazes.

"What's for supper?" he mumbled.

"Shrimp stir fry," Brenda muttered.

"Aren't we going to talk about what's going on?" I pushed. I certainly wanted more answers. Now that my dirty little secret was out, I figured Richard needed to own up to his own.

"Why were you so angry with Emily?" Brenda asked.

"She wouldn't shut up," he grated.

I hadn't noticed that to be a problem during the time she and I had worked together.

"About what?" Brenda prodded.

"About Jeff. She went on and on about how unfair it was for him to shoulder so much responsibility for the business."

She had that right, although I didn't voice that opinion.

"And?" Brenda was determined to hear the whole story.

Richard took another hit of his drink. "And then after she left, I got to thinking and...."

Embarrassment colored his cheeks.

I took a wild guess.

"About what an ingrate I am. How I've abused your generosity for decades and now my leaving the business was going to leave you in the lurch."

He didn't answer.

"Oh, Richard," Brenda chided him.

"Yeah," he admitted. "But on the drive to the hospital, I remembered all the times you refused to accept my help. How when you were a kid you hounded me to approve your working papers. How you got a job so you could buy your own clothes, and bought a bike so you could be more independent. And all the rest of it."

"I *am* grateful for all the help you've given me over the years," I said sincerely.

"Yeah, and you really didn't want to take on R&A Insights, and I kept pushing and pushing until you finally said yes."

There was that, too.

"I'm sorry," Richard said and turned toward me with anguished eyes. "I guess I lost focus on what I wanted to do. What I wanted *us* to do."

"That's the thing," I said. "It was supposed to be *us*, not you versus me. What happened to that way of thinking?"

Richard seemed to draw inward, shrinking before my eyes —though he was at least six inches taller than me. "I don't know," he said contritely.

"What was so all-freaking horrible in your life that you had to try to diminish Jeffy—to make the cases you took on a competition?" Brenda demanded.

"Yeah. We've worked together on the things that have come up these past three years. What *did* change?" I asked him, hoping he had the balls to actually answer the question.

Again he shrugged. "I don't know. But while I was waiting to get my hand x-rayed, I had time to think about it." His gaze dipped lower. "I was thinking I might need to seek therapy."

Better him than me. I'd tried it twice with disastrous consequences. Not that I thought the whole idea was wrong, just that I'd had the bum luck to get a couple of crappy counselors. And I was never likely to try therapy again. I was pretty sure that no matter what life handed me, I would handle it better alone. That was just me. Richard's mileage was sure to vary.

He turned his attention to me. "I'm sorry I've been such a bastard. I want this business to work. I promise I'll be better in the future. Please—please don't leave."

I stared at him. I believed he was sincere. After all, for most of my life—despite all the crap that had gone on in the past—I believed that for the most part, he *did* have my best interests at heart.

"Okay," I said. "I'll stay for now. But for that to happen, things have to change. We have to be a hundred percent honest with each other, and I don't think we should be working separately on cases. We can have more than one case going on. One of us might take the lead, but we have to keep each other appraised on what we're doing. This has to be a true partnership, or it'll never work."

"I agree," Richard said, and I believed him.

"Okay then," I said, but then I wasn't sure what else to say. I thought back to my corporate days at the big Manhattan insurance company I'd worked for. "Should we spend a day and have a serious talk, with Emily included, where we hash out the goals of the business and where we think we should concentrate our efforts?"

"Emily asked if we had a mission statement and a business plan."

"I did advocate for them," I pointed out.

"Yeah, and I blew you off. I apologize. You were right, and Emily was right to point that out to me."

"Can we start tomorrow with a clean slate and move forward?" I asked, not sure of what the answer might be.

For a moment, I thought Richard might give into tears, as his eyes were shiny and his mouth trembled. "Yeah."

"Sounds like an excuse for a bagels and cream cheese breakfast at R&A Insights," Brenda suggested.

"It sure couldn't hurt," I agreed.

"Okay. Then that's what we'll do," Richard said.

"And you need to spend more time at the business," I insisted. "After all, it was *your* brainchild."

"You're right," he meekly agreed.

Holly had lost interest now that no Cheerios were falling from the sky and moved to stand beside Richard. He petted her head, and I could just see her eyes above the crest of the table and heard the thump of her tail against the kitchen floor.

"Did you say we were having shrimp for supper?" I asked Brenda.

She rose from her seat. "Yes. And I guess I'd better get to it."

"Need any help?" I asked.

She gave me what I could only say was a grateful smile but shook her head. "I've got this."

I hefted my beer bottle and took a swig, which was now room temperature. Well, I wasn't likely to toss it down the sink and figured I'd finish it anyway.

Richard continued to stroke the dog's head while Betsy started singing—not that there was a coherent tune, but that little girl was a bucket of happiness. Oh, how I wish I could feel that vibe for myself, but at least I didn't feel as miserable as I had a few hours before.

Instead, and for the first time in a long time, I felt hope.

Chapter 25

I spent way too much time putting together the words for a prototype mission statement for R&A Insights. I'd scoffed at such endeavors when I worked at big corporate entities, but now I embraced the concept because if we were going to be successful, we had to have a complete understanding of what the business was about and how we were to accomplish our goals. I despised corporate America, where I'd been treated so badly, but there were some practices big companies embraced that could be successfully adopted by smaller entities.

The next morning, I hit the local bakery and picked up half a dozen bagels, a tub of cream cheese, and headed to the office. I made a pot of coffee, set the bagels on a paper plate on the side table in the conference room, collected a few knives from our storage cupboard, as well as paper napkins, and waited.

Richard was the first to arrive.

"Welcome back," I said.

"Thanks," he muttered, still trying to avoid my gaze despite what I'd considered a breakthrough the evening before.

"I sent you an e-mail with some suggested wording for our

—" It made me cringe to say it. "—mission statement and some goals for the business."

"I looked at it at home," he said and hung up his coat. "I've got a few suggestions, but they're pretty minor. I'd type them up, but—" He hefted his broken hand.

I hadn't printed any pages because my home printer was still in my apartment over the garage and by the time I finished, I hadn't wanted to brave the cold to do it.

"Can you print out three copies so that we can work on it?"

"Sure thing." His shoulders were slumped as he entered our office. It would take a day—or more—for him to buck up. That was okay with me. I could wait.

When Emily arrived a couple of minutes later, she seemed surprised to find the R&A partners in attendance.

"I saw both your cars in the lot," she said as she hung up her coat and hat. She took a tote bag back to her desk and took out a box of packets of hot chocolate, placing it on the shelf below the coffeemaker. She lowered her voice. "Am I in trouble with you?"

I shook my head. "You speeded things up," I said wearily.

"I'm sorry, but if things were going to go sour, I figured it was better if it happened sooner rather than later."

I nodded.

Emily craned her neck to look into our small conference room. "Bagels," she said, pleased. "I didn't have time for breakfast. Thanks." Then she scrutinized my face, not looking pleased. "Was that another of your psychic intrusion into my mind and feelings?"

"Richard's wife suggested them. But you don't have to have one if you don't want one it."

"Oh, I want one. Maybe two." She shrugged her shoulders. "I didn't have time to make lunch."

"Then feel free to have as many as you want—and take any leftovers home."

She gave a sigh. "You're too good to me, Jeff."

I wasn't. I was practical. That was all.

I turned toward my brother's and my shared office. "Rich, are you ready for work?"

"Coming," he called.

Emily was terribly concerned about Richard's hand, but he brushed it off with a terse, "I whacked it good," and we moved on.

Since none of us had had breakfast, we all feasted on the bagels, with Richard and me pouring cups of coffee and Emily preparing cocoa for herself, then took seats at the conference table to eat and chat.

We went over the mission statement, tweaking it here and there, and then the goals for the business.

"Dr. Alpert, do you honestly believe Jeff has psychic abilities?" Emily challenged when we went over the part that mentioned restless spirits.

"If you'd asked me a couple of years ago, I would have said no. But I've interacted with one restless spirit for myself. It only happened once, but it *did* happen. She wasn't a figment of my imagination."

He was speaking of Sophie, which reminded me that I needed to connect with her again—and soon.

"I still find that hard to believe…even though you *seem* to be able to tap into my thoughts," she said, glaring at me.

"You've got that wrong. I can tap into what you're feeling. I'm sorry I can't turn it off, but I make a deliberate effort to try not to tune into you. If you're feeling overly emotional, I suggest you try to tamp it down. I know that won't be easy. But if you feel you need to leave us, then I'll understand."

Emily frowned. "I…I like it here. I really don't want to leave."

"Great, because we like having you here," Richard said. Whether he actually felt that way after what they'd discussed the day before wasn't my business. Emily was competent and generally affable, which was as much as we could expect...at that moment.

After we'd gone through the mission statement and goals, we moved on to sharing what Richard and I had learned about the disparate cases we were working on.

"It sounds like both cases are a bust," Emily commented honestly. "Are we likely to make a nickel on either of them?"

"No. But then, as we mentioned in our mission statement, profit isn't our primary goal," Richard told her.

Emily didn't seem pleased by that pronouncement. "How are you guys going to move forward on your cases?"

I wasn't sure.

"I'm still checking out Marcel Clark's schoolmates. Is that something you'd be willing to help me with?" Richard asked Emily.

"Of course. Let me know who you want me to contact and I'd be glad to give it my best shot. I *want* to be an integral part of this business."

I glanced at Richard and figured we'd made a good decision to hire Emily.

"Great," Richard said. He turned his attention to me. "I'm interested in that death doula. Have you done a concentrated background check on her?"

"Just cursory. But I also know that despite my first impression, she isn't a fake. She knows that Louie's spirit is present."

"And you haven't quizzed her on it?" Emily asked.

"We've sort of danced around the subject," I said.

"Maybe you ought to dance a little more energetically," she suggested.

I caught sight of Richard, who wasn't successfully stifling a smile.

For the first time since we'd opened our door for business, it actually seemed like we were all on the same page. Would that last more than a few hours, let alone a couple of days? Only time would tell.

"Maybe we should have a morning meeting at least a couple of times a week," Emily suggested. "Just so that we could catch up on what we're all doing. What do you think?"

"It's a great idea," Richard agreed.

I liked the suggestions Emily was bringing to the conversation.

In fact, I was liking Emily a whole lot more.

After that, we had a frank discussion about our cases and the frustrations we were dealing with.

"It seems to me, that you've got a more dire situation," Richard finally admitted. "With Susskind literally at death's door."

"Yeah, but just because he dies doesn't mean I can't keep working with him."

"You think?" Richard challenged. "That's not how it worked out with your friend Dave."

He was right about that. But I hadn't mentioned that Louie had already threatened to haunt me if I crossed him.

Emily shuddered, looking a bit freaked out. "And you think this kind of talk is normal?" she asked Richard.

"As I said, I've had to change a lot of my thinking since Jeff came back to Buffalo."

"But can we make this work if you both believe it and I don't?" she asked.

"You don't *have* to believe," I told Emily. "Don't listen or pretend it's fiction. I don't care."

Emily wasn't satisfied with that comment, but Richard and I moved on.

"What can I do to help?" Richard asked.

"Abe Bachman is being a real pain in the ass. The first time I met him he was wary, which was to be expected. The last time I spoke to him he was downright belligerent. Something's fishy at the brewery, so I can understand that he and Bethany were on guard, but it seemed to me he was being particularly wary, more so than Bethany."

"Interesting," Richard said.

"I think they're sleeping together," Emily muttered.

Richard turned his questioning gaze on me.

"It didn't occur to me until she mentioned it the other day, but I think she might be right."

"Are either of them married?" Richard asked.

"No," I answered. "Would that have any bearing on our investigation if they were?"

Richard shrugged. "Give me what you've got on the guy and I'll start looking."

"What can Emily and I do to help you with your case?" I asked my brother.

He waved me off with his good hand. "It's been a cold case for more than twenty years. If we don't work on it for a few days or even weeks, no one's life is going to change."

For some reason, his words caused a chill to run down my spine—as clichéd as that sounded.

"But what about Mrs. Clark? What if what you uncover exonerates her son?"

Richard frowned. "From what I've observed, she would rather I drop off the face of the earth than probe into the circumstances surrounding her missing son."

Emily shook her head. "I'm a mom. If something happened and Hannah was in trouble, I would move heaven and earth to prove her innocence."

"But what if she *wasn't* innocent?" I asked.

Emily blinked, as though that thought would never have occurred to her.

"I'm going on the assumption that Marcel *is* innocent," Richard said. "But even if he is and he's been hiding, which I believe is true, I have to be able to prove it. Much as I think the cops may have made a wrong assumption of his guilt, I haven't come across any evidence to the contrary."

"But you haven't been able to gather much if any real evidence, either," I countered.

"No," Richard agreed, sounding defeated.

"We'll get back to that," I assured him, "but I agree Louie should get our full attention—for now."

"And what if you save the brewery from being sold?" Emily asked. "What happens next? After he passes, is the nearly dead guy going to end up in heaven or wandering the earth like Jacob Marley in *A Christmas Carol*?"

It was a good question. "To be honest, I don't know."

"But you say you've been in contact with spirits. Why *don't* you know?" Emily pressed.

"Because everybody is different. Some people, like Louie, have unfinished business. But when my friend Dave was murdered, he was just…gone. I have no idea why."

Emily didn't seem to like my explanation. It wasn't grounded in the here and now. Nothing my regular senses could comprehend, and there seemed to be no way I could convince her.

"So what's our plan for the rest of the day?" Richard asked.

I liked that he wanted to move forward, even if it wasn't on his case.

"If you're willing to look into Abe Bachmann's background, I'll quiz Omega Dustin on what she thinks is going on."

"Are either of you likely to find anything of significance?" Emily asked, scowling.

I gave her a wry smile, echoing Richard's words of minutes before. "Maybe."

Emily frowned. "Is that any way to run a business?"

"When your business is gathering information, you just do it. Then you have to try to make sense of it," Richard told her.

I couldn't have said it better.

THE MORNING'S meeting had gone much better than Richard could have anticipated, and for the first time, he actually felt energized about the business. But then reality raised its ugly head.

He stared at his computer screen and scowled. Jeff had started a background check on Abe Bachmann but hadn't gotten very far, concentrating his efforts on other aspects of his case. But as Richard dug into the man's background he found there wasn't much to suss out. The man hadn't been mentioned in the Gusto section of *The Buffalo News* when the brewery and the items on its menu were reviewed. But other than that—nothing. The name itself was suspicious. Not to put too fine a point on it, but it was a very Jewish name. Sure, there were black Jews, but was this guy really Jewish?

Richard couldn't find anyone who fit those parameters within Erie county. Of course, the US was a big country—and people assumed names and lived underground for decades, but it was getting harder to do. A child named Abraham Bachmann was born in Buffalo in 1964 and had died in infancy. What if Abe was passing himself off under that name?

And why had he thought the brewmaster fit that criterion?

Because he trusted his gut.

The thought bothered him. Within R&A Insights, a lot of their decisions seemed to be based on emotion instead of pure facts. Richard considered himself to be a man based in science … but science had failed him when it came to understanding his brother and his paranormal abilities.

In the best of all worlds, staking out the guy would be the

best way to learn the man's habits. R&A Insights didn't have the manpower to do that—at least not then and maybe never. So what else could Richard do to trace the guy?

Richard knew exactly what he could do—and how to cover his tracks when hacking into supposedly secure databases. He knew Jeff didn't approve of such tactics. But … what if that was the only way to find out certain facts?

He considered consulting Brenda, the firm's moral compass about accessing such data and knew what she would say.

No. No. And no!

Richard stared at his keyboard for four or five minutes before making his decision. He shut down his R&A computer and then pulled opened a drawer in his desk and removed a black case that contained a laptop he hadn't mentioned to Jeff as owning.

He got up from his desk and headed for the firm's reception area.

"Leaving already?" Emily asked as he headed for the coat rack.

"I have some things I need to do."

"Will you be back soon?" she asked, sounding unsure.

"Today…I'm not sure. But I plan to spend a lot more time here at the office."

She smiled, looking pleased. "I'm so glad to hear you say that." But then she looked embarrassed. "I'm sorry if I shamed you yesterday, but—"

Richard waved a hand in dismissal. "Never mind. You were right. You opened my eyes to my bad behavior and I'm grateful."

Emily gave him a beatific smile, as though indicating a weight had been lifted from her soul. "Thank you."

"No problem. See you later."

"You bet," she agreed cheerfully.

Richard left the building and walked through the salt-bleached parking lot to his Mercedes. He got in, started the car, and drove to the nearest Starbucks. After parking, he went inside, bought a latte, and settled himself at a back table to boot up what he thought of as his stealth computer. He'd fixed it so that it would be incredibly difficult to trace, and never used it within the R&A Insights network. Theoretically, his efforts should cover his tracks. He wasn't all that worried.

He took a few minutes to think about the situation. What he needed to do was hack into the Horse Hockey Brewery's computer network. For someone with his abilities, it should be child's play. It wasn't. In fact, it took nearly two hours before he managed to infiltrate the brewery's internal system, finding his way through Microsoft's cloud to get there. The first place he looked was in their employee tax records. For some reason, he wasn't surprised to find that Abe Bachman wasn't listed as one of its employees. There was no record of him, and no social security number to tie him to any government entity. Abe Bachman was a ghost. Living, but with no record to tie him to the real world.

And why was that?

It was something he and Jeff would have to figure out.

Chapter 26

"Where the *hell* have you been?" Louie shouted at me when I appeared at the door of his hospital room. I didn't answer as his bleary-eyed daughter sat at his bedside, holding his inert body's hand. She looked up when I cleared my throat.

"Oh, Mr. Resnick," she said wearily, sounding like she'd gone ten rounds with a heavyweight champ.

"How's he doing?" I asked.

Teresa heaved a sigh and I thought for a moment she might succumb to tears. "The doctors keep saying he's beating all the odds because he's still here. I hope that means that—" But then she didn't continue. As Omega had said, Teresa knew her father was on the cusp of dying and I could tell she had mixed emotions about the length of time it was taking. She loved him, but this terrible, protracted death watch was doing a number on her—and she felt guilty about wanting it to just end.

"Omega will be here soon, won't she?" I asked.

"Yes." And unspoken was the phrase *thank God.*

"If you need to leave, I'd be glad to sit with your dad until Omega gets here."

"Are you sure about that?" Louie taunted. After all, he'd chased me away the last time I'd visited.

A light blazed in Teresa's eyes and she let go of Louie's hand as though acid burned. "Are you sure?" she asked, echoing her father's words, but even as she spoke, she began packing up her things.

"Of course," I replied.

"Bless you."

"Eh, bless the pope," Louie's disembodied spirit growled. "She sits there reciting the rosary hour after hour and it ain't helped me one damn bit." No, but it gave *her* a sense of peace. Still, I knew better than to debate Louie—over *anything*.

Teresa donned her coat, grabbed her tote and purse, pressed a kiss on Louie's body's forehead, and, muttered a good-bye before fleeing the room.

I looked after her and felt sorry for her, wishing I could do something more to lessen the burden on her soul. Instead, I pushed the door nearly closed and sat down on the chair Teresa had just vacated.

"Well?" Louie demanded.

"Well, what?"

"Have you saved my brewery?"

"Not yet."

"So what's holding you up?"

It was time for some honesty.

"The more I look into things, the less they add up."

"Add up?" he asked suspiciously.

"Yeah. Things you've told me don't mesh with what I'm learning."

"Like what?" he challenged.

"Nick's interest in the Great Lakes wrecks. It's not his—or your—money that funds it. He's established a limited liability company to fund his endeavors. It turns out a lot of other people who're interested in Great Lakes history are willing to pay to learn and/or explore what's out there."

"What else?" Louie demanded. Had he just accepted what I'd told him about Nick, or had he already known about the LLC and just forgotten to mention it?

"There's an awful lot of bad beer sitting on your warehouse floor."

Louie's brow furrowed. "Who says it's bad?"

"I do."

Louie had the decency to look guilty, but he didn't offer to explain why the kegs, bottles, and cans weren't being distributed and sold. "Anything else?"

I wasn't sure I wanted to share more. He'd already threatened me. Ghosts weren't supposed to have any power over the living. *Supposed* was the key. I'd witnessed just how much energy a supposed spirit could muster and it had been deadly.

"Yeah. What's in it for you if I save the brewery from being sold? I mean, you're not exactly in a position for it to matter anymore."

"Well, it does matter. I'm doing this for Bethany."

"Why?"

"Because she's the only one in my family who cared about it. And if it got out that—" But then he didn't continue the thought.

"What kind of trouble would she face?" I asked.

Louie's glare was the epitome of malevolence.

"Maybe I should ask Bethany."

"You leave her out of this," Louie growled.

"What are you afraid of?"

"I ain't afraid of nothin'," he bluffed.

"What have you done that could come back and bite Bethany?"

"Not a damn thing."

I scrutinized Louie's spirit face. He was lying through his

protoplasmic teeth. "Then I guess there's nothing else I can do for you."

"The hell you can't."

"Then give me some direction."

Louie looked pensive.

"Look, Nick and Teresa can do whatever the hell they want once you're dead. There's nothing I can say to persuade them otherwise, and Bethany's in the same position," I pointed out. "You had to have figured that out by now. So what's keeping you from leaving this earthly coil—besides just stubbornness?"

Non-corporeal Louie looked away. Whatever secret he was holding onto, he wasn't yet—maybe never—willing to divulge it. But whatever it was, he knew that once he was gone that the secret was likely to be ruinous to Bethany. The idea gave me another angle to explore…but nothing was going to happen on that day.

A noise at the door alerted us to another's presence.

"Oh, Mr. Resnick. I expected Mrs. Barton to be here," Omega said.

I stood. "She had to leave."

"Escape, more like it," Louie groused.

"And how is Mr. Susskind today?" Omega asked, casting a glance at the silent figure on the bed.

"The same," I said and gestured for her to take the seat I'd just vacated. "His grip on life remains baffling."

She nodded. "It is so with those with unfinished business on this earth," she said quietly, shrugged out of her polar fleece jacket, and took the bedside chair.

My life would be so much better if Louie's bodily functions just shut down and he croaked. I wondered if Omega, a death doula, had a way to nudge him closer to the great beyond—and get him out of my life forever. Sophie had said Richard and Omega were the catalysts to send Louie on his way to whatever awaited him. But how…and when?

I chose my words carefully.

"Do you know of any way to ease poor Louie's suffering?"

"I *ain't* suffering!" Louie declared.

Omega's expression was enigmatic. "I'm not sure what you mean, Mr. Resnick."

I took a few moments to consider my reply. "I sense that there's a reason poor Mr. Susskind clings to life, despite his incapacity."

"And that is?"

"Something he might not want to be revealed."

"You're treading on shaky ground," Louie warned me.

"The unfinished business?" Omega asked.

I nodded.

Again she nodded. "Do you think you could find the cause of his spirit's unrest?"

"Ha! I dare you," Louie taunted once again.

"I'm not sure. But I'm willing to try."

Omega nodded. The thumb and forefinger of her left hand cupped her chin. "You best be careful," she said, just barely audible.

"Why?" I asked.

"Alice," she said succinctly.

A sudden arctic blast wrapped around my heart—perhaps my soul. But that one noun—name—gave me pause. How could she know what I'd been through with Alice Newcomb?

"Tell me," I muttered.

She shook her head, then tilted it toward the bed where Louie's comatose body lay. Omega wasn't about to voice what she feared—or perhaps knew—about future events.

"I think you'd better go," Omega whispered.

I slipped my hand into my slacks pocket, grabbed the business card with the note I'd scribbled earlier asking her to call me, and then reached for her hand, slipping it into her palm.

"Take care," I said, and turned for the door.

"Wait, where are you going?" Louie bellowed, and I high-tailed it out of there and headed for the stairwell, hoping like hell Louie wouldn't be able to follow me.

Yet.

THE DAYS WERE DEFINITELY GETTING LONGER as the vernal equinox approached. I'd checked the Internet to find that sunset on that day was at seven twenty-three.

I left the Sisters hospital parking lot and was heading east. Luckily, I had to stop for a red light when my ringtone disturbed the quiet. I extricated my phone from my jacket pocket, glanced at the screen, and saw it was Maggie. I thought about ignoring it, but then on impulse tapped the call and speaker icons before setting the phone on my lap. "Hey, Maggs." It wasn't the most enthusiastic greeting.

"I wanted to call and thank you for taking care of my little problem yesterday."

Little problem?

"My tenants were so happy to come home from work and find the bathroom in tip-top shape."

I said nothing. She could have called the evening before—or at least texted—but then I'd turned off the phone so I wouldn't have to talk to her. Still, there were no missed calls or text messages to indicate she'd even attempted to acknowledge how I'd saved her bacon the day before.

"Are you still mad at me?" she simpered.

"To be honest, you're not my favorite person right now."

"Why not?" she asked, her tone flattening.

"Maggs, I'm not a plumber. And with what I had to deal with yesterday…." I didn't finish the sentence and hoped she caught my drift. "Have you looked into finding someone to manage the property while you're gone?"

"Well, not yet," she admitted.

"You'd better make it a priority because I can't be available to rescue you every time there's a problem at the house."

"Well, you've only had to do it once," she replied rather testily.

"Maggs, you've only been gone a week. What other problems are those people likely to cause tomorrow, next week, and beyond?"

"To be honest, I don't know where to start. Maybe you could help me with that, too."

"Google is your best friend," I deadpanned.

"Well, you don't have to get snarky," she retorted. "What are you *really* angry about, Jeff? That I accepted the phenomenal opportunity of a lifetime to work in San Diego?"

"No, you seem to have forgotten that we're connected and I know damn well that you're fucking some guy and were too chicken shit to tell me, and that was the *real* reason for your leaving Buffalo."

A long silence filled the thousands of miles of airwaves between us.

"Well," Maggie said finally. "I have a meeting to go to. I'm sorry but I haven't got the time right now for the meaningful conversation this situation deserves."

"When *would* be a good time?" I asked.

"Soon."

"How soon?"

"Soon," she repeated. Seconds passed. "I'd better go. We'll talk soon." And with that, the call ended.

Had I just burned a bridge by confronting her? If so, I couldn't say I felt too bad about it. Would she call back anytime soon? I wasn't sure I cared. What bothered me was that even if we weren't on speaking terms, we shared a bond. Was it spiritual or physical? I wasn't sure and I had no clue how to force a disconnect.

As I drove on, the angrier I became. She hadn't denied sleeping with some other guy. She'd known she was caught. Did she feel guilty about it? If so, I sure hadn't felt any of those vibes, either.

If nothing else, we knew where we stood. Maggie caught, and me cuckold.

I drove on toward Richard's house, swallowing hard, my hand gripping the steering wheel.

My dead wife had played me for a fool—and now Maggie had done the same thing. Was it a personality flaw that I seemed to connect with women who were destined to hurt me? Or was I just a bad judge of character? The opposite could be just as true. Was I attracted to women who were less committed than me? I was never a mainstream guy…so, yeah, maybe I set myself up as a patsy—attracted to women who really weren't all that into me.

And then there was the small flame of attraction I felt toward Emily. There was no way I would act on it. Such an interest in the time of the #metoo movement would be seen as predatory. Still, there was some kind of magnetism between us. Admittedly, it was more on my part than hers, and I was determined not to act on it. Even so, I would have to tread softly.

I braked for another light. I was getting way ahead of myself. Emily had only shown contempt for me. There was no way she'd ever look at me as a potential lover. Maybe I was destined to be alone. Well, at least I had a cat for company. And maybe…just maybe…I'd get my brother back.

Monks lived out their entire lives without a woman to love. Maybe that was my fate as well.

The thought depressed the hell out of me.

Chapter 27

Richard retreated to his study to contemplate the things he'd learned and been told. The information Detective Destross provided indicated that a witness had fingered Marcel Clark as the arsonist. Unfortunately, the name of said witness had been redacted. Why? Who'd done it and how long ago? Richard had supposedly been provided with all the documentation related to the arson investigation. What was the point of excluding the name of the informant? Had someone gotten to—bribed—the officer in charge of the case?

Richard was determined to find out. He didn't bother with e-mailing and instead called Destross directly and was pleased when the detective answered on the second ring.

"To tell you the truth," Destross admitted rather sheepishly, "I hadn't noticed the redaction. I'm juggling three pending cases. Off-loading cold cases to you guys will be a boon to the department—that is if you come up with answers."

"Oh, we think we have, but without corroborating evidence —in this case witness testimony—there's not much we can do."

Destross was quiet for a long moment. "I spoke to my former colleague. It seems he's had a change of heart about speaking out about this case. I assume the redactions were made to shield the name of the witness."

Not very likely. Richard didn't voice that sentiment. "It would be helpful if I could talk to that individual," he said tactfully.

Destross sighed. "Okay. Give me ten or fifteen minutes and I'll get back to you."

They ended the call.

In the interim, Richard again ran through the names of the high schoolers Marcel Clark might have been friends with. He didn't have psychic insight like his brother, but he'd always depended on gut instinct to guide him, but for some reason he felt strongly that it was a schoolmate who'd pointed the finger at Marcel as the suspect in the arson.

And what would have persuaded a friend—or more likely an acquaintance—to testify against a teammate? Probably a legal charge against that individual—and most likely for a minor infraction that might've been seen as a major impediment to graduation or something else. A college application perhaps?

As promised, the detective called back within minutes.

"I assume the colleague you've mentioned is Peter Jones. Are you willing to give me his contact information?"

"I can't. However, should you find out that information on your own…." He let the sentence hang.

Peter Jones was a pretty ordinary moniker. "I don't suppose you could give me an inkling on *how* to find someone with such a common name?"

"I'm sorry, I can't divulge that information," Destross said. "But I can tell you about my favorite place to get a fantastic fish fry—in East Aurora." Destross went on to describe the quaint restaurant that made great drinks, provided huge beer-battered haddock fillets with fries, coleslaw, and mac salad, with a side of seeded rye bread.

"I'll have to give that tavern a try," Richard said. "Thanks for the tip."

"Not at all. Let me know if I can give you any other restaurant suggestions."

"I'd appreciate that. If I come up with anything else on the Clark arson, I'll be in touch."

"You do that," Destross said, and ended the call.

Richard replaced the receiver and sat back in his big leather chair. Well, now he had a place to start looking for former Detective Peter Jones. He straightened again and typed the name and village into his browser. It took only moments before he had an address and phone number.

On impulse, he picked up the phone's receiver once again, punching the number into the keypad. It was answered in two rings.

"Hello?" a female voice answered.

"Hi, I'm looking for former Buffalo police detective Peter Jones."

"That's my husband," the woman said.

"Would it be possible for me to speak to him? I'm working on a cold case for the Buffalo PD and would like to ask him some questions."

Silence answered his inquiry. He waited. And waited.

"Mrs. Jones?"

"Let me see if he's up to talking to you," she said.

"Okay," he said, and heard a clunk as the receiver was set down.

Seconds turned into minutes until he heard a weak male voice say, "Hello."

Richard introduced himself and told Mr. Jones just what his relationship was to the Buffalo PD's cold case unit.

"John Destross is a good cop. But I specifically asked him not to give you my contact information," Jones said.

"He didn't," Richard said. "My partner and I are consultants. Finding people is what we do."

Jones didn't reply, but he didn't hang up, either so Richard told Jones about the Clark arson investigation he was following up on. "How much do you remember about that case?"

There was a long pause before Jones said, "Some."

"The name of the witness who pointed the finger at Marcel Clark was redacted. Is there a chance you remember who it was?"

Another long pause followed the question. "I'm sorry, but I don't."

It was entirely possible he didn't remember the name of the teen who'd turned on his peer. But that didn't mean he didn't remember why it had happened. Richard asked the question.

"Mr. Alpert, those events happened a long time ago."

"But the case is still open—unsolved. I understood you wanted to see this investigation closed. If you can shed any light on what went on all those years ago, you could not only help a man who was unjustly accused, but bring the person who made the false accusation—or the person who coerced that person—to justice."

"And what is justice?" Jones demanded.

"For one thing," Richard said, losing patience, "it's not letting an innocent man take the blame for something he didn't do."

Another long silence followed before Jones spoke again.

"I've confessed my sins to Father Greely and have been absolved of them."

"That's all well and good, but there's an innocent man out there who still has a bogus murder charge hanging over his head," Richard pointed out. "Knowing that has to weigh heavy on your soul."

"I told you," Jones said, his voice sounding stronger, "I've been absolved," he said sanctimoniously.

"I doubt God would see it that way. Not if you let an innocent man be punished for a crime he didn't commit."

Another silence met that statement and for a moment, Richard thought the old man might hang up on him.

"We have nothing to talk about," Jones said finally.

Richard's seldom raised ire threatened to show itself. "Apparently so. And may God have mercy on your soul."

Seconds later, the call was ended.

Richard hung up the receiver, absolutely disgusted. That Jones, who'd brought the case to Destross's attention, was now willing to go to the grave knowing he was responsible for an injustice—believing confessing such a moral lapse could be forgiven just by admitting it—made Richard question his own religious beliefs, which was disquieting.

He sat there for a long while, berating himself for not immediately going back to work to see if he could suss out the identity of which of Marcel Clark's schoolmates had lied about the young man, accusing him of arson.

R&A Insights looked good on a business card, but was the enterprise Richard had concocted going to be worth the effort when even the police who'd worked these cases weren't to be trusted to do the right thing—or even tell the truth?

Feeling discouraged, he thought about the year's lease he'd signed on the office space, and the fact that they had an employee with a dependent child. Richard stared at his desktop. As head of the whole enterprise, he had an obligation to both Emily and Jeff to make the business a success. He resolved he'd work at being a true partner in the future. He owed Jeff that, not to mention more than a heart-felt apology.

The landline rang, startling him. Richard picked up the receiver. "Hello."

"Mr. Alpert?"

It was Jones all right, but instead of sounding defiant, he sounded cowed.

"Yes."

"I … My wife has uh, convinced me that I may want to rethink about answering your questions."

At least someone in that family had character.

"Wives often show great wisdom. I know mine does."

"Yes, well. I don't remember the name of the young man who claimed Marcel Clark set fire to his home but I do remember why his name was redacted."

"And?"

Silence followed for long seconds.

"I'm not proud of some of the things I've done in the past," Jones admitted, hence the need to unburden himself to a priest.

Seconds passed. Jones was taking his time to get to the point.

"Did you take a bribe to pressure that young man to make false statements to the police?" Richard asked.

More silence followed the question before Jones answered.

"That may have happened," the ex-cop admitted.

"I don't suppose you remember the name of the person who offered you the bribe."

"I do."

Again, the older man was quiet. Richard wasn't about to lead his witness by blurting out the name he was sure he already knew, so he waited.

"The man worked for Empire Properties. I don't remember his first name, but I know the surname: Susskind."

Bingo!

Richard didn't comment on Jones's last statement.

"I take it you're not surprised," Jones said.

"No," Richard answered succinctly.

"Then you *are* making headway in that cold case."

"Can you tell me anything about the witness who fingered Marcel Clark?"

"Only that he was a basketball teammate."

At least that piece of information narrowed down the search.

"Would you be willing to report your complicity in framing Marcel Clark?" Richard asked.

"You realize that would destroy my reputation, and I'll have to die with that knowledge."

Richard wasn't about to accept that guilt trip. "Mr. Jones, your reputation was in tatters the moment you accepted the bribe." Surely, there had to have been many others, as well. Once a louse, always a louse.

Richard heard the man sigh. "If nothing else, I might regain my wife's respect. She's let me know how much I've disappointed her—and on a regular basis."

Richard wished he could meet—thank—the woman for pressuring the old, sick man to do the right thing.

"Thank you for speaking with me today, Mr. Jones. Your help will change the life of the man who was wronged."

"It's sure about to change mine," Jones muttered.

"Will you speak to Detective Destross and tell him what you know?"

"I suppose I can," the old man said wearily.

"I'll have him get in touch with you."

"Very well," Jones said, sounding defeated. He ended the call.

Once again, Richard replaced the phone's receiver and sat back in his chair. Without corroborating testimony, all he had to present to Detective Destross was hearsay, and useless to prove Marcel Clark innocent of a potential murder charge.

Now he just had to worry about Jones getting cold feet.

He looked at the clock. He'd email Destross about his

discoveries, but he wasn't sure he wanted to talk to Jeff about it. Not yet. He wanted to think about it. Write up his notes.

Was he being secretive, or was he being thorough?

Maybe a little of both, Richard decided.

But he wouldn't sit on this information for long.

A sound in the hall alerted him to Brenda's presence. "Dinner will be ready soon. I assume you'll want a drink beforehand."

"I'll have one as soon as Jeff gets here."

Brenda nodded. She studied his face. "Is something wrong?"

"I may be close to cracking the case."

She brightened. "Really. When will you know for sure?"

Richard shrugged. "Maybe tomorrow."

"Are you going to tell Jeff?"

"Tomorrow."

Brenda frowned.

"I've been thinking. If I'm going take a greater interest in the business, I should devote more of my time at the office during business hours. I don't want to be bringing work home with me. We had too much of that in California."

"We sure did," Brenda muttered. "But you will fill him—and me—in on what you've learned tomorrow?"

"Definitely."

"Okay."

"Where's Betsy?"

"She fell asleep in her highchair. I'd better get back to her. I only meant to be gone a minute," Brenda said and scooted off.

Richard followed her. He hadn't imbibed yet that day. He'd earned his Scotch…and soda. Adding the latter would make Brenda happy and perhaps ween him back to an acceptable liquor level, if that was possible.

Baby steps, he thought. From now on, he would push forward…even if only with baby steps.

Chapter 28

Despite the damage to the planet, Richard and Jeff had a tacit understanding that they would not be carpooling to their office on a regular basis. Jeff had already left for the day before Richard was even out of bed. But he'd showered, dressed, and accepted a brown-bag breakfast of a thawed bagel smeared with cream cheese that Brenda offered as he headed out the door.

That morning, there was music in the office. Nothing loud or obnoxious, but low key and coming from a small radio that sat on the little fridge behind Emily's desk.

"Hey, Doctor A," she called cheerfully in greeting as he arrived for a second day in a row. It felt good. Not as good as when he'd worked at the think tank in Pasadena, where he'd spent so many years and thought of the people he worked with as friends. Emily wasn't a friend, but she might be one day. It was too soon to tell.

"Morning," he said and struggled to get out of his coat. Emily jumped to her feet and assisted him, hanging up his coat just as Jeff emerged from their shared office. "'Bout time you got here," he said, but he didn't sound angry. In fact, Richard thought he sounded pleased.

"Sorry. I was up during the night thinking about things."

"Work things?" Jeff asked.

Richard nodded. "Let's get some coffee and talk about it."

So, they poured cups of java, doctored them up, and retreated to the conference room for a chat.

When Richard opened the bag, he found not one but two bagels. One an everything, which he thought was probably meant for him, and the other a sesame.

"Looks like Brenda packed a breakfast for both of us."

"You've got one helluva lady there," Jeff said rather wistfully.

"You don't have to tell me."

Paper plates and cutlery from the day before were still stationed on the side table against the far wall, and they grabbed napkins before taking seats on opposite sides of the conference table.

Richard passed the sesame bagel to his brother before he settled his own on a napkin. He didn't possess the kind of sensitivity his brother had, but he could tell just by studying Jeff's face that something wasn't quite right."

"Talk," Richard said.

While pulling apart the halves of his bagel into smaller bits, Jeff relayed his most recent encounter with the disembodied spirit of Louie Susskind.

"I'm sorry you've had such a rough time with the old guy."

"Yeah, when I consulted Sophie about him, I was bummed when she said I'd have to figure this out on my own."

"That doesn't sound encouraging."

"It wasn't."

"What are you going to do?" Richard asked and took a bite of the bottom half of his bagel.

"I'm not sure that staying away from the hospital is a good thing. I mean, it could anger him even more," Jeff said. He looked worried, and the hairs on the back of Richard's neck bristled.

"I keep remembering what happened with sweet Alice Newcomb," Jeff continued.

Alice had been a restless spirit Jeff had encountered the summer before. She'd enlisted his aid to find her murderer—and he'd done it, much to her chagrin. But when confronted with another murderous soul, her fury had proved deadly. It seemed inconceivable that a disembodied spirit could inflict such violence.

"When I was lying in bed awake last night, I had an absurd thought," Richard began, wondering why he would even voice his late-night thoughts.

"Yeah?" Jeff said.

"There seems to be some weird juxtaposition of the things we've looked into in the past few years. It's almost as though fate drew our divergent inquiries together until we found that they intersected."

Jeff picked up his coffee mug and stared into it. "In what way?"

"First, let me tell you what I discovered yesterday about the police investigation into the Clark arson and Empire Properties."

"So you think Louie had something to do with the arson?"

"Supposedly, he's been keeping a big secret, right?"

"Right."

"Well, what if my missing arsonist suspect is the same person as your brewmaster?"

"The odds are astronomical," Jeff said skeptically.

"Not when you think about it. You had ties to Krista Marsh, and I had ties to Wes Timberly."

Jeff looked away, utterly disgusted. "I try not to think about her *and* the havoc she caused me."

"We also figured out that Maria Spodina had a link to Alice Newcomb."

Jeff continued to look skeptical. "Are you suggesting that when we take on disparate cases, they'll always align in some way?"

"Not at all, but you have to admit it's happened more than once in our endeavors. If nothing else, it's either pretty damned coincidental or—"

"Or what?" Jeff asked, his tone a challenge.

"Fate."

Jeff's expression grew even more somber, and he shook his head. "I don't like that explanation. Fate means we have no control over our lives. That we're prisoners to some higher power. And I, for one, don't believe in a higher power."

Richard did, but with caveats. "Then how do you explain it?"

Jeff looked uncomfortable. "I've often invoked the idea of Karma, but I don't really believe in that, either."

The brothers were quiet for a minute or two, sipping their coffee and nibbling their bagels, pondering just what made their alliance so strong when it came to ferreting out the truth to help them solve crimes. Or at least, that was what Richard was thinking. He was never sure what was going through his brother's mind.

"So," Jeff began, "you think Marcel Clark and Abe Bachmann *might* be the same person?"

"I'm not ruling it out. But think about it: one of them disappeared and the other appeared at just about the same time. Marcel Clark was a brilliant chemistry student. Abe Bachmann is an equally talented brewmaster. They're about the same age. They're both black."

Jeff shook his head, looking uncomfortable. "If you're right, and I'm not saying you are, how do you prove it?"

"Let's go back to our office and do a little experiment," Richard suggested.

Jeff shrugged and rose to his feet. "I'm game." He picked up his plate with the rest of his uneaten bagel and coffee cup and preceded Richard out of the conference room.

Once in their shared office, Richard moved to sit behind his desk. He powered up his computer before typing the URL for a particular website and hit the search button. In no time flat, a screen came up that asked for a picture to be uploaded. Richard clicked the box and found a picture of Marcel Clark from a file on the cloud. He asked the program to add twenty years to the face of the young black man in the picture and hit enter. Seconds later, an altered image replaced the one on the screen.

Jeff leaned in for a closer. "Goddamnit. I think you're right," he said incredulously. "It's the spitting image of Abe Bachmann. How did you know?"

Richard frowned. "I took a wild guess."

Jeff straightened, looking somber. "Okay. Say Abe Bachmann actually *is* Marcel Clark, what do we do with that information?"

Richard related his conversation with retired BPD Detective Jones the evening before.

"That's fantastic," Jeff said enthusiastically.

"If he lives long enough to give a formal statement."

Jeff immediately sobered. "Damn."

"I was thinking we might also want to visit the arson scene."

"Are the remnants of that house still around?" Jeff asked.

Richard nodded. "It didn't burn to the ground. Like most of the area, it was renovated two decades ago. Last night I did some research and found that the current owners bought the property ten years ago. It was featured in a historical tour of the neighborhood a few years back in *The Buffalo News* and a WKBW TV feature. I'll send you the links."

"Is it likely we can get a personal tour?"

"I don't think asking to visit the room where Mrs. Johnson died would be well received. Still, there's no reason you can't visit the property to see if you can glom onto something. If nothing else, you can stand on the sidewalk in front of the place. If it's been shoveled, that is."

"I'm willing to do it, but I'm not hopeful."

"It would only take a few minutes. I think we ought to go for it."

"If you want," Jeff said with a shrug, still sounding skeptical.

"Let's finish our bagels and coffee and hit the road," Richard said.

"Agreed."

But during the little eat-a-thon, the brothers didn't have that much to talk about. The one thing they did agree to was to go in Richard's car. Ten minutes later, they were on the road.

The neighborhood's Victorian and Edwardian homes had undergone a miraculous transformation during the previous three decades. The area that had once been considered slums had been transformed through sweat equity and a huge infusion of capital to be a shining example of a section of Buffalo that had been brought back to life.

Gentrification revived old neighborhoods, but also uprooted its denizens who could no longer afford to live there. Of course, the city encouraged that kind of renovation. The more a structure could be improved, the better the city's tax coffers.

But as Richard had observed, after the fire, Mrs. Clark's family had been displaced from her former neighborhood only to be relocated to one that hadn't seen such improvements.

The Northbend Neighborhood where old Mrs. Johnson had died still featured several empty lots where the houses that had once inhabited those spaces had been razed. Richard parked his Mercedes in front of a beautiful Victorian Painted Lady. Even in the last stages of winter, they could see that the place had been lovingly landscaped and the home meticulously maintained.

They exited the car, and Richard hung back as Jeff strode a few steps up the snow-blown driveway of the home that had once housed the Clark clan.

He stood there for a long time, staring at the restored building, seeming to commune with the place. Then, with his back toward his brother, Jeff crouched down and grabbed a handful of crumbly dirt beside the snow that had receded, rubbing it between his fingers until the last of it had fallen to the cold ground again.

Finally, he stood.

"Well?" Richard demanded.

"It's hard to say," Jeff said, looking just a little confused. "I mean, I'm getting vibes from the current owners. They love this house. They've put a lot of effort into the landscaping because they haven't had to do much to the house itself. The previous owners brought it back to its former glory."

"So you're not getting any vibes about the Clark family?"

"I'm not sure," Jeff said enigmatically. "I mean, there's some kind of understated sadness about the place, but I can't pinpoint what it was and what went on in the past." He frowned. "Sorry."

"Hey, this was a long shot at best."

Their heads jerked up as the home's front door opened and a woman of about fifty with gray-streaked hair, a blue polar fleece jacket, and magenta sweatpants stepped onto the covered veranda. "Can I help you?" she asked.

Richard figured *what the hell* and stepped forward. "We've

been admiring your lovely home. Would you have a few moments to tell us about it?"

Apparently, that was the correct opening question, for the woman beamed and moved closer to the edge of the porch, while Richard and his brother stepped forward.

"What would you like to know?"

"We're particularly interested in the more recent history of the home. To narrow it down, about twenty years ago."

The woman shook her head. "I'm afraid I can't speak to those days."

Just as Richard had thought.

"But … the former owners had their own opinions about what happened before they bought the place," she continued.

"Would you have contact information for them?" Richard asked, despite knowing he could look that information up online.

The woman lowered her gaze, looking sad. "We communicated with them for the first couple of years we owned the house, but first the husband died and then the wife stopped responding. I'm sad to say I'm pretty sure she's passed away, too."

"What did they tell you about the house?" Jeff asked. "Anything detrimental?"

The woman's mouth took a downward turn. "Only that there was a death in it before they bought it. I wouldn't have thought they'd mention it since that's not what any real estate agent wants to be said about a place when it's on the market."

"What exactly did she say?" Jeff asked.

The woman looked thoughtful. "Just that it had happened more than a decade before when there'd been a fire in the house and that she'd never felt any negativity. In fact, she felt the house welcomed the improvements they'd made to it."

"Did the former owners mention anything left by the

former tenants?" Richard asked, not expecting a positive response to the question.

The woman looked thoughtful. "Well, we do have a box of old stuff in the attic."

Richard shot a look at his brother, who looked just as intrigued.

"What's in it?" Richard asked.

She shrugged. "I'm not really sure. I went through it shortly after we bought the house, but I can't remember exactly what's in there."

"Would it be terribly inconvenient if we had a look?" Richard asked.

"Why would you want to?" the woman asked suspiciously.

The brothers exchanged a knowing look, but it was Jeff who addressed the question.

"We're a consulting firm," he said, extracted his wallet from the back pocket of his slacks, removed a card, and handed it to her. "I'm Jeff Resnick, and this is my partner, Dr. Richard Alpert. We've been asked to look into the death that occurred here. It's a cold case that the Buffalo PD wants to close."

The woman scrutinized the card. "Well," she began doubtfully, "I'd like to help the authorities, but…."

"If you'd like to speak to Detective Destross of the Buffalo Police Department, I'd be glad to give you his number," Richard volunteered.

She shook her head. "You look like trustworthy guys." She threw a glance over her shoulder to the house, then seemed to make a decision. "Come on in."

And with that, she ushered them onto the porch and into the house.

The entryway had been beautifully restored with varnished gumwood trim and attractive vintage-style tile just inside the door. A huge oak hall tree stood against the left-hand wall inside a plaster arch. A large speckled mirror dominated the structure, which held brightly polished brass hooks with a ledge above a small drawer. Stands on either side held an assortment of colorful umbrellas and canes—more for decor, Richard decided, than anything else.

"And your name is?" Richard asked.

"Sarah Peters. My husband and I have lived here for the past ten years."

"You've got a beautiful home," Jeff said, looking past her into the parlor.

"Why don't you take a seat and I'll go find that box. It might take me a few minutes."

"Thank you."

She waited to make sure they sat down on the home's style-appropriate furniture before she mounted the stairs to the attic.

"She's sure trusting," Jeff muttered. "I sure as hell wouldn't have invited two strange men into my home and left them alone."

"You're paranoid," Richard said, but if he was honest, he felt the same way.

And it turned out that Sarah wasn't as trusting as they'd thought as a full-grown rottweiler suddenly appeared in the doorway to the room where they sat.

"Hey, pooch!" Richard called and moved to stand, but the dog growled menacingly.

He sat back down.

"He—or she—is no friendly beast like Holly," Jeff observed.

"I guess not."

The dog seemed content to keep an eye on the intruders in its home, and Richard was just as glad to stay in his seat and not provoke the animal.

It was Jeff who finally broke the quiet. "Is it likely anything the former owners scavenged during the renovations to the house will help us in our investigation?"

"Who knows," Richard said. He looked around the room. "This is a great place. I really like what they've done restoring the woodwork and all the Victorian wallpaper and dècor."

Jeff frowned. "Feels like a museum, if you ask me," he reflected.

The Alpert house was, for the most part, a relic from the 1940s when it had been built. "Does my home feel like a museum to you?"

Jeff shrugged. "It's not my taste, but then I'm prejudiced. That house has a lot of negative energy—at least for me."

Richard could understand it. And yet Jeff had *asked* to return to it in his time of need. Was that something they might want to discuss at some point, but not just then?

Richard changed the subject. "Are you going to visit Louie today?"

Jeff's expression soured. "I suppose I have to, but I sure hope he's calmed down since we last spoke. Unfortunately, I don't have anything new to tell him. Until he's dead, he seems to be confined to that floor of the hospital. After that…." He let the sentence hang, but Richard could see the worry in his brother's expression.

"What was your initial opinion of the guy, and how has it changed?" Richard asked.

"At first he seemed pretty rational, but the more I've interacted with him, the more hostile he's become. It really unnerves me how he feels toward Omega. What has Abe had to contend with working for the guy?"

"Maybe you should start referring to him as Marcel," Richard suggested.

"Not yet," Jeff said. "Not until we know for sure."

They heard footsteps trundle down the lovingly restored

staircase, and the dog rose to its feet as Sarah returned with a saggy cardboard carton.

"Good boy," she praised as she passed the rottweiler and entered the room. She placed the box on the tufted leather hassock that served as a coffee table and sat on one of the upholstered chairs. "This is everything. Feel free to rummage."

Jeff nodded in Richard's direction. "Go for it."

Richard sat forward and pulled open the interwoven flaps to reveal the pitiful collection of objects within. A singed photo album sat on the top of the small pile. He removed it, and two decades after the fire, it still reeked of acrid smoke. He opened the pages, sharing the contents with his brother. They took in page after page of black-and-white and time-bleached color photos, studying the faces of the people portrayed. Adults, children, teens. But one face seemed to stand out to Jeff. He tapped his finger on the photo of the black teen. "That's him. That's Abe."

Sarah looked up. "Do you know this family?"

"We're pretty sure we do," Richard answered. "I know it's a lot to ask, but I've been in contact with the family pictured in this album. Would you consider—?"

"Turning this stuff over to them?" she asked. "Of course. The former owners asked my husband and me if we'd mind trying to find the family of those pictured. We had the best of intentions, but then we didn't know where to start as they hadn't had any luck."

Richard sorted through the rest of the box's contents. A soot-darkened broach with some missing stones, along with some official papers: an honorable discharge certificate, a high school diploma, and a couple of birth certificates.

"It all seems so sad," Sarah said. "If you can return these items to their rightful owners, I'd sure like to know about it. Maybe even meet them," she said, and Richard saw her eyes were welling with tears. "You see, I was adopted. Though I've tried to find my birth family, even using those ancestry websites, I haven't had any luck. If I could help a family reconnect to their past, it would sure make my day."

"I assure you, the family pictured in this album would be extremely happy to have it. They suffered terribly after the fire. In fact, one of their own was accused of setting that fire. We don't think he was responsible. We're trying to prove it."

"Well, good luck to you," Sarah said.

Richard replaced the box's contents and folded in the flaps once more. "I know the family will be grateful to be reunited with these links to their past."

"If they'd like to visit the house, I'd be glad to give them a tour of what the former owners and we've done—unless you think that wouldn't be appropriate. I know the home was pretty dilapidated before the former owners bought it. It was said the landlord who owned it refused to make the repairs that were so desperately needed. That could have been the cause for the fire."

Except that it wasn't. Arson was the cause.

Richard shot a look at his brother, who gave him the briefest of nods.

"I'll let them know of your generous offer," Richard promised.

"I'd appreciate it if you'd get back to me—just to let me know…." Her voice trailed off.

"Of course."

Richard rose to his feet, and once again the dog growled menacingly.

"Earl, quiet!" Sarah ordered.

"Thanks so much for your generosity. No matter what happens, we'll be sure to contact you again to let you know if we're able to resolve the situation," Richard said.

"Let me give you my phone number," the woman said, waiting until Richard could jot it down.

She preceded them to the entryway and grabbed the dog's collar just as it lunged at them and barked.

"Thanks again," Richard said.

"Yeah, thanks," Jeff echoed as they quickly took their leave.

Richard carried the box to the car, setting it on the back seat before the brothers got into the Mercedes.

"That went a helluva lot better than we could've ever expected," Jeff said.

"Yeah, but what will happen when we present the family with their long-lost heirlooms?"

"We?"

"Well, Brenda and hopefully me."

"If they weren't willing to meet you before, what makes you think they'll agree to meet with you now?" Jeff asked.

"I hope Brenda can convince the matriarch to let me tag along."

"And if she can't?"

Richard shrugged and started the engine, shifting into drive and pulling away from the curb. "I may have to resort to blackmail. I won't give up the goods unless they meet me face to face."

"That's a risk. Are you really that big a jerk?"

Richard's hand tightened around the steering wheel. "No. But it's the only leverage I have."

"And how will you bring up the subject that we may have found their long-lost kin?"

"That's a good question." For which Richard had no answer. "If they refuse, I'm won't deny them the photos and other precious items."

"I would hope not," Jeff said, leaning back in his seat.

Richard braked for the light at the end of the street and checked traffic before turning right.

"When will you contact them?" Jeff asked.

"There's no time like the present, or at least when I get home and give Brenda a show-and-tell performance."

"She seemed very protective of the family."

"She's a compassionate person. I wouldn't have expected anything else. What're your plans for the rest of the day?" Richard risked a glance askance. Jeff looked thoughtful.

"I'd sure like to get Abe on his own to see if I could get him to open up, but he's been kind of hostile toward me. If he's lived undercover for two decades, he probably sees me as someone who could expose him, thinking it could lead to a jail sentence."

"But if he's innocent—"

"We don't know that for sure."

Richard braked for another red light. "Yeah. Which means we're still on the hook with Detective Destross to give him a viable suspect."

They drove in silence for a few minutes.

"You hungry?" Richard asked.

"Sort of."

"Let's catch some lunch. Maybe we'll come up with some bright ideas over a burger."

"Stranger things have happened."

When Jeff was around, strange things always happened.

Chapter 29

As it was close to noon, Richard steered the car to a tavern near our office, where we had lunch. They served Horse Hockey pale ale on tap, so we ordered it along with our sandwiches. It was okay—but nothing special. Why a big conglomerate wanted to buy the business was beyond me.

Richard drove us back to the office, where we parted company. He headed for home, and I killed time at the office until it was nearly time for Omega's next shift at the hospital with Louie. After our last encounter, I didn't want to be alone with him—not that I thought Omega could do anything to quell his wrath, but it wouldn't hurt to have a kindred spirit nearby.

While I pretended to do work in my office, Emily gave herself a manicure. We really needed to find more for her to do.

I drove back to Sisters Hospital and, once again, waited until I saw Omega walk into the building. I hurried to join her.

"Mr. Resnick," she said in greeting.

"Call me Jeff," I reminded her. "I'm sorry I left you in the lurch yesterday. To tell you the truth, I didn't feel safe with Louie after his meltdown. You may not believe it, but I've seen what havoc a disembodied spirit can wield. It wasn't pretty." She paused to give me a strange look. Was it disbelief or one of understanding?

"What happened after I left yesterday?"

"As I said, I'm not as in tune with Mr. Susskind as you are, but he was in a rage for many hours."

"Did it negatively affect you?" I asked, concerned.

She waved a hand in dismissal. "Not at all. I sang to myself the songs of my grandmother and mother, and eventually he calmed down."

We came to a bank of elevators, and I pushed the UP button. "I have several questions I need to ask him. Do you think it unwise if I confront him with them?" I asked.

"You have a job to do—which he has tasked you to do. If you aren't getting the answers you need elsewhere, you must try to get them from him."

The elevator opened and several people disembarked. We entered and I pushed the button to Louie's floor. "What was his condition when you left him this morning?"

She shrugged. "Unchanged—which is still confounding his doctors. He seems to be tethered to this world until something can be found or done to ease him into what lies beyond. It is the way with those whose life on this earth is incomplete."

The elevator opened and we stepped onto Louie's floor. I admit it; my gut tightened as I remembered the awful wrath sweet Alice Newcomb had unleashed against the woman who had not only done me wrong—as clichéd as that sounded—but ruined the lives of so many others, as well. Hell hath no fury like a woman scorned … but I had a bad feeling that Louie Susskind might be an even more powerful nemesis.

Coward that I am, I let Omega precede me into Louie's

room. As usual, his spirit sat on the stone window sill and looked up as she arrived to relieve her client. Teresa Barton hurriedly gathered up her things.

"Omega, glad to see you," she said as she shrugged into her coat.

"Has there been any change in his condition?"

Teresa shrugged. "Not a thing." I wasn't sure if the woman sounded relieved or discouraged.

Louie saw me standing at one side of the door's threshold. "Resnick—what the hell are you doing here?"

I didn't answer. I wasn't about to until his daughter took off.

"I'll see you in the morning," Teresa told Omega and grabbed her oversized purse, tossing it over her shoulder as she practically fled the room and I wondered if she was catching all the negativity her father's spirit was spewing.

"Have a good evening," Omega called after Teresa, but the woman didn't turn to acknowledge the well wish. Still, Omega didn't seem fazed by the slight. Instead, she shrugged out of her coat, hung it on the back of the chair beside the bed, and settled her things on the bedside table to begin her long nightly vigil.

"Resnick!" Louie's spirit hollered once more and I finally stepped into the room. "We've got unfinished business," he bellowed and stood up, looking incredibly ferocious for someone short in stature and not really there.

"You've got that right," I said as I unzipped my jacket. "If I'm supposed to save your brewery, there are some things I need to know."

"Like what?"

"Well, it would help if I actually knew about who you are. Where you came from. Why the brewery means so much to you."

"What could the past possibly have to do with the here and now?" the old man challenged me.

"That's the thing—I won't know until I know."

"You're full of shit."

"And I can't help you if I'm not clued in. Accept that, or I'm willing to walk."

"I told you—you *owe* me," Louie growled.

"And I don't believe you have the kind of power you say you do. In fact, I'm the one who told you that you *might*—and that's a pretty big assumption—be able to hang around once your body dies. I'm willing to take that chance that you can't come after me once the guy in that bed passes on," I bluffed.

Louie's expression soured and he seemed to shrink just a little as he took his seat on the window sill once more. "Go on," he grumbled.

Omega had settled herself on the chair and seemed to have tuned out of our conversation. Was it self-preservation, or didn't she give a shit?

It seemed incredibly warm in that room. Hospitals, I've found, are either way too hot or way too cold, which can't be good for anyone's well-being. I leaned against the wall of what suddenly seemed a catastrophically small room.

"Tell me your background. I want to know all about you."

Louie scowled. "I was born, I went to school, I went to work. I got married, had kids, and now I'm nearly dead. What else is there to know?" he demanded.

"There are a lot of years between all those events. Why are you afraid to tell me about them?"

"I'm not afraid of anything." It was his turn to bluff, for as soon as he said the words, his gaze shot to his dying self and his expression grew fearful. The idea of leaving this earth scared the shit out of him.

"How far did you go in school? High school? College?"

"I dropped out in the tenth grade and went to work. My

father was dead, and our family needed the money. There, are you happy?"

"It must have been a hard life. What did you do?"

"At first, I worked in a grocery store stocking shelves."

Reading between the lines, I'll bet he also stole as much as he could get away with stuffing into his coat pockets and maybe brown paper bags.

"And after that?"

"I got into real estate. I was pretty good at it, too."

"You sold houses?"

"I started working construction. It paid a helluva lot more than retail, that's for sure."

"And how long did that last?"

He laughed. "Until I married the boss's daughter. Then he brought me into the business."

Empire Properties—just as Richard had learned.

"What was your role?"

"At first, just following him around. The old man would buy up real estate—usually odd lots—and develop them."

"Develop them how?"

"Put houses on them and sell 'em, what else?"

"Tell me more," I encouraged.

"There's nothing to tell. We bought undervalued properties, improved them if we could, and either rented them out or sold them to the highest bidders."

"And where did you buy these properties?"

"Wherever we could. Why is this so important to you?" Louie demanded.

"I'm trying to understand where you came from and how you got to where you are. Working real estate and brewing beer aren't exactly trades that go together."

For some reason, I glanced at Omega and noted her expression was enigmatic. I wasn't sure she gathered what Louie was saying, but she was trying hard to appear as though she wasn't adamantly listening to my end of the conversation.

I tried not to notice.

"A man can't have a hobby?" Louie finally answered. "I loved beer. I was fascinated by the idea of making it. It's too bad I had to wait forty years before making that dream come true with our brewery."

Our brewery. Who did he include in that statement? Him and Bethany or was he including the rest of his family?

I asked.

"Nick was never interested in beer—unless it was for free. The worst thing I ever did was send that kid to law school. He turned on me like a snake."

"And why was that?"

"Because he got caught up on all liberal feel-good save-the-planet crap, and especially the Great Lakes."

"You don't think that's a good thing?" I asked.

"Shit, no. It's every man for himself, and if you don't believe in it, you're an asshole."

From what I'd seen, Nick Susskind had nothing but empathy for the souls who'd lost their lives on the Great Lakes. What was wrong with that? But Louie seemed to view compassion as a weakness instead of a virtue. That said, if Nick knew Louie's shameful secret and had kept it secret, did that make him as bad an SOB as his old man?

I changed tacks. "And how long ago was it that you began making beer?"

"I started home brewing when the kids were little. My batches got bigger and bigger, so I started researching craft brewing. When my father-in-law died, the wife inherited everything, and the idea of actually starting a craft brewery was suddenly possible. When Bethany showed an interest, instead of college, I sent her to learn the trade at a little brewery in Vermont of all places."

"And?" I encouraged.

"She came back after a two-year apprenticeship with a lot of ideas. I had the business smarts, and she had the big batch brewing experience."

"Would you say Bethany's your favorite because she was interested in your hobby?"

"That's a crappy thing to ask a father," Louie groused.

"But is it true?" I pushed.

Louie turned his gaze out the window. "Probably. Nick and Teresa were more their mother's kids than mine."

"Bethany's the youngest, right?"

"Yup."

Had Louie been more invested in his original career when his two oldest were born? It wasn't surprising that the youngest should be his pride and joy when she became his biggest cheerleader for opening a brewery.

When it came to my investigation, Bethany wasn't high on my list of things to contemplate. What I needed to push him on was his brewmaster … and I wasn't sure how to approach it.

I decided bullshit was my best friend.

"And how has Abe Bachmann impacted your business?"

Louie shrugged. "I told you. He's just an employee."

"Then why is he the brewmaster instead of Bethany?"

"Extenuating circumstances," Louie hedged.

"Which were?"

"None of your damn business."

What had he decided not to tell me?

"You say Abe is just an employee, but the brewmaster is the most important person when it comes to making beer."

"So *you* say."

"Then who do *you* think is the most important person at Horse Hockey Brewing?"

"The boss, of course."

"Bethany."

"*I'm* the boss," Louie roared.

"Not anymore. Even if he," I nodded toward the guy on the bed, "should make it out of here, he's more likely to end up in a nursing home than walk the aisles between the steel vats at Horse Hockey Brewing."

"Are you actively trying to piss me off?" Louie growled.

Yeah, I was, and that wouldn't get me answers.

"What's Abe Bachmann's background? How long has he been with the brewery? How much do you trust him?"

"Why do you care?" Louie's eyes were blazing now.

"Because I think he sabotaged a hell of a lot of beer."

Louie gaped at me. "What?"

"The production line is down, and there are cases and kegs of beer sitting on the warehouse floor, with not much is going out the door. You asked me to save your brewery—I'm trying to do it. Now, are you ready to tell me about Abe Bachmann?"

"He'd never betray us," Louie muttered.

"Then who else has a mighty big grudge against the brewery?" I pushed.

Before he could answer, a scrubs-clad tech with her computer on wheels entered the room. It was time for Louie's body's vitals check.

"Do you want us to leave?" I asked.

"No. It'll only take a minute."

It took nearly five by the time she'd charted everything, and by then, the shock had worn off and the incorporeal Louie's expression was of pure anger. I could almost see the wheels turning in his brain, trying to figure out what he should say and do next—and mostly to deflect me.

"All done," the bright young woman said, but then her gaze lingered on Louie's body for a moment, and she frowned, shaking her head. It wouldn't have been the best thing to do had we been relatives, but it proved that time was growing short for Louie Susskind.

Omega and I glanced at one another as the woman trundled her cart out of the room. Omega had only heard one side of my conversation with Louie. I wondered what she made of it.

Louie was the first to speak. "Why do you think Abe has something against the brewery?"

"Is it the brewery, or might it be someone *at* the brewery?"

"He gets along with everybody." The words sounded fine, but his tone indicated something else.

"Things are changing at the brewery. Selling it to a big company could destroy everything you've built."

"We're fighting against that," Louie asserted.

"Bethany and Abe are fighting against that. Nick and Teresa aren't. What better way to make the brewery unsalable than to taint its product."

"That's stupid. If we get a bad reputation—" Louie began.

I cut him off. "The tainted beer isn't leaving the warehouse, but it is a mighty big problem for anyone looking to buy the assets."

Louie shook his head. "We aren't actually negotiating with anyone to sell."

"*You* aren't. What about Nick? He's a lawyer. He's got lots of friends in high places. Once you're out of the picture, under the terms of your will, he'd own one-third of the brewery." I was bluffing since I had no clue what was in Louie's will, but I could see by his expression that I was right.

"Sabotaging a single batch of beer wouldn't hurt the brewery too badly," I continued. "But what about the next time the idea of selling comes along? Nick seems like a man who gets what he wants." Not unlike his father, although I'd say a lot less ruthless. "If the first deal falls through, I'm sure he'll try again. And even if the brand can't be sold, the equipment sure can."

The anger seemed to be draining from Louie's face. He'd said Abe would never betray him, but it was apparent he felt his son had.

"Is there a reason—beyond money—that Nick wants to sell the brewery? He seems like a pretty successful attorney."

Louie shook his head. I had a feeling the two had clashed throughout Nick's life. It was an interesting angle to explore, but I needed to get back to discussing Abe. There'd been real friction when I'd pushed.

I usually get vibes from touching people, but I was pretty sure my touching Louie's unconscious body wouldn't give me any further insight. That said, I was now sure Louie knew about the tainted beer. Hell, it had probably been his idea. But something had flashed in his eyes at the thought of Abe betraying him. I decided to push it.

"Let's get back to Abe," I said. Louie glowered at me. "How long has he worked for you?"

"The brewery's eighteen years old."

"That wasn't my question."

"I don't know," Louie said and looked away.

"I think you do," I pushed. "Maybe he'd worked for you for just about twenty years."

Louie still wouldn't look at me.

I leaned against the wall. It was getting hot in that awful little room. I should have taken my jacket off when I arrived, but there really wasn't anywhere to put it.

"The thing is…when I looked into Abe's background there isn't much of a paper trail."

"What does that mean?"

"Well, the guy's obviously in his early forties, but there's no real record of him until about twenty years ago. He didn't just spring from the head of Zeus like Athena, so where did he come from? He's got a very Jewish name, yet he wears a chain around his neck with a crucifix. I didn't get the feeling that he's a messianic Jew, either."

"You should never trust your feelings," Louie growled menacingly.

I glanced at Omega, who looked like she wanted to laugh and was doing her best to stifle it.

"It seems that Abe has no home," I continued. "His official address is a PO box. He doesn't seem to have a savings or checking account, either—at least that I could find."

Louie's glare had turned malevolent. "Lots of black people don't have bank accounts," Louie countered.

And how would he know that?

"It all seems just a little funny," I continued. "What do *you* know about his background? Why did you hire him? Did he have experience in beer fermentation? Where did he work before he came to work for you?"

"Why the hell don't you ask him that?" Louie practically shouted.

If Omega couldn't hear the nearly dead guy, she sure seemed to pick up on his escalating anger, for her eyebrows rose, and she swung her gaze to the inert form on the hospital bed. A moment later, she suddenly rose from her seat. "Enough!" she called. "That's quite enough."

Louie's spiritual head jerked in her direction. "Can she hear me?" he demanded.

"No, but she's aware of what's going on."

"I think it's time for you to leave, Mr. Resnick," Omega said.

"Jeff," I reminded her once again.

She nodded, but I was pretty sure she'd never address me by my first name. "I think you have enough to pursue your next line of inquiry."

"What the hell is she talking about?" Louie demanded.

I started for the door. "I'll see you again soon, Louie."

"The hell you will."

I turned at the door. "We have a verbal contract," I reminded him.

"Not anymore."

I turned away. I was in too deep to stop now.

Chapter 30

Richard entered the house, carrying the saggy cardboard carton. He bypassed the butler's pantry and set the filthy thing on the kitchen table. He had a pretty good idea of what Brenda would say about it. She was nowhere in sight, but her van was still in the garage, so she had to be somewhere in the house. He opened the door to the basement, but no sounds of the washer or dryer greeted him. Betsy usually went down for a nap after lunch and awoke about now, so Brenda was probably upstairs.

Tossing his coat over the back of a chair, he headed for the fridge, opened the door, and thought about having a beer. But it wouldn't be happy hour for another couple of hours. He closed the fridge door and contemplated heading for his study when Brenda entered the kitchen.

"What is that filthy box doing on my nice clean table?" she demanded.

"Just the ticket I need to get in to see the Clark family."

"What's in it?" Brenda asked, leaning forward and sniffing, apparently not liking what she smelled.

"Jeff and I went to the home where Mrs. Johnson died."

Brenda's eyes widened, but she said nothing.

"The previous owners collected things they thought might one day be returned to the family, although they didn't know who they were. They held onto them for the entire time they owned the home and left them with the new owners, hoping they could pass it on."

"And this is your leverage to meet them?"

"I really need to talk to Mrs. Clark. It'll be your job to get me in."

"She was pretty adamant that she didn't want to talk to Mr. Whitey White."

"There's a photo album full of family memories in that box, among other things. It's up to you to convince her to talk to me."

"And if I can't."

"Nothing says I have to give it to her any time soon."

"You think I should blackmail the poor woman so she can have her family heirlooms?" Brenda stormed.

"If she says no right away, holding them back for a few days or weeks might soften her resolve."

"That's despicable."

"I didn't say I wouldn't let her have them, but I need to talk to her. I can't learn what I need to know to prove her son innocent by going through a third party. You see that, don't you?"

"Well," Brenda began, but she wasn't at all pleased. "I guess not."

"The thing is…we think we've found the long-missing son."

"Where?" Brenda asked, looking dumbfounded.

"Working as the brewmaster at Horse Hockey Brewing."

To say Brenda looked skeptical was putting it mildly. "Go on."

"We think he's been in contact with his family all along."

"And you intend to badger the man's mother to find the truth?"

"Not at all. But the woman who gave me the contents of that box told us the owner of the Clark's rental house refused to make necessary repairs. What better way to force them out? He could evict them if they didn't pay the rent—but that process could take months. With the entire neighborhood being revived through gentrification, apparently desperation drove him to set the house on fire?"

"That doesn't make sense. Where's the profit if the home was inhabitable—"

"Even if the house was destroyed, which it wasn't, the lot could be sold and something else built on it. If nothing else, it would get rid of another neighborhood eyesore."

Brenda looked distinctly unhappy. "I suppose you want me to call Mrs. Clark this afternoon to arrange another meeting."

"If you could. Try and set it up for tomorrow morning so we can get someone, either Jeff or Emily, to look after Betsy."

"Yes, *Boss*."

"Please call Mrs. Clark," he said, hoping his tone was conciliatory.

"I will," she muttered, not looking at him.

Richard reached across the table to grasp her hand. "Brenda, isn't our aim to find the truth? And in this case, I don't for a second believe Marcel Clark was responsible for the fire that killed his grandmother. Wouldn't it be best for him, for his whole family, if we could prove his innocence?"

She nodded, but there were tears in her eyes. "It just seems so pushy to intrude on her grief."

"Brenda, the fire was over two decades ago."

"Yes, but that poor woman is still suffering. She lost her mother and her son."

"If Jeff and I are right, her son is alive and well—and she knows it. If we can prove his innocence, he can come out of the shadows and resume his real life—his real name."

It took a few moments, but then Brenda did nod. "Okay. When do you want me to call?"

"How about now—before Betsy wakes up from her nap?"

Brenda looked as enthusiastic as she would have been to have a tooth pulled.

Richard headed for his study, with Brenda following slowly behind him. He retrieved the phone number, punched it into the black push-button phone on his desk, and handed her the receiver.

The phone was so old it didn't have a speaker feature, but Richard listened intently as Brenda spoke.

"Mrs. Clark? This is Brenda Stanley. We met last week. Yes. I'm calling because my husband's firm has been in contact with the new owner of your former home. They gave him a box with mementos that the former owners rescued after the fire. It was their wish that they be returned to your family. Would it be convenient for me—and my husband—to bring them to you tomorrow?"

Brenda didn't speak for long seconds, listening to the voice Richard could barely hear on the other end of the line.

"My husband would like to present it to you himself. After all, the box was entrusted to him to—" She stopped speaking and bit her lip. She looked to Richard as if to tell him that his plan wasn't going to work.

He held out his hand to take the receiver.

"Mrs. Clark—"

Richard snatched the receiver from her hand. "Mrs. Clark? Richard Alpert here. I don't want to play hardball, but if you want your mementos back, you will have to talk to me. And I know all about Marcel and the name he's been hiding under all these years."

"Do you mean to threaten me if I don't agree to see you in person?" the woman asked.

"Not threaten. My firm isn't engaged to prove people

guilty. We're determined to prove Marcel innocent. I want to give you back your possessions and tell you why our firm believes we can exonerate him. Please give allow me to do so."

A long silence followed his plea.

"Why should I trust you?" Mrs. Clark asked, the vulnerability evident in her voice was heartbreaking.

"Because I think I can help heal the terrible wrong that's taken place. Please give me the chance to try."

Another long silence followed his words.

"You may visit me tomorrow morning."

They sorted out the timing. "Very good. We'll see you then."

"Just what is in this box you say you've got?"

"For one, a photo album. Hopefully, it'll bring you more happiness than pain."

"I've experienced twenty years of pain, sir. I would dearly love to have the opportunity to experience even one moment of joy. It's been so damned long."

"We'll see you tomorrow, Mrs. Clark. And thank you."

She said no more and broke the connection.

Richard returned the receiver to its cradle. "We're good to go," he told Brenda.

"Good?" She shook her head. "That remains to be seen."

I'D DONE a lot of surveillance in the early days of my insurance career. Oh, those golden times of peeing in a bottle, of feasting on a bag of pistachios, cracking the carcasses and tossing them onto the passenger side floor of my car so that my-then wife could complain about the crunch under her Jimmy Choo shoes.

Yeah. Once upon a time.

It was dark when Abe Bachmann left the brewery. I'd

searched for a car registered in his name via the DMV website—don't ask how—and found none. But several vehicles in the lot were registered under Louis Susskind's name, including delivery trucks, Bethany's car, and the SUV that Abe—Marcel—drove.

I'd parked in a seedy strip mall across the street from Horse Hockey Brewing, sitting there listening to a podcast about getting a garden ready for spring, when I saw the black SUV leave the brewery's lot. Bethany Susskind had left in her car ten minutes before. The brewery was now abandoned for the night.

I had to wait for traffic to clear before I could pull out of the lot and follow my prey. Luckily, I was able to catch up within a long block. Transit Road is a four-laner, and I kept Abe in sight without making a spectacle of myself. And I was pretty sure Abe hadn't spotted a tail.

When he turned right on Sheridan Drive, I was only a car length behind him. He drove a few blocks west before turning right onto Saber Lane. When he pulled into a driveway of a split-level house, I passed it before circling the block. By the time I returned, the lights inside the home blazed, and I noted the number on the mailbox. I didn't need to hang around because I wasn't yet ready to confront Horse Hockey's brewmaster and headed back to the main road before I started for home.

I was too late for supper, but Brenda had saved me a plate of baked chicken, peas, and mashed potatoes. I nuked it, grabbed a beer from the fridge, and took them both to my room, hot to get on my computer. Louie had lied to me, and he'd been more than a little vague. Now it was time to figure it all out.

I'm so thankful for the Internet. Not having to slog through books, magazines, and old newspapers was so much easier than how it had been for generations of investigators before me, and I knew a lot of tricks.

I learned that Bethany Susskind was divorced—no kids—and had been for years. She was good on televised interviews, but it seemed that until recently, the brewery had a company spokesperson to handle the bulk of the brewery's PR. Was she one of the people let go during the recent slowdown?

Bethany lived in a swank, gated community in North Amherst. Despite her address, her attire and manner seemed pretty down to earth. From what I'd seen of her older siblings, they seemed to have tried to rise above the family's more humble beginnings. The house Abe had gone home to was owned by—surprise!—Empire Properties.

I'd drained my beer and eaten nearly all my by-now cold dinner by the time I found everything I was looking for. I can't say I was surprised, but I would have to put that newfound knowledge to use the next morning.

I returned my plate and bottle to the kitchen, rinsing the first, putting it in the dishwasher, and setting the bottle out in the butler's pantry to be recycled.

Herschel came padding into the kitchen, ready for his dinner, and I fed him something stinky before exiting the kitchen. On my way back to the stairs, I met Richard, with Holly dutifully following in his wake.

"What happened with Louie?" he asked.

I gave him a short version and some of what I'd discovered during my Internet sleuthing. "I've uploaded my notes to the R&A cloud. Feel free to read them."

"And Emily, too?" he asked.

"I've already encouraged her to do so. Whether she does it or not…." I let the sentence hang. "How about you?"

"We've got an appointment to see Mrs. Clark tomorrow to give her that box of mementos."

"Great. And I'm going to try to talk to Abe. Maybe we start wrapping this up soon."

"Good luck."

"You, too."

I headed up the stairs to my temporary digs, and he started off toward the kitchen. I hadn't had much time to think about my personal situation, which was actually a relief. That I hadn't heard from Maggie also made me feel more settled.

It wasn't that late—for the grownups in the house—but I got ready for bed anyway, leaving the door open a crack for Herschel. I didn't feel like watching TV, so instead, I climbed into bed, pulled up the covers, turned out the light and stared at the ceiling, thinking about what I'd said to Richard when it came to wrapping up our cases. Yeah, our conversations with the Clark family members might bring some clarity, but there was still the problem of Louie and the brewery. I didn't give a damn whether the brewery sold or how much the Susskind children inherited. It still bothered me that Louie might haunt me for the rest of my life.

I'd seen the kind of havoc a restless spirit could muster, which had scared me shitless. Pondering experiencing that kind of vitriol again kept me staring at the ceiling long after Herschel had come to bed, nestling himself against my knee and purring until he drifted off to dreamland.

I wasn't quite as lucky.

Chapter 31

I was up bright and early the next morning, not knowing what time Abe Bachmann would likely leave for work. I parked a few doors down from his house around seven and waited. My toes were frozen, and I was on my third podcast when he exited the house and headed for his car. I scrambled out of mine and jogged to intercept him.

"Marcel Clark!" I called.

Abe stopped dead, then turned around, searching to see who had called him out. Not recognizing anyone, he turned around.

"Marcel," I called again and approached within ten feet of him.

If looks could kill was an old cliché, but when Abe/Marcel recognized me standing before him, he looked like he could have cheerfully murdered me.

I stepped up to him. "Can we talk?"

"It looks like I've got no option," he growled.

"There's a Tim Horton's on Transit Road. Let's get some coffee."

"And if I don't want to?"

"I suppose I could have this conversation with Bethany—or how about Nick Susskind? I wonder what he would have to say about what I know."

Abe/Marcel said nothing.

"Louie Susskind said you're just an average employee. Nothing special."

The man's eyes blazed. "The guy's nearly dead," he said.

"Eh, not as much as you might think," I told him.

"And what is it you think you know?" Abe/Marcel demanded.

"That's what we need to talk about."

One of Abe/Marcel's neighbors left his house, heading for his car. Abe/Marcel managed a wan smile and waved. The neighbor waved back, retrieved the ice scraper from his car, and started working on the windshield.

Abe/Marcel's SUV had a remote starter. The car was warmed up and ready to go. At least Louie had provided his employee with a good vehicle.

Abe/Marcel looked back at me. "Okay. Timmy's it is."

I got back in my car, and Abe/Marcel followed me. We parked our vehicles and entered the coffee shop, where I encouraged him to get not only coffee but a pastry of his choice. These were R&A Insights bucks I was spending. He chose a bagel and lox. He might not be a landsman, but he sure acted like one.

"What do you want from me?"Abe/Marcel demanded after we sat down with our breakfasts. It was my first—and probably his second.

"Not a damn thing," I said, which wasn't exactly true. "I didn't lie to you and Bethany. Louie Susskind hired me to save his brewery from being sold to the highest bidder. But since our first meeting, I've learned that Mr. Susskind isn't the most honest person I've ever dealt with."

Abe/Marcel sipped his coffee and didn't refute that statement. It was then I again noticed the gold chain with a crucifix hanging around his neck.

"My partner and I have pretty much figured out what's going on at the brewery, and your past," I told him, watching his eyes widen just a bit. "I've documented it all, and I've got a contact with the Buffalo PD's cold case unit, so don't think about trying to silence me because I've covered my ass left, right, and center. And I've got you pegged."

Abe/Marcel's lower lip quivered, and his eyes filled with tears, which I hadn't expected.

"That said, I don't think you had anything to do with your grandmother's death. That the cops fingered you was wrong and shitty. They scapegoated you as a suspect because it was convenient."

Was there relief in the poor, tormented man's eyes?

"I'm pretty sure I know what happened—and I suspect you know now, too."

"Keep talking," Abe/Marcel said, his tone tight.

"From what I can figure, Louie's father-in-law owned the house that your family lived in. They wanted you out, and I believe Louie set the fire."

Abe/Marcel's gaze dipped and a tear cascaded down his cheek.

"Of course, you didn't know that then," I continued. "But you only recently learned what happened. How?" I asked.

Abe/Marcel shook his head and sipped his coffee before answering. "Louie," he said simply. "We kind of argued a few weeks back. He called me an ingrate. He reminded me that he'd saved me from life in prison because the cops wanted to pin my granny's death on me."

"They did. But I wouldn't be surprised if Louie pointed them in your direction in the first place."

"Yeah. I got the same feeling lately," Abe/Marcel admitted.

"Why?"

He shrugged. "I can't remember his exact words. He was talking to himself at the time, but when I thought about all the shit that's gone down over the years, I could only come to one conclusion. Louie had really fucked me."

"And that's why you sabotaged a big batch of beer?"

"I take the fifth," Abe/Marcel said. "But you won't hear me say that to anyone in authority."

"Hey, I don't blame you a bit. Louie took your life away from you. You've been living in hiding for *half* of your life. If you let us—my partner and me—help you, we'll do our best to prove you innocent and give you back your life."

"Yeah, and at what price?" Abe/Marcel asked suspiciously.

"That's the thing. Bethany never asked me what our fee would be."

"And what is it?" Abe/Marcel asked belligerently.

"A buck. One dollar. A bill with George Washington's face on it."

"What the hell?" Abe/Marcel asked. To say he looked skeptical was an understatement.

"That's it. It may seem hard to believe, but we're not in this for the money."

"But you stressed you wanted to be paid," he said, sounding exasperated.

"Yeah, I do. I want that goddamn buck."

For a long moment, Abe/Marcel just stared at me, then he reached for his wallet and pulled out a dollar bill, handing it to me. "Are we square?"

I accepted the bill. "Damn right."

He nodded, but he didn't look happy.

I pocketed the bill and faced him once again. "Does Bethany know you sabotaged the beer?"

"Know about it? She helped me do it. She doesn't want the brewery sold out from under her."

It made sense. They had different reasons to try to make

the brewery unsalable, but they were partners in crime. And yet, it was only a crime if they tried to profit from the act.

"Do you mind if I ask what your relationship with Bethany is?"

"Do you mean am I fucking her?" he asked me.

"Well, yeah," I admitted.

He shrugged. "We had a relationship a few years ago, after her divorce, but it kind of fell apart. She's my best friend—the only friend I've got, really. Because of my circumstances, I haven't had a lot of opportunities at relationships."

I could see why.

"R&A Insights' plan is to give you back your life. And we will do all we can—even hiring an attorney and going to court if we have to, to do so." Richard and I hadn't talked about it, but I was pretty sure he'd be okay with that.

"And all you get for your trouble is a buck?" Abe/Marcel asked, still skeptical. "Why's that?"

"It's kind of hard to explain … but we have a generous benefactor. Someone with deep pockets who's more or less given us cart blanche to help people who don't have the resources to pull themselves out of trouble."

"Why would someone do that?" Abe/Marcel asked.

"Because they can," I explained simply.

He shrugged. "Well, I'd be eternally grateful. I haven't been able to have a Thanksgiving, Christmas, or birthday celebration with my family for twenty long years. I don't know my nieces and nephews. I haven't hugged my mother or my sisters in just as long. You can't imagine what an awful life I've had because the cops decided to pin Louie's crime on me."

Yeah, I could imagine it—but I would never be able to feel the depth of his despair and loneliness. Hell, I'd been lonely after my wife's death—I felt lonely since Maggie's defection, but not two decades' worth of that kind of agony.

"I'm sorry," I told Abe/Marcel. "I'm sorry you've had to

endure this isolation for so long. And I promise you, our firm will do all we can to make it up to you."

"And how are you going to do that?" Abe/Marcel asked sarcastically.

I didn't yet have that answer—and I told him so.

"I don't know that I can trust anyone in Louie's family—even Bethany," I admitted. "So I'd appreciate it if you'd keep our conversation private—at least for the next few days."

"Why? Do you think something is going to happen that will impact the brewery?"

"I don't know. But please, whatever you and Bethany are thinking, don't do anything that could adversely affect the sale of it."

"So, you're on Nick's side? You think we should sell?"

"Not at all. But if the brewery can't fulfill orders, then you're just as fucked. You've got to deliver product to stay in business. Pitch the ruined product. And start strategizing other alternatives. Like Bethany buying out her siblings."

"And where would she get that kind of capital?" Abe/Marcel

"I told you. Our benefactor has deep pockets. If you can devise a plan, you might find a partner willing to help you out."

Okay, I was totally bullshitting him. But I was pretty sure I could convince Richard to partner in a fledgling business until it could stand on its own. I crossed my fingers really hard on that account.

"Okay," Abe/Marcel said. "I'll lay low and I won't talk to Bethany about our conversation. But I have to tell her something."

"How about that you're cooking up a plan but need some space to think it through?"

"It's weak, but it might work."

"There's just one more thing."

"Oh, yeah?"

"Roberto Gonzalez."

Marcel's gaze dipped to the table's top.

"What do you know about his death?"

Marcel looked guilty.

"Was it an accident … or negligence?"

"Let's just say a good man died because safety rules had been relaxed."

"Are you willing to testify to that?"

Marcel looked distinctly uncomfortable. Had he sent that death announcement to me hoping I might get someone looking into the brewery. Or had Bethany sent it? I couldn't think why. Or had another of the brewery's few remaining workers found my discarded business card and decided someone needed to know Gonzalez's death could have been prevented? It was something Richard would have to run by Detective Destross.

I ate the last of my doughnut and gulped the rest of my coffee. "Can I have your phone number to keep in touch?"

For a moment, I thought Marcel might refuse, but then he gave it to me and I entered it into my phone's contact list. "Thanks."

We left the coffee shop and headed for our cars. "Later," Abe/Marcel said.

I nodded and got into my car. He left the parking lot first, and we turned in different directions. I wasn't sure what my next step should be but I thought I should have bought something to go for Emily for breakfast and cursed myself for not remembering. I was beginning to care about her far too much.

AFTER DROPPING Betsy off at R&A Insights, and being assured that Emily was okay with taking care of her until Jeff arrived, it was a silent drive to visit Mrs. Clark. Richard couldn't understand his wife's reluctance to visit Marcel Clark's mother. If things worked out, they'd be able to give Marcel his life back and reunite him with his family. How could that be detrimental?

Still, Brenda had a touch of what her grandmother had called "the second sight." It was nothing like Jeff experienced, but that she felt uncomfortable was something he needed to pay attention to.

"What's wrong?" he asked, giving her a sideways glance.

Brenda's gaze remained focused on the road ahead of them. "I'm not sure. I just feel … unsettled."

"In what way?"

"That's it; I don't know. And it worries me."

Richard thought about what he should say next. "Is it possible we could be bringing this woman joy? I'm not talking about bringing her son back to her—we don't know how that's going to work out. But seeing that photo album, touching the things her family once owned, might be of great comfort to her."

"Maybe," Brenda said, not sounding at all sure.

"If nothing else, we've brought those items back to her family."

"Yeah," she grudgingly agreed.

Richard braked for a red light. "What's got you so upset?" he asked, saying the words gently.

"I don't know. Something just feels wrong."

Richard decided not to push her—at least not then.

He parked the car in front of the Clark home once more. The walk had been shoveled after the last snowfall, and the uneven concrete was bone dry. Richard got out of the car and retrieved the box from the trunk. Then he and Brenda started up the walk to the house. Richard hung back as Brenda ascended the steps and knocked on the sun-blistered painted door. What looked like oak graining peeked out between the faded, peeling red paint that had once graced the wood. Brenda had to knock again before Mrs. Clark opened the door.

It was the first time Richard had seen the gray-haired black woman, whose face was lined with wrinkles, no doubt due to the decades of sadness she'd endured.

"Thank you for seeing us," Brenda said sincerely. "May we come in?"

"Yes, of course," Mrs. Clark said, but when her gaze traveled to Richard, it wasn't as welcoming as her words, and he felt humbled.

Mrs. Clark beckoned them into her living room, which was furnished in a shabby, orange suite of furniture which was straight out of the 1970s and no doubt a thrift-store purchase, but the room was immaculate, and he caught a whiff of freshly baked bread.

Mrs. Clark encouraged them to sit on the couch, and Richard set the box on a rectangular maple coffee table with plate glass protecting its pristine surface.

"This is my husband, Dr. Richard Alpert," Brenda said in introduction. "He's one of the founding members of R&A Insights."

"So you said before," Mrs. Clark said, her gaze not at all welcoming.

"Thank you for seeing us," Richard said.

Mrs. Clark nodded. "And what have you brought me?"

Richard pushed the box forward. "The current owner of your former home wanted you to have these items and hoped they'd comfort you."

The look Mrs. Clark gave him had little to do with comfort. It wasn't exactly hostility, but it wasn't quite friendly, either.

She took one of the chairs opposite them and stared at the seedy-looking carton for a long moment before she pulled open the interwoven flaps and withdrew the first of the pathetic items within. It was the soot-darkened round broach. She fingered the pin, trying to clean away the remnants of the fire with her right index finger, her eyes filling with tears. "This was mama's. Our daddy gave it to her for their tenth wedding anniversary. She wore it with pride to church and on special occasions," Mrs. Clark said, her voice breaking. She pulled a used tissue from her sweater pocket and tried to clean off the worst of the soot on what had once been sparkling rhinestones. She looked at it for long moments before carefully setting it aside on the table.

Next came the photo album. Although it had been two decades since the fire, it still reeked. She set the book on the coffee table and opened to the first page with its collection of black-and-white pictures that looked like they'd been taken in the 1950s. The people were slightly out of focus, but she obviously recognized them as tears rolled down her cheeks, and she kept swallowing. With a heavy sigh, she turned the first leaf over and stared at a color picture of a smiling woman holding a baby no more than a month or so old. Then the quiet sobs turned into a howl, and she slammed shut the album, and clutched it to her chest.

"Oh, Lord," she cried and completely broke down, wailing inconsolably. Brenda jumped up from her seat, rushed to Mrs. Clark's side, and tried to wrap her arms around the crying woman, but the old lady pushed her away.

"Who's in that picture, Mrs. Clark?" Brenda asked.

The woman sniffed. "That's my mama and me. That was the first picture ever taken of me. There are so few from those days," she said, her tears escalating.

"If the album is too painful for you to look at just now," Richard began, "perhaps you'd like to look at some of the other items that won't be as emotionally devastating."

Brenda shot him an annoyed glance but said nothing.

Mrs. Clark seemed to think over his advice and then

nodded, setting the album on the table as well. She found another tissue in her sweater pocket and blew her nose loudly. "I don't think I can handle the rest of what's in this box just now," she said, hiccuping between sobs. "Oh, Lord, I miss my mama," she cried and doubled over. Brenda knelt beside the crying woman and rested a hand on her shoulder. This time, Mrs. Clark fell into Brenda's waiting arms. But her soothing voice and embrace made no impact on the grieving woman's wrenching sobs.

Witnessing that level of misery was more than a little jarring for Richard, who rose from his seat and found himself inching just a little further back from the volatile emotions exploding around him like Fourth of July fireworks. He hadn't expected to witness such an eruption of despair and felt embarrassed to witness it.

Without a word to Brenda or Mrs. Clark, Richard left the room. For a minute or so, he stood in the home's entryway but then decided it might be best to relocate to the car.

He sat there for almost an hour, again having to start the engine every ten minutes or so to keep the temperature tolerable. He'd never treated someone who'd had a post-traumatic meltdown, and Mrs. Clark's excessive distress had rattled him.

Eventually, a car pulled up in the driveway, and a woman got out and approached the house. Ten minutes later, Brenda finally reappeared. She exited the home and walked down the shoveled walk to join him in the car.

"How is she?" he asked tentatively.

"Not very well. I told her I would stay until she could call someone to come be with her. She asked me to call a church friend. She apologized profusely for taking up our time knowing, we've got a little one."

"We need to get that poor woman some help," Richard said, his throat tight.

"She's never gotten over the fire—and who could blame

her, losing her mother and her son—not to mention everything she owned."

"I'd hoped seeing some of her family treasures would have been healing."

Brenda looked at him. She didn't say it aloud, but her expression said *I told you so*.

"What happens next?" Richard asked.

"Haven't we done enough damage?" Brenda demanded.

"The goal is to reunite this family," he reminded her.

"And how do you propose to do that?" she asked, her tone icy.

"Are you willing to continue working with me on this?"

"In what way?" she asked, not sounding so formidable.

"This case has taken on a new aspect. There are public options for people who need mental health counseling."

Brenda let out a snort of derision. "And we both know how useful they are. Overloaded psychologists who have to justify every moment of their day with an eye on the clock and a ton of paperwork to fill out for precious tax-based reimbursements."

"What do you suggest we do?"

"Dammit, Richard—cough up the bucks to help that poor woman!"

"Okay, okay! But would she accept that kind of help?"

Brenda sighed. "I'd do my best to talk to her about it," she said.

Richard braked for a red light and glanced across at his wife. "Any ideas on how to address that?"

Brenda frowned and didn't immediately answer.

The light turned green, and Richard tapped the accelerator.

"What if…" Brenda began. "What if you set up a fund to help people with mental health issues? God only knows you've got enough money to do so."

"And?" he prompted.

"Your own mother had serious mental health issues, and not a damn soul stepped up to help her. You could name it in her honor, and the first recipient of that foundation could be Mrs. Clark."

Richard didn't need time to think the proposition over. "I like it. I like it a lot." He managed a smile. "Brenda, you're a genius."

There was no note of pleasure in her voice as she commented, "I'm practical."

"Hey, lady, what's wrong? We're doing it. We can make a difference."

"Only one small life at a time," she said, defeat coloring her tone.

"It's a first step. Everything starts with one step. Hopefully, we can move forward." He thought about what he wanted to say. "Would you be willing to set up such a foundation?"

She took her time before answering. "I might. But it wouldn't be something I could do alone, and it wouldn't be my passion."

"I realize that."

"We can talk about it," Brenda said neutrally.

"How do you think Jeff would react ?"

"He'd be for it, but I can't see him being all that invested in it, either. Seems to me he's tried his hardest to distance himself from the years he spent with a mentally ill parent."

He had indeed.

Richard changed the subject. "Do you want to go out to lunch or something?"

"To celebrate? Hardly. Let's just get our girl and go home. I just want to go home."

So did he. But he still had work to do.

Chapter 32

It was after nine when I made it to the office for the day, and as I stepped into the building I heard a familiar cry. Well, not cry—terrible wail was more like it. CP was crying her heart out.

I entered the office to find a distressed Emily holding my sweet girl, bouncing her up and down and not making a dent in that little girl's anguish.

"Baby girl," I called, and CP turned her tear-streaked face in my direction—and then held out her arms.

She practically leapt into my embrace, grateful to recognize a friendly face.

"Don't cry, baby girl," I crooned as I rocked her, and she immediately quieted.

"Wow, you've got the magical touch," Emily said. "She's done nothing but scream since the doc and his wife dropped her off."

CP nestled her damp face against my neck, her little fingers clutching the fabric of my jacket. "I've helped take care of this little girl since the day she came home from the hospital, haven't I, CP?"

Betsy gave a little squeal of delight.

"Why do you call her CP? I thought her name was Betsy."

"It is. But she's my little Cherry Pie—hence, CP." I wasn't up to telling Emily about the little dresses featuring cherries I'd bought that sweet girl that ranged from infant to 6x before she was even a twinkle in her father's eye. I'd purchased every size I could find and hoped she would love the pattern as much as I did.

I bounced that girl up and down and in no time she was back to being a bucketful of giggles. But when I looked at Emily, I found her frowning.

"What's wrong?" I asked.

"How are you so good with a baby when you've never had one?"

I shrugged. "CP and I have an understanding."

Emily looked at me skeptically. "How can an adult man and a baby have an understanding? Is it some kind of psychic thing?" she asked derisively.

"Yeah." CP started singing to herself, a tuneless song, and no one could dispute that she felt better—if not happy.

"Maybe you should try to bottle whatever it is you have and try to sell it," Emily said, but her tone wasn't exactly friendly.

I shook my head. "It only works with people you love. And I love my little girl, don't I, CP?"

The baby squealed with delight, giving my soul a much-needed lift.

I turned my attention back to Emily. "I'm sorry you had to deal with CP. We'll try not to have that happen in the future."

"I don't mind. I'm just sorry I couldn't soothe her. She really only wanted her family," Emily said, tweaking the little waddle beneath CP's chubby chin, which made Betsy giggle.

"You miss the times when Hannah was little," I said, which wasn't much of a guess. I could pretty much read Emily, which

I wasn't about to tell her. She was already freaked out about how much I could discern about her.

"Kind of," she admitted. "But I want my daughter to be bold, to find her place in life. Goodness knows that's going to be hard enough." She looked somber. "Are you going to stand around in your coat?"

I shook my head. "Now that CP's calmed down, I'll put her on the floor. She'll be okay." And to prove it so, I placed the baby on the floor, took off my coat, and hung it up. But the baby held out her arms for me, grunting for me to pick her up. I wasn't about to deny her.

"Time to go to work, big girl," I told CP, and we headed for my office.

"About time, too. You're an hour late," Emily said, following us in.

I sat down at my desk and pushed the button to boot up my computer. "Not really. I've already had an interview with a person of interest."

"Interest?"

"Yes. Have you read the notes Richard and I've filed on the computer?" She could do that now that Richard had tweaked the system.

"Yeah, but they don't mean much."

"Oh, but they do. Instead of working on two disparate cases, our investigations are entwined."

"How is that possible? He's working on a cold case. The arson. And you're working on the brewery case, which is based in the here and now."

"That's right. But it turns out that the person the cops thought started the fire in Richard's cold case is actually the brewmaster at Horse Hockey Brewing. It was the brewery's owner who started the blaze," I said as I bounced CP on my knee. "Back in the day, Louie worked for the company that owned the property and wanted to oust the tenants."

"Shut up!" Emily said, disbelieving.

"No, really."

"How is that possible?"

"That's the thing. There seems to be some cosmic force that brings the things we're looking into to mesh. You'd probably call it God's divine plan."

"I call it bullshit," she said, crossing her arms across her chest. She glared at me. "And what do you intend to do about what you *think* you've learned?"

CP reached for a pen, about to put it in her mouth when I took it from her and shoved it into the desk's center drawer. "Well, that's the thing. I'm not exactly sure *what* we can do to give the poor guy his life back. But we think we've figured out what happened. Now we have to convince the police to do something about it."

"Isn't that a conflict of interest?"

I grimaced. "Sort of. But he paid our fee, so now *he's* my client."

"What? Isn't that unethical?"

"Why?"

"I thought the guy in the coma hired us?"

"Sort of. But he had no way to pay—being halfway to dead."

"So you switched teams just like that?" she asked, appalled.

I let out a breath as CP jostled to turn on my lap, standing and yanking on one of my ears. "Just like that."

"And how much did you charge the guy?" Emily demanded as I pulled CP's chubby fingers away from my head.

"A buck."

"A dollar?" she asked, appalled. "You charged him a friggin' dollar?"

"Yeah. Do you have a problem with that?"

"How are we supposed to turn a profit when that's all you charge?"

"Who said we have to make a profit?"

"Isn't that the whole idea of going into business?" she asked in astonishment.

"For most people. We aren't most people."

I bounced CP a little more, and she giggled. I really needed to get one or more of her toys from the stroller so I wasn't the focus of all her attention.

Then it occurred to me that I had the dollar bill Abe/Marcel had given me and that we ought to frame it and hang it on the wall like restaurants do. Yeah, the idea appealed to me. I'd have to go on Amazon and see if I could find an appropriate frame. Maggie would have cried foul and said I could find one at a yard sale—or at least that she could. She was into reusing and recycling, and I certainly wasn't opposed to it, but it was March, and there weren't any yard sales, and the whole thrifting business—at least with yard sales—wasn't my thing.

Thinking about Maggie put me into an instant funk that even CP's giggles couldn't lift. Why did I have to think about the woman? I was trying hard *not* to think about her.

"What's the matter?" Emily demanded. Jeeze, her voice sounded harsh.

"What do you mean?"

"In a heartbeat, you went from almost happy to downright depressed."

"That's a pretty big range of emotions you're accusing me of experiencing."

"Well, is it true?"

I blinked at her, startled by her depth of perception. I hadn't given her credit for that. Was that a *faux pas* on my part?

"I was just thinking that we should frame that dollar bill and that my—" I chose not to say girlfriend because I was pretty sure Maggie no longer held that place in my heart. "—

friend Maggie would want me to get a used frame. You know. Save the planet and all that."

"Well, it's a great idea. I need to go to the thrift store to get shoes for Hannah. If you want, I could look for a nice frame for your dollar."

"You're still buying Hannah's clothes at the thrift store?" Weren't we paying her enough to buy new items for her daughter?

"And before you judge me, yes, I still buy clothes, shoes, and lots of other stuff used. There's a huge problem with commercialism and how much waste there is on the planet. Don't you even *care* about plastic in the ocean?" she asked, her eyes wide.

"Yeah, I do."

"Then *we* should do something about it," she declared.

We?

A ripple of something ran through me. I'm not sure what it was. Validation? Appreciation? Hope?

Was I as bad as Maggie, looking beyond our relationship to what might be next? Yeah, I was becoming more and more attracted to Emily, and with it came an onslaught of guilt.

"What do you propose?" I asked her, trying to keep my hormones in check.

"Well, we could go to a thrift store at lunchtime and look for a frame."

"And then?"

"I didn't bring my lunch today. We could go to McDonald's —Dutch treat," she said.

"I think R&A Insights could spring for a Big Mac." Or something much nicer.

"Well, then, let's do it," Emily said.

CP squealed with delight as she found another pen on my desk. She examined it and in no time figured out how to pull off the cap—which I intercepted before she could shove it into her mouth.

"What if Rich and Brenda don't come back until after lunch?"

"We don't exactly play by the clock here at R&A Insights," Emily reminded me.

No, we didn't. But I did need to reconnect with Omega and Louie later that afternoon. Still, we had nothing else to do to kill time before then.

"Okay. Thrift store and lunch it is."

Emily nodded before turning back to her post in the outer office.

CP giggled as she pounded her little fists on my computer keyboard, and I was glad I hadn't turned on the machine. "Come on, big girl, let's find some better toys," I said and grabbed the baby and stood up, heading back for the reception area and her stroller, where a cache of toys was stored behind the seat. I didn't look at Emily, who was seated behind her desk, as I steered the stroller back into my office. I wouldn't get any work done—like recording my notes on my interview with Abe/Marcel—until Richard and Brenda retrieved their daughter. That was okay. But a part of me wished they'd hurry and get back. I was more than ready to spend a little quality time with Emily.

EMILY DIRECTED me to her favorite thrift shop, where not only did we score a beautiful gold frame for Abe/Marcel's dollar bill, but she found shoes and a pretty Easter dress for her daughter.

We didn't go to McDonald's. Instead, I took Emily to the Falcon's Nest, near our office. It was probably a mistake because being older than her—and the clientele in the place was certainly a lot older than me—she gave the place a distinctly jaundiced eye.

"Would you like something to drink?" the waiter asked after we'd been seated at a corner table.

"I'll have a Jack Daniel's on ice," I said.

"I'll have a ginger ale," Emily said.

"Are you sure that's all you want?" I asked.

Emily looked just a little wistful. "Yeah," she said flatly.

The waiter left us menus and disappeared.

"Thanks for helping me find that frame. It looks great. Where do you think we should hang it?"

Emily gave a sort of grimace. "Well, not in the reception area. And maybe not your office, either."

"There's the conference room or the washroom. Which is your preference?" I deadpanned.

"It's too bad we don't have a real closet," she muttered, picking up the menu.

"So, you think my idea to hang up our first dollar is bad?"

"Well, it's kind of … tacky."

Good grief. Was she a snob?

Feeling chastised, I picked up my menu. I'd let Richard decide. If he thought the idea was stupid, then I could live with it. I sure wouldn't feel bad about hanging the damned thing in my own digs.

Oh boy. *My* home. The place I'd moved out of because I wasn't comfortable about being alone. But I wasn't sure I felt that way anymore. Now that I felt more secure about where my relationship with Maggie was bound, I felt much better about myself. If Emily would be a part of my future wasn't relative. I felt stronger knowing that I could figure out my future. I might only be a guest in Richard's house for another day. I was pretty sure I was almost ready to return to my apartment across the driveway. Herschel had quickly adapted to life in the Alpert home. He'd probably miss being apart from Brenda and CP.

Holly—not so much, but he'd come to tolerate Maggie's—no, now Richard's—dog.

Emily studied the menu as though it had been written in Sanskrit. "Don't like what you see?" I asked her.

"Well, it's kind of heavy on red meat."

"If you like cheese, the Welsh rarebit is good."

"I've never had it before—never even heard of it."

"Then maybe you're in for a treat." I told her what the dish entailed.

"I'll give it a try," she said reluctantly.

When the waiter returned with our drinks, we ordered. I got a beef on weck sandwich. I knew from experience that the Falcon's Nest made a good one.

After the waiter left, we looked at each other self-consciously. "So," Emily said at last, "what's your next move?"

"With Louie Susskind?"

She nodded.

I wasn't sure how to answer. I needed to confront the guy, but how would that go? I wasn't comfortable detailing my thoughts and fears to an audience I didn't entirely trust.

"I'm pretty sure the—" I was about to say *death* doula, but decided to respect Omega's description of her job, "end-of-life doula might be of some use to me in that regard."

"In what way?"

"She's a kindred spirit."

"In what way?" Emily reiterated.

"In that she has an empathetic connection with the people she deals with at the end of their lives."

Emily didn't seem to like that explanation, which left us looking at each other in awkward silence. Finally, I cleared my throat.

"Would you like to come with me to the hospital this afternoon?"

"What for?"

"If nothing else, to meet Omega."

"Don't they limit patients to two visitors at a time?"

"We might be able to fudge it. I've only seen Louie's daughter, Teresa, or Omega visit him."

"Nobody else cares about that poor dying man?" Emily asked.

"I get the feeling Louie hasn't endeared himself to many."

She frowned. "That's sad."

That Emily, who'd been mistreated by her Ohio family, could muster empathy for another was telling. Or was I just trying to convince myself she had virtues worth admiring?

Emily toyed with the edges of her linen napkin before opening it and setting it on her lap. "Okay."

I wasn't sure what she meant. "Sorry?"

"Okay, I'll go to the hospital with you. I don't suppose I'll be able to speak to Mr. Susskind."

"I wouldn't think so."

"Then I guess I'll go just to keep you company. I haven't got anything else to do at the office this afternoon."

I could have done without the second part of her acceptance.

Our meals arrived in record time. For someone who'd never heard of good old-fashioned Welsh rarebit, Emily tucked in with gusto, eating every bite. It took everything I could do to eat my sandwich, and I left nearly all the fries that accompanied it. But damn, the pungent horse radish on that salt-and-kimmel roll tasted damn good.

Emily and I lingered at the table, and I encouraged her to choose dessert while I indulged in another beer. She chose crème brûlèe—something else that young one had never tried before. I was opening her eyes to a myriad of new taste sensations. I had to remind myself that I had another fifteen years of experience under my belt than she did. It made me feel old.

I knew Omega didn't show up at the hospital until around

four o'clock, so after lunch, I drove Emily to the local big box office supply store, where I snagged a couple of flash drives, and she chose a few pink, purple, and blue gel pens. Getting to indulge in such a simple purchase for the office seemed to fill her with a giddy joy, reinforcing the age chasm between us.

Finally, I drove us to Sisters hospital, parked the car, and we avoided the nurses' station while I led Emily to Louie's room. But when we got there, the name on the whiteboard outside the room said PARKER. I peeked inside and saw an elderly white woman on the bed with a mass of wild hair that would have made Medusa proud.

I steered Emily toward the nurses' station and waited to get the attention of the guy manning the desk. Finally, he put down the phone.

"Excuse me, but where's Mr. Susskind? I visited him just yesterday and—"

"I'm so sorry, but Mr. Susskind passed away during the night."

Dead? Louie was dead? No one had contacted me to let me know. I would've thought Omega would have done so. She had my card. I'd practically begged her to call me.

Why hadn't she called?

"I'm so sorry for your loss," the nurse said.

I was too flabbergasted to reply. Instead, Emily spoke to him as I walked away, heading back to the room where Louie's spirit had settled on the window sill just about every time I'd visited. He wasn't there. Did that mean I'd be free of him—that his threat of haunting me was over? I didn't know. But now I had to figure out what came next.

"Are you okay?" Emily asked.

"Yeah," I assured her, but I wasn't. Where did Louie's death leave me—our—investigation into the fire at the Clark home? Was I supposed to keep trying to save the brewery from being acquired—or worse—closing?

I was on auto-pilot navigating back to the parking garage, with Emily trailing in my wake.

"What happens now?" Emily asked after we climbed back into my car.

"By now, Louie's body has probably been transferred to a funeral home. I need to know which one. I need to know if he's transitioned or is still tied to this earth."

Emily studied my face, scowling. "When people die, they go to heaven."

"Not hell?" I asked.

She had no answer.

"What do we do now?" she asked.

"We?"

"Well, I can't say I'm not intrigued."

"First, I should take you back to the office so you can go home and pick up your daughter."

"I can call her after-school sitter. I've done it before. I'd kind of like to know what happens next."

"You don't want to wait until tomorrow?"

She shook her head.

I shrugged. "Okay."

Chapter 33

I left Richard a text, telling him Louie had died. Before I could send more than that terse sentence, my phone pinged—a text from Omega.

Mr. Resnick. Mr. Susskind has died. He is at the Thomas Funeral Home on Main Street. The family is on their way to discuss the arrangements. Please come.

That she asked me to join her there was a little concerning. Why would she need me to be there?

On my way, I texted back. Of course, then I had to Google to find out *where* the funeral parlor was located on Main Street. It's a pretty damned long ribbon of asphalt. Once I did, I again texted Richard and asked him to join us there, giving him the address.

Still silence on the brother front.

"We're off," I told Emily as I backed out of the parking space. Once I paid the fee, I filled her in on everything.

I braked for a red light and caught sight of Emily looking at me. "What?"

"Things seemed to be at a standstill just minutes ago, and

now they've escalated. Is this a normal part of an investigation?"

"Yes and no."

"Like…how?"

"Sometimes things snowball, but more often, it's just slogging along."

The light changed to green.

"What do you think we'll encounter at the funeral home?" Emily asked.

"I have no idea," I answered honestly. I wasn't sure what to think about Omega inviting me to come. I was pretty sure the family wouldn't want me there. And what would Nick say if/when Richard showed up? Was Omega looking for an ally? Knowing Louie's volatile personality, did she expect his spectral self to cause a disruption? Worse—did she expect *me* to be able to control his caustic eruptions should they manifest?

Her previous warning to remember my experience with Alice Newcomb troubled me.

Emily and I didn't speak much during the drive to the funeral home. A couple of cars dotted the lot, but I got the feeling they were employee vehicles. As it was nearing the close of business hours, they might be getting ready for a viewing that evening.

I kept thinking back to the hour I'd spent arranging for my dead wife's funeral, such as it was. I buried her. She didn't want to be cremated, and aquamation and composting weren't available then and still weren't in New Jersey, where she was laid to rest. I'm not sure she'd have gone for either of those, anyway. Shelley thought she was invincible. Not when it came to a Glock firing a bullet into the back of her skull.

"What are you thinking about?" Emily asked.

"When I had to make burial arrangements for my wife," I answered honestly, glad my voice hadn't cracked. I'd fallen out of love with Shelley by then, but it was still one of the most difficult days of my life.

"Wife?" Emily repeated in disbelief. "I didn't know you'd been married."

"There's a lot about me you don't know."

"How did she die?"

An impertinent question, but I didn't blame her for asking. She wouldn't be expecting the answer.

"She was murdered," I said matter of factly, although the memory was still too sharp not to sting.

"Oh, my God!" Emily cried. "How?"

"I don't think I'm up to telling the story today. Ask me again some other time."

"I will," she said, and I could tell by her tone that she meant it.

The Thomas Funeral Home was a large brick building with a colonial vibe—probably built in the late 1960s or early 70s. I'd never noticed it on my travels up and down Main Street and had never heard of the enterprise, which meant it was probably one of the few mom-and-pop funeral homes around. I was surprised the Susskind family hadn't gone with one of the big chain establishments.

I parked the car near the main entrance, and Emily and I got out. "Are you sure you want to do this?" I asked her.

"I'm an R&A Insights Associate. I'm not going to be its receptionist forever," Emily declared.

It pleased me to hear her say that.

I reached for the brass handle of one of the big double doors and paused. "If something should go down, please do whatever I ask you, no matter how illogical it might seem."

Emily studied my face. "What are you expecting to happen?"

"I'm not sure. I just want you to be safe."

"I'm not a kid," Emily said.

No, but she had never experienced what I had when it came to the paranormal. If she wasn't worried, I would have to do it for both of us. And, perhaps, Richard, too. He had a clue about what we might encounter. At least, I hoped he did…that is if he ever showed up.

I ushered Emily inside the funeral home, which seemed to be awfully warm. A sign to the right announced the name of the deceased person featured that evening. When we peeked inside the opened door of the smallish room, we saw a table near a window that overlooked the parking lot with a wooden cask sitting upon it. No doubt the earthly remains of one Priscilla Mason. A picture board stood on an easel nearby with photographs chronicling the woman's life from black-and-white infancy to Kodacolor prints unto old age.

We backed out of the room.

"I've never been to a funeral parlor before," Emily remarked somewhat sheepishly.

"Really?"

She nodded. "Because of my circumstances, my Ohio family didn't mix much with family or had many friends. Nobody in our circle died. I haven't known my New York family long enough to lose one of them to death."

I nodded. "You're lucky," I said succinctly.

I looked around. Nobody stood behind the home's reception desk. I assumed Omega would be around to meet us, but she was nowhere in sight, either.

"Hello!" I called. "Anybody here?"

It took nearly a minute before someone emerged from a door behind the reception desk. A gaunt, black-suited man who had to be in his seventies spoke. "I'm Derek Thomas. May I be of help?"

"Yes. Omega Dustin asked me to meet her here. I'm working on behalf of the Susskind family."

The older man nodded. "Ms. Dustin is with the deceased. Would you like me to ask her to join you?"

I looked at him, fought the urge to say "duh!" and merely nodded.

"Very good," he said solemnly and turned toward the back room again.

Emily was giving the place a thorough once-over, looking a little green.

"Are you okay?" I asked.

She gave a little shudder. "This building gives me the creeps."

"Why?"

"Well, I've never been in a place that takes care of dead bodies—let alone seen one before."

I'd seen far too many.

"You won't see Louie."

She heaved a sigh of relief yet still seemed troubled. "But…Mr. Susskind…?"

"He's probably in the basement—in cold storage."

Revulsion crept across her features. "This is kind of like those NCIS TV shows."

"Not exactly. They show bodies in a morgue. I'm sure Louie came directly here from the hospital. No autopsy needed."

Emily continued to study the place. Across from the reception desk was a lounge, presumably for family members with a wine cooler filled with water bottles, a little glass bowl with peppermints, and brochures for the home's services. Emily emanated vibes that let me know she was quietly freaking out, but she seemed to handle her anxiety well. I thought about complimenting her on it but decided not to. She didn't like to be reminded that I could sense some of what she was experiencing.

Omega emerged from a door at the far end of the corridor.

She looked haggard. She'd never appeared that way in all the sleep-deprived days I'd known her.

"Mr. Resnick," she greeted me wearily.

"Jeff," I automatically corrected her, knowing she would never call me by that name. "Are you okay?"

"It has been…an experience," she said simply.

I gestured toward the lounge. "Let's sit and talk."

She nodded, and I introduced her to Emily once we'd all sat down. Omega nodded, but she looked wiped out. Almost as though she'd been through a battle.

"What happened?" I asked.

Omega's gaze drifted toward the corridor as though she expected an enemy—Louie?—to leap out at any moment.

"Mr. Susskind's death was not easy," she began.

"I assume he went into cardiac arrest."

She nodded, and again her gaze traveled first to the floor and then the corridor beyond, almost as though she expected Louie to appear.

"What did you sense?" I asked quietly.

Omega looked at Emily and then back to me as though questioning whether she could speak freely. I assured her she could. She opened her mouth to explain just as we heard voices outside the room. It seemed that members of the Susskind family had arrived.

"Have you spoken with the family?" I asked Omega.

Omega turned her gaze toward the subdued voices. "Only Mrs. Barton. I'm afraid I woke her at two this morning to tell her the sad news."

"Sad for whom?"

"For her," Omega clarified. She didn't seem a bit sad. In fact, if I didn't know better, I would have thought the spectral Louie had accosted her.

"What did Louie do to you?" I asked as gently as I could.

Omega had no time to answer. Family members Nick and

Bethany assembled in front of the reception desk, with Abe/Marcel tagging behind them, almost as an afterthought. He caught sight of me but quickly looked away.

The group was greeted by the same older man who'd belatedly welcomed Emily and me. They introduced themselves.

"Will Mrs. Barton be joining you tonight?" the old man asked.

"No," Nick said authoritatively.

Since he seemed to be speaking on behalf of the family, Bethany turned and caught sight of me. "What are *you* doing here?" she demanded. "Your services are no longer needed."

Nick pivoted to take me in. "Services? Why would you need a photographer?"

"Photographer?" Bethany repeated dumbly. "He's a private investigator."

"I'm a consultant," I corrected her.

Nick's cheeks flared red. "Consultant? You passed yourself as a photographer when you came to my office."

"It's my side hustle."

Nick turned on his younger sister. "Why on God's earth did you hire a consultant—and for what?"

"It was Dad's idea," Bethany said. "At least that's what *he* told me." She leveled a glare in my direction.

"Your father hired me," I remarked. "And I've been paid my retainer, so I'm still on the clock."

"Paid your what?" Nick asked.

"Who?" Bethany demanded. "Who paid you?"

"I'm not at liberty to disclose that information," I said, working to keep my expression bland and not daring to look at Abe/Marcel. He seemed to be doing his best not to look at me, too.

"You should go," Nick told me. "Now."

"I was invited here."

"By whom?"

"By me," Omega said, rising to her feet.

"And who are you?" Nick demanded.

"She's the death doula Teresa hired," Bethany told him.

"We no longer need your services, either," Nick declared.

"You may not," Omega said quietly, "but I am here at Mrs. Barton's request."

"What for?"

"Part of my job is to prepare the body for its final journey."

Nick looked angry. "What?"

"It's part of my job to wash the body and prepare it for internment."

Nick shook his head. "That isn't going to happen. Dad's going to be cremated."

"That decision is out of my control," Omega said. "It was Mrs. Barton who hired me," she reiterated.

The elderly mortician held a leather binder in his left hand and spread his right hand out as though in invitation. "Let us all convene to the conference room to discuss the disposition of Mr. Susskind's remains," he said quietly.

Nick glared at Omega and me. "You are *not* invited."

I couldn't argue with that statement, but Omega stood proud, her back straightening. "Mrs. Barton has told me her wishes. As she's not here, I'm to speak on her behalf."

Bethany shook her head. "Whatever," she practically grunted.

Nick shifted his gaze to Abe/Marcel. "You don't need to be here, either."

I could feel a flair of anger from the attorney—maybe even hatred—aimed at Horse Hockey's brewmaster.

A noise at the end of the corridor and the home's entrance caused us to turn. It was Richard. He passed through the double doors and walked toward us. "Am I late to the gathering?" he asked blithely.

"Dr. Alpert. What are you doing here?" Nick demanded.

"Moral support," he said simply.

"How did you know dad died?" Nick asked.

Richard shot a look in my direction and I shook my head ever so slightly. Now was not the time to disclose our relationship. Emily took a small step forward, but I grabbed her arm, giving her a warning look. She stepped back.

"I called the hospital," Richard said. "I'm so sorry for your loss. Is there anything I can do to help?"

"Dad's beyond help now," Bethany said sourly.

A low rumble coursed through the building.

We all looked at each other.

"An earthquake in Buffalo?" Richard questioned. He must have lived through scores of them while living in California.

I glanced at Omega.

"That wasn't an earthquake," she said quietly.

We heard the sound of a high-pitched yelp, and all eyes turned to the door to the basement where Omega had emerged not long before. A guy in protective garb covering his day clothes burst through the door. "Holy shit!" he cried.

"What's wrong?" the elderly mortician behind the desk asked.

The guy grasped his protective goggles, yanking them off, looking scared shitless. "I was working on Mr. Armstrong when all the bottles started tumbling off the shelves. Then I swear—as God is my witness—I saw Mr. Susskind's body convulse."

"Dad's alive?" Bethany blurted, her eyes wide.

"He can't be," Mr. Thomas declared.

"He isn't," Omega said definitively.

Nick and Bethany turned to look at her.

"His body has failed, but his spirit is very much alive. And angry."

Nick looked at her for long seconds before his expression hardened. "Bullshit."

"I suggest we all gather in the conference room," the rattled mortician proposed in a placating tone.

This time, Nick and Bethany didn't resist, and the older man led the way with Richard, me, Emily, Omega, and Abe/Marcel following in their way, while the guy in the protective gear scurried into the office behind the reception desk, seeming to want no part of continuing working anywhere near Louie's body.

The conference room was actually more of a showroom with a long table at the south end big enough to seat twelve people. Three of the four walls held displays of smaller than normal caskets with gold, silver, and bronze handles, silk linings, their hides spray-painted with Detroit-precision-formulated lacquers. Floating shelves featured various porcelain, wood, and enameled urns to hold the ashes of those exposed to cremation's flames. Others had funereal jewelry, brochures for florists, and plaques of beachscapes and rainbows boasting platitudes of comfort to ease the suffering of the bereaved.

Once we'd all settled at the table, Mr. Thomas spoke again. "Now, what did you have in mind for Mr. Susskind?"

"What's your cheapest option?" Nick asked callously.

"Nick!" Bethany protested.

"Dad's estate will pay for his burial. He wouldn't want us to waste money."

"He wouldn't want to be treated carelessly, either," Bethany declared.

"We take pride in preparing our clients for their last journey," Mr. Thomas said in a voice that oozed tranquility.

"Cremation or composting. What's your cheapest option?" Nick reiterated.

A tight-lipped Bethany fumed. "I have power of attorney," she declared.

"That expired last month when Dad assigned that task to me," Nick told her. He pulled a sheaf of papers from his inside suit pocket and laid it on the table for all to see, indicating Louie's signature. Bethany studied it and positively fumed. She hadn't believed me when I'd told her what Louie had done.

"May I ask who the executor of the estate is?" Mr. Thomas asked.

Bethany turned a triumphant glare in her brother's direction. "Me."

Mr. Thomas took great pains not to look at either of them. "Very good." He opened his leather binder as another vibration shook the building.

Omega groaned, and I turned to see her wince as though in pain.

"Are you all right, Ms. Dustin?" Mr. Thomas asked.

She shook her head. "Mr. Susskind's spirit is restless because of a dark secret he kept for many years…" She cast a look in Abe's direction. "I'm just beginning to understand…."

Nick and Bethany exchanged panicked expressions, but I noted that Abe looked resolute. "Whatever secrets Dad carried, he's taking them to his grave," Nick declared with a look in Abe's direction.

Then he *had* known about the blackmail Louie used against the Horse Hockey's brewmaster.

"I'm not so sure," Abe/Marcel said.

"Shut up," Nick ordered. It was a threat, and we all knew it.

Mr. Thomas ignored the tension in the room. "I understand you've already reserved a grave."

"Yes," Bethany said. "He'll be buried next to our mother."

Again, another tremor rumbled through the floor beneath our feet. An uncomfortable pressure seemed to surround me, and I found myself clenching my hands, the hairs on the back of my neck rising to attention.

"What's going on?" I asked Omega *sotto voce*.

"We are about to be joined—" But before she could finish

the sentence, the door from the corridor blew open, and a hot breath of air whooshed past us.

"What the—?" Richard muttered.

With dignity, Mr. Thomas rose from his chair and started the five or six feet toward the door, but then he halted, his body jolting as though he'd been punched in the gut. He doubled over with a groan and staggered to his right until he stumbled into the wall with windows overlooking the side parking lot.

Closest to him, Bethany jumped to her feet and caught the old man before he could fall to the carpet just as a terrible wail seemed to issue from the area right outside the room.

Omega was instantly on her feet and rushed to the head of the table, straightening to her full height—which couldn't have been more than five foot two.

Emily leaned against me. "What's going on?" she asked, sounding panicked. "You said I wouldn't see him!"

I didn't have time to answer as the floor beneath us rumbled once again, and then suddenly, the incorporeal Louie stood in the open doorway, his shadow of a body glowing as though bathed in phosphorescence.

Back at the hospital, I'd been the only one who could see and hear Louie, but it was evident by the shocked expressions of the others in that room that they saw him, too.

And they were terrified.

Mr. Thomas writhed on the floor in a semi-fetal position, but the rest of us, save for Omega and me, looked upon Louie's spectral countenance with horror. Prepared as he was, even Richard had gone pale.

"What do you want?" Omega demanded of the entity standing in the doorway, looking sick and haggard, unlike the spectral Louie I'd encountered so many times at the hospital.

Louie raised his right arm, his index finger pointing in the general direction of the table.

Feeling queasy from the hyper-emotion suddenly

bombarding me from nearly everyone in the room, flashing back to the tremendous burst of energy I'd encountered the summer before from a shattered spirit.

"Him." Louie pointed straight at Abe/Marcel, who sat at the far end of the table.

Bethany turned toward her former lover, her eyes dilated so wide they looked black. I could see her visibly shaking before she, too, collapsed in a dead faint onto the floor next to Mr. Thomas.

"Dad?" Nick asked, his voice shaky with disbelief.

Louie turned on his son, raising a hand, and with it came a volley of energy that knocked Nick off his feet.

"Get under the table," I told Emily, who sat frozen in her seat, looking at Louie as though—and in fact—she'd just seen a ghost.

"This can't be real," she breathed.

"Oh, I'm real all right," Louie growled and lumbered into the room but in his current state, he seemed to have lost the dexterity he had when his body still lived, only now his spirit boiled with a scorching malevolence. "You," he breathed, glaring at the brewmaster.

"The rot that seethes through Horse Hockey Brewing revolves around Abe," I said.

All eyes turned toward him.

"Don't go there," Abe grated.

"You say that but you don't mean it," I continued.

"Well, I second what he said," Louie growled.

"You don't get a vote," I told him.

An angry Nick had crawled onto his knees and couldn't seem to tear his gaze away from the image of his deceased father.

"It all started with gentrification," I began and laid out the terrible things Louie had done, from setting the fire that killed the old lady to pinning the blame on Marcel and forcing him to work for the family for decades under the threat of turning him into the authorities.

Slowly, Abe rose from his seat. Louie had dominated his life for at least two decades, calling all the shots, but as I continued presenting the facts, I sensed that Abe—Marcel—had finally had enough.

"You don't scare me—not anymore," Marcel declared.

"Step out of line, and Nick will report you to the cops. You'll be charged with killing your sainted grandmother," Louie threatened.

Marcel shook his head, raising his chin defiantly. "I've got a team to prove my innocence. I'm not running away. Not ever again."

"Team?" Louie thundered.

"Marcel looked in my direction.

I gave a nervous laugh and shrugged. "He paid our fee."

"I'll deal with you next, Resnick," Louie threatened before turning his ire back on Marcel.

"You don't own me anymore, *dead* man."

"You're going to jail—if only for insurance fraud," Louie thundered.

"*I* didn't make a claim."

"No, but Bethany has," Louie gloated, "and she'll blame you. Nick will prove it in court."

Had Nick been in on the fraud all along?

A sly smile crept across Marcel's face. "Bethany didn't make a claim."

Louie's eyes glowered a frightening shade of crimson. "I told her to."

Marcel's tone was deadly. "And she decided not to," Marcel countered.

"Why would she defy me?" Louie stormed.

"Because you're a dead man and you can't threaten us anymore."

Louie's eyes blazed red like burning coals, like something out of a horror movie. "The hell I can't." The specter charged forward, but Omega stepped before him, blocking the way.

"No, old man. Your time on this earth is over."

Lighting seemed to crackle around us, and the drapes on one of the windows burst into flames as Louie advanced toward Omega, who held her ground.

"Dad, no!" Nick shouted, still on his knees, but Louie paid no attention to his oldest child and headed straight for me, Emily, and Richard, who stood in his way of confronting Marcel.

Emily screamed.

"Down," I shouted, grabbing her by the back of her coat, hauling her off the chair, and shoving her under the table. Richard flew at Marcel like a left tackle, knocking him to the ground.

A howling wind roared around us, almost deafening in its intensity, shaking the building with the force of a 9.0 earthquake.

I glanced over my shoulder and caught sight of Omega as she intercepted the specter. Her hands reached out and connected with whatever was left of Louie Susskind. Instantly, they were engulfed in orange and red flames. Louie's soul screamed, his face twisting in agony, but Omega stood strong, holding on to the apparition, shouting words unintelligible to me.

The struggle seemed to go on for ages and ages but must have been only seconds.

And then the building blew up.

Chapter 34

Some might say it was a miracle that nearly everyone in the Thomas Funeral Home survived. The only casualty was Omega. There was no sign of her body.

We made a motley crew lurching away from the wreckage. My ears were ringing as I staggered to my feet and extricated Emily from under the shelter of the table and helped her to stand. Her face was caked with plaster dust, and her hair seemed to be standing on end. She looked like she'd been tazed. Richard pushed away the pieces of plasterboard that had fallen on him and Marcel.

"You okay, Rich?" I asked.

"Yeah, you?"

"Yeah."

Emily coughed.

Richard, Marcel, and I helped pull the rest of the survivors out onto the freezing parking lot, where we waited for the fire and rescue people to arrive.

The entire building had been flattened, and the guy we'd seen escape to the home's office looked shell-shocked, stumbling out of the wreckage to join the rest of us.

"What in God's name happened?" he asked.

Nobody answered his question. Nobody would have believed us.

"We should go back to find Omega," Richard said and took a step forward.

I grabbed the sleeve of his coat. "She's gone."

His gaze caught mine. He looked dazed. "But—?"

I shook my head. Whatever had happened, Omega had sacrificed herself to save the rest of us from the malignancy that was Louie.

Bethany sat on the damp asphalt, her knees in the air, rubbing her head and looking distinctly unwell. Marcel crouched beside her. "It's okay. I'm here." At his words, she leaned into him.

"Nick, what do we—" Bethany began.

"We don't say a goddamn word," Nick warned his sister. "Do you understand me? Don't say a word until I figure out where we stand legally. And you, too," he warned Marcel, who seemed much more interested in Bethany's welfare than her own flesh and blood.

Bethany pulled away from Marcel and took a long look at her brother before turning away and vomiting onto the ground.

That's pretty much how I felt about him, too.

The next couple of hours transpired in a blur. Sirens screamed to announce the appearance of fire trucks and rescue vehicles. The strobing lights were enough to give me the beginnings of another of my skull-pounding headaches. Still, I fought against it and tried to answer the cops' questions as accurately as I could without telling them what had actually gone on before the funeral home exploded.

A team from the gas company showed up and sealed off the lines. Everyone with any authority seemed to think the incident was the result of a gas breach. Nobody who'd survived the blast said a damn thing to dispute it.

It was almost ten when I drove Emily back to R&A Insights to pick up her car.

"Are you sure you don't want me to go with you to pick up Hannah? I'd be happy to take you guys home."

"But then I wouldn't have my car to get to work tomorrow."

"We won't be opening tomorrow," I told her.

"Are you sure?" she asked.

"Positive. The three of us need to recover from this whole ordeal."

Emily seemed to think over what I'd said. "Well, I do have a lot to process. So much of what happened tonight goes against everything I was taught and believed." She looked at me with sadness. "I'm sorry I doubted you. What a terrible life you've been given to experience what no one should have to see and hear."

I didn't know how to reply to that. Still, I felt better about having her as a part of the business. Maybe it could work out.

Emily sighed. "Call me when it's time to go back to work. After what happened tonight, I'm sure we'll get a lot more business."

I wasn't so sure.

IN THE WEEKS THAT FOLLOWED, I did my best to get my life back in order. Two days after the explosion, I moved back into the apartment over the garage on Richard's property. After needing to spend time with my family to keep my sanity, I now found I needed to spend some time alone to preserve it.

I hadn't heard from Maggie. I knew she kept in contact with Brenda, mostly asking for updates on Holly, but because of me, Brenda had soured on her friend. Hey, it wasn't my fault the woman was fucking around with someone else.

Or maybe it was. Maybe I just wasn't good enough for her.

I didn't like to think about it.

I ended up thinking about my role in life, or at least my place in the world at large.

Despite what she'd said the night of the explosion, Emily took a couple of weeks off to think things through. We told her to take all the time she needed. I kept going into the office because after resolving the Clark investigation, we did start getting calls that might lead to jobs. Nothing big or exciting, but it was enough to get Richard into the office on a regular basis.

The events of that terrible March evening had a sobering effect on the Susskind family, who quickly sold the brewery, and probably for less than they might have received—just to get out from under the scandal. I hadn't spoken to Marcel since the night of the explosion, but Brenda kept in contact with his mother. A lawsuit against the Susskind family was a real possibility. And thanks to Richard's generosity, they had the means to pay for it. I wondered about the other players. Richard discovered that Nick was coming off a divorce that had cost him plenty, which was why he'd pushed so hard to sell the brewery, while Teresa grappled with her family problems sans help from Omega. Bethany was at loose ends, but I knew she'd eventually find work at another craft brewery, although probably not in Western New York. Marcel was spending time getting to know his family again. The poor guy deserved it.

So, things had worked out. Sort of. But something was missing, something that kept nagging at me. It wasn't just Omega's death. In fact, after the explosion, I tried to find out more about her, feeling responsible even though she'd told me we all had our destinies. Had sacrificing herself to stop Louie's malignant spirit from harming others been her destiny? And though I'd witnessed the event, I still didn't know what actually happened.

I guess that's why I ended up at Sophie's bakery late one Thursday night in early April. The light at the back of the shop came on as soon as I rang the bell, and my psychic mentor quickly ushered me inside.

"It's cold—hurry, hurry," Sophie scolded as I pulled the door shut me and followed her into the back of the shop.

"Cocoa tonight?" she asked.

I nodded and took my usual seat at the rickety card table.

In minutes, a steaming mug of hot chocolate sat before me, along with a plate of macaroons. Sophie took one of the cookies and bit into it, studying me as she chewed. "You are very unhappy."

It seemed like a natural state for me.

"Tell me," she said, her voice soft.

I sipped my cocoa and thought about how to phrase all the crap circulating through my brains.

"Part of it is Omega. Her dying like she did. But the weird thing is when I tried to find out more about her … there was nothing to find."

Sophie raised an eyebrow.

"There's no record of her. Her website is gone. Even the domain name is up for sale." Sophie looked at me quizzically. She'd passed on years before the Internet was even a thing. "There's absolutely no trace that she ever lived." I glanced up and into Sophie's dark brown eyes. "What do you make of that?"

She nodded sagely, and I thought she was about to say something profound, but then she merely shrugged.

"Omega was a living, breathing woman. The hospital staff knew her. So did Louie's daughter. Weeks ago, I was able to find her on Google. Now there's no trace. The Internet is forever. You just can't erase yourself."

"So you say," Sophie muttered, sounding only half interested. "What else is wrong?"

This was the thing that had been weighing heaviest on my soul. "I didn't solve anything. I wasted my time, my client's time—"

"No, no, no," Sophie admonished me. "You did what you were supposed to do."

"Fail?" I asked.

"You did not fail," Sophie told me.

"Well, I didn't succeed."

"Have you ever thought that your role here on this earth might be something different?"

"Different? How?"

"That *you* might be the catalyst for change?"

If she was trying to make me feel better about myself, it wasn't working.

"Change? People don't want change. They want answers. As a consultant, I'm supposed to provide them. And it wasn't me who connected the brewery and Marcel Clark. It was Richard."

"Ah, but if you hadn't been involved, would he have made that connection?"

Maybe. Maybe not.

"You're far too hard on yourself." Sophie pushed the plate closer to me. "Have a cookie. You are too skinny."

Now she sounded like a grandmother.

She asked about Betsy, and I pulled out my phone and scrolled through all the pictures in my gallery. Sophie's eyes lit up with pleasure. Once a grandma, always a grandma—even if Betsy had no biological link to her.

Once we'd gone through all the pictures, Sophie sobered. "Have you heard from your Maggie?" Sophie asked.

"Well, she's not mine anymore."

Sophie merely nodded.

It took me more than a minute to work up the courage to speak again.

"I've been thinking about asking someone out to dinner, or at least lunch."

Sophie's eyes widened.

"She has a daughter."

Again Sophie nodded but said nothing.

"Anyway, as Maggie's apparently moved on, I thought I may as well do it, too."

"You and your Maggie have unfinished business," Sophie said solemnly.

I shook my head. "Maggie and *Richard* have unfinished business. He's taking care of her dog. And I suspect that could be a real problem. He loves that dog. I don't think he'll want to give her up without a fight."

Sophie nodded and began nibbling on another cookie. I sipped my cocoa.

"This woman," she began, referring to Emily. "She's quite a bit younger than you."

Why did she always know about stuff I'd prefer to keep to myself?

"Yeah. But Richard and Brenda have an age difference and they've done all right."

"The age difference between you and this young woman is even greater," Sophie said casually.

I frowned. "Hey, all I was thinking about was inviting her—and her daughter—out to lunch or dinner."

"You like the little girl?" Sophie asked.

"I owe her a cut-out cookie."

"And her mother?"

"To start, I'd like to establish a friendship. And if that goes nowhere…." I left the sentence hanging.

I guess I was looking for Sophie to give me her blessing to

move on from my relationship with Maggie, which had gone from stagnant to pretty much over.

"Maybe you should take up a hobby," Sophie advised, which seemed like a non sequitur. She was trying to tell me something by not saying a thing. It was something she often did that drove me crazy.

I tipped my mug back and drained it.

"I should get going. I need to get to work by eight."

Sophie nodded and stood. She led me back through the shop. At the door, she offered her cheek for a kiss. "Come see me again soon. We'll have things to talk about."

Crap. I didn't like the sound of that. But I also knew she'd be a sympathetic ear, even if she couldn't—or wouldn't—offer me valuable advice.

I kissed her good-bye and closed the door behind me. I watched as she walked to the back of the bakery and the light winked out.

Then I walked back to my car and drove home.

Epilogue

It was on a Monday morning when Emily finally returned to work, a day I'd been looking forward to.

"Welcome back," I greeted her and had a pot of hot water for her cocoa at the coffee station. I also bought a couple of her favorite chocolate chip muffins and an everything bagel for me. Richard wasn't due for a few hours as he was tagging along with Brenda for Betsy's well-baby check-up. That was okay. I wanted to talk to Emily about what had happened and how we could all move forward.

We settled at the table in the conference room. Me at the head of the table, and Emily at my right side. She eyed the framed one-dollar bill that hung on the south wall and frowned. I ignored her reaction. Richard didn't have an opinion either way on whether it should be there.

I won. Yay.

"How's Hannah?" I began. "Is she happy with her bedroom makeover?"

Emily frowned and looked down at the paper plate before her, breaking off the top of her muffin and reducing it to smaller, bite-sized pieces. "Not exactly." She offered no other explanation. Instead, she changed the subject. "Have you guys taken on a new case?"

I nodded. "It's nothing remarkable. Nothing that requires my special services."

I waited for her to comment on my extra-sensory abilities, but she didn't. She was exuding weird vibes, primarily sadness, although I didn't know why. It wasn't the first time I'd caught that sense of despair from her, either.

"You know," I started and paused, trying to think of something positive to say that might cheer her up. "I'm glad you came back to work. For a while, I wasn't sure you would."

"I need the money," she said bluntly. "Especially now."

It was my turn to experience plummeting spirits.

"Don't get me wrong," Emily backpedaled. "You and the Doc are the best bosses I've ever had. And…I'm pretty sure I can get used to the other stuff that goes on in your investigations."

That was more than I could have hoped to hear her admit.

"I'm glad you're willing to accept that part of me."

"Yeah, it's been a challenge," she admitted. That she'd been willing even to contemplate it without a jaundiced eye was a win as far as I was concerned.

"Hey, how would you like to go to lunch this afternoon to celebrate your return to the office?"

"I'd like that," Emily said. "But as my employer, there's just one thing I think you should know."

"What's that?" I asked, delighted by her affirmative answer on the first part of her sentence and paying no attention to the latter part.

Emily looked me straight in the eye. "I'm pregnant."

About the Author

The immensely popular Booktown Mystery series is what put Lorraine Bartlett's pen name Lorna Barrett on the New York Times Bestseller list, but it's her talent -- whether writing as Lorna, or L.L. Bartlett, or Lorraine Bartlett -- that keeps her there. This multi-published, Agatha-nominated author pens the exciting Jeff Resnick Mysteries as well as the acclaimed Victoria Square Mystery series, Tales of Telenia adventure-fantasy saga, and the Lotus Bay Mysteries, and has many short stories and novellas to her name(s). Check out the descriptions and links to all her works, and sign up for her emailed newsletter here: http://oi.vresp.com?fid=b4e19560e9

If you enjoyed ***SHADOW MAN***, please help spread the word by reviewing it on your favorite online review site. Thank you!

Connect with L.L.Bartlett on Social Media

www.LLBartlett.com

Also by L.L. Bartlett

THE JEFF RESNICK MYSTERIES

Murder On The Mind

Dead In Red

Room At The Inn

Cheated By Death

Bound By Suggestion

Dark Waters

Shattered Spirits

Shadow Man

JEFF RESNICK'S PERSONAL FILES

Evolution: Jeff Resnick's Backstory

A Jeff Resnick Six Pack

When The Spirit Moves You

Bah! Humbug

Cold Case

Spooked!

Crybaby

Eyewitness

A Part of the Pattern

Abused: A Daughter's Story

Off Script

Writing as Lorraine Bartlett

The Lotus Bay Mysteries

Panty Raid (A Tori Cannon-Kathy Grant mini mystery)

With Baited Breath

Christmas At Swans Nest

A Reel Catch

The Best From Swans Nest (A Lotus Bay Cookbook)

The Victoria Square Mysteries

A Crafty Killing

The Walled Flower

One Hot Murder

Dead, Bath and Beyond (with Laurie Cass)

Yule Be Dead (with Gayle Leeson)

Murder Ink (with Gayle Leeson)

A Murderous Misconception (with Gayle Lesson)

Dead Man's Hand (with Gayle Leeson)

Life On Victoria Square

Carving Out A Path

A Basket Full of Bargains

The Broken Teacup

It's Tutu Much

The Reluctant Bride

Tea'd Off

Life On Victoria Square Vol. 1

A Look Back

Tea For You (free download in most countries)

Davenport Designs

A Ruff Week

Recipes To Die For: A Victoria Square Cookbook

Tales From Blythe Cove Manor

A Dream Weekend

A Final Gift

An Unexpected Visitor

Grape Expectations

Foul Weather Friends

Mystical Blythe Cove Manor

Blythe Cove Seasons (free download in most countries)

Tales of Telenia

(adventure-fantasy)

STRANDED

JOURNEY

TREACHERY (2024)

Short Women's Fiction

Love & Murder: A Bargain-Priced Collection of Short Stories

Happy Holidays? (A Collection of Christmas Stories)

An Unconditional Love

Love Heals

Blue Christmas

Prisoner of Love

We're So Sorry, Uncle Albert

Sabina Reigns (a novel)

Writing as Lorna Barrett

THE BOOKTOWN MYSTERIES

Murder Is Binding

Bookmarked For Death

Bookplate Special

Chapter & Hearse

Sentenced To Death

Murder On The Half Shelf

Not The Killing Type

Book Clubbed

A Fatal Chapter

Title Wave

Poisoned Pages

A Killer Edition

Handbook For Homicide

A Deadly Deletion

Clause of Death

A Questionable Character

A Controversial Cover

WITH THE COZY CHICKS

The Cozy Chicks Kitchen

Tea Time With The Cozy Chicks

The Cozy Chicks Picnic

Ingram Content Group UK Ltd.
Milton Keynes UK
UKHW020707210423
420559UK00015B/1051